AFFECTIONATELY YOURS...

Caesar wasted no time executing his plan to bring Nixie and Jed together. Success would be his, and all too easily. All they needed was to spend some time together and let nature take its course. He'd even waited to see if they'd figure things out by themselves, but instead of following their natural inclinations, the two young fools had been avoiding each other!

Now it was up to him. He'd thought of the perfect plan. He'd spent a lot of time writing out these letters, striving for the exact right tone, one that would lead the recipient to believe more than casual interest from the sender, but nothing so forward as to lead to suspicion of impropriety.

Impropriety would come later. Right now, he merely wanted to get the two alone....

Praise for Cynthia Sterling's *A Willing Spirit*:

"This is beautiful. Splendid! 4½ Bells!"
—*Bell, Book, and Candle*

Jove titles by Cynthia Sterling

PATCHWORK HEARTS
A WILLING SPIRIT
GREAT CAESAR'S GHOST

Great Caesar's Ghost

CYNTHIA STERLING

JOVE BOOKS, NEW YORK

If you purchased this book without a cover, you should be aware that this book is stolen property. It was reported as "unsold and destroyed" to the publisher and neither the author nor the publisher has received any payment for this "stripped book."

This is a work of fiction. Names, characters, places, and incidents are either the product of the author's imagination or are used fictitiously, and any resemblance to actual persons, living or dead, business establishments, events or locales is entirely coincidental.

HAUNTING HEARTS is a registered trademark of Penguin Putnam Inc.

GREAT CAESAR'S GHOST

A Jove Book / published by arrangement with
the author

PRINTING HISTORY
Jove edition / January 2000

All rights reserved.
Copyright © 2000 by Cynthia Myers.
This book may not be reproduced in whole or in part,
by mimeograph or any other means, without permission.
For information address: The Berkley Publishing Group,
a division of Penguin Putnam Inc.,
375 Hudson Street, New York, New York 10014.

The Penguin Putnam Inc. World Wide Web site address is
http://www.penguinputnam.com

ISBN: 0-515-12730-2

A JOVE BOOK®
Jove Books are published by The Berkley Publishing Group,
a division of Penguin Putnam Inc.,
375 Hudson Street, New York, New York 10014.
JOVE and the "J" design
are trademarks belonging to Penguin Putnam Inc.

PRINTED IN THE UNITED STATES OF AMERICA

10 9 8 7 6 5 4 3 2 1

*This one is for the Bad Girls.
Thanks for everything, dear friends.*

Great Caesar's Ghost

Chapter One

TEXAS, MAY 1893

Great Caesar's Celebrated Curative was known to ease stomach discomfort, cure dyspepsia, silence snoring, stop coughs and congestion, and remove warts, but as far as Caesar Hawkins could determine, it had no effect whatsoever on bullheadedness. At least not where his son, Jedediah, was concerned. If anything, the young man had grown even more hardheaded in the months since the accident. Take right now, for instance. A half hour before showtime and the boy was digging in his heels.

Jed folded his arms across his chest and glared at his father across the narrow confines of the caravan, the headquarters for Great Caesar's Medicine Show. "I intend to do the show by myself and that's that!"

A more timid man might have shrank back from Jed's imposing height and broad shoulders. The boy took after his father, with the same robust appearance and handsome profile. But the streak of obstinance—well, that must have come from his *mother's* side of the family. *"By thunder, if I could, I'd go out there and teach you how to really put on a show!"* Caesar growled.

"But you can't, can you?" Jed's shoulder's sagged, and his tone softened. "You can't do things your way anymore, Papa, so what's wrong with giving my way a try?"

Caesar's stance sagged, too. He didn't like being reminded of his "condition." He hated having to watch from the wings while Jed preached the wonders of the formula *he* had perfected—Great Caesar's Celebrated Curative. But that didn't mean he couldn't offer the boy some badly needed direction. *"You'll never draw a crowd without a pretty girl on stage,"* he said.

"The floozies you bring around here aren't my idea of pretty. And they certainly aren't girls."

There he went being uppity again. *"People don't just want to be sold a product,"* Caesar huffed. *"They want to be entertained."*

Jed scowled. "When you started out, you worked by yourself."

"That was different. I'm the Great Caesar Hawkins. I have an instinct for this business."

"And I don't. Is that what you mean?"

Caesar winced. That was exactly what he meant, but Jed didn't have to sound so offended. *"Your showmanship is improving, my boy. You just haven't developed a...a stage presence yet. But you will. I know you will."*

Jed drew himself up to his full height, his head almost grazing the curved ceiling of the caravan, and assumed an equally lofty tone of voice. "How are people supposed to have any respect for what we do if you have some scantily clad female parading around on stage?"

"The people who come to see us want to have a good time, and maybe improve their health in the process," Caesar said. *"Respect has nothing to do with it."*

"I intend to change all that."

Caesar sighed. If Jed wasn't careful, his drive for respectability would put them out of business altogether. But there was no arguing with the boy. Caesar realized he needed to take matters into his own hands. *"Fine then. You go on and get ready for the show. I'll amuse myself visiting the rest of the fair."*

This announcement didn't seem to make Jed feel any more at ease. His scowl deepened. "Now, Papa, remember what we talked about. You have to behave yourself."

"I didn't lose my mind *in the accident,"* Caesar snapped.

He nodded. "Sorry, Papa. Just . . . be careful." Jed turned and plucked his jacket from a hook against the wall.

Caesar drifted out of the wagon and into the alley behind the midway. Here was the real action at any fair. As he looked down the wide lane behind the show wagons, Caesar spotted the Carrelli brothers rehearsing their tumbling act. Their patched trousers and undershirts would soon be replaced by the bright pantaloons and tunics that served as their stage costumes. Mrs. Ramirez walked by, carrying a kettle of her savory chili, followed by Pepita Thompson and her trio of trained dogs, out for a walk. The air rang with mingled voices in many languages, the lively music of the steam calliope from Wilson's carousel, and the laughter of the crowds on the midway behind them.

The smells of roasted peanuts, axle grease, and horse manure mingled in a heady perfume that, to Caesar, had always meant home. Or as close to home as a traveling man ever came. Except for the brief interval of his marriage to Jed's mother, over three decades ago, Caesar had spent almost fifty years on the road between small towns and carnivals and fairs across Texas and Louisiana.

You'd think his own son would heed that kind of experience, wouldn't you? But then, young people today, they never listened to anyone. He'd show the boy. He'd— Oho, what was this?

A veritable vision in pink and white stepped into view. She might have been the inspiration for one of Mr. Gibson's advertisements. Her high-piled blond hair gleamed in the sunlight, and the full sleeves and pinched-in waist of her candy-striped dress accented a very attractive figure. Caesar grinned. Obviously not a carnival worker, the town miss appeared to be lost. Lovely brow creased in a frown, she moved from wagon to wagon peering up the steps of each, as if looking for something. Of course, from the back, most of the show wagons looked alike.

Now there was a young woman customers would line up to look at. Nothing "floozy" about her! His pretentious son might even approve of a woman like this. *"Psst! Over here, Miss."*

The young woman looked up, startled.

"May I help you?" Caesar asked.

The woman peered at the shadows from which his voice emerged. "I . . . I'm looking for the Gospel Wagon," she said. She squared her shoulders. "I'm supposed to sing with the McKenna sisters at three o'clock."

It was almost three now. Perfect. He opened the door at the top of the steps leading up into the wagon and held it wide. *"Very good, Miss. We've been waiting for you."* If she wondered why he was hiding behind the door, it didn't matter to him. *"Better hurry,"* he urged. *"The show's about to start."*

As he'd hoped, the young woman took the bait. With a look of relief, she hurried up the steps and into the wagon. Chuckling at his own cleverness, Caesar slammed the door behind her and made his way toward the front of the wagon. This was one performance of Great Caesar's Medicine Show he didn't want to miss.

Nixie Dengler jumped as the door of the caravan slammed shut behind her. Blinking at the sudden dimness, she gradually could make out calico curtains on either side of a narrow passage leading toward the stage at the rear of the wagon. The stage area was further divided from this passage by a set of red velvet drapes. Yes, this looked like backstage at the Gospel Show, but where was everyone?

Surely they hadn't started without her. She'd meant to be on time, but a combination of nerves and a second cherry phosphate had necessitated a quick trip to the women's latrines, and then she had become disoriented in the press of people. Thank goodness, the gentleman outside had spotted her . . .

Great Caesar's Ghost

All thought flew from her head as a man emerged from between the velvet curtains and started down the passage toward her. He was dressed all in white, his broad shoulders practically filling the passageway. Was he one of the evangelists with the show?

"Who are you?"

She jumped at the suddenness of the question and the harshness of his tone. "N-Nixie Dengler," she stammered.

The man frowned. "What kind of a name is Nixie?"

She flushed. "My real name's Nanette. But my father has called me 'Nixie' since I was a little girl. It's some kind of German water sprite."

"And who's your father?"

"Dr. Hamlin Dengler."

"Your father's a doctor?" The frown deepened.

Why all these questions? She struggled to quell her irritation. Maybe the preacher just wanted to know about everyone in the show, even local volunteers like herself. "My father operates the health resort at Welcome Springs."

"Then what brings you here today?" Was she imagining it, or did his voice hold an edge of impatience?

"I'm one of the singers. I—"

"Singers?" The man positively scowled. If this was an evangelist, his specialty must be fire and brimstone. "I suppose my father sent you?"

"Your father?" Nixie's heart pounded. A terrible suspicion swept over her. Maybe she wasn't in the right place after all.

"Who sent you in here?" the man demanded.

"I . . . I don't know. I didn't exactly see him—"

"That was my father all right." He folded his arms over his chest and looked her up and down. "You're a sight prettier than most of the women he hires. I suppose it wouldn't hurt to give you a try." He grabbed her hand and tugged her toward the stage. "We'd better hurry. The show's about to start."

"I don't think—" She tried to free herself, but her hand was trapped in his warm grasp.

"I'll do the thinking." He pulled her through the velvet drapes and gave her a gentle shove toward the side of the stage. "Just do what I tell you and you'll be fine."

She opened her mouth to protest, but her captor had turned away. The murmur of voices drew her attention to the area in front of the stage. "Oh my!" she gasped. At least two hundred people crowded around the small stage, with more arriving by the minute. Her legs began to tremble beneath her skirts at the thought of standing before all those people. She'd been nervous enough about singing with the McKenna sisters, but the Gospel Show never drew a crowd of this size.

"Ladies and gentlemen, may I present my lovely assistant, Miss Dixie."

Her captor's booming voice startled her from her daze. "That's Nixie," she hissed, but he ignored her.

"Friends, my name is Jedediah Hawkins, and I'm here to talk to you today about the marvelous healing powers of Great Caesar's Celebrated Curative." His voice carried over the crowd, rich tones vibrating right through Nixie. He smiled and his face was transformed into breathtaking handsomeness. He gestured toward the crowd. "Do you feel overwhelmed by the burdens of life, friends? Do you suffer from poor health, ill temper, or fits of melancholy? Then draw near and hear the message I bring to you today."

Realization swept over Nixie like a bucket of cold water. Somehow, she'd ended up on the stage of a . . . a medicine show!

Mr. Hawkins stood before the crowd with his arms uplifted like the revival evangelist she'd mistaken him for. She wanted to run away and hide, but her feet remained frozen to the stage. "I bring to you today the solution to many of the ills that plague you," Mr. Hawkins continued. He turned toward Nixie. "Miss Dixie, would you be so kind as to hand me one of those bottles?"

She stared at him, uncomprehending.

"The bottles!" he said through clenched teeth. "Behind you. Hand one to me."

She turned and almost knocked over the table holding a pyramid of bottles, the amber glass glinting in the sunlight. Snatching one up, she hurried over to Mr. Hawkins with it.

"Will you loosen up?" he whispered. He rolled his eyes. "Why couldn't Papa at least have found me a girl with talent?"

No talent! She bristled. Why, she'd been the understudy to the second lead in last fall's production of *The Little Match Girl*, and she sang every Sunday in the choir at the Wesley Fellowship Church. What did this . . . this snake-oil salesman know about talent?

Chin up, she stalked back across the stage and stood beside the table, glaring at him.

He held up the bottle and studied it, brow furrowed as if considering a great mystery. "Everything we need for good health and full life has been provided for us on earth," he said.

"Amen!" came a voice from the crowd. Others murmured in agreement.

Mr. Hawkins nodded. "The secret is in finding out the right combination of elements to cure the ills that plague us." He extended his empty hand toward Nixie once again and snapped his fingers.

"The stool. He wants the stool." Nixie jumped as the gravelly voice that had gotten her into this mess in the first place came through the curtain behind her. *"He's going to sit down and he needs the stool."*

She looked around and spied a tall stool next to the table. Glancing over her shoulder, she saw that though Mr. Hawkins's face remained passive, his eyes sparked with impatience.

With an exaggerated smile, she picked up the stool and sauntered toward him, as if she had all the time in the world to make her delivery. She set it down behind him and made a great show of dusting off the seat cushion. A thrill of delight ran through her when the crowd responded with laughter.

At last, he lowered himself to the stool and nodded to

her in a gesture of dismissal. "Please, have a seat, Miss Dixie."

She strolled back across the stage, feeling the gaze of the crowd following her. Someone had shoved a chair over to the table. She studied it. When she sat, she'd be almost hidden behind the tower of bottles. A meek little servant, awaiting Mr. Hawkins's next bidding.

I should leave right now and hurry over to the Gospel Wagon, she thought. *I might still have time to make the performance.* She glanced at Mr. Hawkins's handsome, haughty profile. He probably thought she was shaking in her boots because of him. He'd have no reason to think differently if she ran away.

"My father, Caesar Hawkins, spent many years as a student of the elements," Mr. Hawkins said. "He spent many more years perfecting the formula for his remarkable Curative. He was . . ." His voice faded as he watched Nixie walk toward him, carrying her chair.

Smiling to the crowd, she placed the chair next to the stool, then sat with her hands demurely in her lap, and gazed up at Mr. Hawkins. "Do go on with your story," she said.

His eyes narrowed in warning, but she continued to stare up at him, feigning wide-eyed innocence. He wrenched his gaze back to the crowd and continued speaking. "Caesar Hawkins . . . He spent years studying herbs and flowers and all manner of plants."

His voice was deep, with a soothing, hypnotic tone. As he told a tale of his father and the healing secrets he'd discovered, Nixie found herself drawn in to the story. She might even have believed he was sincere about the wonders of his product. But then, traveling salesmen could lie with all the charm of the serpent in the Garden. Like Eve, Nixie had learned that lesson the hard way.

She tore her attention from his words, and let her gaze drift over him. Though he dressed like a wealthy dandy, up close he showed signs of neglect. His hair curled up at his collar, in need of a trim, and that collar was noticeably frayed. She'd wager Jedediah Hawkins had no woman in his life to see to these details.

She had never seen a man in a white suit before. Her father always wore black. Some of the younger men of her acquaintance might hazard gray or brown, or perhaps even a daring blue. But none had ever appeared in white.

Whether it was the color or the cloth, she was sure a man's shoulders had never looked as broad as Mr. Hawkins's did. They seemed wide and solid beneath the perfect tailoring of the suit coat, and she felt an illicit flutter in her stomach as she let her gaze linger upon his broad back. She'd mistaken Mr. Hawkins for a man on the side of the angels, but now it was obvious he was the most handsome devil she had ever seen.

Troubled by such thoughts, she quickly dropped her eyes, but found herself looking through veiled lashes at Mr. Hawkins's long legs, stretched out before him as he leaned against the stool. She couldn't recall paying much attention to a man's legs before. Did they all possess such muscular thighs, such long proportions?

She shook her head to clear it. "Is something wrong, Miss Dixie?"

Looking up, she found Mr. Hawkins staring at her. A burning flush crept up her neck as she became aware of the crowd watching her as well. She swallowed, trying to think of something to say. "That story of yours," she said after a moment. "Is it true?"

He clamped his lips together in a tight line and blew a breath out his nose. "So you're a skeptic, are you?" he mumbled under his breath. He shook his head. "I should have known."

The laugh he gave sounded forced. He looked back at the crowd. "A lot of you out there are probably wondering the same thing, aren't you?" he asked. "Can one product truly possess all the amazing powers with which this one is endowed?"

Nixie saw heads nodding, and allowed herself a small smile of satisfaction.

Mr. Hawkins stood. "Yes, my story's true. And today,

I'll let you in on a little secret few are privy to." He nodded toward the table at the far end of the stage. "Miss Dixie, will you be so kind as to bring me the small blue flask behind the bottles of Curative?"

For the first time, she noticed the ornate blue-glass bottle on the table. Propelled mainly by curiosity, she went to fetch it, though she took her time doing so. It wouldn't do for Mr. Hawkins to think she was hurrying because of him. She returned to his side and held the bottle up, examining it, ignoring his outstretched hand. Inside, she could make out half a dozen shriveled pods of some plant material. "What is it?" she asked.

The lines around his mouth deepened. "This is the secret to the potency of Great Caesar's Celebrated Curative. A plant whose medicinal power my father discovered in his years of study. Half a dozen of these go into every batch of Curative."

She eyed the contents of the bottle skeptically. "They look like shriveled up okra pods to me."

The crowd erupted in laughter again. Jed Hawkins curled his hands into fists. "You may laugh," he said, "or you may avail yourselves of the opportunity to test my claims for yourself. Satisfy your own curiosity as to the power of Great Caesar's Celebrated Curative." He held the amber remedy bottle aloft. "One dollar a bottle. If it does not alleviate most common dyspepsia, malaise, fatigue, aches and pains, summer complaints, and a host of other ailments—when used according to the directions on the bottle—your money will be cheerfully refunded."

A murmur swept over the crowd. People began to press against the stage, arms outsretched. "Give me two bottles, Dixie honey." An old man pressed two bills into Nixie's hand.

"I'll take one!" A very large woman waved a dollar at her.

"Here." Mr. Hawkins shoved a bottle of Curative toward her. "Give the people what they want."

Nixie slipped the flask of "secret ingredient" into her skirt pocket and began handing out Curative and collecting money. When she glanced back, she could see the top of Mr. Hawkins's head, sunlight glinting on the golden strands in his hair as he sold bottle after bottle of his product.

At last, the crowd dwindled. "Thank you, folks," Mr. Hawkins said as the last few customers drifted away. He shut the lid on his metal cash box. "Be sure and tell your neighbors."

He was still smiling when he took Nixie by the elbow and led her through the red velvet curtains behind the stage. "Just what did you think you were doing?" he asked, turning on her, his smile abruptly absent from his face.

Nixie drew herself up to her full five feet, which still left her a foot shorter than Mr. Hawkins. "Why are you so upset? The audience liked me."

"They were laughing at you when they should have been listening to me."

She raised her chin. "Well maybe you take things too seriously. You should be thanking me for injecting a little humor into your show."

He put his hands on his hips and leaned toward her, so that the scents of bay rum, masculine sweat, and another, more woodsy fragrance filled her nostrils. She could feel the warmth emanating from his body, see the pulse pounding at his temple. "Your job is to *assist* me," he said. "That's all."

"My *job*?" She practically shrieked the word. "How can you say that? I was lured in here, then forced out on that stage against my will, where you attempted to make me the laughingstock of everyone . . ." The enormity of what had happened overwhelmed her. What if someone she knew had seen her with Jedediah Hawkins? Being a twenty-five-year-old spinster was already enough to set tongues wagging if she so much as looked at a man. Forsaking the McKenna sisters for a patent medicine peddler would keep the gossips busy for weeks to come.

"I have to go!" she blurted, shoving past him.

"Wait!"

His cry only spurred her onward. She raced down the wagon steps and darted among the milling people in the alley outside, ignoring the curious glances and startled cries that followed in her wake. When she reached the midway, she forced herself to slow down and walk as quickly as she dared in the direction of the Dengler family buggy. How was she ever going to explain her absence from the Gospel Show to her family?

"Whoever she was, she was good for business." Caesar, backstage once more, thumbed through the stack of bills in the cash box. *"It's a new sales record."* He grinned and shut the lid with a solid *click*. *"I guess they like that virginal look."*

"Hmmmph!" Jed turned away. He could still see the little blonde's eyes blazing at him, all bowed up like a cat with her tail trod on. How was he supposed to know she wasn't an actress his father had hired?

He scratched the back of his neck, frowning. He'd admit no actress he'd ever seen had looked like that—hair the shade of new corn silk, a perfect peaches and cream complexion, and a slight dusting of freckles across her upturned nose. And those eyes—golden-green hazel, like verdigris on bronze, practically shooting out sparks when she'd glared at him.

He chuckled to himself, recalling the way she had paraded across the stage with that stool and pantomimed dusting it off. He'd been annoyed with the delay at first, but then, the audience *had* laughed.

"I liked the way she scooted her chair right up next to you on stage, then looked up at you with those big doe eyes," Caesar said. *"The audience liked it, too."*

Jed nodded. He'd been all too aware of her, sitting so close. For the first time in memory he'd been rattled, almost losing his place in his spiel. Doe eyes? More like a tiger's gaze. Despite her virginal appearance, there'd been something not quite innocent in the young woman's study of him.

"Any chance we can get her back?" Caesar asked. *"She was great for sales."*

Jed unbuttoned his collar and shook his head. "Not

likely. She was mad enough to spit nails when she left here."

"We could go after her. Where did she say she lived? Something Springs?"

"Welcome Springs. Her father's a *doctor* there. Can you imagine?" He sighed and tossed the loosened shirt collar aside. Truth be told, he wouldn't have minded getting to know the lovely Miss Dengler better. But wasn't that the way it always worked? About the time he developed an interest in a woman, it was time to move on to the next town, the next show, the next night alone.

"I always got along pretty well with the medical establishment," Caesar said, from somewhere over by the wardrobe chest. *"At least, those enlightened enough to listen to my theories with an open mind. Perhaps I could talk to Dr. Dengler . . ."*

Jed sighed. "Papa, you can't just go up and start conversations with people anymore."

A long silence. A chair across from Jed moved back a foot, and the seat sagged as if a weight were settling in it. *"I suppose the accident did cramp my style somewhat,"* Caesar finally said.

Jed turned away, not wanting his father to read the disappointment in his eyes. The "accident" had been an explosion that destroyed their wagon and everything in it, including Caesar Hawkins himself. But Caesar, in customary fashion, ignored any reality he didn't agree with. Jed hadn't yet figured out how to handle a ghost who refused to believe he was a ghost!

Chapter Two

Nixie was red-faced and out of breath by the time she came in sight of the Dengler buggy. Her father and mother sat in the front seat, her mother holding a blue frilled parasol to shield her from the sun. If the folding buggy top had worked, they might have raised it for shade. But the top had needed repairing since the previous spring, when her brothers, Lou and Pete, had "accidentally" shot arrows through it while pretending to be wild Indians.

Said brothers were chasing each other around the buggy wheels when Nixie arrived. "Look who's here!" ten-year-old Lou called out. "Nanette the nanny goat! Nanny goat!"

"Baaa. Baaa!" Fourteen-year-old Pete blatted out his imitation of a goat.

Nixie fought the urge to wallop them both upside their heads. She walked to the buggy with as much dignity as she could muster. "Oh, there you are, dear," her mother said, smiling down at her.

Even having borne three children, Nadine Dengler looked disconcertingly young, with the same fair hair and

GREAT CAESAR'S GHOST   15

skin as her daughter. On more than one occasion, she had been mistaken for Nixie's sister.

"Nixie, girl, where have you been off to?" Her father turned in his seat and beamed at her. Hamlin Dengler reminded Nixie of a jolly German shopkeeper, perhaps a butcher or a baker. He seemed too round and red-faced and perpetually cheerful to fill the role of physician.

"I . . . I got lost in the crowd," she answered as he helped her into the seat behind him. "I'm sorry I missed the singing."

"We missed it, too, dear," her mother said, half-turning to look at her. "Your father was telling Mr. Carruthers about his plans for the boardinghouse."

She nodded and held back a sigh. The Dengler boardinghouse had been a work-in-progress for three years now, a half-finished shell in front of the family's cramped home. A sign by the road advertised WILLKOMMEN INN. COMPLETE WATER CURES AVAILABLE. OPENING SOON. Three years in the Texas sun had faded the once-blue lettering to a dull gray, and visitors seldom inquired about the project anymore. But her father swore one day the building would be finished, and then Welcome Springs would really be famous.

"So you got lost, did you?" her father said. "And here I was hoping some handsome stranger had swept you off your feet and you'd eloped!"

He and Nadine laughed together at this, one of the family's favorite jokes. Nixie blushed and busied herself smoothing the skirt of her new dress. At twenty-five, she knew it was likely she'd never marry, but her parents couldn't seem to let go of the hope that some man would come along and carry her away.

As for handsome strangers appearing to sweep her off her feet, she might as well believe in love potions—or patent medicines.

She slipped her hand into her skirt pocket, searching for the peppermint drops she'd put there earlier. Instead, she felt the hard smoothness of a glass bottle. She gasped, remembering the blue-glass bottle of the Curative's "secret ingredient." Would Mr. Hawkins come after her now, as if she were a thief? Perhaps she should return it?

She banished the thought from her mind. The last thing she wanted was to face haughty Mr. Hawkins again. No doubt, he had plenty more of the "secret ingredient" where this came from. Maybe she'd give the bottle to her father later, and he could amuse himself figuring out the identity of the mysterious pods.

Pete and Lou squeezed in beside her, filling the buggy with the little-boy smells of dirt and horehound candy and penny firecrackers. With a lurch, the buggy started forward.

Nixie looked out over the fairgrounds, at the still-crowded midway, where many families would roam far into the night, eating roasted peanuts, riding the carousel, and gaping at the bearded lady and the iron man.

And buying bottles of Caesar's Celebrated Curative. The brightly painted wagon loomed before her, its side ablaze with an advertisement for the miraculous tonic. She stared openmouthed at the painting of a woman dressed in what might have passed for a Roman toga, who was smiling and holding a familiar amber bottle.

As Nixie watched, a man stepped down from the wagon. Jed Hawkins had removed his suit jacket and stood in shirt-sleeves and white waistcoat, watching the crowds pass by.

Watching *her* pass by. His gaze locked on hers as if directed by some unspoken command. The warmth of those eyes drew her, as did the pure, masculine power of the man behind the look.

Flushing, she wrenched her gaze away, but not before she felt again the curious fluttering in her stomach and the racing of her heart.

The next morning, Great Caesar's Medicine Show left behind the dust and clamor of the fairgrounds and hit the open road once more. The sun bathed the fields alongside the road with a soft light, and a warm breeze stirred the yellow tickseed and scarlet and golden firewheel blooming in profusion among the knee-high grass.

Jed raised his head and filled his lungs with the warm,

sweetly scented air. He couldn't imagine a finer morning for travel, or a finer place to be than Texas in May.

"Best take we've had in a good while." The wagon seat creaked as Caesar settled in beside his son. *"The cash box is full and our supply of Curative is almost exhausted."*

"We'll have to stop soon and mix up another then," Jed said. He'd found it odd at first, conversing with his father's disembodied voice, but he'd grown accustomed to the awkwardness of it.

"It's all due to that girl—Dixie, Nixie, whatever you called her. I told you a woman would make all the difference."

How like his father to refuse to give Jed any of the credit. "I'm willing to concede that a nice, *respectable* woman could have a place in the show," he said.

"Exactly. A woman lets the other women know it's okay to come over and listen to the spiel. And if the gal on stage is pretty, the men will come to take a closer look and stay to buy."

Amazing, how his father could twist any story to his own advantage. "Of course, no respectable woman is going to agree to travel alone with me," he said. *Let alone with a ghost*, he silently added.

"Hmmm. I suppose you could marry someone."

Jed snorted. "And what woman is going to want a life of traveling around the country in a medicine show wagon? Not that I'm ever in one place long enough to court anyone, anyway."

"Miss Dengler seemed interested in you. And you seemed to like her well enough."

Jed glanced sharply in the direction of Caesar's voice. He didn't have to see his father to know the smug expression he'd be wearing. Yes, the delectable Miss Dengler was pretty. It would be a long time before the image of her pale blond hair and green-gold eyes faded from his mind. But what of it? "Miss Dengler detests me."

"You liked her, though, didn't you? I could tell because you wouldn't call her by her right name. You always did tease the girls you liked best."

He shrugged. "She was easy to get a rise out of, that's all."

"You lost your place in your spiel, too. You never do that. You wouldn't have done it if you hadn't been rattled."

"I wasn't rattled. I was distracted by that business with the chair."

"You liked her. Maybe there's hope for you yet."

"It doesn't matter," Jed said, annoyed. "Miss Nixie's gone home to Papa and a whole porch full of beaux waiting for their turn to sit in the swing with her."

But had she? He'd seen that she was no giggling girl. Not old, but a grown woman past the age when most married. Why wasn't a woman as pretty as Nixie Dengler wearing a ring on her hand? Wouldn't her papa let her wed? Or was something else keeping her from the altar?

He smiled to himself, remembering how she'd looked, standing up there on that stage beside him. She was a tiny thing, with a nice, rounded bosom and a waist small enough he imagined he could span it with his hands. He'd wager it wasn't merely rows of ruffles padding her bodice.

No, Nixie Dengler didn't strike him as the type to employ such subterfuge. She'd stood up to him, refusing to back down or run away. There was no coy miss hiding behind blushes or veiled lashes. She, no doubt, advocated women's suffrage and temperance and all manner of high moral causes. That was probably the real reason she remained a spinster. What man would want to face such a lioness over the breakfast table every morning?

Though there was something to be said for a wildcat in one's bed at night . . .

He pushed the thought away and snapped the reins over the horses' backs. "Why don't you go back there and see if we have everything we need to make a new batch of Curative?" he said.

The wagon seat creaked and the door behind him opened and closed as Caesar made his way back into the wagon. Jed turned his mind to the schedule ahead. They were due in Rock Springs tomorrow, which meant they'd have to put up a batch of Curative tonight in order to be assured of having enough . . .

"*Where's my secret ingredient?*" The door separating the body of the caravan from the driver's seat opened once more. Jed felt his father's hot breath on his shoulder. "*I can't find the bottle.*"

"It should be where it always is, with the rest of the props for the show."

"*It's not there. Are you sure you replaced it after the performance yesterday afternoon?*"

"Of course I did. I—" He froze. Cold memory swept over him . . . a picture of Miss Nixie Dengler holding the bottle aloft, refusing to hand it to him. He'd had to exercise all his self-control to keep from snatching it from her. He couldn't recall seeing it after that. "Nixie Dengler had it last," he said softly.

"*Are you saying she stole my secret ingredient?*" Caesar's indignant roar made the horses fold back their ears.

"No, I don't think she *stole* it." Now why had he said that? After all, he didn't know much about Nixie Dengler. Except that she seemed far too open and honest to ever be a thief. "What would she want with that bottle anyway?"

"*That's what I'd like to know. And what I intend to find out.*" The wagon shook as Caesar crawled through to the front seat once more. "*We're driving to Welcome Springs right now to have a talk with Miss Dengler.*"

"Papa, she may not even have it."

"*She was the last to see it. At the very least, she may be able to tell us where she put it.*"

Jed groaned. "Why don't you just open another bottle? It's not worth the trouble."

Silence. Not a good sign where Caesar Hawkins was concerned. Jed gripped the reins more tightly. "Papa, why don't you open another bottle?"

"*Because that was the last one.*"

"The last one?" Jed couldn't believe it. "If you'd let *me* take charge of mixing the batches, this wouldn't have happened," he snapped.

"*I worked years to perfect that formula,*" Caesar

growled. *"You'll get it from me when I'm ready and not before."*

Jed ground his teeth together. "Then we'll stop in Rock Springs early and purchase more of whatever you need from the druggist there."

"Can't do it." Caesar sounded morose. *"It has to be special ordered. It could take weeks."*

Jed stared straight ahead. At moments like this, it was probably just as well he couldn't actually see his father. If they could look each other in the eyes right now, they might be tempted to physical blows. When he finally spoke, his voice was strained. "Fine. We'll go to Welcome Springs." He directed a stern look in his father's direction. "But *I'll* do the talking."

Nixie frowned at the row of figures in the ledger before her. Getting the accounts to balance was worse than trying to thread a needle while looking through a knothole. Nothing ever lined up quite right.

She raised her head and addressed her father, who was standing beside her desk in the combination parlor and waiting room, polishing his reading glasses. "When you went out to Mr. Prophet's place to set his leg the other day, how much did he pay you?"

Ham Dengler held the glasses to the light and squinted at them, then went back to buffing them with his handkerchief. "Nothing. Edward has six children to feed, and he cannot work while he is laid up with that leg. He will be good for it later."

Nixie could feel the furrow between her eyes deepen. "In the meantime, *we* have to eat, too. You could have asked him for *something*."

Ham replaced the glasses in his coat pocket and came and patted her on the shoulder. "Not to worry, Nixie girl. There is plenty of money to be made here in Welcome Springs. Once the boardinghouse is open and word gets out . . ."

She couldn't hold back a sigh as she listened to her father's familiar refrain. "Next time, Papa, won't you please remember to at least *ask* for your fee? I'm sure more people would pay if you gave them the opportunity."

He smiled and nodded. "Of course, dear. I will try to remember."

She watched him walk into his office, knowing her plea was more than likely already forgotten. Her father's head was too full of wild dreams and plans for the future to be cluttered up with such mundane matters as buying food and clothing and paying off debts. When Dr. Dengler saw his next patient he would no doubt spend the better part of the visit debating whether Welcome Springs would be the next Carlsbad or Baden Baden. And then it would be up to Nixie to send a note to the Patterson farm, or Mr. Hodgkins's store—wherever the next patient resided—begging them for what should be offered willingly for her father's services.

She closed her eyes and massaged her neck. She was going to end up humpbacked as an old woman, worrying over the books. But if she didn't see to them, who would? Certainly not her father. And her mother, bless her heart, did well to make correct change at the mercantile. It was up to Nixie to keep things in order.

A solid knocking on the door interrupted her musings, and she sat upright. Maybe it was a patient. At least she could collect in person from those who came to the house.

Pausing first at the mirror in the hallway to smooth her hair and straighten her skirt, she grasped the china knob and yanked open the door.

And stared up into the face of Jedediah Hawkins.

She caught her breath and put one hand to her throat, as if to still the suddenly frantic hammering of her heart in her chest. Surely it was only the unexpectedness of his arrival that caused her to react so fiercely, and not his breathtaking handsomeness, nor the way his fudge-brown eyes seemed to look right into her soul and read her most secret and forbidden thoughts.

Jed looked the picture of a dapper man-about-town, dressed in a black morning coat and trousers and a waistcoat of black-and-gray striped silk over a white shirt. His sun-streaked brown hair fell boyishly across his forehead when he doffed his black bowler and nodded. "Miss Dengler. We meet again."

She straightened her spine and reminded herself that no matter how attractive he was, he was still a medicine show performer. Not a man with whom a respectable young woman would choose to associate. "What can I do for you?" she asked in her most formal voice.

"I wonder if I might speak with you for a moment?"

"About what?" She didn't trust this silver-tongued devil. Not for one second.

He nodded toward the parlor. "Perhaps it would be best if we spoke inside."

He had a point. Even now their next door neighbor, Mrs. Frisco, was probably watching them from behind her lace curtains, ready to tell the whole town about the *handsome* young man who'd visited the Denglers. "Of course." She held the door wide and he walked past her into the hall. She led the way back toward her father's office, all the while aware of Jed Hawkins's eyes on her as she crossed the room. The sensation of being so closely watched raised prickles on the back of her neck.

She took her place once more behind the desk in the front parlor, painfully aware that she and Mr. Hawkins were alone in the room. He glanced at the open ledger on the desk before her. "I can see I've interrupted you. Finish your work. I don't mind waiting."

Good. Maybe if she kept him cooling his heels long enough, he'd leave. She pretended to study the ledger, but her eyes were continuously drawn to the man who seemed to fill the small room with his presence. He was still holding his hat, turning it slowly in his hands while he looked over the titles of the books on the shelves behind the sofa.

As if feeling her gaze, he turned and smiled, his whole face alight with the expression. She jerked her head down, embarrassed to be caught staring at someone who was, after all, a stranger.

"Miss Dixie, is it?"

She flinched. "It's *Nixie*. Miss Dengler to you, if you please, Mr. Hawkins."

He grinned. "Then it is 'Miss.'" He put his hands on the back of a Queen Anne chair and turned it around so that it faced the desk. "Tell me about Welcome Springs." He sat and balanced the bowler on one knee.

"Surely you didn't come here to ask about Welcome Springs," she snapped.

He shrugged. "Maybe I'm thinking of adding it to my regular circuit. You're the only person I know here to ask."

She'd hardly characterize their brief interaction as a pleasant acquaintance, but short of calling for her father to throw Jed Hawkins out, what choice did she have? Knowing Ham Dengler, he'd invite the patent medicine peddler to stay for supper.

"The town was founded in 1868 by Hiram Guenther, who named it Welcome Springs for the abundant mineral springs in the area," she recited. How many times had she heard her father give this same speech? Only Hamlin Dengler always managed to convey the information with more enthusiasm than Nixie could muster at the moment. "We have a four-room school, Baptist, Methodist, Lutheran, and Catholic churches, an ice cream parlor, livery stable, mercantile, and men's and women's bathhouses." She raised her head and discovered Jed Hawkins watching her, still smiling. For some reason, she found the scrutiny irritating. "It's a nice, quiet town, Mr. Hawkins. Nothing to interest a . . . a rambler like you."

He sat back in his chair. "What makes you think I'm a rambler?"

"Oh, really." She shook her head. "Just look at you, with your fancy clothes and fancy painted wagon. You make your living traveling from town to town selling your medicine."

He looked up toward the ceiling, seeming to consider her assessment. "I suppose I do enjoy traveling." He looked back at her. "But I come by it honestly enough. I grew up in a wagon very much like that. My father—"

"Yes, I know. Your father invented Great Caesar's Curative, and you're following in the family footsteps." She closed the ledger and glared at him. "Just another snake-oil salesman in a long line of snake-oil salesmen."

His smile vanished, and the light went out of his eyes. Nixie immediately wished she could take back those wounding words. He stood, worrying the brim of his hat between his fingers. "That's what you think I am—a charlatan? A con man who fills bottles with whiskey and pepper and calls it medicine?"

He set the bowler on the desk, then took an amber bottle from his pocket and pulled the cork. Looking around, he spied her father's collection of shot glasses on a shelf below the books. He grabbed one and filled it from the bottle. "Go ahead, try it," he said, shoving the glass toward her. "Unless you're one to accuse a man without weighing the evidence for yourself?"

It was her turn to smart at his accusation. Glaring at him, she snatched the glass from the desktop and raised it to her nose. It smelled herbal, rather pleasant even.

"Go on. Drink it up."

Taking a deep breath, she opened her mouth and tossed in the full contents of the glass, the way she'd seen her father drink bourbon. A sweet, clean flavor flooded her mouth. She looked up at Jed Hawkins in surprise.

"That's pure clover honey, fresh water, a special blend of herbs, and my father's own secret ingredient." He put both hands flat on the desk on either side of his hat and leaned toward her. "My father spent years perfecting the recipe."

Nixie bit her lower lip. It wasn't like her to insult people. What was it about Jed Hawkins that made her behave so out of character? She struggled to put together the words of an apology. "Mr. Hawkins, I—"

The door to her father's office flew open and Hamlin Dengler emerged. "What is this shouting I hear?" he asked.

Mr. Hawkins straightened and extended his hand. "Jed Hawkins. And you must be Dr. Dengler."

"I am pleased to meet you." Ham Dengler gave Mr.

Hawkins a hearty handshake. "Is there something I could do for you? Some medical problem?" He looked Jed up and down. Nixie thought she'd never seen a healthier male specimen.

"I met your daughter yesterday at the fair," Mr. Hawkins said, as if this explained his presence here.

Dr. Dengler's face bloomed with a smile. "Ah! You have come to call on Nixie. How delightful!"

Nixie wanted to crawl under the desk. Jed Hawkins must think she was absolutely desperate, for news of a caller—a total stranger—to be greeted so enthusiastically.

"And where did you meet our Nixie?" Dr. Dengler asked. "Perhaps you heard her sing. She has a voice like a nightingale, I always say."

"Papa, really!" she scolded, annoyed at the blush she knew stained her cheeks.

"Actually, I met Nixie at my show," Mr. Hawkins said.

"Ah! You are with the Gospel Show." Dr. Dengler's grin broadened. "Then perhaps I should address you as Reverend Hawkins."

"Actually, I run a medicine show."

Dr. Dengler's smile faltered. He glanced at Nixie. "You were at a medicine show?"

Nixie's stomach clenched. She was going to strangle Jed Hawkins. She really was. "Papa, it was all a terrible mistake. I was looking for the Gospel Wagon and—"

"And your daughter was kind enough to assist me in a moment of need," Mr. Hawkins said. "I stopped by today to thank her."

Dr. Dengler relaxed. "Ah, that is our Nixie. So kind and generous."

From sinner to saint in the blink of an eye, that's me, she thought. "Well, now that Mr. Hawkins has paid his respects, I'm sure he needs to be going," she said, preparing to show their guest to the door.

"Oh, I'm in no hurry," Mr. Hawkins said, smiling sweetly.

"Tell me, what products do you represent in your show?" Dr. Dengler asked.

"Only one, Dr. Dengler. A formula my father perfected—Caesar's Celebrated Curative."

"The name sounds vaguely familiar to me." Dr. Dengler pulled up a chair. "Please, sit down and tell us more."

"Papa, really, I'm sure Mr. Hawkins doesn't want to—"

"I always enjoy talking about the Curative." He picked up the bottle from which he'd served Nixie and handed it to the doctor. "It's a product unlike any of the quack potions hawked by the more unscrupulous of my profession. My father developed this after years of study of herbal medicines."

"How remarkable!" Dr. Dengler declared. "I, too, have an interest in natural healing." He leaned forward. "I have found the mineral waters here in Welcome Springs to be more powerful than most physics on a number of common ills. Every year, people come from far and wide to subscribe to my water treatments."

"Yes, I understand that bathing in and drinking from mineral springs can be most beneficial," Mr. Hawkins said.

"Please, tell me more about your father's Curative."

Nixie rolled her eyes and sank into a chair. She recognized defeat when it stared her in the face. No doubt her father and Mr. Hawkins would go on like this for hours.

When their visitor reached the part in his story where he told about his father's "secret ingredient," he glanced at Nixie. Guilt stabbed at her. The blue bottle containing the mysterious brown pods was sitting on her dresser upstairs at this very moment. Did he know she'd accidentally taken it? Maybe that was the real reason for his visit. If so, she'd happily return it and send him on his way.

But first, Ham Dengler insisted on sampling the Curative for himself. "Marvelous!" he declared, smacking his lips. "In fact, I would say it is much too delicious to be a medicine."

Mr. Hawkins laughed. "My father didn't believe something should have to taste bad in order to do good," he said. "Part of his secret was in developing a pleasant-tasting concoction that people would actually use."

"I must have this Curative of yours to try on my patients," Dr. Dengler said. "And you, sir, must do us the honor of staying for dinner. In fact, stay as long as you are able."

Mr. Hawkins glanced at Nixie. Surely he knew already what *her* opinion on the matter would be! "I hadn't planned on staying that long," he said.

"Nonsense. It is almost noon now. Every man has to eat."

Few people could withstand her father's infectious cheerfulness. She wasn't surprised when Jed Hawkins relented. "All right. It's good of you to offer."

"It is settled, then. We will have a nice meal, then perhaps we can persuade you to keep company with us even longer." Dr. Dengler beamed at his daughter. "What do you think of that, Nixie girl?"

She looked away from her father's obvious elation, and found herself trapped beneath Jed Hawkins's steady gaze. "Yes, Nixie girl, what do you think of that?" he murmured, so softly that she was the only one who heard, the only one who saw the spark of challenge ignite in his brown eyes.

Chapter Three

Nixie rushed up the stairs to her room, shutting the door behind her. As if she didn't have enough annoyances in her life, along had come Jed Hawkins to subject her to more ridicule and whispers.

"I love you. I love you." With a whir of yellow-and-black-barred wings, a green bird with a yellow head sailed across the room and landed on her shoulder. The parakeet laid his head against her cheek and made clucking, comforting noises under its breath.

Nixie smiled and stroked the bird's soft stomach with the tip of one finger. "I love you, too, Sweet William," she crooned.

The little bird sidestepped his way across her shoulder and cocked his head to eye her quizzically. "Nanny goat. Nanny goat," he squawked.

Nixie laughed. "That Peter. I told him and Lou to leave you alone. Now look what they've taught you."

William fluffed up his feathers, then began tugging on the lace at the collar of her shirtwaist. She sat on the edge of her bed, beginning to relax as she watched the bird's antics. She'd complained mightily when her father had accepted the parakeet in payment of an overdue medical bill. She told him he should have negotiated for something they could eat or wear.

But now she wouldn't have traded William for a whole store full of food or dresses. Anytime she was feeling out of step with the rest of her family and the world, she had only to come up to her room and confide her woes to her little companion. The bird's open adoration salved her bruised feelings, and his playful acrobatics were a sure cure for the mopes.

Mr. Hawkins would probably advertise his Curative as a more appropriate remedy. The man seemed to think it would cure everything. Her gaze rested on the little blue bottle on her dresser. She was sorry she'd ever laid eyes on that bottle, or on Jed Hawkins. He was bringing nothing but trouble into her life.

Liar, a voice inside her head whispered. Jed Hawkins wasn't to blame because he tempted the wild, undisciplined side of herself that she could never quite tame. While other women contented themselves with home and family and church, why was she forever fighting daydreams of exotic adventure, far-off lands, and totally unsuitable men?

Men like Jed Hawkins. He might as well have been a pirate or a gypsy king or the leader of an outlaw gang or any of the others who populated her secret fantasies. He was every bit as unsuitable for a proper young lady.

She looked across at her reflection in her dressing table mirror. She did her best to be a proper young lady, but she was always making mistakes. For instance, a proper young lady would never have gone out on that stage in the first place, and she certainly wouldn't have stayed there.

"Nixie, dinner's almost ready. You'd better come down."

Her mother's voice outside her door pulled her attention from the bird, back to her earlier worries. She couldn't hide from Jed Hawkins forever.

She glanced at the blue bottle once more. At the first

opportunity after dinner, she would return the bottle of "secret ingredient" to him and urge him to be on his way.

"Oh, aren't you looking pretty today. Isn't Nixie pretty, dear?"

Nixie nodded to the elderly couple who were just coming out of the parlor as she made her way toward the dining room. "Hello, Mrs. Chapman. Mr. Chapman." She raised her voice so that Mr. Chapman would be sure to hear her. He and his wife must have been past seventy, but they'd been coming to camp at the Denglers' for the past three summers. Every year, Dr. Dengler opened his house and grounds to people who came to bathe in the springs, which gave the town its name, and take the "water cure" Dr. Dengler had devised. The Chapmans claimed the waters did wonders for their rheumatism. They stayed in a little wagon fitted out with a feather mattress, and talked fondly of the day the boardinghouse would open.

Another guest, Dory Evans, stopped Nixie in the hall just past the Chapmans. "Miss Dengler, I've been thinking of changing my hairstyle. Could you show me how to do my hair up like yours?" She put a hand to the mouse-brown locks arranged in a friz of curls on her forehead and smiled, revealing prominent teeth.

"I don't know why you bother keeping up with fashion, Dory." Dory's older sister, Dinah Merchant, came to stand behind her. "You don't think a new hairstyle will make you pretty, do you?" Dinah's own gray-streaked chestnut locks were drawn back in a severe chignon at the back of her head, adding to the pinched appearance of her face. This was the sisters' first visit to Welcome Springs, and already Nixie had developed a dislike of Mrs. Merchant.

"I'd be happy to help you with your hair, Miss Evans," Nixie said, turning a smile on Dory. "I think the fullness of this style would be very flattering."

Dory's smile expanded. Though it was true she was terribly plain, her bright eyes and ready grin lent her an engaging expression.

The sisters and the Chapmans followed Nixie into the

dining room, where the rest of the family, and those campers who paid extra to take their meals at the house, were already waiting. Nixie moved past Theo Stebbins, who flushed bright red and held her chair out for her.

Dr. Dengler sat at the head of the table, with Miss Evans on one side and Mrs. Merchant on the other. Next came Mr. Stebbins, then Lou and Pete, with the Chapmans across from them. Finally came Nixie, next to her mother at the end of the table, and Mr. Hawkins opposite Nixie.

She avoided looking at the man across from her until after her father had intoned grace and her mother began passing bowls of food. When she finally raised her eyes, she found Jed Hawkins watching her. "Hello again, Miss Dengler," he said.

"Hello, Mr. Hawkins," she said coolly.

She reached for the basket of bread in front of her, then jerked her hand away as her fingers brushed his. The brief contact set up a curious tingling in her skin.

"Not mutton again!" Lou's loud protest distracted her. She looked down the table to see him staring in disgust at the platter his father passed to him.

"Now, son, we should be thankful for Mr. McGregor's generosity," Mrs. Dengler said. "Try it with some of this fresh applesauce."

Nixie shot a sympathetic look in her younger brother's direction. Tonight made three times this week they'd dined on mutton. As for Mr. McGregor's generosity, next time he came around with a sheep in payment of his bill, she had a mind to tell him they'd just as soon have cash. Or at least chicken or beef.

"Mrs. Merchant, I trust you and your sister are settling in nicely?" Dr. Dengler addressed the woman to his right.

"We find the atmosphere here to be relaxing, though perhaps not as elegant as some," she said.

"I'm enjoying it very much," Miss Evans said. "Everyone we've met has been so nice."

"As a spinster, Dory has led a rather sheltered life, and therefore has never developed very discriminating tastes." Mrs. Merchant addressed those around her. "I, however, traveled a great deal with Mr. Merchant, before his untimely demise, and have somewhat more sophisticated preferences."

"I . . . I think everyone here has been very nice, too." Mr. Stebbins's face turned almost as red as his hair as everyone at the table turned to look at the normally silent boarder. "I . . . I mean . . . Well, they have been," he added and ducked his head.

"We've been coming here every summer for the last three years." Mrs. Chapman patted Miss Evans's arm. "It may not be elegant, but we favor the homey atmosphere ourselves. We're not much for crowds."

Mrs. Merchant frowned as her sister's smile widened at this apparent victory.

"So, Mr. Hawkins, what do you think of our little town?" Dr. Dengler's voice boomed from the end of the table.

Nixie pretended interest in her plate, but through a veil of lashes, she studied their guest, curious to hear his impression of her hometown.

"Welcome Springs seems a very pleasant place," he answered.

"Don't you agree that Welcome Springs is a place with potential?" Dr. Dengler waved his fork before him like a magic wand. "We have sunshine, fresh air, the abundant mineral springs. I tell you, in a few years people will be flocking here to vacation and take the waters."

Nixie concentrated on cutting her food into small bites. What must a sophisticated man like Mr. Hawkins, a man who had traveled all over the country, think of her father's wild dreams?

"I quite agree, Dr. Dengler. Welcome Springs has the makings of a first-class resort."

Nixie choked on a mouthful of potatoes and stared at Jed. He had turned to address her father. "Water cures are all the rage these days. Not only is the mineral water healthful, but people enjoy getting out in the fresh air and sunshine. The social aspects of it are as attractive as the health benefits."

"Exactly!" Ham pounded the table so hard that the water glasses danced on the damask cloth. "I've said the same thing myself."

"The only thing you don't appear to have is lodging for all these potential visitors." Jed speared a bite of mutton and chewed thoughtfully.

"My boardinghouse will take care of that," Dr. Dengler said.

Nixie wished the floor would open and swallow her whole. The boardinghouse again! Her father's pipe dream.

"A boardinghouse. An excellent idea." Jed Hawkins nodded. "When do you expect it to open?"

"Ah, that is one problem," Dr. Dengler said. "Construction is not moving as swiftly as I would like. You would not believe how difficult it is to find steady workers for a project such as this, Mr. Hawkins."

Or ones who will work for practically no pay, and a lot of vague promises for the future, Nixie thought bitterly. The last group of workmen had walked off the job when her father had tried to persuade them to take subscriptions to the springs in exchange for their labor.

"I'm sorry to hear that," Mr. Hawkins said. "From what little I saw, the town could use some sort of lodging facility."

From there, her father and Jed Hawkins fell to discussing the health benefits of mineral springwater versus water from creeks or wells. Pete and Lou argued over whose turn it was to fetch wood for the cookstove. Mrs. Chapman asked Mr. Stebbins if he would come with her and her husband on an excursion to view the Indian rock paintings south of town. She invited Mrs. Merchant and her sister along as well.

Nixie concentrated on her plate, letting the different threads of conversation weave a cocoon around her. Sitting among the bustle of family and guests, she was free to explore her own thoughts, invisible to those around her. If they thought about her reticence at all, they would simply dismiss it as "Nixie's way." Surely one of the advantages to being a spinster was the freedom to indulge in eccentricities—from talking to a parakeet, to not participating in dinner-table chatter.

She was aware that her withdrawal had not gone completely unnoticed. The tingling sensation returned, and when she raised her head, she found herself staring into Jed Hawkins's dark-brown eyes. She steeled herself against the censure or amusement she expected from such a worldly showman, but the look he gave her sent a ripple of shock through her. Past the sun-god good looks and public smile, Jed Hawkins was lonely. It showed in the longing buried in the depths of his gaze, a longing that matched the unspoken desires of her own heart.

Her heart pounded as she tried to summon the irritation he had sparked in her earlier. She wanted to fight off the tender emotions that swelled within her. But the only anger she could find was at herself, that she could lose control of her carefully marshaled defenses so easily.

The moment dinner was over, Nixie shoved back her chair and hurried from the table. The sooner Jed Hawkins left town the better. She didn't like the way he made her feel, or the memories he stirred within her.

Jed leaned against the fence behind the Dengler house and watched the horses clip the short grass of their pasture. *"Rather pleasant place, I think."* His father's voice sounded low in his ear. *"I wouldn't mind staying a while."*

Jed glanced around to make sure no one was watching him. He didn't want to develop a reputation as the kind of man who talked to himself. "We're leaving as soon as I get that blasted bottle from Nixie Dengler."

"No need to bite my head off." The fence wire bowed inward, as if someone leaned against it. *"You don't seem to be in too much of a hurry to depart, either. We've been here hours and I haven't heard any mention of that bottle."*

"I'm waiting for the right opportunity. I didn't want to make a fuss in front of Dr. Dengler, and I couldn't very well bring up the subject at the dinner table."

"The doctor's quite a pleasant fellow, isn't he? Much more open-minded than others of his ilk. And his daughter,

GREAT CAESAR'S GHOST 35

well..." Caesar gave an appreciative chuckle.

Jed felt a pang of regret at the mention of Nixie. She was so beautiful and bright: everything a man could want in a woman. "She detests me," he said, spirits sliding further.

"I wouldn't say that, Son." The fence wire *twang*ed as Caesar moved away from it once more. *"After all, you inherited my good looks. I can guarantee you Miss Dengler has noticed that. And you can be quite a charming fellow when you choose to be."*

Jed didn't choose to stay and try to charm Nixie Dengler. She'd made her opinion of "snake oil salesmen" infinitely clear. He failed to see what he had done to upset her so. All right, they had gotten off to a shaky start on the stage, but that was an honest mistake. She didn't have to hold that against him forever. He'd noticed she could be pleasant enough to other people, but the moment she was around him, her hackles raised up like a kitten confronted with a growling dog.

Only this dog might have enjoyed a chance to at least pet the kitten, he thought ruefully. He shook his head and turned away from the fence. He could see no chance of that. He'd be lucky if the feisty Miss Dengler didn't claw his eyes out before he managed to get out of town.

He stuffed his hands in his pockets and began walking on past his wagon, which was parked behind the house. Two other wagons sat a little distance away, drying laundry and ash-filled fire rings beside them. Further on, three tents were arranged with their backs to the pasture fence. Next to these, under the shade of an oak, four men sat engaged in a game of dominoes.

Jed might have appeared to walk alone, but he knew his father was beside him, though he made no sound. The man who had made such a big impression on him in life still managed to exert a strong influence after death.

They walked away from the campground, along the side of the Dengler residence to the building that towered before it next to the street. The shell of the Willkommen Inn rose three stories high, unpainted boards weathered silver.

Through the empty cutouts for windows he could see the unfinished interior walls, lathe awaiting plaster in some places, paint halfway to the ceiling in one room. Scraps of lumber, bent nails and broken brick littered the floors, sawhorses still arranged and tools sitting idle as if abandoned in the middle of the day.

"Looks like the doctor has quite a grand place planned here," Caesar observed.

Jed stepped through the open back door and looked down the wide hall that divided the boardinghouse in two. How many such places had he and his father spent time in when he was a child—dozens, even hundreds? All smelling of cooking cabbage and antimacassar oil and lemon floor polish, the mattresses too lumpy and the towels too thin.

Even so, they had been a welcome change from sleeping in the wagon, or on the ground between the brightly painted wheels. Jed couldn't remember what it was like to live in a real house, with a room of one's own and the same surroundings every day for years. There must have been something like that at one time, when he was very small, before his mother died and Caesar took him on the road.

He stooped and picked up a length of beaded molding. Looking up, he saw a similar wood trim running the length of the room next to the ceiling. Hamlin Dengler had indeed planned a beautiful place.

"So what do you think of the Willkommen Inn?"

Jed whirled and saw Nixie standing in the doorway, and for a moment he stopped breathing. Her face was in shadow, but the light shining behind her illuminated her figure. His eyes traveled up from the toes of her kid boots peeking beneath her skirts, over her rounded hips to the indentation of her waist. He imagined he could hear his heart pounding in the stillness, and felt the sudden tension in his chest.

Then she stepped into the room and walked toward him. The frown on her face banished his delight in seeing her. "Go ahead and laugh, Mr. Hawkins," she said. "Half the town does, behind our backs." She looked at the piece of molding in his hand. "They think Papa is crazy to believe that Welcome Springs could ever be more than another small town with bad-tasting water."

"Why should they laugh? Other towns have done well selling water cures." He tapped the molding against his palm. "They come for the same reason they buy the Curative. People are hurting and they want to get well."

She flushed and looked away. "About your Curative . . . I'm sorry I said what I did. It was rude and uncalled for."

He could tell the words took effort. Of course, a woman so proud wouldn't bend easily. Well, he had his pride, too. He wouldn't let her see how much her apology mattered to him. "You're a young woman who says what she thinks. Some people would say that's an admirable quality."

"You mock me now, Mr. Hawkins." She walked over to one of the spaces for a window and stared out across the yard toward his wagon.

He looked past her, to the array of tents and wagons. "Do all the campers come here to take water cures?"

She glanced over her shoulder at him. "Most of them buy subscriptions, yes."

"And what is the subscription for?" He didn't really care about the answer. He merely wanted to keep her talking.

"A bath a day for three weeks, and as much water as they care to drink."

He nodded. "Let me see if I can guess. The tall, skinny fellow in the black galluses—he must be suffering from consumption."

"Mr. Harrison seems to be well on his way to recovering, and intends to stay the summer."

"And the red-haired man next to him. He's easy. That skin inflammation must be quite embarrassing."

"Mr. Stebbins is quite self-conscious about his eczema."

Jed was beginning to enjoy this guessing game. Maybe if he kept it up, Nixie Dengler would relax a little. "But the other two, the roly-poly chap, and the one with the moustache—I can't make out what's troubling them."

She blushed to the roots of her hair, and quickly turned

her back to him once more. "It really isn't proper for me to discuss my father's patients with you—"

He suppressed a grin. "Ahhh. Obviously, the gentlemen in question suffer from a . . . ah . . . 'social disease.' I had heard water cures were quite popular for that sort of thing."

She did not answer, though he could see the flush along the back of her neck deepen. He came to stand behind her, close enough to smell the lemon she must use to rinse her hair and the starch of her shirtwaist. What was it about this woman that attracted him so? Though he'd tried to deny it, from the first moment he'd seen her on his stage, staring at him with a challenge in her eyes, he'd been drawn to her. It was all he could do now not to reach out and pull her to him.

He heard her breathing quicken and watched the rise and fall of her breasts beneath the starched cotton cloth. So the cool Miss Dengler felt something for him as well. Or was it merely fear he mistook for arousal?

"You act as if you want me to go away, Nixie," he said. "And yet we've only just met."

She looked over her shoulder at him, frowning. "I don't even know you. I couldn't care less what you do." She faced the window once more, one hand to the back of her neck, rubbing it as if it ached.

"What's wrong. Does your neck hurt?"

"I suppose you think your Curative would fix that, too." She sounded annoyed.

"No. I know something better." He reached out and brushed her hand away, then began massaging the knot at the top of her spine. "I used to do this for my father." Of course, his father had never felt as soft and delicate as Miss Dengler.

She stiffened, freezing like some wild animal at the first touch of the trap. Then, as he continued to soothe and rub, she relaxed and leaned against him, her eyelids drooping and a smile of pure pleasure curving her lips. He brought his other hand up to join the first, working his fingers in circles across the tense muscles of her shoulders. He looked down at the soft nest of her hair fanning out from its top-

GREAT CAESAR'S GHOST 39

knot at the crown of her head, and bent to inhale deeply of its lemon freshness.

She was so lovely, but more than mere beauty drew him. Nixie Dengler looked as fragile as a spring blossom, but inside, she was as strong as an ironwood tree. He had recognized that strength when she'd challenged him before his audience the day before. Now that he was in Welcome Springs, Jed knew the source of Nixie's strength.

Nixie had the strength of deep roots, home, family, and a place where she belonged. After years of wandering, the idea of such roots held a powerful pull for Jed. It was almost as if, by touching Nixie, he might claim a little of her kind of strength for himself.

Suddenly, like someone awakening from a dream, she snapped open her eyes and pulled away from him. "What am I doing?" she cried, her hands flying up to cover her suddenly flushed cheeks. Without another word, she ran from the room, racing across the yard as fast as her feet would take her.

Jed leaned against the open door and watched her go, depression following quickly on the heels of his cooling desire. Was Nixie Dengler so terrified of all men, or was he the only one who stirred such fear? Despite her apology, did she still see him as nothing more than a traveling humbugger?

"Well, are you going to just stand there and let her run away from you like that?"

His father's brusque question startled Jed out of his reverie. "I'll be damned if I chase her down," he grumbled.

"You were doing pretty well there for a minute. Reminded me of myself in my salad days. Another minute or two and you'd have been spooning proper."

"I didn't come here to 'spoon.' " Jed stalked out of the half-finished building. "In fact, the sooner we leave here, the better."

"Fine with me. Except you still don't have the bottle of secret ingredient."

His father's words stopped him halfway across the yard. He glanced at the house, at the curtains billowing out an open upstairs window. Was that Nixie's room? Was she hiding there now, or had she run to Papa to complain that the *snake-oil salesman* was also a masher? What of it? Come sundown, he didn't intend to be anywhere near the place. "I'll get the bottle right now," he declared, and started toward the house.

The side door he entered led to a kitchen. Two boys, Nixie's brothers if he remembered rightly, sat at the kitchen table polishing off a plate of cookies. The youngest looked up and wiped the crumbs from his mouth with the back of his hand. "Hullo. You're that medicine showman, aren't you?"

"That's me." He glanced around the simply furnished room, half-hoping to find Nixie waiting besides the massive black stove, or seated at the opposite end of the wooden table. But except for the boys, the room was deserted.

"Say, mister, you ever seen one of them exotic dancers?"

The oldest boy spoke, his voice shooting up a register at the end of the sentence, startling Jed almost as much as the question. "What do you know about exotic dancers?" he asked.

The boy shrugged. "Nothin'. That's why I'm askin' you. I figured bein' with the fair and all, you might have seen one."

As a matter of fact, Jed *had* seen a pair of Egyptian belly dancers perform at a fair in Fort Worth once, but he wasn't about to confess that to the boy. The Denglers, or at least Nixie, had a depraved enough picture of him as it was. "I don't usually travel with the fair," he said, hedging the question.

"Oh." The boy looked disappointed.

"You want a cookie?" The younger boy held up the last one on the plate.

"No thank you." Jed looked around the room once more. "Have you seen your sister?"

"Nixie's upstairs in her room," the youngest boy answered. He shoved the cookie into his mouth. "You can go on up."

Jed hesitated. It wasn't exactly proper for a man to visit

a young woman's bedroom. He glanced up the stairs. Still, it was broad daylight, and he wouldn't be long. Only long enough to fetch the bottle and leave.

The decision made, Jed took the steps two at a time and arrived in a narrow hallway lined with doors. He paused outside the first door and studied the piece of paper tacked to the center wood panel. KEEP OUT was lettered across it in schoolmarm script. Ah hah. This was the place.

He knocked, softly. After a moment, the door eased open and Nixie peered out. As soon as she saw him, she started to close the door, but he put out a hand to stop her. "We need to talk," he said.

"I don't know why you think I'd have anything to say to you." She pushed against the door, but he held firm.

"I believe you have something that belongs to me."

Guilt flashed across her face. She glanced past him into the hall. "What if someone sees you up here?"

"Give me the bottle and I'll go away."

Worry lines creased her brow. "All right, I'll get it."

She left the door open and walked across the room. From his station in the hall, Jed could see a single bed and a diminutive dresser, done up in pink and white. A girl's room, though Nixie was well past girlhood. The only odd note was a tall black wire cage in the corner, which housed a small green-and-yellow bird.

"I didn't mean to take your silly old bottle," she said. "It's right here, on my dressing t—"

Her horrified gasp alarmed him. After a moment's hesitation, he rushed to her side. "What is it? What's wrong?"

She pointed toward the dresser. "The bottle! It was right here before dinner, and now it's gone."

Chapter Four

Jed walked over and studied the cluttered dresser top. A varied assortment of bottles and flasks and tins practically obscured the surface. Ribbons tangled with lace collars and tumbled over powder puffs. A flower-garden aroma of perfume filled the area, clouding his senses. What did women *do* with all this froufrou? He picked up a length of cloth, which he realized, with a start, was an embroidered garter.

"I told you, it's not here!" She snatched the garter from his hand, blushing the color of ripe peaches.

Jed was suddenly aware that they were alone in her bedroom, the bed itself not ten steps behind them. Was it his imagination, or was it overly warm in here? "Then where is it?" he snapped.

She glanced over the surface of the dresser and picked up a shiny glass marble. "My brothers! They know they're not supposed to play in here, yet they do it all the time."

"I saw them in the kitchen when I came in," he said.

"Just wait until I get my hands on them!" She stormed out the door and down the stairs, Jed in her wake. Rushing into the kitchen, she snatched the youngest boy up by the collar. "Louis Wilson Dengler, where is it?"

The boy's eyes grew round as quarters. "Where is what?" he choked.

"The blue-glass bottle that was on my dresser. I know you took it."

Lou shrugged out of her hand. "We just wanted to borrow it for a little while," he mumbled, eyes on the table.

Nixie looked angry enough to pop a vessel. Jed could see stubborn looks stealing over the boys' faces. If she wasn't careful, they'd never find the bottle. Time to take matters into his own hands. He slid into the chair next to the oldest boy, Pete. "Actually, that bottle belongs to me," he said, assuming a friendly tone. "It's fine with me if you boys wanted to look at it, but I need it back now."

Pete glanced at him, then reached into his pocket and reluctantly pulled out the bottle and set it on the table. Jed picked it up, already knowing the worst. "It's empty," he said softly.

"What did you do with the stuff that was inside it?" Nixie asked.

Pete made a face. "We tasted them pods and they weren't any good, so we threw them out."

Nixie's bent toward violence was growing more attractive by the minute. "You threw them out?" Jed gasped. "Where?"

"We dumped them in the springs." The younger boy grinned, revealing a space in his front teeth. He shook his head. "The fish didn't care for 'em either."

Jed felt as if a big wind had sucked the energy out of him. "It will take weeks to reorder those ingredients," he mumbled.

Nixie turned on her brothers with a fury that would have been admirable if he hadn't been so caught up in his own worries. In any case, the boys appeared indifferent to her harangue, as if this was nothing they hadn't heard before.

He flinched as an icy hand gripped his arm, and stifled a groan at the sound of a low chuckle in his ear. "What are you laughing about?" he mumbled to his father.

"I just think it's funny how things work out," Caesar said. *"You were so dead set against hanging around here. Now it looks like we'll have to stay a while after all. One of these days, you're going to learn to listen to your old man."*

One of these days, his old man was going to start listening to him. He glanced at Nixie, who was still lecturing her brothers. He might as well wish for Miss Nixie Dengler to suddenly develop tender feelings for him. The odds of either happening seemed about even.

Later that evening, Jed sat on the wagon steps, elbows propped on knees, staring toward the Dengler home, the shell of the Willkommen Inn rising beyond it. Laughter drifted to him from the front of the house. At least someone was having a good time this evening. Was Nixie in that bunch? Was she entertaining her friends with tales of the snake-oil salesman's ill fortune?

"What are you moping about?" Caesar demanded from somewhere near Jed's right elbow.

Jed's frown deepened. "I suppose it doesn't bother you a bit that we could miss the best part of summer waiting for an order of secret ingredient for the Curative to come in?"

"Oh, it won't be so bad as that." He felt Caesar settle onto the steps beside him. *"We've got a right pretty camping spot here, and those marvelous springs—"*

Jed straightened. "I don't have any intention of staying here. We're headed out in the morning."

"To go where? Don't be ridiculous! There's no reason to leave this lovely place."

"And no reason to stay here, either." Another burst of laughter from the Dengler home. Which one of those voices belonged to Nixie?

"Nonsense. Dr. Dengler is the perfect host. There's no need for us to go anywhere else."

Except that the thought of Nixie Dengler looking down her pretty nose at him for the next few weeks made his supper feel like a lump of lead in his stomach.

GREAT CAESAR'S GHOST 45

"I'm looking forward to experimenting with the local mineral water and enjoying this agreeable climate," Caesar continued, oblivious to Jed's dark mood. *"We passed a bandstand on the way into town. I imagine there are summer concerts, and probably dances, too."*

That was just like his father, wasn't it? Always full of plans. But what about Jed's own plans? After all this time, did his opinion count for nothing?

"Not to mention this gives you the opportunity to get to know Nixie Dengler better."

The mention of Nixie snared Jed's attention once more. "I don't intend to waste any more time with Miss Dengler."

"I can't believe a son of mine is willing to give up the fort so easily!" The air around them practically quivered with Caesar's indignation. *"Where did I go wrong, boy? Don't you enjoy a challenge?"*

"Hmmph!" Jed grunted. "As if *you* were ever an expert on women."

"I'll have you know I had quite a reputation with the ladies when I was your age, young man!"

Outside of his mother, Jed had never seen his father with anyone who might have been called a "lady." "I don't see the point in discussing it further. We're leaving in the morning, and that's that."

"You've forgotten one thing, though, haven't you?"

Jed cringed at the taunt ringing in his father's voice. "What are you talking about?"

"We can't just set out on the road in any direction we please. The ingredients for the Curative have to be shipped to us from the pharmaceutical supply house, and for that, we have to stay put long enough for it to get to us."

Jed's jaw ached from clenching his teeth, but when he spoke, he made his voice calm, as if his father's words hadn't affected him in the least. "As soon as the ingredients arrive, we'll be leaving. Did you fill out the order form yet?"

Silence.

Jed closed his eyes. "Papa? Did you fill out the order

form to send off to the pharmaceutical supply house?"

"I haven't gotten around to it yet." Caesar sounded completely indifferent.

Jed stood. "Then give the list to me and *I'll* do it. We haven't got time to waste here."

"Ah no. You won't trick me that way." Jed could hear the smirk in his father's voice. *"You won't get me to hand over the recipe for Great Caesar's Celebrated Curative so easily, boy."*

If Jed could have put his hands on his father, he would have shook him. "I am thirty-one years old. Hardly a boy. And it's well past time I knew what is in this potion I've hawked for you all these years."

Caesar chuckled. *"All in good time, my boy. All in good time. When I'm good and ready, I'll turn over your legacy to you, but not before."*

His father's laughter made Jed's blood boil and his head pound. He whirled away, not wanting Caesar to see the fury on his face, or the hurt he feared might show in his eyes. Even dead, Caesar didn't trust Jed with the prized recipe for Great Caesar's Celebrated Curative. A longtime employee would deserve better treatment than this—and he was the man's son!

His agitation drove him away from the wagon. He intended to walk and sort out his feelings, but another burst of laughter pulled him toward the front of the Dengler home. It wouldn't hurt to walk by and let Nixie see that her scorn didn't bother him the least little bit.

Caesar started to go after Jed, but knew it wouldn't do any good. When the boy got in one of his moods, there was no reasoning with him. Seemed like those "moods" came more and more frequently these days.

Of course, ever since he could remember, Jed had been straining at the leash like a headstrong pup, determined to strike out in his own direction. It was up to his dad to rein him in, keep him from having to learn things the hard way, the way Caesar had.

He sighed and settled down on the wagon steps once

GREAT CAESAR'S GHOST

more. Take women, for instance. Jed scoffed at the idea that his old man had ever been a handsome swain, but in his heyday, Caesar Hawkins had had women following him around like bears after honey.

That was before Mona came along, of course. Ahh, now there was a woman and a half! Hair the color of goldenrod, eyes a deep velvet brown— she'd swept Caesar off his feet, instead of the other way around. He smiled at the memory. Make no mistake about it, Mona Simpson had been a real lady of the first water. After she'd passed on, Caesar hadn't found any who came close. Theirs was a once-in-a-lifetime romance, for sure.

So how had he raised a son so inept in the ways of love? Any fool could see Jed and Nixie Dengler were perfect for each other. Jed was the image of Caesar as a young man, and Nixie was enough like Mona to be her kid sister.

Caesar slapped his hand down on the wagon step. By Jove, he wasn't about to let Jed pass up this chance at happiness. There were a lot of things Caesar wasn't able to do anymore since his accident, but he could sure enough help his boy. Maybe a good woman was all Jed needed to ease his restlessness. If Caesar had to help him along a little with his courting, well, what was a father for anyway?

Jed found Nixie's family and half a dozen campers on the front porch of the Dengler home, taking turns cranking a freezer of ice cream. Dr. Dengler stood and waved him over. "Mr. Hawkins! Come join us, please."

He hadn't intended to intrude, but it would be rude to ignore the invitation, and ice cream did sound good. Jed made his way over to the gathering and nodded to everyone. A plain-faced young woman—Miss Evans wasn't it?— smiled up at Jed and folded her skirts close about her to allow him to climb the steps onto the porch, while her sister, Mrs. Merchant, gave him a cool stare. Theo Stebbins nodded formally from his place along the porch railing, next to Mr. Harrison, the camper suffering from tuberculosis. "You arrived just in time," said an older man, Mr.

Chapman, giving a mighty turn to the crank. "Ice cream's about ready."

Pete and Lou Dengler crouched beside the freezer, ready with a bucket of chopped ice and a paper twist of rock salt to add to the freezer, if necessary. Mrs. Chapman waited nearby with a tray of bowls and spoons. With the exception of the two "social disease" patients, everyone in the Dengler household had gathered in anticipation of a tasty treat.

So where was Nixie? Why wouldn't the daughter of the house be here in the midst of fun and laughter? Jed searched the gathering once more. He'd noticed that about her at dinner, too, how she held herself apart from the clamor and conversation. What was it about Nixie that made her different from those around her?

He turned away from the happy crew around the ice cream bucket and found himself facing Mrs. Dengler, who sat in the porch swing beside her husband. Even though she had to be at least fifteen years older than Jed, she was still an attractive woman. Easy to see where Nixie got her good looks. Nadine gave Jed a knowing smile. "Has anyone seen Nixie?" she called. "She won't want to miss out on the fun."

"She's on the back porch with William." Pete looked up from licking the dasher. "Let's leave her there! Then I can have her share."

Who is William? Jed thought, irritation rising. And what were Nixie's parents thinking, letting her sit alone on the porch with the man? Didn't they care about their daughter's reputation? A sinking feeling hit him in the stomach. Or maybe this was her fiancé—

"Mr. Hawkins, how long do you think you'll be staying with us in Welcome Springs?"

Dr. Dengler's question caught him off guard. "I'd meant to leave in the morning, but I'm afraid . . . something's come up."

"Nothing serious, I hope?" Mrs. Dengler leaned forward, all motherly concern. "You look rather upset."

Jed squared his shoulders. "No, nothing to be concerned about. I've run out of one of the ingredients for Great Caesar's Celebrated Curative, one that has to be special ordered from an Eastern pharmaceutical company. It will take several weeks to get here."

"Then you must certainly stay as our guest while you wait for its arrival." Dr. Dengler looked pleased. "I would welcome the opportunity to talk further with you about my plans for promoting Welcome Springs as a health resort."

Jed shifted from one foot to the other. Ham Dengler was such a kind soul, an innocent, really. The kind of man too many people probably took advantage of. "I wouldn't dream of imposing," he said.

"It would not be imposing at all." Dr. Dengler turned to his wife. "Mr. Hawkins would be most welcome, wouldn't he, dear?"

If Mrs. Dengler had worries about adding another mouth to her table, she had the grace not to show it. "But of course, dear." She smiled warmly at Jed. "We'd love to have you with us for as long as you're able."

Now if this wasn't a fix. He couldn't refuse the invitation without hurting the Denglers' pride. But he couldn't very well take them up on it without hurting his own.

"I'm sure you could help me with many good ideas for promoting Welcome Springs," Dr. Dengler said. "With your experience in the field of health products, I am sure you have much to teach me."

Jed looked away from the doctor's open, friendly gaze. His gaze came to rest on the graying hulk of the Willkommen Inn. His earlier conversation with Nixie came back to him—how her father had so much trouble finding help to finish the boardinghouse, which was crucial to his dreams of a booming health resort. He relaxed and turned back to the Denglers. "I don't know about advice, Dr. Dengler, but I do have a strong back and a little construction experience. What if I were to offer to work on the boardinghouse while I'm here, in exchange for a place to park my wagon?"

The doctor's face grew ruddy with excitement. "A place to park your wagon and meals at my table, too. I insist upon it." He jumped up from the swing and pumped Jed's hand. "Surely you were sent here to help make my dreams come true, Mr. Hawkins."

"I'd say that ice cream's almost ready." Mr. Chapman saved Jed from the embarrassment of answering.

Mrs. Dengler rose and put her hand on Jed's arm. "Would you be so kind as to go through the house and fetch Nixie for us?" she asked.

He hesitated. He had no wish to interrupt Nixie and her beau . . .

"It's perfectly all right." Mrs. Dengler nodded toward the door. "Just go straight through to the back."

He made his way through the house, his boot heels echoing on the hardwood floors. Past the front parlor and Dr. Dengler's office, past the dining room and kitchen, on through to a screened back porch.

As he approached, he could see the top of Nixie's blond head showing over the back of the settee cushion. Pausing outside the doorway, he stared at that silken halo, wondering what the ashen locks would look like tumbling down around her shoulders.

The fantasy brought an immediate physical reaction, and he shook the idle thoughts away. The sudden urge to talk to Nixie—really talk to her—overcame him. If he was going to be here for a few weeks, then they needed to reach a truce. She had made it clear enough she wanted nothing to do with him, but that didn't mean he couldn't do his best to change her low opinion of him. The challenge would enliven what might otherwise prove to be a dull summer.

Relieved to see that the other chairs in the room were unoccupied, he started forward, then froze at the sound of her voice. "I love you," she crooned. "You're Nixie's handsome man, aren't you? I love you so much."

The words, spoken with such tenderness, made his heart ache. He'd forgotten about the mysterious William. Even though the man was not in sight, Nixie was obviously not sitting on that sofa alone. Was some fellow from town meeting her here?

Whoever the man was, he certainly had cheek, making love to her practically underneath her parents' noses. It would serve the lovers right if he embarrassed them by interrupting now. He took a step forward, stomping down on the wooden floorboards.

"Oh!" Nixie started, and something flew from her shoulder. She peered around the side of the sofa at him. "Now look what you've done. You've startled William."

Jed looked around in confusion. Whoever William was, he had vanished, leaving Nixie alone on the sofa, a plate of what looked like chopped vegetables and fruit in her hand.

"Come here, sweetie. I won't let that man hurt you." To his amazement, she held out her hand and a green-and-yellow bird fluttered down from a hanging lamp and landed on her shoulder. The bird snuggled close to her cheek and glared at Jed. "I love you," he chattered. "Go away!"

Nixie laughed. "He picked that up from hearing me say it to my brothers so often." She looked fondly at the bird, and stroked his stomach with the tip of her finger.

Jed felt his own stomach tremble at the sight. What would it be like to be the recipient of such tenderness? "I didn't realize you had a bird," he said. Then he remembered seeing one in the cage in her room earlier that afternoon.

She held a bit of parsley between her thumb and forefinger. The bird tore off a bite, still studying Jed out of one eye. "William was given to us by one of Papa's patients in payment for a medical bill. But I'm the only one he really likes."

Jed noted the pride in her voice. But then, didn't everyone crave to be singled out for another's special affection?

Jed moved cautiously to a wicker chair and took a seat close to Nixie. She made a move as if to rise. "No." He put out a hand to restrain her. "Please, don't go. Stay and talk with me."

She remained poised on the edge of the sofa cushion, regarding him with a wary expression that was very similar to that of her pet. He could feel her pulse throbbing in her wrist beneath his fingers, hot and tremulous. Reluctantly, he released his hold on her and sat back in the chair.

He searched for some safe topic of conversation, anything to keep her here with him a while. "Quite an interesting group of guests you have here," he said. "I imagine the ranks will swell as the summer progresses. Lots of people must come here for the waters."

"Not as many as my father would like."

She sounded so sad. "Well, your father is a man of great vision."

"Is that a nice way of saying he's just a dreamer?"

The scorn in her voice startled him. What did Nixie Dengler have against dreamers? He'd thought women found that sort of thing attractive, adventurous, and daring even. "Men of vision put their dreams into action. If your father was content to merely dream, he'd have never laid the foundation for his boardinghouse, or painted that sign."

"Not many people seem to see it that way."

"There you go, frowning again." He smiled, teasing her. "I saw you frowning at me at dinner. You didn't seem too happy with my compliments to your father on his boardinghouse."

She offered the bird a chunk of apple, avoiding Jed's gaze. "I'm sure you meant well."

"But you still don't approve."

"Whatever makes you think that?" She arched her neck in feigned indifference.

He laughed. "My first assessment was right, Miss Dengler. You're no actress. You don't approve of my encouraging your father, and I want to know why."

He felt the sting of the disapproving look she gave him. "You're not the first one to come along and profess an interest in my father's plans, you know. You say nice things to please him, but you don't really mean it."

"What if I told you I'd just agreed to take over construction of the boardinghouse while I'm here in Welcome Springs."

She looked anything but delighted at this news. "And how long will that be?"

Even a day would apparently be too long for Nixie. "I

can't say for sure. I have to wait for the supplies I ordered to come in. Several weeks, at least."

She looked away. "I've seen it before. You'll talk a great show, work for a while, and in a few weeks, when you're tired of it all, you'll move on to some new adventure, leaving Papa with more of a mess than ever."

"You don't have a very high opinion of me, do you?" He spoke with the same teasing quality as before, but it was an effort to do so. It annoyed him that he cared what this prim spinster thought of him.

"I know your type."

"Ah, yes, what was it you called me—a rambler?" He leaned forward, elbows on his knees. "Well, maybe you're right. Is that so horrible?"

She looked at him, eyes dark with concern, worry lines creasing her forehead. "Suppose you stay long enough to finish the boardinghouse. What if after all these years, after all the money and time and worry he's put into it—What if Papa opens his boardinghouse and nothing comes of it? What then?"

He was aware of his knee almost touching her, of her thighs outlined beneath the fabric of her skirt, mere inches from his hand. He forced his eyes to look up, to gaze into her face once more, and cleared his throat. "Then your father will find a new vision—a better one."

She gave him a considering look. "But you think Papa's right? You think Welcome Springs could become famous?"

He shrugged. "Nobody can predict the future. But I think there's opportunity here."

"Opportunity to sell Great Caesar's Celebrated Curative?"

"I haven't any left to sell. At least not until the order from the pharmaceutical house arrives."

Her face flushed. "I apologize about your secret ingredient. I still can't believe the boys behaved so badly."

He laughed. "I'd say they'd been sufficiently punished. You about scorched my ears telling them off. And having to clean the neighbor's chicken house is a pretty terrible fate for a pair of youngsters."

He thought she almost smiled then. He leaned closer, encouraged. "So tell me, why are you sitting alone back here when everyone else is making ice cream out front?"

Her face took on a shuttered look. "I came to feed William. Besides, they'll never miss me."

He started to tell her that wasn't true, that in fact, he'd been sent to fetch her, but the bird distracted him. It peered around the back of Nixie's head and proclaimed, "Nanny goat! Nanny goat! Go away!"

He laughed, some of the tension flowing out of him. "Nanny goat? Where did he learn that?"

Her cheeks blushed a deeper pink. "My real name is Nanette. Pete and Lou taught him to say that. They aren't supposed to come into my room and bother him, but they always do when I'm not looking." She held up her finger and the little bird climbed onto it. "Naughty William," she scolded, lifting the parakeet up to eye level.

William ignored the reprimand and began to preen, running each long wing feather through his bill.

"He's fascinating, isn't he?" Jed said, leaning forward again for a closer look. "His feathers look so soft. Do you think he would let me touch him?"

She looked doubtful. "You could try, but he usually doesn't think much of strangers..."

Her voice faded as the bird stepped onto Jed's finger and bobbed his head. "Pretty boy!" he squawked.

Jed thought Nixie looked disappointed at her pet's easy acceptance of him. "I think he likes you," she said grudgingly.

He turned his head and met her gaze. He had the feeling William had just granted him a singular honor. And though he never would have thought to want a parakeet's approval, he was grateful for it now, if it would in any way improve Nixie's opinion of him. "What about you, Nixie?" he asked softly. "Do you think you could learn to like a rambling patent-medicine peddler like me? I might come to see my stay in Welcome Springs as worthwhile after all."

She turned away, her smile vanished, her skin grown as pale as paper. "I don't know what you were expecting when you came here this evening, but I can tell you I don't intend to make your stay here 'worthwhile.'" She stood and backed away, refusing even to look at him. "And in the future, I'd appreciate it if you'd stay as far away from me as possible. Come here, William, we're leaving."

The bird let out a squawk as Nixie turned to go, and sailed across the room to land on her shoulder. "Now wait a minute—" Jed rose to follow her, but he was intercepted in the doorway by Ham Dengler.

"There you are Mr. Hawkins, Nixie." Dr. Dengler nodded to Nixie, then clapped Jed on the shoulder. "Come, before the ice cream melts. And I want to talk to you about our plan—"

Jed could hear Nixie's footsteps retreating down the hall, followed by the sound of her hurrying up the stairs. What had he said or done to upset her so? Was the thought of even mere friendship with him so distasteful to her?

He frowned. Why should he care what Nixie Dengler thought? A town like this would have dozens of women who'd be more than happy to walk out with him, if all he was looking for was company, or an evening's distraction.

He pushed the thoughts away, trying to concentrate on Ham Dengler's conversation. But he couldn't shake the memory of Nixie staring at him, her hazel eyes filled with anger and more than a little hurt.

Chapter Five

Nixie usually enjoyed swimming. In the cool, mineral laden waters of the spring-fed pool below her house, she could forget the annoyances of everyday life and abandon herself to the silken flow of the water. The voices of those around her receded to distant murmurs as she dove beneath the surface of the pool, and people were reduced to stalklike legs arranged in groups in the shallows, or blurs of wind-milling arms and kicking feet as other swimmers passed by.

But today she found little to please her in or out of the water. Freed from the restraints of her corset, and dressed in her blue serge swimming costume, with its knee-length bloomers and cutaway skirt, she was all too aware of her body's dips and curves. The silken caress of the water kindled a wanton ache within her.

She did not have to look far to find the reason for such thoughts. Jed Hawkins had reminded her all too clearly of her role in life—unfulfilled spinster, and therefore an easy target for scoundrels like him.

She quickened her strokes, cutting across the pool to the far side, unwelcome memories pursuing her. He hadn't wasted any time, had he? Propositioning her his very first day in town? At least the others had waited a few days, and made a pretense of wooing her.

But in the end they were all the same, leering at her and telling her how "accommodating" they'd heard she was. One had even used the same words Jed Hawkins had chosen, saying a friend had told him about the little blond in Welcome Springs who'd make his visit there "worthwhile."

She reached the edge of the pool and turned to swim back toward the bathhouse, grateful for the water that hid the tears stinging her eyes. Six years she'd waited for the stories about her to die down. Two years had passed since the last mention had been made of it, and she'd begun to breathe easier, thinking she might salvage her reputation yet. But somewhere in his travels, the wild tales must have reached Jed Hawkins's ears.

Well, she'd made it clear she had no interest in "accommodating" him. She emerged from the water in front of the bathhouse, tired and gasping for breath. Pulling herself up onto the concrete curb that had been poured around the natural, gravel-bottomed pool, she rested for a moment in the shade of the oak and cypress that ringed the bathing area. Then she stood and wrung as much water as possible from the drooping skirt of her swimming suit and retied the sash into a neat bow. The garment was fashionable, but certainly not practical. Apparently the designers hadn't considered that a woman might actually want to swim in a swimming suit.

She retrieved her frilled mobcap from beneath the yaupon bush where she'd stashed it along with the sandals that resembled a ballerina's shoes and were as uncomfortable for swimming as they were for walking. Coiling her thick blond braid on top of her head, she popped on the cap, and scanned the growing crowd in the section of the springs set aside for women.

Dory Evans waved from a bench in the shallows. Smiling, Nixie walked toward her. Here was someone who could take her mind off herself and her worries.

She greeted Dory and nodded to Mrs. Frisco, who sat on the bench across from Dory. The stout widow, who lived next door to the Denglers, was known for her flower garden and her abilities as a baker, as well as for her abiding interest in anything that happened in the Dengler house.

Still holding the sandals in one hand, Nixie negotiated the rock steps down into the pool. Dory moved over to make room for her on the bench. Nonswimmers could sit here and take advantage of the spring's healing waters, which flowed up to their waists, while enjoying the fresh outside air. Those who wished for more privacy could rent individual bathtubs inside the bathhouses. The separate men's and women's facilities each also had drinking fountains, lockers, and changing rooms.

"You swim like a seal," Dory said, smiling up at Nixie. Dory wore a fanciful bathing dress of pink-and-gray striped cotton, with wide lace ruffles around the hem of the full skirt, and more lace trimming her bathing bloomers at the knees. A raspberry-colored sash was knotted to one side, with streamers falling past her hips, while a turban of matching raspberry fabric covered her hair. The ribbon straps of her ballerina sandals crisscrossed her calves to her knees.

"Nixie swims better than any man I know," Mrs. Frisco said in her thick German accent. She leaned forward and patted Nixie on the knee. "It is not so good for the woman to be better at something than the man, no? What do I tell you?"

Nixie tried to hide her frown. Mrs. Frisco was always fretting over Nixie's unmarried state and offering advice on how she might improve her chances of finding a husband. Nixie looked away from her nosy neighbor and addressed Dory. "What do you think of the baths?"

"Oh, I'm enjoying them so much. It's so beautiful and cool." Nixie followed Dory's admiring gaze around the pool. This time of day, after dinner, dozens of women and children gathered to sit around the tree-shaded pool, or splashed in the deeper water. One large matron floated on a log raft toward the center of the pool, while nearby, a pair of women took turns pouring buckets of water over each other.

"Look, there's Dinah." Dory pointed across the pool.

Dinah Merchant was so swathed in black that Nixie did not immediately recognize her. But when she turned her familiar frown in their direction, her identity was made clear. Nixie smiled in an exaggerated manner and waved wildly, pleased to see Mrs. Merchant's frown deepen at what she no doubt regarded as uncivilized behavior.

"Everyone in town must be here," Dory said.

"Everyone comes now, during the hottest part of the day," Mrs. Frisco said. She scooped up a handful of water and let it flow over her shoulder. "Of course, the men have their own pool, through those trees there." She nodded toward a path leading into the woods to their right.

Dory looked down and smoothed her swimming dress down over her knees. "I wonder if Mr. Stebbins likes to swim?"

Nixie bit back a grin as she watched Dory's cheeks flush as pink as her bathing dress. "Mr. Stebbins is a very nice man, isn't he?"

Dory raised her head. "The nicest! And now that his rash is clearing up, I think he's quite good-looking, too. Not that appearances are the most important thing about a person, of course, but . . ."

"But it doesn't hurt if a man is nice looking," Nixie said, thinking of Jed Hawkins's broad shoulders and handsome face. The thought of him in a swimming costume made her heart beat a little faster.

Dory giggled, then put a hand to her lips as if to keep in the sound. She glanced at Mrs. Frisco, who sat with her eyes closed, drowsing against the side of the pool. Then she leaned closer to Nixie and lowered her voice. "So you don't think I'm foolish to hope that . . . Well, that Mr. Stebbins might . . . might *like* me?"

Nixie shook her head. "No, of course not! Why shouldn't he like you?"

Dory bowed her head. "Please don't tell Dinah I said anything to you. I know she'd make fun of me if she knew."

Nixie vowed the next time she went swimming she'd be sure to grab Dinah Merchant by the ankles and pull her under. Of all the hateful things to do to her own sister—

"And what are you girls whispering about over there?" Mrs. Frisco sat upright and fixed them with a gimlet gaze. "Something interesting, it is certain, the way you both are blushing. Or do you need a dose of mineral water for the summer fever?"

Dory looked horrified. "I think I'd have to be really sick to actually want to drink the water." Her nose crinkled up in distaste.

Nixie laughed. "Most people don't care for the taste of the water at first, but you get used to it."

"Have you lived here all your life?"

"Almost. We moved here when I was still a baby."

"No wonder you swim so well, growing up with this practically in your backyard."

"Aye," Mrs. Frisco agreed. "I used to see her taking to the water like a fish when she was no more than a mite."

Nixie could not remember a time when the springs had not been a part of her life. The shaded pools were as familiar to her as the rooms of her house, serving as playground, retreat, and sanctuary over the years. She turned her attention back to Dory. "Where did you grow up?"

"Near Dallas. Daddy had a lot of land and cattle on different ranches. We girls were supposed to stay in town with Mama, but I went out with Daddy whenever I could." A mischievous look came into her eyes. "Dinah always hated it that I could ride better than her. Daddy taught me to stay on a horse practically before I could walk."

Nixie pictured a tiny, bucktoothed girl, clinging to a horse and riding alongside a leather-clad cowboy. The image made her smile.

"I think it is time to take a little swim and exercise these old bones." Mrs. Frisco heaved her bulk out of the pool, water sluicing off her black serge suit. She shook her finger at Nixie and Dory. "You girls had better not be sitting here all afternoon gossiping. You will not have those young figures forever. You should do what you can to keep them now."

"I'm afraid I don't know how to swim." Dory's voice quivered in dismay.

"Come on. I can teach you." Nixie stood and offered her hand to her new friend.

Dory looked doubtful. "I don't know. I'm not very graceful."

"Is that something else your sister told you?" Nixie shook her head. "I haven't seen any signs that you're especially clumsy, but in any case, you don't have to be graceful on land to be graceful in the water." She grabbed Dory's hand and tugged. "Come on. I've taught lots of people. It'll be fun."

Dory grinned. "All right. I'll do it."

They ran, laughing, toward the opposite end of the pool, where graveled shallows offered the perfect starting place for a swimming lesson. As Nixie coaxed and coached, she found her dark mood of earlier in the day completely lifted. How could anyone feel gloomy with sunlight and sparkling water and the company of a new friend?

Yes, it certainly was a glorious day to commune with nature, Caesar thought as he settled more comfortably on the thick branch of a cottonwood that jutted out over the water. He smiled down on the bevy of women clad in damp, form-fitting swimming costumes. Sun, fresh air, and beautiful scenery. What more could a man want?

A curvaceous young woman in a suit of black wool floated beneath his perch. Ah! It was enough to make a man feel young again! He'd been a great one for swimming in his day. Too bad Jed had never taken to it, even though Caesar had done his best to teach him. The boy had let one little setback put him off water forever.

A young woman's laughter drew his attention to the shallows. A smile spread across his face as he recognized Nixie Dengler. She was standing in hip-high water with a fancier-dressed but plainer-faced friend. Now there was a beauty and a half! The blue serge swimming costume clung to Nixie's full bosom and called attention to her trim waist. Damp tendrils of sunshine-colored hair escaped from beneath her frilly cap, and water droplets glittered in her lacy lashes.

Caesar found himself wishing she'd step out of the water, so he could get a look at her legs. He was sure they'd be as perfect as the rest of her. He bet she had nice ankles. He'd always been a sucker for a well-turned ankle. Mona had had gorgeous ankles. They hadn't had swimming costumes this revealing in those days, but there had been one memorable occasion when he'd persuaded her to go skinny-dipping . . .

He shook himself. Best keep his mind on the business at hand, and that business was hooking Jed up with Nixie Dengler. Too bad he hadn't studied love potions instead of herbal tonics . . .

No, he'd just have to do things the old-fashioned way, forcing them together in certain . . . compromising situations until they realized they were made for each other. Sometimes love happened overnight, but in this case, he wagered he might need a little longer. So he'd better make sure he had all the time he needed.

He searched around in his pockets until he found the sheet of paper he'd made out while Jed was over at the Denglers' last night. He'd intended to drop it into the post this morning, but now he was glad he'd forgotten. If Jed thought to question why the order from the pharmaceutical company was taking so long, Caesar would tell him it had been lost somewhere along the way.

Which, of course, would be the truth. Grinning at his own cleverness, he folded the order form and tore it over and over again, then opened his hand and let the bits of paper drift down onto the water. One by one, they grew waterlogged and sank.

Ah! It was good to have a project again, something important to do. He hadn't felt this good since he'd invented the formula for Caesar's Croup Compound, a recipe he'd been perfecting when the unfortunate explosion put certain ... *restrictions* on his lifestyle.

Preparing to climb down from the tree, he took a last look out over the pool. Such a beautiful place. He'd make it a point to come back soon, but right now, he had work to do.

Whistling to himself, he skirted the pool and headed toward the bathhouse. He'd reached the entrance to the stone building when he heard a high-pitched cry. Was that a child in distress? He stopped and cocked his head to listen. There it was again—definitely a child crying, though very softly.

He glanced around. The women seemed oblivious to the noise, but there was nothing wrong with *his* hearing. He hurried around the side of the building, following the noise. He hadn't gone far when he spied a boy huddled on the ground, cradling one arm and moaning.

Ah hah! It wasn't hard to deduce what had happened here! The broken branch of a cottonwood very much like the one where Caesar had been sitting, lay on the ground not far from the boy, its jagged end jutting skyward. Caesar stood over the boy and shook his head. What were young people coming to these days? If a boy was going to spy on the women's bathhouse, he ought to at least have enough sense to choose a properly sturdy branch.

He bent to help the young scamp to his feet, then noticed the angle of the arm. Something not quite right about that. He bent and spoke in the boy's ear. *"Young man! Are you all right?"*

"I think my arm's broken," the boy said tearfully, bent double in the dirt, his face turned toward the ground.

"I'll have someone to help in two shakes." What this needed was someone with a cool head in a crisis. *"Better find Jed,"* he mumbled as he set out as fast as he could move.

"Nixie! Nixie Dengler!"

Nixie jerked her head up at the sound of her name. Her eyes grew wide when she saw Jed Hawkins making his way toward her through the throng of curious women. Her first instinct was to sink down in the water and hide, but half the women in the area were already gesturing toward her. When she looked again at Jed's face, something about his anxious expression made her stand and wave in response.

"Good, I found you," he said, striding toward her. He paused, gasping for breath, his face flushed as if he had run a long way. His shirt was stuck to his skin in places by sweat, and sawdust clung to his hair.

"Mr. Hawkins, you shouldn't be here," she said when he reached her.

He seemed to notice where he was for the first time. All around, women regarded him with expressions ranging from disapproval to open admiration. "Young man, what do you mean, coming into the women's bathing area?" Mrs. Frisco demanded, arms folded over her ample bosom.

Jed turned to Nixie. She was suddenly conscious of the water streaming from her body, and of the blue serge clinging to her like a second skin. His face flushed deeper. "I need your help. Your brother's fallen and I think he's broken his arm."

The news was like a splash of cold water to her fevered senses. "My brother? Which one?"

"Pete. He's asking for you." He turned as if to lead the way to the injured boy.

"Wait," she called. "We should fetch my father."

"I checked at the house before I ran to the pool. The note on the door says your father went to some farm on a call. I didn't see your mother or any of the others anywhere."

"Mama went to her sewing circle. The others are probably at the bathhouses or pavilions."

"Come on," Jed said. "He's just through here."

All thought of modesty forgotten, she followed him along a path leading around the side of the women's bathhouse. The sight of Pete lying crumpled at the base of a cottonwood tree brought a cry to her lips.

Jed put a calming hand on her shoulder. "I think he's going to be all right."

When she reached his side, Pete raised his head and gave

her a weak smile. "You're not going to bless me out, are you, Sis?"

"Shush." She put a hand to his pale forehead and pushed aside a lock of light-brown hair, soaked with sweat. He lay on his back, cradling his arm, which hung at an odd angle from the elbow. She glanced up at the row of windows near the roof of the bathhouse, then looked over her shoulder, at the group of women, including Dory and Mrs. Frisco, who had followed them. "Would one of you go to fetch my father?" she asked. "See if you can find out who he went to call on. Mr. Hawkins and I will see about getting Pete to the house, out of the heat."

She waited until the crowd had dispersed before she looked at Pete again. "You were trying to spy on the women again, weren't you?"

He nodded and pressed his head into the cradle of her palm. "Jed here found me just in time."

Nixie looked up at Jed Hawkins. "What were you doing here?" she asked, suspicion growing. "Why aren't you swimming with the other men?"

A look of—Was that embarrassment?—came into his eyes. "I don't swim."

She shook her head. "Half the people here don't. But they still enjoy the water."

"I don't." He frowned and looked away.

She continued to watch him. "So what were you doing here? Did you come to spy on the women, too?"

He squatted down beside them, his gaze focused on Pete, as if he wanted to avoid looking at her. "I was working on the boardinghouse and I . . . I thought I heard a cry. Something told me to check it out."

A likely story, she thought.

"It was an angel."

She stared at Pete, uncertain she'd heard him correctly. "What did you say?"

"It was an angel told Jed to come and find me. I heard it right after I fell. It asked if I was all right, then told me it would go for help. Next thing I knew, Jed was here."

"An angel," Nixie repeated softly.

"Stranger things have happened," Jed said. He put a hand on Pete's shoulder. "Do you think we ought to make a sling or something for that arm?"

She frowned and reached for the injured limb. Pete flinched. "Don't touch it."

"We can't leave you lying out here in the heat," she said. "And we can't move you to the house without jostling you. At least if we stabilize your arm, we'll avoid hurting you more."

He bit his lip and nodded.

"We'll need to make a splint," she said to Jed. "We can bind the arm to a stick or something to keep it from shifting overmuch while we carry him."

"You find a stick," Jed said. "We can use my shirt for a bandage." He was already stripping off the garment in question.

Flushing, she turned away to search the undergrowth for a suitable piece of wood. But when she turned back with her offering, she could not avoid the sight of Jed's undershirt-clad torso. The thin knit fabric clung to his broad shoulders like a second skin, more enticing even than naked flesh. A dusting of golden brown hair, glistening with sweat, showed at the triangular neck opening, and Nixie could just make out the flat outline of his nipples, pressed against the taut fabric. She caught her breath and would have dropped the stick had he not taken it from her. "Show me what to do," he said, forcing her wayward thoughts back to the task at hand.

Jed held Pete still while Nixie tore the shirt into strips and bound the stick to the arm. Pete bit his lip and made only a few grunts of pain, but when she was finished, Nixie saw tears shining in her brother's eyes. "Now let's get him to the house," she said, sitting back on her heels.

Jed stood and offered his hand to Nixie and pulled her up in one smooth move. She stood very close to him for a moment, her hand still in his, eye-level to his chest. The scents of masculine sweat and sawdust and sweet herbs assailed her in an intoxicating rush.

Then he released her and bent down, carefully scooping

Pete into his arms. "Just hang in there, young man, and we'll have you home in no time."

Nixie followed them toward the house, hurrying to keep up with Jed's long-legged strides. She was still barefoot, the straps of her sandals wound awkwardly around her arm. Every time she stumbled on an uneven place in the path, or tripped over a root, Jed would pause, looking back toward her. "Are you all right?"

She nodded, motioning him onward. She tried to watch the path, concentrating on where she was stepping. But over and over again, her eyes were drawn to Jed's broad back. She watched in fascination as the muscles moved beneath the sweat-dampened undershirt. He carried Pete as if he weighed no more than a baby, though at fourteen, her brother was already taller and heavier than Nixie herself. Jed was careful to brace the boy's injured arm with one hand so that it was not jostled. The combination of strength and tenderness brought a lump to Nixie's throat. Was this the same arrogant showman who'd propositioned her on her own porch last night?

When they finally reached the house, Jed arranged Pete on the parlor sofa while Nixie fetched a bottle of laudanum from her father's office. She returned to find Jed plumping pillows and spreading an afghan over their patient.

Pete took the laudanum without protest. "Do you think Papa will be home soon?" he asked.

"I hope it won't be too long," she said.

He nodded. "I'm glad Jed found you, so I don't have to wait alone."

Nixie looked over her shoulder at Jed, who had pulled a chair to the end of the sofa and sat watching the two of them. His gaze moved from the injured boy to herself, traveling over her water-soaked suit. His eyes darkened and his breathing deepened. She felt a hot blush color her cheeks, even as her nipples rose to press against the damp fabric of her suit.

"You'd better get out of those wet clothes," Jed said, his voice husky.

Nixie choked out some response, then whirled and hurried for the stairs. It was true she was shaking, not from any chill in the air, but from a fire burning within her that refused to be damped.

Jed held himself very still, gripping the arms of the chair until his fingers ached. He watched Nixie hurry out of the room. She always seemed to be fleeing from him. The more she fled, the greater his desire to capture her.

A deep longing overwhelmed Jed, a mixture of lust and loneliness and need. When he'd gotten over the first moments of concern for Pete, he'd been dumbstruck at the sight of Nixie standing before him, wet swimming costume clinging to every curve of her figure. Water streaming from her body, damp tendrils of hair escaping from beneath her mobcap. She'd called to mind a siren, risen from the deep to tempt a sailor to breach his ship on the rocks. It was all he could do to sit stone-still in the chair, trying to hold his composure.

He was still sitting that way when Nixie returned. She was dressed in a modest gown of rose-striped cotton, with a high neck and long sleeves that were full near the shoulders, and fitted tightly from elbow to wrist.

But damp tendrils still escaped from the coil of braids atop her head, curling around her face like a mermaid's tresses.

"I brought this for you." She did not look at him, but held out a man's shirt, crisp with starch. "It's my father's, so it won't fit you right, but . . ." Her voice trailed away, and she flushed a deep rose that matched the stripes of her dress.

"Thanks." He took the shirt and slipped it on. It was too tight in the shoulders, too short and full around the torso. But he was glad to have it. Being even partially undressed in Nixie's presence was too great a reminder of what he really wanted to do with her.

The front door flew open, slamming back against the wall and rattling the glass in the windows. Dr. Dengler rushed in, red-faced and panting.

GREAT CAESAR'S GHOST

"Oh, Papa!" Nixie cried, running up to him. "I'm so glad you're here."

"Mrs. Frisco found me and told me what happened." He dropped his doctor's bag beside the sofa and knelt to examine his son.

Pete opened his eyes. "Papa," he murmured drowsily.

"I gave him some laudanum for the pain," Nixie said, hovering behind him.

"That's a good girl." Ham began carefully unwinding the torn linen from around the injured arm. "And you did a fine job with this splint, too."

Jed rose and stepped back from the sofa. He felt awkward, an intruder onto this family scene. Nixie and her father bent over Pete, comforting the boy and discussing the injury to his arm. They seemed to have forgotten that anyone else was in the room.

He turned away, throat tight with disappointment. Nixie had her family. He had no one. A ghostly father was no substitute for real human companionship. He couldn't even console himself with the thought of crowds waiting to hear about the benefits of Great Caesar's Celebrated Curative. For the first time in memory, he had nothing and no one with which to devote his energies.

"Where do you think you're going, young man?" Dr. Dengler rose, knees creaking, and addressed Jed. "I haven't had a chance to thank you for helping Pete. Nixie never would have been able to get him to the house by herself."

"There's no need to thank me, Doctor."

"Well, I'm certainly not going to let you leave, not yet. I'll want you to help me move the boy up to his room."

"All right." Jed tried not to look at Nixie, but he could not seem to keep his eyes from her. She was rolling the pieces of his torn shirt into a neat ball, her fingers working swiftly to gather up the fabric and wind it tightly together.

As if feeling his gaze on her, Nixie raised her head. For one brief moment, he stared into the green-gold depths of her eyes. He had expected her to look on him with scorn, as she had before. What he saw instead surprised him. Someone, some time, had hurt the lovely Miss Dengler.

The pain showed in her eyes like an unhealed scar.

Then she blinked and looked away. He clenched his fists at his sides in frustration. What would it take to relieve Nixie Dengler's pain? And what would it cost him to get close enough to do so?

Chapter Six

Caesar wasted no time executing his plan to bring Nixie and Jed together. Success would be his, and all too easily. He'd watched the two of them as they cared for Nixie's brother the other day and it was as plain as spots on a dog that they were already halfway in love with each other. All they needed was to spend some time alone together and let nature take its course. He'd even waited to see if they'd figure things out by themselves, but instead of following their natural inclinations, the two young fools had been avoiding each other!

He pulled two pieces of paper from his pocket and carefully unfolded them. Now it was up to him. He'd thought of the perfect plan. He'd spent a lot of time writing out these letters, striving for the exact right tone, one that would lead the recipient to believe more than casual interest from the sender, but nothing so forward as to lead to suspicion of impropriety.

Impropriety could come later. Right now, he merely wanted to get the two alone.

He read the first note again, the one for Nixie.

> *Dearest Lady,*
> *Nothing would make me happier than for you to do me the honor of walking out with me this afternoon. Please meet me at Indian Springs at half past four.*
> *Signed,*
> *An Admirer*

"A small masterpiece if I do say so myself," he mumbled. He bent and selected an appropriate sized rock from those lining a nearby flowerbed. Something not too large, but with enough heft to travel far. He wrapped the note around the rock and tied it neatly with a bit of string, then made ready to loft it through Nixie's bedroom window.

Stepping back, Caesar took aim, then froze in the middle of his windup. Two open windows on the second story of the house confronted him. Which one was Nixie's? He frowned and studied the two identical openings. Each had lacy curtains fluttering in the breeze. Both were absent screens and high enough in the wall so that he could see nothing of the room inside from his vantage point.

The one on the left was Miss Dengler's. He was sure of it. Should he go up and check?

No. Nixie's was on the left, he was certain. Before doubt had a chance to interfere with his plans again, Caesar pulled back his arm and lobbed the paper-wrapped rock through the open window. It sailed through perfectly, scarcely brushing the curtains.

I still have the old touch, he thought, and set out to deliver the second note. This one was more circumspect, as befitting a proper young lady.

> *Dear Sir,*
> *There is something I would like to discuss with you, if you would do me the favor of meeting me at Indian Springs at 4:30 this afternoon.*

No signature, though he'd done his best to imitate a woman's flowery handwriting. Any man worth his salt wouldn't be able to resist such a mysterious summons.

GREAT CAESAR'S GHOST

Caesar made his way to the Willkommen Inn, where Jed had been slaving away every day since they'd arrived here. *This afternoon's adventure will do the boy good,* he thought. Spying Jed's jacket hanging on a tree near the inn, Caesar slipped the note into the front pocket and hurried away, whistling a happy tune underneath his breath.

Nixie tried to concentrate on bringing her father's accounts up to date, but the incessant hammering from the Willkommen Inn made it impossible to keep her mind on her work. Did Jed Hawkins have to work on the place *all* the livelong day? She'd seen him setting out this morning, tool belt slung about his hips like some gunfighter ready to do battle. She'd glimpsed him once or twice during the day, too, standing in the shade of the live oak out back, drinking a dipper of water, sweat molding his shirt to his muscular back.

Her father raved every night about what a wonderful job he was doing. It's true he was a hard worker, and certainly he'd been strong and reliable when Pete fell and broke his arm. She didn't know what she'd have done that day without his calm, steadying presence . . .

She frowned. It didn't matter how many admirable qualities Mr. Hawkins possessed. The fact remained that he fed her father's fantasies of making the resort a success and distracted him from the real work of looking after his medical practice. And she couldn't easily dismiss the way he'd propositioned her his first night here.

She turned back to the ledger once more, determined to put the Willkommen Inn, and Jed Hawkins, out of her mind once and for all.

"Nixie?" A light tapping on the door frame pulled her away from the books once more. She swiveled in her chair and found Dory Evans peeking in at her. "I hate to disturb you while you're working, but I wondered if I might talk to you a moment?" Dory asked.

"Of course we can talk." Nixie pushed the ledger book away. "What is it? Has something happened?" Dory's face was flushed pink, and her eyes shone feverishly bright.

"Oh Nixie, look what just came through my bedroom window!" She pulled her hand from behind her back and revealed a fist-sized rock.

"A rock?" Nixie looked up, puzzled.

"Yes, I was practicing walking with a book on my head—Dinah tells me it promotes a graceful posture—when it came sailing through the open window and landed on my bed!"

"It's a good thing you weren't in the bed at the moment. Who would be throwing a rock at this house?" A horrible thought came to her. "Do you think one of the boys—?" She started to rise from her chair. If one of her brothers had been heaving rocks at the guests—

"Oh no. I'm sure it wasn't one of your brothers."

Nixie lowered herself into the chair once more. "I suppose not. Pete is still recuperating from his accident and I doubt Lou would get into this kind of trouble by himself."

"It wasn't just a rock." Dory pulled a crumpled piece of paper from the pocket of her skirt. "This was attached to it."

Nixie took the paper and read the note neatly inscribed on it. " 'An Admirer?' " She looked up at Dory again. "Who do you think sent it?"

"I don't know! Do you think . . ." Dory flushed a deeper pink. "I mean . . . Do you know where Mr. Stebbins is this morning?"

"I believe he's helping Mr. Hawkins at the Willkommen Inn. They mentioned something about it at breakfast." Dinah had claimed a sick headache this morning, and Dory had remained upstairs to nurse her sister.

Dory looked down at the rock cradled in her hands. "Do you think he might have sent the note?"

"Attached to a rock? Why didn't he give it to someone to deliver to you, or slip it under your door?"

Dory grinned. "But this is so much more romantic!"

Nixie returned the note to her friend. "What are you going to do? Are you going to meet him?"

Dory carefully folded the note. "Oh, I think I must." She hesitated. "But I wonder . . . would you go with me?"

"Go with you? But Mr. Stebbins, or whoever your admirer is, doesn't want to see me. He wants you."

"Just walk over there with me," Dory pleaded. "Just until we make sure it *is* Mr. Stebbins, and not some stranger up to no good."

Nixie was glad to see Dory hadn't lost all her common sense to romantic fantasies. She nodded. "I'll be happy to go with you and make sure everything's all right."

"Good. I'll meet you down here about a quarter past four and we'll walk over to Indian Springs together." All smiles, Dory hurried from the room.

Nixie turned back to the ledger. But she found it difficult to concentrate. Dory's enthusiasm for her admirer's romantic gesture had infected her. What kind of man would lob a rock through an open window to get a young woman's attention? The gesture seemed entirely too primitive for shy schoolmaster Theo Stebbins.

Now Jed Hawkins—she could see him taking that sort of he-man approach. He had the kind of masculine, take-charge personality that both aggravated and intrigued her.

Nixie sat up straighter in the chair and forced her attention back to the book in front of her. What was she doing wasting time thinking about him? Jed Hawkins was an arrogant wanderer, not the kind of man she wanted anything to do with.

Caesar was waiting by Indian Springs that afternoon when the young women came walking down the sun-dappled path. *What's this—two of them?* He leaned closer and squinted until he recognized Nixie Dengler and her plain friend. The friend was dressed to the nines in a flowered frock, complete with matching frilled parasol, while Nixie had on the same shirtwaist and skirt she'd worn to breakfast. Hmmph. You'd think she'd have dressed up a little more for an assignation.

Still, even in ordinary dress, she left most other women in the shade. But why had she bothered to bring the friend?

The two women paused beside the springs and looked around. "I think it's a good idea we came together, Dory,"

Nixie said. "We have no way of knowing whether the person who sent the note has honorable intentions or not."

"Oh, I do hope they are honorable." The plain one, Dory, giggled. "Or at least mostly so."

Caesar relaxed and smiled to himself. Of course, the young lady was simply being prudent. Another mark in her favor, if he did say so.

The young women tensed, and he followed their gaze up the path. A man headed toward them. Not Jed, but that other fellow, the red-faced one. Caesar frowned. What was he doing here? He hoped the women got rid of him quickly, before he spoiled the plot.

The man stopped. "H-hello, Miss Evans, Miss Dengler."

"Hello, Mr. Stebbins." The plain woman flushed and looked pleased. Nixie merely nodded politely. *She's probably wishing he'd be on his way and quick about it,* Caesar thought.

"L-lovely day out, isn't it?" Stebbins observed. He looked at the sky, at the springs, at the woods around them—anywhere but at the two young ladies before him.

"Yes, it is beautiful," Miss Evans agreed.

"A perfect afternoon for a walk." Nixie elbowed her friend in the side.

The young man tugged at his collar and cleared his throat. "Miss Evans, I wanted to see you?"

She leaned toward him. "Yes?"

He flushed. "I mean, you wanted to see me?"

"Oh, yes!" she breathed.

He looked around, avoiding the eager look on her face. Nixie stared at the ground. Caesar suspected she was biting her tongue to keep from laughing. Truly, he'd never seen a more inept pair. If he hadn't been so busy working with Jed and Nixie, he might have taken the young man aside and offered him a few pointers.

"It is a lovely day for a walk, isn't it?" Stebbins declared, as if the thought had suddenly occurred to him.

"And I . . . I'd be pleased to walk out with you, Mr. Stebbins," Miss Evans said in a rush.

"You would?" He grinned, then offered his arm, and

off they went, leaving Nixie behind, all but forgotten, though Dory paused to wave good-bye and mouth "thanks."

Well, now that they're out of the way, let's get this show on the road! Caesar fished a battered watch from his pocket and checked the time. Four forty-five! It wasn't like Jed to be so late.

He looked up in time to see Nixie headed down the path, back the way she'd come. Had she grown tired of waiting and decided to give up? He hurried along ahead of her, determined to manufacture a distraction to keep her from leaving.

Hmmmm. She didn't look like a jilted paramour. In fact, she looked almost . . . pleased!

He glanced back down the path, toward the retreating figures of Miss Evans and Mr. Stebbins. A horrible thought came to him. Had things gone wrong somewhere? Could it be he'd thrown the rock into the wrong window? And put the other note in the wrong jacket?

Hmmph. Well, even geniuses made mistakes sometimes. He wouldn't let a little setback like this dissuade him from his goal. The Great Caesar Hawkins had more than one trick up his sleeve. Jed and Miss Nixie Dengler would get together and soon, he'd see to it!

"The trick is to get people to concentrate on what you're saying, not actually what you're doing."

Nixie halted on the threshold of the screened porch when she heard Jed Hawkins's voice. She had scrupulously avoided seeing him, outside of the dining room, in the week since Pete's accident. She had no desire to risk more than the merest exchange of civilities with the man. Though he had redeemed himself somewhat by helping her with Pete, she had no doubt that, given the opportunity, he would proposition her again. He didn't strike her as a man who would give up easily.

She frowned, annoyed. The screened porch was her favorite retreat, and she'd been looking forward to sitting there with William. She looked at the bird perched on her shoulder. William moved closer and cocked his head to look up at her, as if awaiting her decision. She started to turn away, but Jed's words caught her attention.

"You don't want people looking too closely at your hands. Remember, the secret to magic is illusion."

"Nanny goat! Hello!"

She flinched and raised a hand to distract the bird, but it was too late. Jed looked around the end of the wicker sofa and grinned at her. "Miss Dengler, come in. I was just showing Pete a few card tricks."

Reluctantly, she stepped into the room. As she walked around the sofa, she saw Pete reclining at one end, intent on studying the cards in Jed's hands. She smiled at her brother and patted his shoulder. "How's your arm today?"

He frowned at the heavy plaster cast supported by a sling fashioned from a red bandanna. "It itches like the devil."

"Have you tried using a buttonhook to scratch?" she asked, sitting in the armchair closest to him.

"Won't reach." He stuck out his lower lip.

"Try a knitting needle." Jed winked at Nixie and extended the cards to her. "Pick a card, any card. But don't tell me which one it is."

Nixie stared at the fan of cards in his hand, struggling to regain her composure, which had fled at his roguish wink. It was all she could do to keep from returning his smile, joining in his game. But that would be encouraging him to think of her as eager to "accommodate" him.

William had no such dilemma to trouble him. While Nixie waited, he sidled down her arm, attracted to the brightly colored rectangles of pasteboard. He launched himself onto Jed's hand and bit into the top of a card.

"William's choosing a card!" Pete squealed, then collapsed against the cushions, giggling.

Jed held up the card the bird had chosen and frowned at the neat wedge that had been excised from the top. "Either that, or he's marking them."

"He likes paper," Nixie said, coaxing the bird back onto her finger. "Most of my books have chewed edges."

"Never mind." Jed inserted the card back into the deck,

shuffled with the skillfulness of a carnival monte dealer, then fanned them before her again. "Come on. Choose a card."

She shook her head. "I don't think—"

"Hurry up, Nixie, so Jed can show you his trick." Pete leaned toward her.

Jed gave her a quizzical look. "I think your sister doesn't want to choose a card from me." He transferred the fan of cards into Pete's hand. "Go on now, you show her what you've learned."

Pete held the cards toward her. "Choose one. Look at it, but don't show me. And don't tell me what you've got."

She did as he instructed, coming up with the six of clubs.

"All right, now wait a minute."

She held the card to her breast as Pete carefully gathered the deck back into a pile and balanced it on the wide arm of the sofa. "Now you put the card you picked back in the deck. Anywhere you want."

She slipped the card into the top third of the stack.

Awkwardly, Pete began to shuffle the deck, worrying his lower lip between his teeth as he struggled to mix the cards without scattering them. As he worked, Nixie glanced at Jed. He was watching the boy, a pleased expression on his face. She felt a stab of regret. How could a man be so thoughtful and patient—spending his spare time entertaining a convalescing boy—and yet be so unprincipled as to proposition her on his very first day in town? Which image was the *real* Jed Hawkins?

"Okay. Now I'm going to show you your card." Pete drew her attention to him once more. As she watched, he began turning over cards. He held up a seven of clubs. "That's not it, is it?" he asked.

She shook her head.

"I didn't think so." He turned over a few more cards and revealed an eight of diamonds. "This one isn't it, either, is it?" he asked, flourishing the card.

"No, it isn't."

"I didn't think so." He tossed the card onto the floor.

William fluttered onto the sofa, next to the stack of cards

and inched toward them. Nixie smothered a giggle. "Tell your bird I don't need his help," Pete said.

He grinned as he spoke. His eyes glowed with excitement, and he seemed to have forgotten about his cast in the thrill of the moment. Nixie had expected him to be depressed over the prospect of a summer with no swimming and no baseball, but he seemed perfectly happy to be lounging about the house. She was loathe to admit it, but she suspected Jed himself, and the attention he paid the boy, had something to do with this change in Pete's attitude.

Nixie felt her heart softening toward the handsome Mr. Hawkins, even as the words to thank him stuck in her throat. Too often before, men like him had used her words, spoken in innocence, against her.

The worst of it was, it would be so easy for her to like Jed. She was drawn to him the way William was attracted to those brightly colored cards. Was it a flaw in her character, this weakness she had for con men and hustlers?

Pete turned over the last card in the stack. "It's not here," he said, looking up at her.

She coaxed William onto her finger once more and lifted him to her shoulder. "Very funny. You didn't look through them all."

"All right. Then you find it." He shoved the deck toward her, then sat back, a smug look on his face.

Nixie looked over to see the same cocky expression on Jed's face. Nevertheless, she picked up the deck and began thumbing through the cards.

After the second pass, she had to concede the six of clubs was not in the stack. "Where is it?" she asked, not daring to look at Jed, but feeling his gaze on her.

"You must have kept it," Pete said.

She shook her head. "I did no such thing—"

"Then how else did this get here?" She gasped as Pete leaned forward and pulled a card from behind her head. Grinning, he showed her the six of clubs.

"That was great!" Jed slapped Pete on the back and grinned at Nixie. "Your brother's got the touch."

Nixie put one hand to the back of her head, as if expecting to find more cards hidden there. "How did you do that?"

"It's magic!" Pete laughed and turned to Jed. "Teach me some more!"

"Tomorrow. You can practice that one in the meantime." He bent and retrieved the card Pete had thrown on the floor. "I liked the throwing of the card. Nice touch. Distracts the audience."

"I thought it up myself." Pete grinned even more.

"Where did you learn card tricks?" Nixie asked, forgetting her resolution not to talk to Jed unless absolutely necessary.

"We once had a magician traveling with our show. He took me under his wing and taught me what he knew."

She frowned. She could see it now—a jaded cardsharp, and a younger version of the handsome man before her. Even then, the thrill of the hustle must have lured him. "I can see how that would come in handy in your present line of work."

"Come on, Jed. Pick a card. Help me practice."

Jed turned his attention to the boy, but Nixie saw the frown that creased his forehead, and felt a heaviness in the pit of her stomach. Why did she have to be such a shrew? Couldn't she put some distance between herself and this man without resorting to cutting remarks?

"What's the matter, Miss Dengler? Don't you believe in magic?" Jed's voice had a teasing quality.

She flushed. "Of course not. There's no such thing."

"How can you be so sure?" He deftly shuffled the cards, a sly smile coming to his face.

"Well, because . . . because I just am."

He ran his thumb along the edge of the deck and looked thoughtful. "Magic is just another name for the unexplainable. You don't understand it, so it must be wrong."

She straightened her shoulders. "No sensible person would believe in such nonsense."

His smile broadened. "Guess not."

What was he grinning about? Was he making fun of her? William moved over and began tugging at a ribbon on the bodice of her dress. She stroked the soft feathers of his belly, trying to calm the storm of emotions that troubled her.

Jed watched Nixie as she petted the bird. He hadn't missed the censure in her remark about his "line of work." So she still saw him as nothing more than a sideshow fraud, out to bilk the public of its hard-earned dollars.

It was just as well she didn't know everything old Tom Satterwhite, the cardsharp, had taught Jed. The old man had fancied himself quite the Casanova, and had taken it upon himself to tutor young Jed in the art of pleasing a woman.

Jed had been thankful for those lessons. Some he'd never had occasion to use—yet. Others he'd practiced until he knew them well. But he'd never drawn upon those skills or others to cheat or defeat anyone. If only Nixie could believe that of him.

As Jed pretended to watch Pete practice one-handed card shuffling, he studied Nixie out of the corner of his eye. She sat upright in the chair, her attention focused on the green-and-yellow bird, who clung to the ruffle edging of her bodice and played with the ribbon streamers of a bow on the collar of the dress. As the bird tugged harder on the ribbon, Nixie smiled and clucked to him under her tongue. The bird responded with similar noises, and began amusing himself with one of the pearl buttons down the front of the bodice.

She stroked the bird's breast with one finger, and the parakeet ran his beak along the edge of the placket where the two halves of the bodice joined.

Their playing had a sensual quality that made Jed's pulse quicken. He could imagine himself toying with those buttons, running his hand along the placket, slipping his fingers between the layers of fabric to feel the lacy undergarments beneath. Nixie would whisper love-words to him, and stroke his chest with her delicate hands.

He tried to push such dangerous thoughts from his mind. Nixie wasn't some carnival lightskirt to warm his bed a few nights before he moved on to the next town, the next show. If he gave in to the desire she stirred in him, he'd be committing himself to a life sentence here on the backside of nowhere.

Even that thought wasn't enough to cool the heat that coursed through him as he watched the bird rub its head against the satin-smooth skin of Nixie's throat. What would it feel like to place his lips just there—

"Nixie loves that silly bird more than anything."

Pete's words brought Jed out of his daydream with a jolt. He looked guiltily at the boy, wondering how much he had let his emotions show on his face. But Pete was teasing Nixie. "You're even jealous if anyone else looks at your precious bird."

"If all you did was look, that would be one thing. But you and Lou come into my room when I've asked you not to, and let William out of his cage, and he might get away or get hurt." She shook her head. "Just yesterday I went in and found him perched on the shade pull. What if he'd gotten tangled in the cord and choked? Or worse, he might escape downstairs and get loose."

"He comes downstairs with you all the time," Pete said.

"But I always make sure the windows that are missing screens are shut tight before I bring William down." She frowned. "Just don't you let me catch you in my room messing with him again."

Pete nudged Jed and laughed. "See, what did I tell you? She's plumb foolish about that bird. I think she likes him better than she does people."

Nixie flushed and looked away. But not before Jed had seen the real concern in her eyes. Pete enjoyed teasing his sister, but this time the boy might have hit on the truth. Maybe Nixie did love her pet more than she loved people. Maybe she'd learned the hard way that people weren't always worthy of her love.

Chapter Seven

Nixie looked away and blinked back angry tears. Pete could be so cruel sometimes. He might as well have told Jed she was an old maid because she'd run off every man who'd ever shown any interest in courting her. She was an eccentric fussbudget who preferred the company of a talking bird to that of a flesh and blood man.

That's what everyone else in the family thought—what most of the people in town probably thought, too. They'd seen a string of men come calling at Dr. Dengler's house over the years, only to leave with hat in hand, after a few days, or weeks, of paying court to the doctor's only daughter.

Must be something not quite right about that girl, they all said. If she was only quieter . . . happier . . . more of a lady . . . smiled more . . . wasn't so proud. Everyone had a reason why Nixie Dengler hadn't married yet. She ground her teeth in frustration. No one ever thought to suggest it was the *men* who weren't quite right. They were the ones who believed those long-ago rumors about her, and they were the ones who left as soon as they found out she had no intention of proving the rumors true. For all his outward charm, she was sure Jed Hawkins was no better than any of the others.

She was trying to gather the courage to leave the porch when Dory Evans swept into the room. "Nixie, I'm so glad I've found you," she said, smiling in a way that made her buck teeth more prominent. She hesitated as Jed rose from his chair and turned to face her. "Oh, I'm sorry, I didn't realize you weren't alone—"

"I was just leaving." Nixie stood and rushed to Dory and took her arm. "Mr. Hawkins is entertaining Pete at the moment and I'm sure they'd just as soon I got out of their way."

Jed opened his mouth as if to protest, but Nixie hurried Dory out of the room. William squawked and dug his nails into her shoulder to keep from being swept off in her haste. "Now, what did you want to see me about?" Nixie asked, stopping when they reached the foot of the stairs.

"I was wondering if you had time to help me with my hair." Dory put one hand to the knot of curls cascading over her forehead.

What Nixie really wanted was to lie down on her bed and nurse the ache that was already pounding at her temples. But Dory's eager smile persuaded her otherwise. An afternoon spent helping her friend might be the perfect antidote for her depression. "Sure," she said, taking Dory's arm once more. "Let's go up to my room."

Once in Nixie's room, William flew to the top of his cage and cast a quizzical eye toward Dory. "Isn't he gorgeous!" Dory exclaimed, coming to stand in front of the cage. "Oh, Nixie, wherever did you find him?"

"One of my father's patients gave him to us." She could already feel some of the tightness easing from her chest, now that she was away from Jed Hawkins's unsettling presence.

She left Dory cooing at the bird while she fetched a brush and comb from her dressing table. "Now sit in this chair here and we'll brush out your hair."

Dory came and sat in the chair before the dressing table. She watched Nixie in the mirror as she began to undo the knot of curls. Her bright-eyed stare made Nixie nervous, and she tried to distract her attention. "So, how was your afternoon with Mr. Stebbins yesterday? Did you have a good time?"

"Oh yes!" Dory's eyes widened in delight. "Such a nice time. The best time I can remember."

Nixie grinned. "I'd say that sounds very promising, indeed." She removed the last pin from Dory's hair and began working loose the curls.

"He's rather shy, but I find that rather . . . endearing, don't you?" Dory didn't wait for an answer, but continued, her words spilling out in an eager rush. "We talked about his work teaching school and what we've each been doing since we arrived in Welcome Springs. I told him you'd been teaching me to swim. Oh—and he complimented me on my dress!"

Nixie pulled the brush through the length of Dory's hair. "All your clothes are very lovely."

Dory ducked her head and smoothed her hand across her cream-colored lawn skirt. Six rows of ecru lace trimmed the bottom of the skirt, and more lace encrusted the wide, round collar of the shirt and trimmed the cuffs of the leg-of-mutton sleeves. "I always have liked pretty clothes," she said. She shrugged. "Of course Dinah says it's like trying to disguise a pig with a satin bonnet."

Nixie paused in her brushing and frowned. "She shouldn't say such mean things to you. It's not true."

"That's merely Dinah's way. She thinks if she can keep me from having false hopes, then I won't be hurt."

Nixie shaped Dory's thick brown hair around her hand. "Just because she's such a sourpuss, doesn't mean she has to try to turn you into one, too."

Dory ran her hand along the edge of the dressing table. "Well . . . Dinah's had a hard time of it." She tilted her head back to look up at Nixie. "Mr. Merchant wasn't really very kind to her, no matter what she says now." She shook her head. "She never should have married him, but she was already twenty-two, and afraid of being left on the shelf, like me."

"How old are you?" Nixie asked, then immediately regretted the question. "I'm sorry, I should never—"

Dory laughed, a light, musical sound. "It's all right. I'm twenty-seven." She winked at her reflection in the mirror. "It always pains Dinah when people think I'm the younger sister, and she's the older, when actually, it's the other way around."

"Well, you do look younger," Nixie said. "You've got very pretty skin."

Dory leaned forward and squinted at her reflection in the mirror. "Except for these freckles and, of course, my teeth." She half-turned to face Nixie. "I've often wondered. Do you think my teeth would get in the way of kissing a man?"

Nixie blushed. "Well, I really don't—I mean, I never—"

It was Dory's turn to flush. "I'm sorry. There I go again, saying the first thing that pops into my head. Another flaw Dinah assures me men find even more unattractive than buck teeth." She turned back to the mirror and shrugged. "Still, I thought maybe you had. Kissed a man, that is. I mean, you're so pretty, and men like you, I can tell."

She concentrated on arranging Dory's hair, hoping her new friend couldn't read her thoughts from her expression. Would Dory be shocked to hear the stories about Nixie that men like Jed Hawkins apparently believed, rumors that she was a loose young woman eager to "entertain" any man who happened to be traveling through? Frowning, she twisted Dory's hair into a psyche knot and rested it loosely on the crown of her head.

Dory gazed at Nixie's reflection and sighed. "Mr. Hawkins certainly is a handsome man," she said. "You sure are lucky to have him for a beau."

Nixie almost swallowed the hairpins she was holding in her mouth. The knot of hair slipped from her grasp and fell around Dory's shoulders. "Mr. Hawkins is *not* my beau!" she protested.

Dory turned to look at her. "He isn't? But I thought—"

Nixie shook her head, feeling her face flame. "Absolutely not!" *Men like Jed Hawkins are never anyone's "beau,"* she thought. The word was too innocent for the relationship he was after.

Too innocent, she forced herself to admit, for the feelings he stirred within her. That was the real reason she avoided the man. With the slightest touch or look he kindled flames she'd just as soon stayed banked. No good could ever come of a dalliance with a rambler like him.

"I'm sorry," Dory said. "I didn't mean to upset you." She picked up a hand mirror from the dressing table. "Show me how you're twisting my hair. I want to be able to do it for myself later."

Nixie refocused her attention on twisting the thick hair into a loose knot and pinning it at the crown while Dory watched in the hand mirror. After a moment, her racing heart slowed and her cheeks returned to their normal color. She was quite calm by the time she spoke again. "It looks very nice if you let a few tendrils curl around your face." She used the narrow end of a rattail comb to pull several strands of hair free from the knot.

Dory smiled into the hand mirror, then turned to face her larger reflection in the dressing-table glass. "It does look better, doesn't it?" she asked.

Nixie stepped back and surveyed her work. The fullness of the style made Dory's face look rounder, better proportioned. The wisps curling from her temples drew attention to her expressive brown eyes. "It's a very flattering style for you," she said. "And much easier than the curls, don't you think?"

"No more burnt forehead from that cursed curling iron!" Dory grinned at her. "Thank you so much for your help."

"It was no trouble. I enjoyed it." In fact, except for Dory's alarming misconception about Jed Hawkins, she'd been a delightful companion, the perfect antidote to what she'd thought of as a spoiled afternoon.

"Then I've another favor to ask of you." Dory ran her hand along the edge of the dressing table.

"What is that?" Nixie asked cautiously.

"Come with us Friday. Dinah and I and the Chapmans are planning a picnic in the hills. It will be a lot of fun, I know."

An afternoon spent in Mrs. Merchant's company didn't sound very pleasant, but the Chapmans were a friendly couple, and Dory would bring her usual cheerfulness to the expedition. "All right." She nodded. "I'll come."

Dory turned back to the mirror and twirled one of the free strands of hair into a corkscrew. "Mrs. Chapman is going to invite Mr. Stebbins to come with us." She sighed and rested her chin in her hand. "Dinah makes fun of him because of his red face, but I ought to know a person's face doesn't tell much about what they're like inside." She gave her reflection a close-lipped smile. "Every time I look in the mirror, I surprise myself. I see this homely face and think, *That's not me at all.* If I forget about the mirror, and think about what I'm really like, I feel almost beautiful."

She turned to Nixie. "I hate it when someone calls me a spinster. Or worse, an 'old maid.' That makes it sound like my life is almost over, when I've still got so many things I want to do. Don't you feel that way?"

Nixie nodded. "Sometimes I do." And sometimes, she felt as if time had stopped for her, freezing her in a life that never moved forward.

Dory stretched her arms over her head. "I still dream about traveling through Europe or even South America. And I want to marry and raise a house full of children. When they're grown, maybe my husband and I will buy a boat and sail around the world." She lowered her arms and smiled into the mirror. "What about you, Nixie? What do you dream about?"

What *did* she dream about? "Nothing much, compared to you."

"Come on, there must be something. If you could do anything, what would you do?"

Nixie busied herself rearranging items on the dressing table. "Well, I used to imagine I wanted to be famous. But of course, that's silly."

"It's not silly. Why couldn't you do something to become famous?"

Nixie replaced the top on a celluloid hair receiver and pushed it aside. "I'm nobody. Just a small-town spinster."

"That's what I've been trying to tell you. Even small-town spinsters can make their dreams come true. Whether it's travling the world or becoming famous—or finding the man who's right for you."

It was a nice dream. A beautiful dream. Nixie wished she could believe in it the way Dory did. "I don't know," she said, shaking her head.

Dory reached up and put her hand over Nixie's. "There's someone for each of us," she said. "I know there is."

What if some of us have waited too long? Nixie wondered. *Or what if we lose our heart to the wrong man, and can't get it back?*

By the time Friday arrived, the picnic party had increased in size, expanding to include not only Dory and her sister, the Chapmans and Mr. Stebbins, but also Mr. Archibald Harrison, the tuberculosis sufferer, who seemed well on the way to recovery.

Nixie's heart stopped for a moment when she saw Jed Hawkins standing at the rear of the wagon that had been hired to take the party into the hills. How could she spend the entire day in his unsettling presence? Worse, had he been invited *because* of her? Did the Chapmans, who'd organized the party, believe Jed and Nixie were sweet on one another, as Dory had thought before Nixie set her straight?

She took a deep breath and scolded herself. There was no need jumping to conclusions. Etiquette required another man to balance out the numbers, and Jed must have seemed the most logical choice. He was young and had more free time than most.

Even though she tried to tell herself she did not care if Jed came with them or not, she couldn't deny the disturbing rush of pleasure she felt upon seeing him. He was wearing the same white suit he'd had on the first day they'd met, the pale fabric accenting his broad shoulders. His sun-streaked hair, slightly longer now, curled at his collar beneath a crisp straw boater.

As if he felt her watching him, Jed turned and smiled, his whole face alight with welcome. She stared into his fudge-brown eyes and felt her stomach quiver. Jerking her gaze away from him, she swallowed hard. What had come over her, that even a look from a man could make her tremble inside?

She unfurled her white ruffled parasol against the bright June sun and went to join Dory and her sister near the front of the wagon.

"Nixie, there you are! Don't you look as pretty as a picture." Dory beamed at Nixie, who returned the smile. Funny, now that she'd come to know Dory, the other woman's teeth didn't seem nearly as prominent as before. "And what a lovely dress that is," Dory added.

Nixie smoothed the skirt of the white linen dress. Trimmed in navy braid, with a wide, square collar, the outfit was crisp, yet casual. She'd made it over from last year's dress, adding the collar and wider sleeves. She'd been pleased with the results, though she had to admit, she felt quite plainly attired compared to Dory's fashionable costume of green-striped cotton, with matching fitted jacket and white foulard tie.

"I'd be afraid of getting grass stains on that white skirt." Dinah Merchant turned from her conversation with the Chapmans and looked down her nose at Nixie. "They'll never come out of that linen, you know."

Nixie bit her tongue to keep from firing back an angry retort. "Hello, Mrs. Merchant," she said. "Are you looking forward to the picnic?"

"Dory has been in a dither about it for days. I shall be glad when it's over." Dinah Merchant retied the strings of her black straw bonnet. As if in consideration of the festive occasion, she wore a dress of dove-gray poplin, with black frogging up the front of the bodice. The color made her look not quite so severe as usual. Or perhaps it was just Nixie's determination to refuse to allow Dinah to prevent her from enjoying the day.

"All right, everyone, let's get going." Mr. Chapman shooed them toward the wagon, which had bench seats arranged on either side of the wagon bed.

Nixie started to mount the box that served as a step into the wagon, and felt a firm hand at her elbow. "Let me help you, there."

She could feel the heat of Jed Hawkins's touch through the thin fabric of her sleeve and sensed his strength as he guided her into the wagon. Then, before she could catch her breath, the moment had passed, and he had turned to lend a hand to Dory.

Dory settled herself next to Nixie on the bench and smiled. "Wasn't a picnic a wonderful idea?" she asked. "I haven't done anything this fun in years."

Jed and Theo Stebbins fit the tailgate into its slots at the rear of the wagon, then climbed in. Theo started to sit at the end of the bench, but Mr. Chapman hailed him. "Stebbins, come up here!" he called, patting the space next to him.

Dory beamed and scooted over to make room between herself and Mr. Chapman. Nixie thought Mr. Stebbins's face flushed redder than usual, but he slid into place as the wagon lurched forward.

Nixie thought Jed had taken the seat at the rear of the wagon, but when she looked around, she saw him making his way toward her. "I believe there's room right here," he said. "If you'll move over a bit, Miss Dengler."

Nixie looked around to find everyone watching her and Jed, either openly, or out of the corner of their eyes. If any other seat had been open, it had mysteriously vanished, as women made a point of arranging their skirts around them and men stretched out their legs.

The wagon lurched forward and Jed braced himself. Fearing he might fall into her lap, Nixie hurriedly swept her skirts out of the way to make room for him. He settled between her and Dory, his body barely an inch from her own. She did not look at him, scarcely nodding her head in acknowledgment of his greeting. As the wagon turned onto the road leading into the hills, she tried to hold herself still, to keep from touching him. But it was impossible to avoid being thrown together on the rough terrain. As the wagon lurched over ruts and potholes, they were constantly pressed together, arm to arm and thigh to thigh. She could feel the heat of his body through the layers of her skirts, and an answering warmth grew within her.

Nixie tried to concentrate on the scenery they were passing. Terraced slopes of limestone hills rose on either side of the road, white-plumed bear grass and burgundy-and-gold Mexican hats bending in the gentle breeze. A doe watched them from the shade of a mott of live oaks, and a scissor-tailed flycatcher made a graceful dive overhead before settling down on the top strand of a barbed-wire fence.

The scene was as familiar to her as the house she lived in, yet she never ceased to think it beautiful. Looking at the flowers, the deer and birds, calmed her in much the same way as when she dove into a pool of water or listened to William's chatter. There was constancy in nature, a fidelity to natural laws that gave order to the days and rhythm to the seasons. Nature was dependable in a way man seldom was.

Jed couldn't deny the pleasure of being so close to Nixie. She was more beautiful than ever in her crisp white dress and sailor hat. Of course, she couldn't even bear to look at him. She'd made it a point to turn away as soon as he'd sat down beside her.

Let her look away. He'd take his pleasure studying her. The curve of her cheek looked as soft as satin, the skin pale and almost translucent, like finest china. His fingers ached to brush across her skin, perhaps to cup her chin and pull her close enough to taste the perfect bow of her lips . . .

As if reading his thoughts, Nixie turned and met his gaze. Did he detect accusation in her eyes, or had his own guilt put the emotion there? He cleared his throat and tried to engage her in small talk. "It's very beautiful, isn't it? The scenery, I mean."

She turned her profile to him once more. "Yes. I find nature more beautiful than anything man can create."

She sounded sad. *Oh Nixie*, he thought. *Who put that melancholy in your voice?* "Nature can be harsh, too," he said. "And unpredictable."

"Man is more unpredictable than nature ever could be," she said with a hint of scorn.

"Man in general, or do you have a particular man in mind?"

She stiffened, and he thought he heard her gasp. A red flush advanced up the back of her neck. Ah, so a *particular* man was responsible for Nixie's low opinion of the gender. Was it Jed himself, or someone in her past? The mystery intrigued him. If her irritation was with another and not himself, then perhaps he might have hope of gaining her confidence, and perhaps even her friendship.

Their arrival at the picnic spot prevented further conversation on the subject. The Chapmans had chosen a site at the base of a hill, with a grove of trees on one side and a narrow creek on the other. "If you'd like to explore a little before we eat, Mrs. Dengler tells me there are paths through the woods and other trails up the hill," Mrs. Chapman said as they all climbed out of the wagon. "And if you follow the creek along a ways, there's supposed to be a very pretty pool."

Jed climbed out of the wagon and reached up to offer Nixie his hand, but she ignored him and jumped to the ground unaided. Fine. If Miss Dengler wanted nothing to do with him, he wouldn't pursue her—not yet anyway. Give her time to cool down, then he might try another approach.

"I'll stay and help the ladies unload the wagon," Jed volunteered as the others formed up groups to go hiking or to head off to see the pool.

"Just what do you think you're doing?"

Caesar Hawkins was the only person Jed knew who could do such a thorough job of conveying rage in a whisper. Jed shouldered a filled picnic hamper and ignored him.

"You had her practically eating out of your hand back there in the wagon, and now you're abandoning her?" Caesar was so close that if he'd been in corporeal form, Jed would have tripped over him. Jed began to whistle, loudly, praying Mrs. Chapman and Mrs. Merchant, who were setting up the picnic things in the clearing, hadn't heard Caesar. Practically eating out of his hand, indeed. Obviously, Caesar had lost part of his sight in that explosion.

"Don't you know anything about women?"

Obviously not, at least in his father's opinion. But then, according to Caesar, Jed didn't know much about a lot of things.

"She's playing hard to get. She wants you to come after her."

"Right. About like people in Iceland want swimsuits."

"Did you say something, Mr. Hawkins?" Mrs. Chapman looked up from unpacking a trunk full of blankets.

"No ma'am. Nothing important." Jed flushed. Damn Caesar! His father was going to get him carted off to the state asylum one day if he wasn't careful.

"It's so nice of you to stay and help us unpack, but I hate to be keeping you from enjoying the day with the other young people," Mrs. Chapman said. "I'm sure if you want to go on, we can manage."

"No, my son would rather waste his time back here while some other fellow with brains romances the lovely Miss Dengler."

"I don't mind helping you out here."

"You don't have to speak so loudly, dear." Mrs. Chapman smiled. "I may be seventy, but my hearing is as sharp as it ever was, Praise God."

"Fine. Don't go. Stay here and flirt with the old lady. I'm sure Nixie will be just fine. I probably imagined that tall, sickly fellow making eyes at her."

Jed froze in the act of lifting a crate of dishes out of the wagon. "What tall sickly fellow?"

"I don't know his name. He had on a gray suit and a

string tie and rather bushy sideburns. Didn't look quite healthy."

The image of Archibald Harrison swam into Jed's mind. "The man is old enough to be Nixie's father," he snapped. "And he was *not* 'making eyes' at her."

"I'm sure he was. Positively ogling her. You were too caught up with her yourself to notice." Caesar sighed. *"Not that any of it matters. You're not interested in her. You couldn't care less that he's alone with her now, doing no telling what."*

Jed delivered the dishes to Mrs. Chapman, indecision clawing at his chest. "I think . . . Well, if you don't mind, I've decided to go walking after all."

"I think that's an excellent idea. If you hurry, I'm sure you can catch up with the others."

"Nixie went with the bunch headed up the hill," Caesar whispered in his ear.

"I know that!" Jed snapped.

Mrs. Chapman's eyes widened. "Well, I'm glad you do."

"I'm sorry, ma'am. I didn't mean . . ." Jed shook his head. "Don't mind me. I . . . I'm not myself these days."

Giving up the attempt at apology, he whirled about and headed up the hill path.

"What's wrong with him?" he heard Dinah Merchant ask.

"Just a little confused, I'd say," Mrs. Chapman said. "Love will do that to a man, you know."

Love didn't have anything to do with it. Anyone who had Caesar Hawkins for a father, especially as a *ghost* father, would be half off their rocker by now.

Chapter Eight

Jed caught up with Nixie and the others as they started up the hill. "Hello, Mr. Hawkins!" Dory Evans was the first to greet him, waving while he was still fifty yards behind them.

The others stopped and waited. Theo Stebbins and Miss Evans looked pleased enough to see him. Nixie's expression was unreadable beneath the shadow cast by her sailor hat, though the way she kept her arms folded across her stomach didn't exactly bespeak an open welcome. Archie Harrison was standing behind Nixie, a little too close for Jed's liking. The older man bent down and said something to Nixie. She shook her head and frowned. Of all the nerve! If the man had insulted Nixie, Jed had half a mind to teach him proper manners . . .

"Guess we're ready to start up the hill now," Harrison said before Jed could confront him. Jed fell into step behind the others on the narrow path leading to the summit. Stebbins and Miss Evans led the way, with Harrison behind them, then Nixie, with Jed bringing up the rear. Their positions made conversation difficult, but it did offer the advantage of a splendid view, one that brought a smile to Jed's face.

The hill path became steeper after a while, and Stebbins was quick to offer his hand to assist Miss Evans up the slope. Harrison reached back to help Nixie, but Jed squeezed up alongside her, one hand at her waist. "Miss Dengler will be fine with me," he said, giving Harrison a dark look.

Instead of responding angrily, Harrison grinned. "Yes, it looks as if she's in good hands."

Jed glanced at Nixie as they started up. Her face was flushed pink, which could, after all, have been caused by exertion. She didn't pull away, but allowed his hand to remain splayed at the base of her spine, pushing her ever so slightly up the slope.

The path widened out toward the top, and Jed moved up beside Nixie. He slid his hand from her waist, down her arm to twine her fingers with his own. In this way he gently pulled her alongside him the rest of the way to the top. She kept her eyes down, concentrating on the placement of her feet on the path.

Jed didn't try to talk, fearful words might remind her that she wasn't supposed to like him, much less allow him the liberty of such physical closeness. He was content to savor the feel of her gloved hand, soft in his, and the lemon and starch smell of her that filled his nostrils with each breath.

They reached the top at last, both somewhat breathless, though Jed couldn't lay the blame for that entirely on the climb. He continued to hold Nixie's hand until she slipped away, and went to stand behind Miss Evans and Mr. Stebbins.

"What a wonderful view!" Miss Evans clasped her hands to her bosom and smiled down on the scene spread before them. They could see their picnic spot below, the quilts Mrs. Chapman had spread on the ground like patches of bright wildflowers amid the prairie grasses.

"Yes, wonderful," Stebbins echoed. He was not looking

at the view, but at Miss Evans herself, who did indeed look more attractive than usual, her cheeks pink from the exertion of the climb, and wisps of hair escaping from their pins to frame her face in soft tendrils.

"I think I like this part of Texas best." Jed moved up behind Nixie and spoke softly, the way he would approach an easily startled animal. "Better than the land to the east. Not so many tall trees here to get in the way of seeing things."

She turned to look at him. "You say that, but in a little while, you'd be restless to move on," she said. "Men like you, who have grown accustomed to traveling, are never happy in one place for long."

He met her gaze, unflinching. "You seem awfully sure of that."

In the silence that followed, they stared at one another. Jed felt the heat of Nixie's gaze, as if she sought to burn away his defenses to judge his true feelings. Why couldn't she see she had no need for suspicion with him? *Others might have been dishonest with you in the past*, he wanted to say. *But I'm not them.*

She turned away, leaving him wounded. He reached out for her, intending to tell her to stop retreating from him, but she hunched her shoulders at his approach, as if fending off blows. "I'm getting hungry," she said. "Why don't we start down?"

Without waiting for an answer, she turned and started back down the path. Jed watched her go, listening to the scrape of her shoes on gravel as she hastened away.

"What's gotten into the girl?" Caesar spoke at his right shoulder.

Jed shook his head. He didn't know what demons pursued Nixie Dengler, but somehow, someway, he intended to find out, and to defeat them all.

By the time they reached the clearing again, Dinah and Mrs. Chapman had unpacked the picnic hampers. Nixie surveyed the feast of deviled eggs, cold roast beef sandwiches, potato salad, pickles, and pound cake with disinterest. Her appetite had deserted her up on the hilltop, driven away by Jed Hawkins's touch. His hand at her back, his fingers twined with hers, had stirred a longing for things she hadn't a right to wish for, and kindled forbidden hungers she'd long fought to suppress.

While Dinah poured lemonade and Dory handed out plates and napkins, Nixie helped Mrs. Chapman uncover the containers of food. Then she settled herself on a shaded corner of the quilt and pretended interest in her plate. To her relief, Jed did not try to sit beside her. She didn't think she could have him near to her just now and hide this cursed attraction she felt for him.

What was it about him? Why did she allow him to stir her this way? Through veiled lashes, she watched as he relaxed at the opposite corner of the quilt. His plate piled high with food, he ate with the same enthusiasm with which he hammered nails or preached the benefits of Great Caesar's Celebrated Curative. A lust for life. She'd read the phrase in a book somewhere once, but had never seen it illustrated so well. Did he have the same energetic approach to the more baser lusts?

She lowered her gaze once more to her plate. Would Jed Hawkins be shocked to know that demure Miss Dengler would have such thoughts? Oh, but there was so much about her he couldn't know. Would never know.

A woman's smothered laughter caught her attention and she raised her head in time to see Dory bat playfully at Theo Stebbins. Stebbins beamed, and continued his pursuit of a green anole who scurried along the edge of the blanket. Nixie smiled. At least someone was following the path of true love unimpeded.

"Really, Dory, don't act like such a silly child." Dinah Merchant's quarrelsome voice quelled her sister's laughter and erased the smile from her face. "After all, a woman your age should know better." The way she said *your age*, a person who didn't know any better might have thought Dory was in her dotage.

"I always like to hear a woman laugh." Jed set aside his

plate and smiled at Dory, which earned him a grateful look from her, though Theo Stebbins continued to look uncomfortable. "I guess we all take ourselves too seriously sometimes." Jed raised his arms over his head and stretched. The sensuous, animal-like movement made Nixie's heart race.

She jerked her gaze away from him, and turned to address Mrs. Chapman. "This picnic was a wonderful idea. Thank you for inviting me."

"Mr. Chapman and I so enjoy being around young people. It keeps us young ourselves."

"We should do more things together this summer," Dory said. "Perhaps we could have a taffy pull or a play party."

"Or a séance."

Everyone turned to Dinah Merchant in surprise. "A séance?" Nixie asked.

Dinah sat up straighter. "Why yes. There's quite a lot of interest in spiritualism back East. Séances are very popular there."

"Are you sure a séance would be quite . . . well, *proper*?" Dory looked doubtful.

"You aren't suggesting I would do anything improper, are you?" Dinah snapped. "I've attended séances in the East. They can be quite entertaining, even educational."

Mr. Chapman pushed his plate aside and neatly wiped his mouth with a corner of the napkin. "Speaking of entertainment, I remember seeing Great Caesar's Medicine Show when we lived in Dallas," he said. "Mr. Hawkins, your father was quite a showman."

Jed nodded. "He was indeed."

"I imagine he pretty much raised you to follow in his footsteps," Mr. Harrison said. "Taught you the tricks of the trade, so to speak."

A certain tightness appeared around Jed's mouth. Even from a distance, Nixie felt the tension in him, though his voice remained calm. "I suppose you could say that. Of course, it wasn't merely show business to my father. Or to me, either. He spent a lot of years developing Great Caesar's Celebrated Curative into a product that would benefit people."

Harrison looked doubtful. "Still, it's entertainment people come for."

Jed nodded. "But what they really want is relief from their problems, whether it's a break from the worries and work of the day or a cure for an illness that's plaguing them. I always try to give them both."

Nixie hadn't realized she'd been staring until Jed glanced her way and locked his gaze to hers. "Of course, some people have yet to be persuaded of the purity of my intentions."

Nixie felt a blush heat her face as everyone turned to look at her. Why did Jed go out of his way to embarrass her like this? Setting her plate aside, she rose as gracefully as possible. "If you'll excuse me, I need to walk off some of this food." She hurried away from the group, eager to put some distance between herself and Jed and the perilous longings he stirred in her.

Jed watched Nixie go, irritation making a knot in his throat. Damn the woman. Did she deliberately try to embarrass him at every opportunity?

The others began to stand and stretch, and Mrs. Chapman and Mrs. Merchant gathered up the plates and went to rinse them in the stream.

"Miss Evans, would you like . . . uh, would you care to . . . um, go for a walk . . . with me?" Theo Stebbins tugged at his shirt collar, as if it were suddenly too tight, and addressed the ground around Dory Evans's shoes.

"Oh, I'd love to, Mr. Stebbins." Dory smiled up at him, adoration filling her expression. Jed looked away. It would be worth a lot to have a woman look at him that way, instead of with eyes filled with scorn. Dory rose and took Stebbins's proffered arm. "A walk would be just the thing," she said.

"Now, Dory—"

Mrs. Chapman shot out her hand and grabbed Dinah Merchant's wrist and put a finger to her lips in a shushing motion. When the young couple had disappeared down a path into the trees, Mrs. Chapman smiled. "Let them go," she said gently. "There's no harm in a little spooning."

Dinah pursed her lips and let out a sigh. But she kept silent, and made no move to go after her sister.

Unable to sit still any longer, Jed stood. "I think I'll stretch my legs a little, too."

Mrs. Chapman smiled up at him. "That's good. And when you find Nixie, don't be too long. We'll be leaving soon."

He hadn't said anything about finding Nixie, but of course, that was what he intended to do. He wouldn't let her continue to avoid him without some explanation. He had done nothing to deserve her disdain, and he wouldn't let her get away with it any longer.

Jed thought he knew which way she'd headed, but once he was on the path, he discovered it veered off in several directions. He charged to the right, only to come up against a wall of undergrowth. Retracing his steps, he headed left, and became caught in a web of vines. Untangling himself, he stood on the path, sweat trickling down the back of his neck, his suit in disarray.

He took a deep breath and took stock of his surroundings. The heavy stillness of the afternoon folded itself around him like a cloak that muffled sound and sense. He felt a long way away from everyone else, both in distance and time. He'd never cared to be close to other people before, but now he wanted—no, *needed* to be close to Nixie. Where was she?

He closed his eyes and tried to picture her, not looking at him with scorn, but smiling, as he'd seen her do with others. Where would Nixie go for comfort and solace? What would calm her troubled spirit and make her happy?

He opened his eyes, a smile curving his own lips. He knew where to find her now.

He came upon her standing by the edge of a wide pool, staring down at the calm water, her image reflected across its sunlit surface. She turned as he approached, then looked away again before he could read her expression.

"I thought I'd find you here," he said, coming to stand behind her, keeping an arm's length between them. "Your father named you well. You really are a water sprite."

"Why did you follow me?" she asked.

He debated pretending that he had not, but she was too bright to be fooled. Besides, he was uncomfortable with lies. "Why are you always running away from me?" he asked. "How can you dislike me when you don't even know me?"

She sighed. "I don't dislike you."

He moved closer. "Is it because I sell a tonic for a living? Would you offer your friendship more readily if I were a teacher, like Stebbins, or some other more 'honorable' profession?"

"I doubt if that would make any difference."

"Then what is it? Why won't you even give me a chance to know you better?"

She turned to face him at last, and he saw again that mixture of pain and trepidation rising in her eyes. "How well do you really want to know me, Mr. Hawkins? Do you care about what I think, or feel, or dream? Or would you prefer to limit your knowledge to the biblical sense only?"

He flinched as if she'd struck him. "Now where the hell did you come up with an idea like that?" he snapped. "Do you think all men are generally up to no good, or would you like to tell me what in particular I've done to deserve this kind of treatment?"

He advanced toward her as he spoke, as if by touching her he could somehow make her pay attention to what he was saying. She took a step back at his approach, so that the heels of her shoes were balanced precariously over the pool.

He was suddenly aware of how deep the water looked, how slick the bank was. An image flashed in his mind of Nixie slipping down that bank, and into the deep water, her long skirts dragging her under. Fear clenched at his heart and he shot out a hand to pull her back from danger. "Be careful!"

GREAT CAESAR'S GHOST

She tottered on the edge of the pool, leaning away from him, trying to regain her balance. And then he had her, pulling her close, keeping her safe. "You almost fell," he murmured. He wondered if she could hear how loud his heart was pounding.

"I'd have been fine if you'd left me alone," she said. But her voice trembled when she spoke, and she made no move to pull away from him.

She seemed incredibly small and delicate in his arms, the top of her head barely reaching his chin. A fierce wave of protectiveness swept over him. He bent his head to breathe deeply of her scent, that clean mixture of lemon and soap and starch he found so provocative.

He gathered her closer, waiting for his racing heart to slow, for his breathing to return to normal. The thought of her falling had frightened him more than he cared to admit. Nixie seemed to be waiting, too. She rested in the circle of his arms, her body pressed against his from shoulder to hip. He could feel the stiff boning of her corset beneath his hand where it rested on her back, just above her waist, and the soft swell of her breasts pressed against his chest.

As his fear subsided, he became aware of her, not merely as a precious thing to be protected, but as a woman, warm and yielding in his arms. He looked down on her and found her staring up at him, eyes dark with a passion that answered his own, lips full and moist and slightly parted, as if in invitation. "Nixie," he whispered her name, all other words failing him. He cleared his throat and tried again. "Nixie, I—"

"Yes," she breathed, and closed her eyes, pale lashes like finest lace across her cheeks.

He lowered his head to cover her mouth with his own, his blood racing, his heart pounding once more, anticipating the taste of her, the feel of her lips pressed to his.

"Hrrrmph!"

The sound was like a rifle shot disturbing the stillness. Nixie let out a cry and wrenched away from him. Jed blinked and looked around, fists clenched at his sides, as if he might thrash whoever had intruded on this moment.

Archie Harrison cleared his throat again and stared tactfully off to his left. "The Chapmans sent me to tell you the wagon is ready to leave."

He let out the breath he had been holding and nodded. "All right. We'll be along in a minute."

Harrison gave a sheepish smile, then turned away. Jed reached for Nixie once more.

But she was already moving past him. "Wait up, Mr. Harrison. I'll walk with you."

By the time Jed reached the wagon, Nixie was already on board, seated between Harrison and Theo Stebbins. She refused to meet his eyes, but a telling flush colored her face as he took his place next to Dinah Merchant.

He forced himself not to look at her on the ride home. Their late arrival back to the group was cause enough for teasing as it was, though thankfully, no one made any unkind remarks.

He might keep his eyes from her, but he could not prevent his thoughts from veering in her direction. She still hadn't answered his question as to why she was so studiously avoiding him. And having experienced her reaction when he'd held her in his arms, he could no longer lay the blame to pure dislike. That hadn't been dislike he'd seen in those green-gold eyes, and surely no woman who hated him would have so eagerly awaited his kiss.

He would have kissed her, if Harrison hadn't interrupted. And what then? How could he have remained satisfied with chaste touching and stolen embraces, once he'd given himself over to the passion she'd awakened in him?

Was that what she had meant by her remark about him "knowing" her in the biblical sense? Had she looked into his eyes and seen the need he felt not only to touch her, but to somehow lose himself in her?

He risked a glance in her direction. She was talking with Harrison, laughing at something he said. But as if feeling him watching, she turned toward him. Their eyes locked for one brief moment, and he saw the fear he'd seen before, overlaying a passion that smoldered still.

What was Nixie afraid of? He was the one who ought to

be worried about his body leading him where his mind didn't want to go. It was one thing to fantasize about an affair with a warm and willing woman. But if he gave free reign to his desires with a respectable woman like Nixie, he'd be honor bound to marry her. The thought made him squirm in his seat—not because he was afraid of marriage, but because for the first time in memory, he found the idea strongly appealing.

When the wagon stopped, Jed was one of the first to climb out. Nixie swept past him and into the house without another word to him or anyone else. As he stared after her, Mr. Chapman handed him one of the large picnic hampers and directed him to carry it into the kitchen.

Jed was setting the hamper on the kitchen table when a cry echoed through the house. The grief-stricken wailing cut through him, sending him bolting out of the room toward the stairs. He met Nixie on the bottom step, and pain twisted in his chest when he saw her anguished face. "He's gone!" she wailed, choking back sobs. "William's gone!"

Chapter Nine

Jed wanted to gather Nixie into his arms, to hold her and somehow soothe away the torment in her eyes. But, still smarting from her previous rejection, he settled for taking her hands. Her fingers were ice cold, and he chafed them lightly between his own in an effort to kindle some warmth. "Are you sure William isn't just hiding?" he asked, his voice calm. "Maybe he's in another room?"

Nixie shook her head and sniffed, but did not pull away from him. "I've looked, and I've called him. His cage is open, and my bedroom door was open. He must have flown out a window."

As fresh tears welled in her eyes, Jed reluctantly released her hands and offered his handkerchief. A crowd had gathered around them, Mrs. Dengler and the returning picnickers wanting to learn the reason for such a commotion. "Those boys must have been playing with him again, after I told them not to." Nixie looked at her mother. "Where are they? I swear I'll—"

"Now, Nixie, violence won't bring your pet back." Nadine Dengler put her arm around her daughter's shoulders and smoothed the hair back from her forehead. "If Pete and Lou are responsible for letting William loose, we'll leave their punishment to your father."

A muffled cry drew Jed's attention and he traced it to the storage closet beneath the stairs. While others offered their assistance in searching for the bird, he yanked open the door to the closet and fished out two red-faced boys. Pete and Lou struggled to escape, but he held them tightly and presented them to Nixie and their mother. "Would you boys like to tell your sister what happened?" he said, his voice grim.

"We didn't mean for it to happen," Pete grumbled. "Stupid bird followed me out the door."

Lou begin to cry. "Nixie, please don't hate us!" he bawled, tears spilling down his cheeks.

Mrs. Dengler came and put an arm around each of her sons. "I'm sure Nixie doesn't hate you," she said. "But she doesn't want to talk to you right now, either. Now come upstairs to your room. You can wait there for your father to come home."

Nixie shot a mournful look at her brothers as they passed her on the stairs. She blotted her eyes with the handkerchief, then made her way through the crowd in the front hall, out the door. "William!" she called. "Sweet William! Where are you?"

"Mrs. Chapman and I will search out back," Mr. Chapman said, his arm around his wife. "Others can try the side yard. If we all look, we'll find the bird."

"Yes, of course," Dory Evans said. "Dinah and I will help."

"Wait a minute." Jed held up his hand and the group fell silent. "If all of you go rushing around the yard making a commotion, you're liable to scare the bird even further away. Better to go about your business and let Nixie call him. She's the one he knows, after all."

"I think Jed's right," Mr. Harrison said. "The poor thing is probably frightened half to death as it is."

As the others made their way upstairs, or toward the

campground, Jed stepped out onto the front porch. Nixie stood clinging to a post and staring up at the live oak tree that shaded the house on that side. "How will I ever find him?" she asked as he came to stand beside her.

"Why don't you go out into the yard and sit quietly," he said. "And wait for William to come to you? I imagine he'll be watching for you. I'll walk around the house and see if I can spy him anywhere."

He led her to a bench beneath the live oak, then set out on a circuit of the house. He had not walked far before he realized how perfectly suited a green bird with a yellow head and black-barred back was for hiding amidst the sun-dappled branches of the live oak and hackberry trees that grew around the Dengler home. As he craned his neck and scanned the treetops, he began to feel his errand was hopeless. If only he knew a magic trick that would make Nixie's pet appear before her.

Of all the times for something to go wrong! Caesar silently cursed the wayward bird and all the turmoil it was causing in the Dengler household. Just when he'd begun to think Jed was finally getting somewhere with the delectable Nixie, that bird had to literally fly the coop and upset everything.

Caesar watched his son now as the boy prowled the backyard. Jed liked to pretend he was above all those messy emotions like passion and jealousy, but his dear old dad knew him better than that. *I knew he wouldn't be able to stand the thought that another man might be after his girl. And she is his, in his heart, even if his head won't admit it yet. All I had to do was plant the idea that that tuberculosis sufferer might be his rival and off he went, like a bullet shot out of a gun.* Caesar aimed his finger at his son and made a firing motion. Ping! *Cupid's dart found its mark.*

Caesar smiled. Ah, the boy would make him proud, yet! He'd really taken things in hand back there at the pool. In fact, if he hadn't been interrupted, he and Nixie would have been all over each other, and probably as good as engaged by the time they got back to the wagon.

"William! Oh William!"

Nixie's plaintive wail brought a frown to Caesar's face. This couldn't have happened at a worse time. Nixie had forgotten about Jed now that her precious birdie was lost.

Well! He straightened and pounded his fist in his palm. The Great Caesar Hawkins wasn't going to let a runaway bird foil his plans. He'd find that feathered critter and send it back to Nixie. Then she and Jed could get on to the business of courting.

He studied the canopy of oaks and elms overhead. Birds belonged in trees, didn't they? Even brightly colored cage birds probably still had that instinct in their tiny bird brains. No doubt the little troublemaker was up there now, surveying the commotion it had caused and laughing little bird laughs.

He wouldn't get away so easily—not from Caesar. Since the accident, Caesar had discovered a few benefits to his condition, one being that reaching the treetops was no struggle. He hovered up amongst the branches and surveyed the territory. Everything was green and still up here, with scarcely a breeze to stir the leaves. Reaching over his head, he took hold of the end of a branch and shook it vigorously. *"Are you going to surrender willingly, bird, or do I have to shake you out of the trees?"* he called.

An angry jay shot out of the foliage above him, squawking as it flew. A black-capped chickadee responded with a rain of chittering sounds, while a tiny hummingbird buzzed his left ear. *So your friends are ganging up on me, are they?* Caesar scowled at the feathered population around him. *Well, they can't hide you forever, by golly.* He grabbed another branch and shook, setting up another chorus of bird protests.

Below him, a door slammed, distracting him from the hunt. He looked down to see a large woman standing on the steps of the house next door to the Denglers'. "Young man, what is going on over there?" she called, looking past a screen of tangled vines that separated her yard from that of the Denglers. Passion flower, wasn't it? He didn't know when he'd seen a bigger mass of the stuff. He shook himself. No time for studying flowers right now. He had work to do.

"I could have sworn I heard someone screaming," the neighbor woman said.

Jed turned and addressed the woman through the curtain of vines. "N . . . Miss Dengler's pet bird has escaped," he answered.

The woman clucked and shook her head. "Nixie Dengler doesn't need a bird. All that girl needs is a good man." She directed a piercing look at him. "What about you, young man? Don't you think it's time you settled down and got a real job?"

Caesar almost laughed out loud at the expression on Jed's face. The poor boy looked like he'd swallowed a mouthful of bad milk. But his discomposure was fleeting. Within seconds, he'd straightened his shoulders and fixed her with his most charming smile. "Why, I do have a job, Mrs. Frisco. I sell Great Caesar's Celebrated Curative, the world's best remedy for dyspepsia, catarrh, neuralgia, and a host of other ills. You might be especially interested to know, ma'am, that older ladies like yourself find the Curative especially helpful for discomforts peculiar to their time of life."

"Hmmmph!" She blushed red and sniffed. "Next thing to show business if you ask me," she muttered as she turned and went back inside, the screen door snapping into place behind her.

Caesar laughed out loud. Learned from the master, the boy had. He knew how to handle hecklers like Mrs. Busybody here.

He glanced at Jed again. The confident manner had vanished and the boy looked as low as a snake's belly. Caesar had a feeling it wasn't just the nosy neighbor's criticism that had him down, though Jed had always been more sensitive about that sort of thing than his father. Jed always wanted everyone to believe in the Curative as much as he did, but Caesar knew it didn't matter what anybody else believed, as long as you knew the truth. That confidence alone would win enough folks over to your side to keep you going.

No, Jed's current mood probably had a lot more to do with Nixie than with criticism of the Curative. Only a woman could sink a man's spirits that far. Lovesickness was one thing Caesar had never developed a remedy for. Though perhaps he should look into it...

Ah, but enough lollygagging. He had work to do. He had to find Nixie Dengler's bird and rescue Jed's love life before the boy's moping drove him to the madhouse. He grabbed another branch, ready to give it a vigorous shake, when a flash of yellow in the corner of his eye stopped him cold.

Slowly, so as not to startle the little nuisance, he turned his head. The bird eyed him with a malevolent gaze. "Go away," it said.

Caesar flinched, startled. He hadn't expected a *talking* bird. *"That's a nice birdie,"* he crooned, inching closer. What was the fowl creature's name anyway? Will something? *"There you are, Willy boy. Come to Caesar."*

"Nanny goat." The bird said, and fluffed its feathers.

"That's good. Stay right there. I've almost got you—"

"Go away!" With a squawk, the little green-and-yellow demon did just that. A lesser man would have fallen, but Caesar merely flailed about for a moment before regaining his perch in the trees. He glared after the departed parakeet. *"You're lucky Nixie Dengler thinks so much of you,"* he muttered. *"Otherwise, I'd be having roast bird for supper."*

Jed continued his search for Nixie's bird, Mrs. Frisco's criticism nagging at him. It wasn't the first time someone had condemned his chosen profession, of course. But lately, he'd begun to question whether selling Great Caesar's Celebrated Curative was such a high calling after all. Did the world really *need* another cure-all—even one as good as the Curative?

And if no one needed the tonic, did anyone really need him?

His dejection growing, he rounded the corner of the house and saw Nixie huddled on the bench, shoulders shaking with silent sobs. Forgetting his own worries, Jed hurried to her side and gathered her into his arms. "Oh, Nixie, Nixie," he murmured, cradling her head on his shoulder and gently rocking her. "Please don't take on so. You'll make yourself sick."

She mopped her eyes with the sodden handkerchief, struggling to choke back her tears. "I know you think I'm silly, to carry on so over a little bird, but you don't understand."

He cupped her feverish cheek in one hand and, with his thumb, wiped away a tear that trickled from the corner of one eye. "Try me," he said softly.

She sniffed, and inhaled a ragged breath. "William is so wonderful—he . . . he l-loves me. Just me." A fresh torrent of sobs overwhelmed her, and she hid her face in his shoulder once more. "You don't know how special he makes me feel!"

Jed heard the anguish in her words, and swallowed against the sudden tightness in his throat. He patted her trembling shoulders and her warm tears soaked through his shirt to dampen his skin. She felt as fragile and precious as a hummingbird. He would have given anything at that moment for the chance to make her feel special.

"I love you." The words were faint and very far away. He raised his head and listened, and they came again. "I love you."

"Nixie, listen!"

She looked up, and held her breath, and the little voice came again. "I love you."

"Call him," Jed whispered.

"William! Sweet William! Come here darling!"

In a blur of green and gold, the parakeet fluttered out of the treetops and landed on Nixie's shoulder. "William. Sweet William," Nixie breathed, fresh tears flowing unchecked.

Jed eased away from her, and stood and offered his hand. She took it, not looking at him, her attention focused on the little bird on her shoulder. William huddled close to her neck and the two conversed in a secret language of coos and murmurs, like long-lost lovers.

They made their way into the house, and up the stairs to Nixie's room. She gave Jed a brief smile, then shut the door behind her. He stood in the hallway for a long time, staring at the closed door and thinking about the woman behind it, who hid such depths of emotion beneath a subdued exterior.

Nixie awoke the next morning to the sound of hammering, coming from somewhere close by. She sat up in bed, gathering the covers around her, and shot a worried look toward the cage in the corner of the room. William saw her watching and greeted her with a loud whistle.

She sighed with relief. So his return had not been a dream after all. The hammering continued as she dressed, reverberating through the room, as though someone were attempting to knock down the walls. A glance out the window revealed nothing.

She started to leave the room, but before she did so, she grabbed a hair ribbon from her dressing table and tied it in a double knot around the door of William's cage. She'd have to cut it off later to let him out, but at least the boys wouldn't be able to get to him.

Humming to herself, she went in search of the source of the hammering. She found Jed Hawkins outside the kitchen, fitting the window there with a new screen. "Good morning," he called, sticking his head over the sash and nodding to her. "Hope I didn't wake you with all this racket."

"Mr. Hawkins is making new screens for the windows," Nadine Dengler said, dishing out a bowl of oatmeal for Nixie. "William won't be able to escape through the holes anymore."

Nixie turned to stare at Jed, who was climbing down from the ladder. "You didn't have to do that!" she called, rushing to the window and looking out at him.

He looked up at her, shoving his bowler further back on

his head so that she had a good look at those fudge-brown eyes. Eyes that telegraphed such confusing messages to her. *Trust me*, those eyes said. But how could she afford to take such a risk? "Your father agreed it was a good idea," he said. "And I've got a lock for your room, too, so certain pesky brothers will have to stay out."

She followed his gaze over his shoulder, to where Pete was cutting screen wire with his good hand while Lou pulled nails from a pile of lumber nearby. "Your father has assigned them as my permanent helpers this summer," Jed said. "That should keep them out of trouble."

She was aware of him watching her, his gaze like a physical touch sweeping over her, recalling the feel of his hand there yesterday, cradling her cheek and wiping away her tears. She did not want to look at him, but could not keep from it. When their eyes met once more, she felt again the rush of blood, like a hot wind in her ears, and the aching tension in her chest, a spring wound so tightly that one touch from his hand would release it and she would throw herself into his arms.

He had almost kissed her yesterday, there by the pool in the woods. She had been stunned, terrified even, by how much she had wanted that kiss. She had anticipated the feel of his lips on her own the way she looked forward to cool water on a burning day.

Only Mr. Harrison's arrival had saved her from abandoning herself to that dangerous desire.

She wrenched her gaze from his, knowing the peril was far from passed. As long as Jed Hawkins stayed in Welcome Springs, he was a threat to the outward appearance of serenity she struggled so hard to maintain.

"Come eat your breakfast, Nixie," her mother said, setting a glass of milk beside the bowl of oatmeal. "Let Mr. Hawkins and the boys get on with their work."

Nixie barely tasted the food, and pushed the bowl away when it was still half full. "I'm not very hungry this morning, Mama," she said, standing and taking the dish to the sink. "I think I'll go down to the pool for a swim before it gets too crowded."

"Yes, you do look a little peaked." Nadine smiled and patted her daughter's cheeks. "I let you sleep in because I thought the excitement yesterday might have been too much for you. Would you like to try some of Mr. Hawkins's Curative? Your father highly recommends it."

Jed Hawkins again! Would the man invade every corner of her life? She shook her head, already moving toward the door.

"Go on, then," her mother said. "The water will do you good."

As usual, the warm mineral waters of the Welcome Springs worked their magic, and soothed Nixie's frazzled nerves. By the time she emerged from her morning swim, her mind was clearer, and she was berating herself for her rudeness toward Jed Hawkins. The man was partly responsible for William returning to her yesterday, and he'd spent his whole morning ensuring the bird could not escape again. Yet she hadn't even thanked him.

She changed out of her swimsuit and started back toward the house. She'd have to find a way to thank Jed properly. It was the least she could do.

Her mind on the task ahead, she scarcely noticed the people moving past her on the path between the springs and the campground, until she almost collided with one couple.

"Oh, Miss Dengler. Do excuse us. I didn't realize we were blocking the path."

She looked up, startled to see Archie Harrison and... was that Dinah Merchant? Yes, that was certainly Mrs. Merchant by Mr. Harrison's side, dressed in a sodden black swimming costume, a man's light blue seersucker jacket incongruously draped about her shoulders. What was Dinah doing out here on the path dressed like that?

Her face a bright red, Dinah pulled the jacket more tightly about her and glared at Nixie. "I am shocked that your father does not do more to combat crime around the springs!" she snapped. "Someone had the audacity to steal my clothing from my locker in the bathhouse."

"But why would someone want to steal your clothes?" Nixie protested.

"Are you saying I would lie about something like this?"

Nixie stifled her irritation. "No, of course not. But perhaps someone mistook them for their own. Or you misplaced them—"

"I'm not so daft as to misplace my own clothing! I tell you, I intend to lodge a formal complaint."

"Mrs. Merchant, you're shivering." Mr. Harrison put a hand on Dinah's shoulder. "Allow me to escort you to the house. We don't want you to catch your death, now do we?"

Dinah's expression relaxed until her mouth was shaped into something very like a smile. "You're so kind, Mr. Harrison. My health is rather delicate, you know. So thoughtful of you to come to my assistance."

Nixie stared after them for a long moment. *What a strange thing to happen*, she thought. Did they really have a clothing thief in the bathhouse? Had one of her brothers . . . ? But no, of course not. Jed was keeping them very busy this morning. The thought of Jed reminded her she had business of her own to attend to. Striking out on a shortcut through the trees, she hurried back to the house, where she collected lemons from the pantry and squeezed them for lemonade. Wrapping up a dozen cookies to go with the drink, she headed toward the boardinghouse with her peace offering.

Nixie found Jed and the boys working in what would be the front parlor, fitting trim around the newly installed glass windows. Jed had removed his shirt, and worked with his back to the door, showing Pete how to measure and cut the trim boards. Lou was on his knees, hammering molding along the floor, the noise of his work covering up Nixie's arrival.

She stood in the entrance to the room, holding a tray with the pitcher of lemonade, glasses, and a plate of cookies, and stared at Jed's broad back, the muscles limned sharply against the clinging fabric of his knit undershirt. He straightened to adjust the angle of a board, and she watched the interplay of muscles beneath his skin.

Every movement of his body spoke to her in a language she could not wholly comprehend, but to which she responded. Her mind might try to avoid any involvement with this charming rambler, but everything that made her a woman pulled her closer and closer to him.

Pete looked up and saw her, and nudged Jed. He turned his head and smiled, sending a rush of warmth through Nixie that had nothing to do with the summer heat. She flushed and looked away while he picked up a towel that lay nearby and wiped the sweat from his torso before pulling on his shirt.

"I brought you some lemonade," she said, hurrying forward and setting the tray on the end of the sawhorse. "And some cookies." She held out the plate.

"Bully!" Pete reached for the plate.

She frowned at him, and held the plate out of reach. "You don't deserve cookies."

Jed laughed and took a cookie from the plate. "Maybe I'll share mine with them," he said. "They've been working pretty hard, and I think they're truly sorry about what happened with William."

"Yeah, Nixie, we're sorry. Truly we are." Lou smiled up at her, all angelic. Despite her best efforts, Nixie could not deny him a smile in return.

"All right, then." She lowered the plate and the boys helped themselves. "Just don't let it happen again."

"I doubt it will." Jed helped himself to a glass of lemonade. "I've threatened to personally tan their hides if it does."

She heard the conviction in his voice and a thrill ran through her to think that he might feel this way because of *her*. "I wanted to thank you for all you've done," she said, trying to keep her voice from betraying any emotion. "The screens and the locks . . . but especially for helping me yesterday. I was so upset, I couldn't think straight." It still made her a little breathless, to think of how close she'd come to losing her pet.

"I was glad to help." He smiled at her over his glass, the gold flecks in his eyes glittering. "Do you feel better today?"

She nodded.

"You've been swimming."

She blinked in surprise. "How did you know?"

He reached out and twirled a lock of hair that had escaped from the pile atop her head. "Your hair is still a little damp." He leaned closer and inhaled deeply. "And you smell . . . fresh, like outdoors and the springs."

She felt the color rise to her cheeks, her throat too tight to speak.

"You like to swim, don't you?" he asked.

She nodded. "But you don't?"

"Never cared for it. Water is for fish." He laughed. "Or water sprites." He winked, a languid lowering of his eyelid that left her trembling with the desire to touch him, or to be touched by him.

She moved away, hoping he could not see his effect on her. "You talk nonsense, Mr. Hawkins." She looked away, at the newly fitted front window. "This looks nice. I had no idea you were such a skilled carpenter."

"My father and I were always building benches or stages or props for our shows. And when money was tight, we'd hire out as carpenters." He walked over to the window and smoothed his hand over the perfectly fitted molding that framed it. "I've spent many a winter framing up or finishing out houses. Once we worked on a crew that was building a bank."

"Papa will be pleased with the progress you're making here."

"What about you? Will you be pleased?"

His gaze pierced and held her, so unsettling she could not answer him. She looked at Pete and Lou, perched on the sawhorses, eating cookies. "You boys bring the dishes to the kitchen when you're finished."

Then she turned and left, forcing herself to walk slowly back to the house, while inside she longed to break into a run—though whether toward Jed Hawkins, or away from him, she wasn't sure.

Jed stood at the side window he'd just finished framing and watched Nixie's departure. Pete came and stood beside him. "Do you like my sister?" he asked.

Jed smiled into his half-empty glass of lemonade. "I'm an easy man to get along with. I pretty much like everybody."

"You don't look at everybody the way you look at Nixie."

He gave the boy a considering look. "The way you look at Becky Simmons?" he asked after a moment.

Pete's face flushed red to the tips of his ears. "How'd you know about that?"

He shrugged. "I hear things. See things."

Pete stared down and scuffed his bare toes against the oak floorboards. "So how do I get Becky to like me?"

"If I knew the answer to that, I'd get Nixie to like me." He glanced out the window again, but the yard was empty. Nixie must have gone inside.

"Oh, she likes you all right." Pete grinned. "She wouldn't have brought the lemonade for me and Lou."

He drained his glass. The liquid was tart and sweet, not unlike its maker, and the fresh lemon scent recalled the way Nixie's hair smelled in the warm sun. "She's just grateful to me for helping her find her bird," he said, setting the glass aside.

Pete shrugged and picked up another cookie. "Maybe so." He bit into the treat. "But when you aren't looking, she watches you the same way you watch her."

Jed picked up the miter saw and began to cut the trim board he'd measured. As the saw sliced through the wood, he savored Pete's words, rolling them over and over in his mind. He wasn't surprised to learn Nixie had been watching him; he'd felt the heat of her gaze on him on more than one occasion. But did she realize where those looks might lead?

He made a last, sure cut and the scrap end of trim fell

to the floor. He examined his work, running his thumb along the surface of the newly sawed edge. At one time he'd enjoyed building things for the sake of the work, never minding that he'd be moving on, not staying around to enjoy the fruits of his labor. But lately, he'd wondered what it would be like to see a building he'd help make be put to use, to stand the test of time.

He didn't know whether it was age, or maturity, or a need to fill the emptiness gnawing at him, but he didn't get much pleasure out of doing for the sake of doing anymore. It was like that with Nixie, too. He'd started out pursuing her because she offered a challenge, but the closer he got to her, the more he realized a few stolen kisses and a little harmless flirtation weren't going to be enough. He wanted to chip away the brittle layers she'd cloaked herself in, and take hold of the tender, passionate woman he'd only glimpsed so far.

And once he had hold of that Nixie, he wasn't sure he'd ever be able to let her go.

Chapter Ten

"Dinah is determined we should have a séance."

"You mean she's actually serious about it?" Nixie looked up from the stockings she was darning. They were on the screened back porch, her favorite retreat, but Dory had been anything but relaxed since they'd settled down with their needlework.

Dory tossed aside the pillow slip she'd been halfheartedly embroidering. "She's hardly talked of anything else since the picnic last week. She says there's a 'ghostly aura' about this place that will be perfect for trying to get in touch with the 'world beyond.'" She fluttered her hands in the air like a revival singer shaking two tambourines. "I declare, I've never seen her like this."

"She doesn't really believe in spiritualism, does she?" Nixie shook her head. "I mean—ghosts and spirits and contacting people on the 'other side?' Not to insult your sister, Dory, but it sounds incredibly far-fetched to me."

"It does to me, too. I don't understand it. Dinah is normally such a *practical* person."

"Maybe she thinks it would be a fun entertainment for the summer guests. If you look at it that way, it's not so bad."

Dory worried her lower lip between her teeth. She seemed to make a decision. "I normally wouldn't mention this to a soul, but I know I can trust you, Nixie."

The solemn expression on her friend's face alarmed Nixie. She set aside her sewing and leaned forward. "I'm flattered you'd confide in me. I promise I'll keep whatever you say a secret."

"This isn't the first time Dinah has expressed an interest in spiritualism." Dory glanced over her shoulder, then lowered her voice so that Nixie had to lean forward even more to hear. "Back in Fort Worth, she was in touch with a spiritual medium, Madame Dubonnet. Have you heard of her?"

Nixie shook her head.

"Well, she was quite famous in our area. The papers wrote articles about her and some of the most socially prominent people in town consulted her. She read palms and cards and all those things, but she was most famous for her séances. A person could attend one by invitation only, and, of course, you had to pay a scandalous fee."

"I take it Dinah attended one of these séances?"

Dory gripped the arms of her wicker chair. "Not one, but several. As many as half a dozen." She shook her head. "I refused to get involved. I even told her I thought the woman was no better than a thief."

Nixie frowned. Such behavior did seem out of character for the ever-so-proper Dinah Merchant. Even though Nixie didn't care much for Dory's sister, she had to admit she didn't seem the type to let a con artist take advantage of her. "Why does Dinah attend séances?" she asked. "I mean, don't people who go to those things usually want to contact a dead relative? Is there someone she wants to speak with, your parents perhaps?"

"She says she wants to talk to Mr. Merchant."

"Mr. Merchant? But I thought you said he wasn't very nice to her."

"He wasn't." Dory looked grim. "Not at all." She knotted her hands in her lap. "I don't mind telling you it's upset me terribly. I thought coming here this summer would take her mind off all that."

Nixie reached out and put a comforting hand on Dory's arm. "Don't fret. I'm pretty sure there *aren't* any spiritualists or mediums in Welcome Springs. We can't very well hold a séance without one of them, can we?"

"Dinah says we can! She says Madame Dubonnet told her how it's done. Anyone can lead the séance and summon the spirits. Dinah says she'll do it."

"Then we'll have to keep putting her off until she forgets about it or gives up."

Dory sighed and sat back. "It's too late for that. She's already scheduled it for next Friday night. She's talked your mother and Mrs. Chapman into helping her out." Dory's lower lip trembled. "Even Theo Stebbins says it will be fun!"

"Oh dear. Please don't cry." Nixie squeezed her arm. "I'm sure he never would have said that if he'd known it was going to upset you so. You and I don't have to participate if you don't want to. We'll both sit out in protest."

Dory dabbed at her eyes with a lace-trimmed handkerchief. "Oh, no. I have to go. I have to be there to keep an eye on Dinah."

"Are you sure that's wise? Knowing Dinah, if things don't go the way she's planned, she'll find a way to blame you."

Dory smiled through her tears. "You're probably right, but I don't mind, really. If I'm not there and things go wrong, she'll have to admit she made a fool of herself in front of everyone. It would crush her, I know it would."

Dinah Merchant was about the most uncrushable woman Nixie knew, but she didn't try to argue the point with Dory. To tell the truth, she didn't want to miss the séance, either. It would be good to see Mrs. look-down-her-nose-at-everyone Merchant brought down a peg or two.

• • •

Caesar loved eavesdropping. People were always talking about how bad it was because sooner or later you'd learn something you didn't want to know, but so far all he'd learned was that other people's conversations could be fascinating, and the information gleaned this way was potentially very useful.

For instance, he'd found Dory and Nixie's conversation about the upcoming séance to be very enlightening. He'd had a little experience in this area himself. In fact, he'd become fairly well acquainted with a spiritualist who was a member of a traveling circus he'd associated with for a while a few years back. Madame Calcutta was a bosomy redhead with a passionate nature who, in the course of their acquaintance, had let him in on a few of the things she did to see that her patrons got their money's worth in every performance. She manipulated doors and curtains with thread tied to her toes. She could crack her toes so that it sounded like someone knocking, and she could throw her voice, too, which was handy for the spirit's sudden appearance. Since everybody knew people changed when they died, all she had to do was talk in a quavery, otherworldly tone and throw out a few bits of information gleaned from a careful questioning of those around the table and she had them hoodwinked, or as she preferred to see it, entertained.

Whether you thought she was an entertainer or a first-rate con artist, she made pots of money in her chosen profession. Last he'd heard, she had set up business in Baltimore and was playing to a full house every night.

Even knowing Madame Calcutta's tricks, Caesar had found the séances he'd attended to be great fun. Nixie and her friend were as bad as Jed, with their shocked attitudes and holier than thou talk. Did young people today have no sense of fun?

To look at Jed, you'd think he'd forgotten entirely how to enjoy life. His constant moping about was beginning to depress Caesar himself. Of course, it was no wonder the boy was down in the dumps, since things were moving like molasses in winter when it came to him and Nixie Dengler.

Caesar was doing everything he could to speed things

along. Why only yesterday, he'd thought to put some pep in the relationship by stealing Nixie's clothing while she'd been in swimming. He'd planned for her to have to walk back home in her cute little swimming costume. Caesar then planned to arrange for Jed to just happen to be on the path to the pool—on some errand Caesar would manufacture—about the time she came walking by.

Could he help it if the clothes he swiped belonged to that sour-faced Dinah Merchant? By the time he'd realized his mistake, it was too late to try the same trick on Nixie.

And now she'd given him the perfect idea for bringing her and Jed together again. What could be better than a *séance* for fostering romance? After all, everyone sat around in the dark and held hands. Scary things happened and women squealed, giving men the perfect opportunity to be strong and brave.

And what if a *real* ghostly being made an appearance? Wouldn't that send them into a tizzy? It might even send Nixie flying into Jed's arms.

Rubbing his hands together, Caesar left the porch, whistling. He had a lot to do to get ready for this séance. He had to polish up the tricks he'd learned from Madame Calcutta. And throw in a few surprises of his own.

Evenings, after he'd finished work on the inn and returned from supper with the Denglers, Jed would sit out on the steps of the wagon, savoring the cooler night air. Sometimes he lit a lamp and took out his sketchbook; other nights he was content to sit in the darkness, letting the muted conversations and distant laughter of the other campers drift around him. This was the sound of home to him, the rhythm that had lulled him to sleep as a child and lent familiarity to every new place. This night music made him a part of something all those people gathered on front porches and snug in their houses could never know: a bigger world with places to go and people to see and opportunities there for the taking.

Lately, however, the music sounded a little flat to Jed's ears. The great adventure of the road didn't stir him as it once had. A different restlessness possessed him now, one that neither a day's hard work nor an evening with charcoal and paper could ease.

"Why so down in the mouth, boy? You look like you just lost your best friend." As always, Caesar's intrusion into Jed's solitude was sudden, but not entirely unexpected.

Jed resisted the urge to look over his shoulder; after all, there'd be nothing there to see. He kept his attention on the sketchpad open on his knees. "I was wondering when we could expect that order of ingredients for the Curative."

"Patience, my boy. It's only been a couple of weeks."

Jed ground his teeth. He hated it when his father called him "boy." He began shading in a portion of the drawing he was working on. "I've been thinking—there's no point in wasting our summer here in Welcome Springs. Why don't we move on? We can have the post office forward the order."

"Why would you want to do that?" Caesar sounded surprised.

Why indeed? Maybe because every time he looked at Nixie Dengler, he fought the urge to touch her. She haunted his dreams and distracted him every waking hour. He'd almost sawed his finger off the other day because he'd been lost in a daydream about her—damp swimsuit clinging to her luscious body, her ripe lips begging for his kiss. He drew a deep breath. A whole summer of such frustrated desire was bound to drive a man crazy.

"The ingredients for Great Caesar's Celebrated Curative are much too precious to entrust to the post office's incompetence," Caesar said.

And too precious to entrust to me, either, Jed thought. "Have you even looked for a local source for the ingredients?" he said aloud. "Give me the list and I'll go over it with Dr. Dengler. Maybe he knows someplace we can get what we need."

"All in due time, Son. You'll have the recipe for the Curative when you need it. Besides, even if the ingredients arrived tomorrow, we couldn't leave Welcome Springs right

away. Didn't you promise Dr. Dengler you would stay and help complete his boardinghouse?"

The charcoal snapped in Jed's hand. There was that. And Nixie expected him to renege on that promise, didn't she? Though she'd warmed to him some since the picnic nearly a week ago, she still kept an exaggerated formality between them. He'd even heard her refer to Stebbins as "Theo," but he was never anything but "Mr. Hawkins." He groaned. He'd never win with Nixie. If he stayed here, he'd have to endure her continued coolness. If he left, he'd only prove her worst suspicions about him.

"Drawing going that badly, is it? Let me have a look."

Jed tried to shield his sketchbook, but it was hard to defend yourself against someone you couldn't see. With one swift jerk, his father tugged the sketchbook from his hand. *"Ah hah! Well, I must say, my boy, it's a very good likeness."*

Jed said nothing, merely snatched the sketchbook back. He started to close it, but Caesar stopped him. *"There's no shame in having tender feelings for a woman, Jed. If I've somehow led you to believe otherwise, then I've done you a disservice."*

Jed's throat tightened at the unexpected seriousness of his father's words. He looked down at the sketchbook. Nixie's image smiled back at him, just as he most liked to imagine her, clad in her swimming costume, golden hair curling softly about her face.

"I see she has excellent taste in her choice of tonics, too." Caesar spoke over his shoulder.

In a moment of whimsy, Jed had sketched a bottle of Great Caesar's Celebrated Curative in Nixie's hand. She seemed to be offering it to the viewer. Many a man would have drunk hemlock if delivered by such a fetching young woman.

"Do you remember much about your mother?"

Caesar had no end of surprises for Jed this evening. He shook his head. His mother had died when he was five. He had a fuzzy memory of a woman in a blue-flowered calico dress, laughing and tossing a cloth ball to him.

"You look more like me than her, but you have her eyes." Caesar's voice softened. *"Eyes I could have gotten lost in. I courted her a year before she'd even agree to walk out with me."*

"A year?" Caesar Hawkins had never stuck to anything for a year. He wearied of a town or even a stage routine in a matter of weeks. "I'm surprised you kept at it."

Caesar chuckled. *"I tried to quit her, but a drunkard would have more luck renouncing the bottle. Your Nixie's like that. You'll think she's fickle, leading you along, and then one day, she'll grab hold of you, and she'll never let go. She wants to be sure, that's all."*

Sure of what? Jed wondered. *Sure of trusting her reputation to a patent medicine peddler like me?*

"That doesn't mean there aren't a few things you can do to hurry her along," Caesar said. *"After all, I've learned a little about women in the years since I met your mother."*

Jed frowned. From what he'd seen, his father's idea of romance was delivering a box of chocolates and a risqué note. Over the years, Caesar had collected lovers like some men collected pipes. He was something of a legend among the itinerant peddlers and travelers in this part of the country, but Jed wanted none of it. He'd had enough impermanence in his life. When he decided on the woman for him, he wanted to know theirs was a love that would last.

Jed snapped shut the sketchbook. "If I decide to court Nixie, I'll do it on my own, without your help."

He'd thought Caesar would sputter and act offended, but he surprised Jed yet again and showed no reaction. He merely clapped him on the shoulder and changed the subject. *"You're going to the séance Friday, aren't you?"*

Jed made a face. "I haven't decided."

"Oh, I really think you should go. It will be great fun."

"How do you know about it?"

"I heard some people talking."

He didn't like the sound of his father's voice. Something entirely too innocent... "Papa, you are going to behave yourself, aren't you?"

"Me? Well, of course I will. I'll be the soul of decorum."

Jed stood. "I don't think you should go. After all, you weren't invited."

"Oh, no one will even know I'm there. I plan on staying back out of the way and watching. You wouldn't deny an old man his only entertainment, would you?"

Jed sighed. Now he'd have to go. If only to make sure his father didn't get into trouble.

"You may come in now. All is ready." Dinah Merchant stood in the doorway of the Dengler parlor and motioned everyone inside. Dressed in her usual black, she wore a lace shawl around her shoulders and what Nixie could only suppose was meant to be a mystical expression on her face.

Nixie moved into the parlor with the others. Under Dinah's direction, the room had been transformed. She'd ordered the furniture pushed back against the wall. Covered with sheets, the sofa and chairs and side tables looked like a half-dozen ghostly figures crouched in the shadows. A single round table sat in the middle of the room, draped in her mother's best damask tablecloth. Candles flickered on the mantel and in a silver candelabra in the center of the table. The smell of wax and herbs and a more exotic, spicy odor hung in the air, adding to the otherworldly atmosphere.

Despite her skepticism, a shiver raced up Nixie's spine. She hesitated a moment before going in so that Jed, who was directly behind her, momentarily bumped into her. The awareness of his solid, masculine presence, and of her body's heightened response to him banished her fear with apprehension of another kind.

"What is that odd smell?" Theo Stebbins followed Jed and Nixie into the room and wrinkled his nose.

"The room has been cleansed with incense and prepared for our communications with the other side." Dinah had adopted a quavery, singsong voice that struck Nixie as funny, but a worried look from Dory quelled her laughter.

Dinah directed them all where to sit. Dr. Dengler had been called to a patient and Nixie's mother was watching the boys. The Chapmans had decided not to join them after all. That left Archie Harrison to Dinah's left, with Theo Stebbins on her right, then Dory, Jed, and Nixie.

They took their seats, knees almost touching around the small table. Nixie tried to make herself as small as possible, but Jed's thigh still brushed her skirts, inches from her own thigh. She could feel the heat of his body, and smell the scent of herbs and sawdust that clung to him. Closing her eyes, she inhaled deeply, a pleasurable warmth flooding her. She was suddenly grateful to Dinah for holding this séance. Here in the flickering candlelight, she could enjoy a physical closeness to Jed without worry that he, or anyone else, might jump to the wrong conclusion about their relationship.

Dinah settled herself into her chair and straightened her shawl about her shoulders. "Mr. Harrison, the lights please," she said.

Archie got up and snuffed the candles on the mantelpiece, leaving the three tapers on the table as the sole illumination in the room. "We must now join hands and spend time in silent meditation as we prepare to communicate with the other side." Dinah extended her hands, and after a moment's hesitation, the others did also.

A shiver raced up Nixie's arm at Jed's touch. Her hand was swallowed up by his, cradled in its warmth. He held her hand gently, but securely. She could feel the callouses on his palm and fingers, callouses that testified to his strength and ability to work hard. The appeal of those callouses startled her. Surely she ought to be more pleased by the smooth skin of a rich man who didn't have to work for a living.

Trying to distract herself from such thoughts, Nixie looked across the table and saw Dory smiling at Theo Stebbins. Perhaps some good would come of this séance after all. Nixie was beginning to think the popularity of such gatherings had very little to do with satisfying spiritual desires and much more to do with nurturing physical ones.

"I didn't realize we were going to sit here all night holding hands, but I can't say as I mind." Jed leaned forward and whispered in Nixie's ear, his mouth so close she imagined his lips grazed her earlobe. The thought sent a rush of heat to her loins. She squirmed in her chair, struggling to keep her breathing even, her expression calm, though inside her chest her heart raced wildly.

"We will now begin." Nixie flinched at Dinah's sudden announcement. Jed squeezed her hand and the heat inside her built.

"I will now summon the spirits to converse with us. Everyone must concentrate. Open your minds to the spirits' presence." Dinah pulled a handkerchief from her pocket and placed it on the table. The monogram *EM* was picked out in black thread on one corner.

"Spirits, I beseech you," she began in a loud voice. "Open the door to the other side so that we may converse with the one I seek. Pass through that celestial portal to visit Earth once more. Come spirits, answer our plea and grace us with your company. Hear us and answer."

"I don't see how a spirit could get a word in edgewise," Jed whispered.

Nixie stifled a giggle, and fought the urge to lean closer to Jed. His body pulled at her like the tide. How long would she be able to resist such a force?

At last Dinah fell silent. Her eyes closed and her chin dropped forward on her chest. Nixie looked around the table. Everyone else had their eyes open, watching Dinah. She glanced at Jed and found him looking directly at her. In the flickering candlelight, she was sure he winked. Hoping he couldn't detect her blush, she tried to slip her hand from his, but he held on tightly.

"I feel the presence of a spirit!" Dinah raised her head and opened her eyes. "Is someone there?"

With a rush of wind, the candles flickered and the curtains billowed inward. A deep voice sliced through the silence. *"Yes. I am here."*

Everyone gasped. Nixie felt the hair rise up on the back of her neck. Jed squeezed her hand and leaned toward her.

"Mr. Merchant, is that you?" Dinah asked.

"It is I."

Nixie looked around the table, sure someone was helping Dinah with this farce. But the others' faces mirrored Nixie's own feelings of fascination, skepticism, and fear. Everyone that is, except Jed, and even he did not look guilty or triumphant, only . . . angry?

"Why are you here?" Dinah asked.

The "spirit" cleared its throat. *"You have something you wish to say to me?"*

Dinah glanced around the table, hesitating. Then she said, "Show yourself to us."

The spirit's sigh made the candle flames bow down. *"Alas, that is impossible,"* it said in a rich baritone. *"It is only with great effort that I can pass through the veil from the other side."*

"Tell us about life on the other side," Archie Harrison said, his face rapt with interest.

"Ah! Such wonders as I cannot convey to mere mortal minds! Riches and grandeur the intellect cannot comprehend. Music more spectacular than any you have ever heard. Gardens that make Eden look like a cow pasture."

"What are the people like?" Dory asked, leaning forward, her initial worries apparently forgotten.

"The people! Oh, I can't begin to describe them. Every man is strong and handsome beyond compare. And the women! The women have such beauty, even the most celebrated belle on Earth would look like a dog compared to the women here."

Jed was squeezing Nixie's hand so hard she was beginning to lose feeling in her fingers. She glanced at him to ask him to ease up, but kept quiet when she saw the expression on his face. He was positively *glowering* toward the invisible "spirit."

Dinah, too, was growing more and more agitated. She jerked her hands free of Theo and Archie and clenched them in her lap, her lips pinched together in a thin line.

"And the food! Dishes that would make the most fastidious gourmet weep for joy. Succulent fruit any time you want. Pastries light as air. The richest puddings. Roast beef

cooked exactly right. Feasting day and night if you like. I can't begin to describe the pleasure."

"Oh, shut up!" Dinah pushed up from her chair so quickly, it fell to the floor with a crash. She turned toward the bodiless voice. "You ought to be burning in the depths of hell for the way you treated me! You were never anything but a worthless excuse for a man. To think I gave up everything for you. You deserve to suffer, you miserable, mean, horrible—"

Dory rushed to put an arm around her sister. "Go away!" she shouted to the voice. "Haven't you hurt her enough?"

"Me? Why I never hurt anyone!" The voice sounded shocked. *"My dear lady, I believe there has been some serious mistake here. Whom did you say you were looking for?"*

A gasp rose up from those seated around the table as the handkerchief suddenly rose and hovered above the table, as if held in an invisible hand. *"Who is E. M.?"* the voice asked.

Dinah and Dory turned to face the table once more. "Edward Merchant, as you should well know," Dinah said gruffly.

"My dear lady, a thousand pardons." The handkerchief floated to the table once more. *"I am afraid there has been a grave error. I am Frederick Merchant, formerly a humble church deacon from Sioux City."*

Dinah's eyes widened. "You're not my late husband?"

"No, Madame." A dramatic pause. *"But I do believe I know the man of which you speak. I will not dignify him with the term 'gentleman.' At the time of my passing, he was talked about among those of us awaiting our judgment as one of the worst sort. As you so correctly surmised, he has been made to pay for the suffering and cruelty he inflicted during his time on Earth."*

"Then . . . he has been cast into the burning pit?" Dinah asked in a whisper.

"Oh worse, Madame. For your former husband has been given the worst punishment of all. He has been sentenced to return to Earth to live his life over. Every bad deed he

ever did will be done to him, and double." The spirit's voice took on a satisfied tone. *"I believe he is destined to live with an ill-tempered wife and seven ill-tempered children, who will plague him every moment of the day and into the night. They will spend his money and abuse his name and make his life more miserable than even the demons below would be able to manage."*

Dinah bowed her head. "Thank you for that information, sir," she whispered.

Nixie glanced at Jed. He was shaking, not with fear, as she had first thought, but with barely restrained laughter. She was about to scold him when the spirit spoke again. *"My pleasure, Madame. So happy to oblige. And now, I'm afraid I grow weary, and must return to my spiritual home."*

In a sudden rush of wind, the candles on the table went out, plunging the room into darkness. Dory screamed. A man cursed. Her nerves stretched thin, Nixie fought panic.

"Dinah has fainted," Mr. Harrison called.

"Someone fetch a light!" Dory cried.

Nixie stood and tried to leave the room, but couldn't even tell in which direction the door lay. She'd been looking directly at the candles when they went out and spots still swam before her eyes. Groping in front of her, she came into contact with a man's broad chest. A startled shriek escaped her, and then someone gripped her arms and pulled her close.

Chapter Eleven

Even in her blindness, Nixie recognized Jed's enticing scent and sure grip. She relaxed against him, grateful for his reassuring presence. Her head fit naturally into the cradle of his shoulder. She had never felt so safe as now, encircled by his arms.

They stood this way for a long moment, the chaos of the room blotted out by the strong beat of his heart beneath her ear. He pulled her closer still, crushing her breasts against the wall of his chest, the hard thickness of his arousal pressed into the softness of her belly.

Nixie knew she should pull away from him with a show of virginal modesty, but such playacting was not in her tonight. She liked the way Jed felt against her, liked knowing, too, that she was responsible for his arousal. Her own body tingled with an awareness of him, and the pleasurable heat of desire.

"Nixie, look at me," he whispered, his lips very definitely brushing her ear this time, setting off sparks within her, like a chain of ten-for-a-penny firecrackers exploding down her spine. She raised her head toward his vague shadow and his lips found hers in the darkness.

No pretense of resistance this time. She sighed and let herself relax against him, giving herself up to the firm caress of his lips against her mouth. A sigh escaped her and he took advantage of the moment to coax her mouth open wider. As his tongue darted between her teeth, her sigh became a gasp and then a groan as his hand slid down from her shoulder to cup her breast. Knowing she was shameless, but unable to help herself, she leaned into his palm, and was rewarded with the exquisite stroking of his tongue inside her mouth, mimicking the brush of his palm across her breast.

The chaos in the room around them receded to a distant murmur, obliterated by the dizzy rush of her own racing blood and panting breath in her ears. How was it that this man, someone she knew little and trusted less, could coax from her such forceful feelings? Sense told her this was wrong, while every nerve in her body told her it was right.

"Oh, Nixie," he breathed, trailing kisses from the corner of her mouth to her ear. One hand slipped to her buttock and he pulled her closer still, grinding his arousal against her until she bit back another moan.

They stood like this for a long moment, so close they might have been one body, too drugged with passion to move or speak. As her head began to clear, Nixie opened her eyes and raised her head. A match hissed, and then bright light hurt her eyes as someone relit the candelabra on the table. For a split second, she stared into Jed's eyes. The fierce possessiveness of his expression tore at her, sending her into a panic. "What have I done?" she whispered, shoving against his chest.

He let her go and she staggered from the room, her legs still too wobbly to guarantee surefootedness. "Nixie, are you—" She shrugged off Dory's hand and hurried away. By the time she reached the stairs, she was running, choking back the sobs that threatened to burst forth at any moment.

• • •

GREAT CAESAR'S GHOST

Jed woke the next morning aching and ill-tempered after a night spent reliving both the embarrassment of Caesar's turn as the "spirit of Mr. Merchant," and the ecstasy of Nixie's passionate response to his kiss. He hadn't been wrong in thinking a fire burned beneath the little blonde's frosty exterior. If only he could get past her initial shyness, he was sure he could win her favorable opinion.

As for his father, he fully intended to deal with *him* as soon as possible. First, he had breakfast to get through, and the task of reassuring Nixie that she had nothing to be embarrassed about. This happy prospect in mind, Jed whistled as he pulled on his jacket and opened the door to the wagon to start the day.

"A lovely morning, isn't it, my boy?"

Jed groaned at Caesar's cheery greeting. He'd been hoping to avoid his father until after breakfast.

If Caesar noticed Jed's response, he gave no sign of it. *"Last night was a rousing success, if I do say so myself. No, don't bother to thank me, boy. I'm always happy to do whatever I can to foster true love."*

"Thank you?" Jed's jaw dropped and he turned to face the general direction of Caesar's pompous comments. "If I could get my hands on you, I'd throttle you. What did you think you were doing, carrying on like that?"

"Just giving the people what they wanted. You know that's always been a guiding principle of mine. Give the public what it wants and they'll come back for more time and time again."

"I'm not talking about selling tonic. I'm talking about scaring folks half out of their wits, and pretending to be somebody you're not."

"Where's your sense of humor, my boy? It was all in fun! No one was truly frightened, at least not after the first few minutes. They were merely intrigued, and entertained." A note of pride crept into Caesar's voice. *"I made a splendid recovery there at the end, don't you think? When Mrs. Merchant started going on about her late husband? A stroke of genius on my part, I don't mind saying."* He chuckled. *"And speaking of genius, my star turn didn't do*

you any harm, either, did it? I couldn't help notice you, um, comforting Nixie there at the end. My word, boy, I thought I was going to have to run fetch the fire bucket and douse you both. He's got the Hawkins's touch! I said to myself. Yessirree. It's easy to see you're a chip off the old block when it comes to knowing how to handle the ladies."

"Enough." Jed didn't even try to keep the note of menace from his voice.

"Yes, you had her right where you wanted her and... what did you say, Son?"

"I said, enough. I don't want to hear another word, and I don't want you to do another thing, to interfere with my relationship with Nixie."

"At least you've stopped trying to deny there is a relationship. You listen to me, boy, and—"

"No. I will not listen. Not anymore." Jed turned away and started toward the Dengler home, but stopped after three steps across the grass. "And I'm not a boy. I haven't been for a long time." He didn't wait for an answer, merely turned back around and headed for the house.

He was sure he would be late to breakfast, but when he reached the dining room, he found that no one else was even seated yet. Dory and her sister were absent, but then they often skipped breakfast altogether, and Theo usually ate at his campsite. Nixie was busy laying silverware at the table, while Mrs. Dengler tried to comfort a squalling Lou. Pete, his unbroken hand shoved into the pocket of his knickers and a sullen expression on his face, looked on. Dr. Dengler stood behind his chair at the head of the table and studied them all with a look of concern.

"What's wrong, buddy?" Jed asked, pausing beside Mrs. Dengler and Lou. "Why the tears?"

Lou buried his head even further into his mother's shoulder. She turned a weary smile to Jed. "Lou is crying because Pete scared him with some awful ghost story he made up."

"I didn't make it up!" Pete scowled at them. "It's true! There really was a ghost. It was the ghost of Mr. Merchant."

"Hrrmph!"

Everyone turned their attention to Dr. Dengler as he cleared his throat. "Nixie, perhaps you had better tell us exactly what happened in the parlor last night," he said.

She flushed, and Jed knew she wasn't thinking about Mr. Merchant's ghost or anything that had happened before the lights went out. She looked at Pete. "How do you know about Mr. Merchant's ghost?" she asked.

Pete stuck out his lower lip. "I was watching through the knothole under the rug in my room. It looks right down into the parlor." He shrugged. "Lou was already asleep and I wanted to see what was going on."

"You weren't invited to that party. You shouldn't have been listening."

"Well, I did. And I know all about the ghost. So there!" He stuck his tongue out. Jed might have laughed if Nixie's expression hadn't been so fierce.

"Nixie, please explain to your brother that what he saw or heard was obviously a misunderstanding on his part." Dr. Dengler laced his hands over his ample stomach. "Obviously, there is no such thing as ghosts."

Nixie looked from her father to her brother and back again, her confusion evident.

"Well, go on," her mother prompted. "Explain to your brothers why there's absolutely nothing to be afraid of."

Nixie folded her arms underneath her breasts. "I can't."

"You can't?" Mrs Dengler shifted Lou onto her other hip and frowned. "Why not?"

"I can't explain what happened in the parlor last night. I don't know what to say."

"Really, Nixie girl. I have always known you to be more sensible than this." Dr. Dengler shook his head, eyes sad with disappointment.

"Shame on you, trying to frighten your brothers this way!" Mrs. Dengler scolded. She cradled Lou's head on her shoulder. "Just because they pester you sometimes, this is no way to take out your frustrations on them."

"Yeah, Nixie! You want me to get in trouble, don't you?" Pete said.

Lou began wailing again. Mrs. Dengler rocked him, murmuring words of comfort, while Pete began to tell his father about what he'd seen through his bedroom knothole.

Nixie hung her head, shoulders sagging. Anger rose in Jed's throat. How dare Nixie's family gang up on her this way. Couldn't they believe she was telling the truth? Did anyone ever think that she might be as frightened and confused by what happened as anyone? "Nixie?" He spoke softly, sure only she would hear him above the turmoil in the family dining room.

She raised her head and looked at him at last. The desperation in her eyes made his stomach hurt. He clenched his hands at his sides and raised his voice so that everyone would hear. "It was me!"

The room fell silent as everyone turned to look at him. "What are you talking about?" Nixie asked.

He took a deep breath. "The 'ghost' at the séance. It was me."

Nixie looked confused. "How could it be you? You were sitting right beside me and I never—"

"I can, uh, throw my voice. You know, ventriloquism." He smiled. "It's an old carnival trick." They had traveled for a while with a circus medium, a Madame somebody or another. Jed thought he remembered her saying this was how it was done.

"What about the handkerchief?" Pete came over to him. "I saw it move and you never touched it."

"Wires." He held up one hand and waggled his fingers. "Nobody can see them in candlelight."

"Why would you want to make fools of us that way?"

Jed flinched, as if he'd been slapped. "I had no intention of playing anyone for the fool," he protested. "I did it to help . . . to help Dinah and to provide a little evening's fun." She wasn't buying it, he could tell. Her eyes flashed with anger and her whole expression was hardened against him. He felt sick.

"All in good fun," Dr. Dengler boomed from the head of the table. He laughed. "I wish now that I had been there. But come everyone, let us eat."

Mechanically, Jed took his place and bowed his head for grace. All the while, he cursed himself soundly. If anyone was a fool in this whole mess, it was him. What had possessed him to think Nixie would appreciate being "rescued" by him? All he had done was bury, once and for all, any chance that the physical attraction she felt for him might grow into something more.

"I see that work on the Willkommen Inn is progressing very nicely, Mr. Hawkins." Dr. Dengler looked up from his plate of fried eggs and ham and addressed Jed.

"Uh, yes sir, it is. Everything is going very well." He glanced at Pete and Lou. "Your sons have been a lot of help to me."

"It is you I should thank, for keeping the little mischief makers out of trouble." Dr. Dengler chuckled. "I am so pleased to see my dream finally on its way to coming true. And to celebrate, I have decided to sponsor a dance. We will celebrate the Willkommen Inn, and our country's independence at the same time."

"We could have it at the pavilion," Nadine Dengler said, smiling at her husband. "A dance under the stars."

"Exactly what I was thinking, my dear. We will hire a band and serve refreshments and shoot off fireworks after dark."

"We must make you a new dress, Nixie," her mother said. "Something red, white, and blue for the holiday."

"I . . . I don't know if I'll be going to the dance," she said, aware of Jed's eyes fixed on her.

"Of course you'll go," Nadine said. "We'll all go, if we're to be the hosts."

Nixie stared at her plate and nodded. "Of course."

Jed looked across at her downcast face. Would he ever persuade Nixie to put aside her wrong impression of him? Could he hope she would consent to let him lead her out onto the dance floor, to take her into his arms and whirl her around to some lively tune beneath the stars?

He gripped his fork so tightly it threatened to bend in his hand. He would dance with Nixie. When the music began to play, he would step up and take her hand. And he wouldn't take no for an answer.

Nixie vowed to put Jed Hawkins's kiss out of her mind, as a moment of indiscretion best forgotten. But the memory slipped into her consciousness at the most inopportune moments, a demon intent on demolishing her hard-won composure.

She would wake in the middle of the night with the vivid recollection of being held so securely in his strong arms. Or while floating in the warm waters of the springs, she would remember warmer lips caressing her, skillful tongue teasing her to new heights of sensation.

Hot embarrassment rushed over her whenever she recalled the way he'd deceived them at the séance. How could he live with himself after he'd taken advantage of Dinah's distress that way? Not to mention the way he'd taken advantage of Nixie herself. If only she could take back those moments after the lights went out, when she'd made the worst sort of fool of herself!

The memory brought tears to her eyes, tears she either cried into her pillow or allowed to mingle with the water from the springs. Worst of all was the knowledge that for a moment at least, she'd allowed herself to think that Jed was different. When she'd wrapped her arms around him and yielded to his kiss, she'd felt, not just physical passion, but a sense of contentment, like a sigh from somewhere deep inside her. The uneasiness that plagued her, the feeling that she never quite fit in, had vanished in Jed Hawkins's arms.

When he'd revealed his deception at breakfast the next morning, she'd lost all confidence in her ability to judge a man's true intentions. To Jed Hawkins she would never be more than a pleasant pastime, a way to fill the days before moving on to the next town, and the next willing woman.

She dreaded the approaching Independence Celebration Dance. It was one thing to avoid Jed during the day at home, quite another to take care not to cross his path at an occasion filled with music and starlight and romance, especially when all she could think of was how it might feel to be swept away in his arms. Whirled around the dance floor until she grew breathless and dizzy.

She thought of feigning illness, but that was not so easily done when one's father is a doctor. Besides, taking the coward's way out would only prove to Mr. Hawkins that he'd affected her. Better to go and literally face the music. When he asked her to dance, as she felt sure he would, she'd have the pleasure of snubbing him in front of everyone.

The afternoon of July 4, Nixie found herself in her room with Dory Evans, surrounded by petticoats and corset covers and ruffles and ribbons, the scent of powder and eau de cologne mingling with the enticing aroma of barbecue that wafted through the open windows.

"Oh, where did I put my rose powder?" Dory rummaged through the disarray of bottles and boxes on the dressing table. "I know I brought it with me."

"There, to the left of the charcoal pencil, next to William." At the sound of his name, the bird fluttered to Nixie's shoulder. Together they studied her reflection in the mirror.

"If it was a snake it would have bit me." Dory unscrewed the lid to the little pot of pale pink powder and dabbed some of the contents onto the end of a camel-hair brush. She swept the brush across her cheeks and studied the effect in the mirror. "You don't think it's too much, do you, Nixie? I don't want to look like a Jezebel."

"You look fine," Nixie said, putting her hands on the other woman's shoulders. "Very natural."

"Only better, I hope." Dory smiled and picked up the charcoal pencil and began adding color to her brows. "Dinah has a conniption every time she sees me using cosmetics. She says it's wrong to try to change the looks God has given us."

"I don't notice your sister giving up her corset or her curling iron. What's the difference in those things and powdering your nose to cover up freckles?" Nixie leaned closer to the mirror and swept a powder puff across her own forehead. William squawked as a cloud of French talc settled over him. He flew into his cage and began to preen.

"I think William shares Dinah's views of cosmetics," Dory said, laughing. She pushed back from the vanity and turned to the bed, where their dresses for the dance lay across the spread.

"This is the prettiest shade of green," Dory said, fingering the seafoam-colored silk of Nixie's gown. "It will be perfect with your hair and eyes."

"Mama wanted red, white, and blue, like yours," Nixie said, coming to stand beside her friend. "But green is more practical and will do for summer and fall both." She picked up Dory's candy-cane striped dress, with its wide collar and cuffs of navy blue. It was the sort of dress she would have preferred. She sighed. No, it was better to be practical. "You'll look patriotic enough for both of us." She helped Dory into the dress, then began to fasten the row of buttons up the back.

"Do you think this looks all right?"

"It's a beautiful dress." She leaned forward and picked up the navy sash from the bed and wrapped it around Dory's waist. "And you're beautiful in it." She grinned. "Mr. Stebbins won't be able to take his eyes off of you."

"Oh, do you think so?" Dory whirled around to face her. "Do you think he'll ask me to dance? We've hardly had a chance to exchange more than a few words at a time since the séance." She frowned. "Dinah hasn't let me have a minute alone with him, but I intend to find a way to speak to him tonight—that is, if he's even interested."

"Of course he's interested." Nixie moved around behind Dory and finished tying the sash into a large bow. "Haven't you noticed the way he goes out of his way to be near you?"

"But maybe he's simply being polite. Or worse, he feels sorry for me." Her eyes widened in horror at the thought. "It does happen, you know. Some men feel very, I don't know, *virtuous* or something, whenever they pay attention to a spinster. They see it as a kind of charity work."

Nixie frowned. "Is that what your sister told you?"

Dory hung her head. "She says either that, or if Theo has any interest in me, it's because I have money. Daddy left us quite a lot you know, and Theo is just a schoolteacher."

Nixie put her hand on Dory's shoulder. "And does it matter to you that Theo might not have much money?"

Dory raised her head. "Of course not." She sighed. "Poor Dinah. She's only judging by her own experience. After she married Mr. Merchant, she found out he was almost bankrupt from bad investments. Once, when they were having an argument, he told her he'd only married her to get out of debt." She hugged her arms across her chest. "Can you believe what happened at the séance? I've never believed in spirits and such before, but how else do you explain what everyone saw, and heard?"

Nixie frowned. She hadn't said anything to her friend about Jed's confession. At the time she'd told herself the tale wasn't hers to tell, but she couldn't let Dory go on believing in such nonsense. "It wasn't a real spirit, Dory. It was just Jed Hawkins having fun with us all."

"Mr. Hawkins?" Dory's eyes widened. "But how?"

Nixie busied her hands straightening the disarray on the dressing table. "He learned to throw his voice from some people who worked in a carnival. And he used wires to make the handkerchief move." She sighed. "I guess he thought it was funny, making fools of us that way."

"I'd say we made fools enough of ourselves, holding a séance like that." To Nixie's surprise, Dory laughed. "I ought to thank him, though. Dinah has been much more at ease since then, and she's lost all interest in spiritualism."

Nixie thought of Dinah's reaction to the revelation that her late husband was being made to suffer as he'd made her suffer. She had to admit, that had been a clever touch on Jed's part. "I suppose the saying is true: Revenge is sweet."

Dory smiled and nodded. "Don't be too hard on Mr. Hawkins. I'm sure he was only trying to help."

"The way Dinah thinks she's helping you by keeping

you and Mr. Stebbins apart?" Nixie deftly changed the subject.

Dory turned to study her reflection in the mirror. "I've tried to tell her it's a mistake to judge all men by the actions of one, but she won't listen."

"Well, you don't have to listen to her, either. I'm sure Mr. Stebbins likes you very much."

Dory's smile returned. "Come on," she beckoned. "I'll help you into your dress."

Nixie forced her mind from thoughts of Jed Hawkins and stepped into the confection of sea-green silk and ecru lace. Though practical in color, it was far fancier than any other gown she owned, with a full eight inches of ruffled lace at the hem, accented with a green silk bow every twelve inches around the wide belled skirt. More lace hung from the cuffs of the full sleeves, trailing past her elbows. A scarf of cream-colored satin filled in the low, square neckline, and the cream satin sash tied in a wide bow at the back, with streamers hanging well past her knees.

"You'll be the belle of the ball," Dory said as she adjusted the bow, then moved back to admire her work.

"No. Mary Sue Flourney or some other seventeen-year-old will claim that honor." She picked up the long white gloves that lay across the end of the bed and began to pull them on. She glanced at her reflection in the mirror, next to Dory's dressed-up image, and smiled. "But we won't disgrace ourselves, I don't think."

"Come along, girls, the buggy's waiting!" Nadine Dengler's voice rang up the stairs.

Nixie fastened the door of William's cage while Dory slipped into her own gloves. Then, grabbing up a fan, she followed her friend down the stairs and out to the family buggy.

Mr. Chapman drove the buggy, with Mrs. Chapman beside him. Nixie and her mother and Dory squeezed in the back, but their finery made for a tight fit. "It's a good thing your father and the boys went on ahead," Nadine Dengler said as she folded her skirts around her legs.

"He's been running back and forth between here and the

pavilion all day," Nixie explained to Dory. "He wants everything to be absolutely perfect."

In fact, Ham Dengler had spent most of the previous week making arrangements for this evening, dispensing money from the family funds at an alarming rate. When Nixie had questioned him on the need for such expense, he'd waved her away. "Think of it as an investment, Nixie girl. What we spend promoting the boardinghouse and the springs now will pay off tenfold in years to come."

As Mr. Chapman turned the buggy onto the street leading to the pavilion, Nixie stared in dismay at the spectacle before her. The lattice-shaded pavilion was draped in red and blue bunting, with more bunting stretched out to form arches across the streets approaching the building on four sides. The bandstand Jed had spent most of two days constructing sat next to the pavilion.

As they drew nearer, Nixie noticed a large sign forming the skirting around the bandstand. HAPPY INDEPENDENCE DAY, FROM THE NEW WILLKOMMEN INN—OPENING SOON!

Her father looked up from adjusting this broadside and spotted them. He hurried to meet the buggy, grinning as he assisted them to the ground. "What do you think, Nixie girl? It is magnificent, is it not?"

She managed a smile and patted his hand. "It looks wonderful, Papa. But do you think . . . Well, should we tell people the inn is 'Opening Soon?' It isn't finished yet."

"It will be in a matter of days," Ham looked back at the sign, grinning. "No harm in letting folks get their reservations in now, if they wish."

She nodded, feeling a little queasy. The sign in front of the inn had proclaimed "Opening Soon" for three years now. Some people had even suggested changing the wording to "Opening Sooner or Later." This banner would provide more fuel for their jokes.

But she wouldn't spoil her father's holiday by pointing this out. She fixed her smile more firmly and squeezed his arm. "Everyone is going to have a wonderful time tonight," she said.

He patted her hand. "Nothing like a dance under the stars." He gathered his wife close with his other arm. "We might have to steal away and do a little spooning of our own—show these young people how it is done."

Nadine laughed and playfully tapped Ham's shoulder with her fan. Nixie released her father's arm and let her parents walk the rest of the way to the pavilion alone.

"What should we do first?" Dory latched on to Nixie's arm and pulled her close. "Stay with me. I'm so nervous."

Nixie surveyed the scene before them. Couples and men and women in groups of three or four walked around the cleared area inside the pavilion that had been designated as the dance floor. Some older folks were already seated in folding chairs around the edge of the dance floor, talking and sipping lemonade, which was being dispensed by the Ladies of the Eastern Star from a table at the back of the building.

Mrs. Frisco smiled and nodded from her chair near the band. "It is good to see you young people out enjoying yourselves," she said as Nixie and Dory approached. She looked Nixie up and down. "You look very lovely tonight, dear. I would not be surprised if you did not catch some young man's eye yet." She reached out and patted Nixie's hand. "Do not be nervous. I know you are the shy type, but it appears standoffish, no?"

Nixie accepted the familiar advice without comment. She knew she was past the point when any of the "young men" would pay attention to her, and the older ones had given up long ago. She moved on around the dance floor, Dory following close beside her. They passed the oak tree where the Masons sold barbecue sandwiches and sausages. Younger boys and girls raced around the edge of the building, playing tag, or shooting off penny firecrackers until some adult chased them away.

"Look, there's your brother, Peter. Doesn't he look handsome?"

Nixie smiled when she spotted Pete. He did look quite handsome, with his hair slicked back and his suit neatly pressed. He'd argued to be allowed to wear long pants to the dance, but Nadine had placated him by promising that when he turned fifteen in a few weeks, she would buy him a pair of trousers, a coveted sign of manhood, at least in Pete's eyes. As it was, Nadine had ended up having to let out the knickers he wore, since he'd shot up several inches seemingly overnight. He was leaning against one of the supporting pillars of the pavilion, watching the children play, a look of feigned indifference on his face. But Nixie was willing to bet at least part of her brother wished he were chasing around in the dirt with the others, for all he was trying so hard to act grown up.

"There's Mr. Hawkins." Dory pointed across the pavilion, where Jed was helping to set up more chairs.

Nixie looked away, before Jed saw her. With any luck, he'd be too busy most of the evening to notice her. "Don't look now but he's headed this way." Dory's voice in her ear set her stomach to somersaulting. But when she looked around she saw, not Jed Hawkins, but Theo Stebbins, walking across the empty dance floor toward them.

"Good evening Miss Evans, Miss Dengler." Theo tipped his straw hat and smiled nervously. Though he spoke to both women, it was Dory who clearly held all his attention. "Uh, lovely night, isn't it?"

"Very nice," Dory said. She opened her fan and began wafting it in front of her face. "It was so kind of the Denglers to sponsor this dance."

"Yes, it was." He swallowed hard and tugged at his collar. "I was wondering, Miss Evans . . . that is, I thought perhaps—"

Nixie looked away, hoping to make things easier on Theo. What she saw made her eyes widen in apprehension. "Excuse me a moment, please," she mumbled to the couple beside her, and hastily set off across the dance floor.

"Why Mrs. Merchant, aren't you looking lovely?" Nixie seized Dinah Merchant by the arm and held on for dear life, pulling her in the opposite direction from Dory and Theo. "I was just going for some lemonade. Wouldn't you like to join me?"

"Not really, Miss Dengler." Dinah scowled toward Dory and tried to pull away, but Nixie held on. "My sister—"

"Your sister isn't going to come to any harm standing in the middle of at least a hundred other people," Nixie said. "You can keep an eye on her just as well from the refreshment table."

"There is no need to hold on to me as if I were some aged grandmother in danger of falling," Dinah protested.

"I'm not worried about you falling," Nixie said, continuing to hold fast to the other woman's arm.

The band began to play, and as if he'd performed one of his magic tricks, Jed Hawkins appeared at her side. "May I have this dance, Miss Dengler?" he asked, bowing before her.

Her resolve to avoid him at all costs faltered now that he was beside her. Dressed in his white suit, hair freshly trimmed and topped with a straw Panama set at a rakish angle, Jed was the picture of the handsome rogue, sure to break any young girl's heart. *I'm not a young girl*, Nixie told herself. *I should know better*. But her willpower weakened against the onslaught of his devilishly handsome smile.

Part of Nixie screamed to accept the invitation, but another part warned of the danger of spending even a few moments in this man's arms. Then there was the problem of what to do with Dinah. She smiled as an idea came to her. "I'm very sorry, Mr. Hawkins, but I . . . I have something else I have to do right now. I'm sure, however, that Mrs. Merchant would love to dance."

Jed raised one eyebrow in surprise, as Dinah began to protest. But Nixie shoved the other woman toward him, and Jed obligingly took her hand and led her onto the dance floor. Nixie sighed in relief as she watched them depart.

At that moment, Dory Evans and Theo Stebbins swept by. They were smiling, oblivious to anything but each other. Would she ever know a love like that—so pure and certain, untroubled by worries and the memories of past mistakes? An overbearing sister seemed a small obstacle to true love compared to the hurdles Nixie faced.

When the waltz ended, Nixie joined the applause and prepared to resume her role as Dinah's keeper. But before she could find Dinah, she felt a masculine hand on her shoulder, and heard Jed's voice in her ear. "I believe this dance is mine," he said.

"But what about Mrs. Merchant?" she asked, as the band began a lively number and he swept her onto the floor.

"Your father is looking after her." He grinned. "After that, Archie Harrison is going to take a turn, then Mr. Chapman will take over."

She shook her head in amazement, but had no time to think, as the quick steps of the dance required all her concentration. For all the lively pace of the music, she felt her heart must be racing faster.

They did not speak until the dance ended, when without comment, he led her toward the refreshment table. "Thank you for the dance, Miss Dengler." He handed her a glass of lemonade and toasted her. "You're looking very pretty tonight. The color of that dress suits you. But then, I should have known a mermaid would choose sea-green."

She looked away, fighting the blush that engulfed her at his words. "Look, there's Pete." She nodded across the room, a smile spreading across her face. "He's with Becky Simmons. He's been sweet on her for months, but I never thought he'd have the courage to speak to her."

"Perhaps he learned everything he needed to know from watching me," Jed said, chuckling.

Nixie stiffened. "I suppose you see yourself as quite the ladies' man."

"No, I wouldn't say that. My father had that title in our family, not me."

She waited for him to say more, but he remained silent. "Was it just you and your father then, traveling together all these years?" she asked.

She could feel his eyes on her, but she refused to look at him. After all, she didn't want him to think *she* was going to be another conquest. "Yes. My mother died when I was five, so Papa took me with him. I suppose it doesn't sound like much of a life for a child, but I can't complain."

"You must miss him a great deal—your father."

"Yes . . . and no."

This odd answer startled her into looking at him once more. His lips curved in a half-smile, and mischief danced in his eyes. "Sometimes it's like he's right here with me still." He emptied his glass and set it aside, eyes locked to hers. She began to feel very warm. "Don't you think it's time you called me Jed? And I could call you Nixie." He moved closer, the scent of herbs and shaving soap enveloping her. "I'd say we know each other too well by now to remain so formal."

She wrenched her gaze away from him, willing herself not to think of how well she remembered the feel of his mouth on hers, or the touch of his hands on her body. She swallowed hard, and sought some distraction on the dance floor.

Once more she spotted Dory waltzing in Theo Stebbins's arms. If Nixie had been asked to paint a picture of love, that was the scene she would have sketched: a couple twirling arm and arm, with eyes for no one but each other. Would she ever know that innocent bliss? The thought that she might not filled her with bitter longing.

"It's warm in here. Why don't we step outside for some air?" Jed's voice, soft in her ear, disturbed her thoughts.

She told herself she shouldn't go with him, even as she allowed him to take her elbow and guide her onto a darkened path leading away from the pavilion. She could not stand on the edge of that dance floor and watch all those happy couples for a moment longer. The darkness, even in the company of Jed Hawkins, was a welcome refuge.

Thick-trunked live oaks arched over the path, blocking the light from the pavilion and shielding them from view. The gunpowder scent of firecrackers hung heavy in the air, mingling with the smoky remnants from the barbecue pits. She inhaled deeply of this rich perfume, trying to clear her muddled head. As the music receded into the background, she was conscious of the sound of her own breathing, rapid and shallow, keeping time with her racing heart.

"Are you afraid of me, Nixie?" Jed stopped and turned to face her.

She looked up at him, his face a map of shadows in the

darkness. But she could well imagine the look of concern that matched the tone of his voice. No matter her doubts about his character, she knew Jed Hawkins would never physically harm her. "No," she said after a moment. "I'm not afraid of you."

"Then are you afraid of these feelings between us?"

She tried to turn away, but he wrapped his hands around her arms and held her. "Th-there's nothing between us," she stammered.

With his thumb, he stroked the inside of her wrists, sending tremors through her. He bent his head and spoke in a whisper, his hot breath tickling her neck, like kisses feathered down her spine. "Nixie, I feel things with you I never felt with a woman before. Don't tell me it's not the same for you."

She could summon no words to deny him, could not bring herself to lie while her whole being yearned for him.

He moved his head and his lips found hers in the darkness. Releasing her arms, he let his hands fall to his sides. Then he waited, holding himself still, his mouth barely covering hers.

She felt his breath, warm on her cheek, and the velvet caress of his lips scarcely touching hers. She closed her eyes and swayed, a magnet seeking its opposing pole, an electric current leaping a gap to complete a circuit. With a sigh, she pressed her lips against his more firmly, and wrapped her arms around his neck to pull him close.

He gathered her into his arms, a gesture of welcome that warmed her from the inside out. Snuggling against him, she relished the feel of his hard, male body and the pressure of his warm, demanding mouth. He kissed her eyes, her cheeks, her neck, before returning his attention to her lips. He tasted their surface with his tongue before exploring the tender interior of her mouth.

She copied his movements, a thrill running through her as he murmured his pleasure in response to her tentative explorations. She grew bolder, gently sucking on his tongue, running her fingers through the hair at the nape of his neck. All memory of the dance faded, all sight and sound of anything other than the two of them and this heady rush of desire that demanded to be satisfied.

He backed up, pulling her into the deeper shadows beneath a tree, bracing his back against the trunk. The rough bark grazed her hands through her gloves as she wrapped them around his neck once more and pressed against him. She was barely aware of the sensation, her senses so engulfed in the smell, the feel, and the taste of this man.

His hands moved down her back until they grasped her buttocks, pulling her against his thigh. Then he reached up to cup her breast, thumb stroking the taut peak. She let her head fall back, smiling at the shudders of delight coursing through her.

"Nixie, Nixie listen to me." His urgent whisper roused her at last. She looked up at him, sleepy-eyed with desire. "We have to stop this," he said. "Someone's liable to find us here and . . ."

His words began to register in her numbed brain. The reality of what was happening hit her with the force of a fist in her gut. She wrenched away and stared at him, open-mouthed in horror. She was doing it again. After all the promises she'd made to herself, she couldn't believe she had let things go this far. "No!" she cried, tears of frustration tightening her throat. "I mustn't—we can't—" She shook her head and whirled around and ran back up the path toward the pavilion.

She found Pete standing with some friends by the refreshment table. "Tell Mama and Papa I went back to the house," she said, grabbing him by the arm. "Tell them I'm not feeling well, and I'm going to lie down."

She didn't give him time to answer, but turned and ran, as the first sobs tore from her throat.

Chapter Twelve

Jed stared after Nixie, feeling as if he'd been caught up in a whirlwind and set down on his head. One moment she had been returning his kisses with a passionate fervor that made him half-mad with wanting her. The next minute she was running away as if he were her worst enemy.

He jerked off his hat and slapped it against his thigh. What had he been thinking, walking her out into the darkness like this? Hadn't he known what such a move would lead to?

"Congratulations, my boy. Looks like you've melted Miss Nixie's frosty shell once and for all. And my, what a warm and willing miss she turned out to be." Caesar's chuckle vibrated in the air around them. *"I must say, even in my heyday, I don't know if I could have done any better. And to think I was beginning to doubt you had it in you."*

"She's not one of your carnival lightskirts!" Jed glared into the darkness, all his frustration and despair condensed into a white-hot anger. "She's a respectable young woman who deserves better than to be spied on by the likes of you."

"Don't forget that I'm your father. You've no call to think yourself any better than me. Everything you have in this world and everything you are, you owe to me."

Jed flinched. Was what his father said true? Was he really the Great Caesar Hawkins made over again? Nixie certainly saw him that way, as an itinerant huckster who couldn't be trusted.

"Well, what are you standing around here for? Aren't you going after her?"

He bowed his head. "She doesn't want anything to do with me."

"Then I'd like to see her kiss a man she's really interested in!" He felt a hand on his shoulder. *"I know you don't think much of my advice, but I'm going to give it to you anyway. The only thing Nixie Dengler is unsure of right now is herself. I'll not deny that she's a perfectly respectable young lady, but it's been my observation that church-going virgins and carnival lightskirts have more in common than you might think. They're both women inside, and neither one of them gives their hearts lightly."*

"Nixie isn't giving her heart to anyone, least of all me."

Caesar released him, his chuckle ringing out once more. *"You may think she was kissing you with her lips just now, Son, but from where I stood, I'd say she had her whole heart in it."*

Jed looked in the direction Nixie had run. He imagined he could still feel the heat of her breath against his throat. Her scent still lingered in the air around him, fueling his desire the way smoke from the barbecue pit might arouse other appetites. He had never wanted a woman the way he wanted Nixie.

"All right," he said to his father. "I'll go after her." He shoved the hat back on his head and set off around the pavilion.

"I'll come with you," Caesar said.

Jed froze in his tracks. "No." He took a deep breath, fighting to subdue his anger. "Look," he said to the empty darkness around him. "What I'm saying right now, I'm not saying as a son to a father, but as a man to a man. Stay out of this. If Nixie and I are going to settle things between us, we need to do it alone."

The noise of the celebration echoed in the gap left by his father's lack of reply. The band struck up a polka and the pavilion fairly shook with the sounds of energetic dancing. Jed's stomach knotted and he started to move on. *"All right."* The words came so softly, he thought at first he might have imagined them. Then Caesar spoke louder. *"I suppose if you haven't learned anything from me by now, there's nothing more I can teach you."*

"Thanks, Papa."

"Well, don't stand around here all night—go after her. And good luck, Son."

Feeling lighter, he shoved his hands in his pockets and quickened his pace toward the house. It was long past time he and Miss Nixie Dengler had a talk.

Not a light glowed within the Dengler home. No one stirred in the campground, either. The whole town was over at the pavilion, celebrating the Fourth and Dr. Dengler's generosity. Jed stood in the yard below Nixie's window for a long while, then stooped and gathered up a handful of gravel. Lobbing it toward the side of the house beside the window, he called out her name. "Nixie! Nixie, come out and talk. I swear I won't lay a hand on you. But we have to talk!"

The only answer was the sound of cicadas, whirring in the trees. Dejected, he turned away to walk back to his wagon.

But before he reached his campsite, he crossed the path leading to the springs. There was a chance . . .

He saw the lantern long before he saw her. He stood in the shadows outside the light and listened to the sound of water lapping at the concrete curb around the pool. The smell of moss and minerals rose up to fill his head with its muggy perfume.

Then he spotted her, a lithe figure cutting through the water, moving in and out of the beam of the lantern's light. He watched her for a while, admiring the smooth movement of her arms, the sleek curves of her body. She seemed as at home with the springs as any sea creature. Could he possibly claim that sense of belonging for himself? Could he make Nixie love him and thereby share a little of her world?

When he moved closer to the pool, his shadow fell across the water. She paused in midstroke and raised her head to stare at him. "I thought I might find you here," he said, taking a step forward. "Nixie, we have to talk."

She shook her head, and before he could argue, she dove, disappearing beneath the black water, a circle of ripples marking where she had been.

"Nixie, come back here!" He paced the length of the pool, knotting his hands into fists in frustration. "Dammit, woman, don't run away from me again!"

But the water was eerily silent, still.

He stopped, and stared into the pool. In the darkness he had no way of knowing its depth. The water looked like ink, impenetrable, suffocating.

His heart hammered in his chest as he waited. "Nixie!" he shouted again. "Nixie, are you all right?"

No answer. She had disappeared. Vanished into that dark water.

An image of her, lying pale and lifeless in the midst of that blackness, flashed across his mind. Not stopping to think, he began to shuck out of his jacket, to pull off his shoes.

Only when the water closed around him, and his feet failed to find purchase on the bottom, did his panicked brain remind him that he didn't know how to swim.

Nixie stood beneath a sheltering rock overhang, water lapping at her waist. She watched Jed Hawkins pace the length of the pool, heard his angry shouts. From this vantage point, she could see him, but he couldn't see her. He would think she'd run away again, and he'd be furious.

Let him fume, she thought. *I won't come out and talk to him. Not tonight.* Not while the memory of his hands on her body, of his lips on hers, still burned.

She no longer thought him a truly bad man. She wanted

with all her heart to believe he had not deliberately set out to seduce her. But he was a man from a different world, a place where the line between entertainment and deception stretched exceedingly thin. He was heir to the Great Caesar Hawkins, raised on the pitchman's pursuasive patter and the applause of the crowd. She was a small-town spinster, confined to a world of mundane matters. Regardless of the strength of the attraction between them, they couldn't deny that difference. One day, the difference would prove too much, and he'd leave her. She didn't need crystal balls or magic cards to predict that part of their future. Better to avoid him now and save herself pain later.

She almost laughed when he began to take off his coat. Jedediah Hawkins, who professed to hate water, was going to get wet. And all because he couldn't stand for a woman to get the best of him.

But her laughter turned to alarm as soon as he hit the water. His wild thrashings were not the moves of a practiced swimmer, or even a competent dog-paddler. "Nixie!" Her name was a strangled cry, torn from his throat as he sank beneath the water. The cry of a drowning man.

In a matter of seconds, she was at his side, struggling to get a grip on his thrashing arms. She managed to raise his head enough for him to gasp for air, and then he pulled them both under, his heavier and much larger body like a lead weight around her shoulders.

"Be still!" she shouted, but it was as if he had not heard her. His eyes glazed with panic as the two of them sank yet again. Water filled Nixie's mouth and nose, choking her. She kicked hard, bringing them to the surface again, where they bobbed up, coughing.

"If you don't be still, we're both going to die!" she shouted into Jed's ear. But he only gripped her tighter, and thrashed more furiously about.

"Stop that this instant!" she shouted, and bit down hard on the only part of him within reach, his ear.

He howled in pain, but she held on. Some instinct must have told him to stop fighting her, rather than risk losing an earlobe. "That's better," she said, her teeth still clamped on his tender earlobe. "Now stop moving and let me get us out of here."

She towed him the few dozen yards to the edge of the pool and shoved him up onto the bank, then pulled herself up to collapse beside him. For a long moment they lay where they fell, gasping and coughing. Finally she turned on her side and looked at him. "Are you all right?"

He nodded as another fit of coughing shook him. She sat and began pounding his back. "What did you think you were doing, jumping in like that, if you couldn't swim?" she asked.

"I . . . I thought you were drowning," he gasped, shoving his wet hair out of his eyes.

"I swim in this pool every day. Why would I suddenly drown in it?" The idea was absurd.

"You might have gotten a cramp. You could have hit your head. How should I know?" He glared at her. "All I know is one minute you were here, the next minute you weren't. I had to do something."

That he would risk his life for her, even foolishly, touched her more than she wanted him to know. She stood so that he couldn't see her face, and held out her hand. "Let's walk back toward your wagon. You'd better get out of those wet clothes before you develop a chill. No telling how much water you breathed in. You could end up with pneumonia."

He ignored her outstretched hand and struggled to his feet on his own. While he gathered up his discarded coat and shoes, she took up the lantern, then led the way back to his wagon.

She didn't ask if he wanted her to stay, merely followed him inside and set the lantern on the table. There was a gas burner in the corner, and she found a tin of matches and lit it. Then she picked up a tea kettle and went out to fill it from the water barrel at the back of the wagon.

"Where's your tea?" she asked when she returned.

"Up there." He pointed to a cabinet over her head and started to open it for her, but she pushed him away.

"Get out of those wet clothes and crawl under the covers at once," she ordered.

He started to protest, but she gave him her sternest look. "Don't you think I've learned a thing or two in all these years of helping my father? You've got to get warm and dry at once or you could end up very ill."

Not waiting for a reply, she turned her back to him and began rummaging in the cabinet for tea and sugar. She pretended not to hear the sounds of Jed removing his clothes, but her ears were attuned to every rustle of fabric, every whisper of a button released from its buttonhole.

She filled a tea ball with leaves and suspended it over a chipped enamel mug she found hanging on a hook over the table. "There's another cup hanging to your left," he said. "And if you look behind the jam on that shelf by the window, there's a bottle of brandy."

She made two cups of tea and added brandy to one. "I think we could both use some of that," he said.

She hesitated, the bottle in her hand. She could count on the fingers of one hand the times in her life she'd been served alcoholic beverages. But she felt the need for something to still the trembling that had suddenly overtaken her. She added a generous splash of brandy to her own cup.

When she turned, she saw Jed propped up in the bed on one side of the wagon, quilts tucked up under his arms. His naked shoulders and arms still had a damp sheen about them. He'd slicked his hair back from his forehead and it curled around his ears. He smiled and took the cup from her hand, then a look of concern crossed his face. "You're shaking. Here, wrap up in this." Before she could speak, he set his tea on a crate that served as a bedside table and plucked a patchwork coverlet from the bed and swept it around her shoulders. "Now sit in that rocker there." He nodded to a chair that faced the bed.

"I really ought to go," she said, as she lowered herself into the chair.

"Drink your tea before *you* catch pneumonia." A hint of a smile tugged at the corners of his mouth.

The hot, sweet brew burned a path to her stomach, radiating through her. She closed her eyes to savor the sensation, and pulled the quilt around her, imagining that some of Jed's own warmth had been transferred through the cover to her. When she opened her eyes, he was watching her.

"I guess I should thank you for saving my life," he said.

She shook her head. "You're the one who jumped in to save *me*." Her heart fluttered at the thought. "I still can't believe you'd do that." The whispered words were barely audible above the low hiss of the lantern.

He lay his head back on the pillow, balancing the cup on his chest, and let out a deep breath. "It's been a long time since I've been that frightened. First for you, and then when that water started closing in over my head."

"Maybe you should take swimming lessons."

He closed his eyes and was quiet for so long she thought he must have fallen asleep. But just when she had decided to get up and tiptoe out of the wagon, he opened his eyes. "I almost drowned once before. When I was seven."

She waited, the tea growing cool in her cup. She wanted to ask what had happened, but didn't dare. The horror of that long-ago event was etched on Jed's face. To pry seemed too intrusive, too personal.

He tried to smile at her, and failed. "My father was trying to teach me to swim."

"I can see why you don't like water." She set her cup aside. "Did you ever try again when you were older?"

He stared down into his cup. "My father wanted me to jump right back in that day. Maybe I should have." He wrapped both hands around the teacup. "I think worse even than the memory of all that water washing over my head was the thought that I might fail again and have to see the look of disappointment on Papa's face."

All his pride and swagger had been washed away, leaving a vulnerability that touched her more than she liked. The story made it all the more amazing that he had jumped in after her.

Was she more to this man than pleasant company with whom to while away the hours? Had there been true feelings behind what she had judged as merely practiced charm?

Only moments ago she had shivered with cold; now the wagon seemed too warm. She felt light-headed from the effects of the brandy, and a whirl of confusing emotions. "I'd better be going." She stood and started to slip the quilt from her shoulders. "If you're not feeling better in the morning, you should have Papa check you over."

"I'm not feeling bad. Just tired." He lay back against the pillows and stared up at the ceiling. "I don't always sleep well. It's lonely here in the evenings, by myself."

She heard the longing in his voice, echoing a kindred emotion in her heart. "I'll stay a little while longer," she said, sitting in the rocker once more.

He looked at her, an intense, questioning gaze. "Will you?"

She swallowed hard, but didn't answer his question. Instead, she looked around the wagon, at the neatly fitted cabinets, the folding table and benches, the bags of herbs suspended from the low ceiling and the calico curtains that, when drawn together, would screen the bed and other furnishings from view, leaving the wagon as she'd seen it that day at the fair, with only a narrow aisle clear to the stage that opened out at the rear. The familiar scent of lamp oil mingled with the more exotic aromas of mint and rosemary and pine. She studied the books fitted neatly into shelves made into the walls. But in her mind's eye she saw only the man in the bed beside her, lamplight polishing his bare skin to bronze, and dancing in his brown eyes.

"It's a different sort of life, isn't it? Traveling, I mean."

"Different. You see a lot of interesting places. Meet a lot of people."

"But you never really have a home." She turned to meet his gaze, to brave the fires that burned in his brown eyes.

"No. Wherever I go, I'm always an outsider, the odd man out."

She nodded. "I've felt like that before."

"Have you?" He raised up on one elbow and leaned toward her. "But this is your home. You belong here."

She shook her head. "There's a difference between belonging some*where* and belonging to some*one*." *Someone who will stay with me forever,* she silently added.

"Yes, there is, isn't there?" His voice was soft, wondering. When she raised her eyes to meet his again, she saw that he understood what she was saying, even what she was feeling.

She leaned toward him, the quilt slipping from her shoulders as she grasped his hand. Even as she realized what she was doing, she wondered that she would risk this much. It was like taking the first step into deep water, and hoping, if you sank over your head, you could find your way to the surface again.

At the touch of Nixie's hand, Jed sat upright in bed. Her fingers were cool against his fevered skin. They trembled as they brushed his palm.

He closed his eyes as their lips met and breathed in deeply the mingled perfumes of lemon and wet serge and the mineral tang of the springs, like a man filling his lungs before a dive beneath the waves.

Her lips were tender and pliant, responding to every pressure or nuance of his caress. She opened her mouth beneath his and her tongue darted out and brushed across his teeth, inviting him to follow along in a teasing exchange of sensation.

Letting the bedcovers fall to his waist, he reached out and gathered her close, until she was half-sitting in his lap, her arms wrapped around his neck. As his mouth continued to savor the sweet-tart taste of her, his hand shaped itself to the firm curve of her thigh. He followed the line of her leg to one slim calf, naked, her skin like warm satin beneath his calloused fingers.

As he plunged his tongue deeper within her mouth, he felt the vibration of her soundless moans against his lips. Her enthusiasm made his own need more urgent. She rolled toward him and he felt the hard tips of her breasts through the still-damp fabric of her swimming costume.

With effort, he struggled to raise his head, to find the

breath to speak. Nixie stared at him with passion-fogged eyes. "This is what you want?" he asked.

"Yes." The word was a sigh. She closed her eyes and leaned toward him once more.

And this is what I want, he thought as he lowered his lips to hers once more. For better or worse, he'd make his claim to Nixie's body and to her life. He'd tie himself to her, like a man building a house around a tree with deep roots, and hope she had the strength to hold him fast.

He groped at the buttons of her swimming costume, desperate to feel her naked beside him. Brushing his hand away, she deftly unfastened the garment, then pushed it down to her ankles and kicked it to the floor. Then she unwound the braid from the top of her head. She started to leave it trailing down her back, but he reached out and slipped the ribbon from the end, and began to separate the strands, until her hair hung in a golden curtain around her shoulders.

Shoving the quilts aside, he gathered her to him. She curved her body around his, her softness surrounding his hardness, sending tremors of pleasure through him.

Separating from her as little as possible, he lowered his head to her breasts, laving each tip in turn with his tongue. She tossed her head back, arching her torso against his almost painfully. He listened eagerly for her passionate cries, music that would fuel his own growing need. But though her body responded ardently to his every move, she remained mute. He paused in his attentions to reassure her. "You don't have to worry anyone will hear you," he said.

A look of confusion passed through her eyes.

"I want to hear if I please you," he said.

She smiled. "You're doing fine." Her voice was soft and husky, driving him to new heights of distraction. When he was sure he would go mad if he waited one moment longer, he rolled over until Nixie was on her back, and kissed her lips. "Are you ready for me?" he whispered, watching her face, lips full and moist from his kisses, eyes heavy-lidded with passion.

"Yes." She reached for him, trying to pull him near. "Oh, yes."

His hand shook when he touched her. He wanted this to be good for her. He didn't want her first memory of sex to be some brute who'd used her only for his own pleasure. So he paused to breathe deeply, until he felt he'd regained more control, then he took his hand and gently parted her legs.

Oh, she was ready, slick and throbbing with need. He cupped his hand over her womanhood and she shoved against him, hard. He parted the golden curls with one finger and began to stroke her, gently at first, then harder as she moved against him in a frenzy of need. She threw her head back and bared her teeth. He thought any moment she would scream out her ecstacy, but it was the sudden tensing of her body and the tremor beneath his hand that told him she had climaxed, and not her voice.

He moved over her while she still lay trembling and gasping for breath. God, she was beautiful, skin rosy in the lamplight, hair a shimmering curtain against the pillow. He stroked the creamy mounds of her breasts with his hands, and began to ease into her, waiting for resistance, praying he wouldn't hurt her too much before he found his own release.

She opened her eyes and smiled up at him, then welcomed him inside her without hesitation. She gripped his back as he began to move inside her, and began to rock with a rhythm that matched his own.

He was lost to sensation, the sweet, exquisite pleasure of two bodies moving as one, man and woman made for each other. He couldn't have said where Nixie left off and he began, as if they had melded together in an act as old as time.

But release when it came was as new as if he'd never loved before. It left him shuddering and gasping for breath, lying in her arms and repeating her name over and over.

She stroked his hair and his back, holding him against her breasts in an embrace he never wanted to leave.

After a while he realized he must be crushing her. He

rolled over onto his side and gathered her to him. "Nixie, Nixie," he murmured, burying his face in the silken fall of her hair. "I love you."

She began to shake, and he wondered at the strength of her passion. Then he realized she was sobbing, as her tears began to dampen his chest.

"Nixie, what is it?" He lifted her head. "Did I hurt you? I tried to be gentle, but—"

"You didn't hurt me." She bit her lip and wiped her eyes with the back of her hand. "You couldn't hurt me."

"What is it then?" He raised up on one elbow.

"Didn't you know?"

He shook his head, confused. "No. Tell me, please."

"I'm not a virgin!" She shoved her hair out of her eyes and stared at him, her expression bleak.

He blinked, the words not registering at first. "I don't understand," he said after a moment.

"I'm not a virgin," she said again. She turned away and began to weep.

The sound of her crying tore at him. "It's all right," he said, drawing her close once more. "Shhhh. It's all right." He kissed the top of her head and stroked her back, a knot of pain growing in his stomach. Had he made the right decision, committing himself to this woman?

Her sobs grew more anguished, rocking him with their strength. "Nixie, who hurt you so?" he whispered after a while.

She sniffed and rested her forehead against his shoulder. "I was nineteen," she gasped, choking back tears.

He continued to stroke her hair, waiting, not wanting to know, but unable to tell her to stop.

"My best friend, Lena Mae Marx, had just gotten married and moved away. All my friends were married. Some had babies already. My aunt Hilda was living with us then, Papa's oldest sister. She was sixty-two and had never been married. I was so afraid I'd end up like her."

She turned so that she was looking away from him, her cheek soft against his shoulder. "He was a drummer, come to town to sell shoes," she continued. "He was handsome, charming. I was flattered when he paid attention to me instead of some of the younger girls. I thought he was . . . maybe my last chance.

"So I let him take me out in his buggy. Alone."

"And he took advantage of you?" Jed's voice sounded odd to his ears, thin, strained.

She nodded against him. "But afterward, he said we'd be married, as soon as he'd saved enough money. The next day he left town."

"And you never saw him again." Jed held her tight against him, murderous rage rising in his throat. "Why, I—"

"No. I did see him again." She raised her head to look at him. "He came back the next month. I know I shouldn't have gone out in the buggy with him again . . ." She ducked her head. "But . . . I liked it."

He put his hand to her feverish cheek. "Nixie, you don't have to be ashamed of that."

She pushed his hand away, fresh tears welling in her eyes. "But I was so stupid to believe him! He said he hadn't saved enough money yet, but that he'd have enough soon."

She sighed. "The next month, I refused to go out with him. I said I was tired of waiting, that we had to marry." She swallowed hard. "He laughed at me."

"Oh, Nixie, no."

"He said I was a stupid child. He said he never intended to settle down. He didn't have any use for a wife to tie him down. He accused me of awful things—said he knew there were other men, that he wasn't my only lover. But it wasn't true!"

She covered her face with her hands, and he thought she would dissolve into tears once more. But she took a deep breath and began speaking again. "A few weeks later, another drummer came by. He said he'd heard I was 'real friendly,' and that I'd 'show him a good time.' "

She uncovered her face and gave him an accusing look. "You heard the stories, didn't you?"

He shook his head. "I swear I didn't. And even if I had, I wouldn't have believed it of you." He could scarcely believe what she was telling him now. He reached for her again, but she pulled away, turning from him and picking up the swimming costume from the floor.

"Nixie, listen to me," he said, sitting up on the side of the bed. "I'm not like those other men. I'm not looking for someone to 'show me a good time.' "

She stepped into the swimming costume and began to button it up the front, ignoring his words.

"Nixie, I love you."

She whirled to face him, cheeks flushed, eyes flashing. "That's what he said, too." She tucked her hair behind her ears and turned away again. "I have to go before my family gets home and I'm not there."

He tried to get out of bed and follow her, but the quilts were a tangle around his feet, and by the time he'd extricated himself, she was gone, the door closing softly behind her.

"I love you," he repeated. But she hadn't understood the meaning in the words the first time he'd said them, anymore than she could hear them now.

Chapter Thirteen

Nixie patted a powder puff under her eyes and frowned at her face in the mirror. The talc did little to hide the dark half-moons showing through her pale skin. She'd cried most of the night before finally falling asleep, only to awaken more exhausted than ever.

"Nanny goat, nanny goat. Hello!" William chirped from his cage, rattling the door with his beak. "Hello!"

She went to the cage and stuck her little finger through the bars to stroke the bird's soft stomach. But even her pet's antics couldn't cheer her this morning.

She didn't feel like eating. But she couldn't stay in her room avoiding Jed Hawkins the rest of the summer. Better to face him now. She knew what he must think of her, after the way she'd behaved last night. Not only had she accepted his invitation into his bed, but once there she'd acted with all the wild abandon of the worst sort of woman. Hadn't the shoe salesman told her as much? Only a woman of loose morals would thrash about and cry out so, he'd said.

She covered her face with her hands, as if to bury the shameful memories. Even Jed had seen her true nature, encouraging her to voice her pleasure with him, like the showgirls and adventuresses he must be used to. She'd tried so hard to remain passive and demure, as a lady ought, but something within her wouldn't let her play that role.

She took a deep, shuddering breath. No sense dwelling on her sins. What was done, was done. Now she'd have to do her best to set things right with Jed before he got any ideas about continuing what they'd started last night. What had happened between them was regrettable. It was a mistake. It was . . .

It was wonderful. Beautiful. Magnificent. With a sigh, she sank onto the stool in front of her dressing table. Her mind told her what had happened between her and Jed last night was wrong. But in her heart she knew the memory of their loving was something she'd treasure in the lonely years to come. In Jed's arms she'd felt cherished, special . . . loved.

No! She pressed the heel of her hand to her forehead as if to ward off the thought. Of course Jed Hawkins didn't love her. He was a man accustomed to telling people what they wanted to hear, whether it was the news that his tonic would cure what ailed them, or the revelation that ghosts could be made to appear in the Dengler parlor. A man like that couldn't be taken at his word.

Could he?

"What does it matter anyway?" she said aloud, startling William, who fluffed his feathers and cocked his head to gaze at her with one dark eye.

"Even if he does love me, it doesn't matter." She stood and faced her image in the mirror. Some folks might call her pretty, but certainly not pretty enough to lure a man like Jed away from the romance of the road. He was used to the applause of a crowd, and the excitement of different places and different adventures. Life in a sleepy town like Welcome Springs, with a very ordinary woman like Nixie, would pale in a few weeks, or months, or years. And then he'd leave her.

She clenched her fists and straightened her spine, replacing her sad mope with a look of determination. She wouldn't let that happen. Jed couldn't very well leave what he didn't have, and he wouldn't have her.

Reluctantly, she left her room. The sooner she was done with this morning, the better.

"Nixie! Oh, Nixie!" Dory Evans hailed her from the landing and ran up to meet her, taking the steps two at a time. "I'm so glad you're up." She arrived at Nixie's side pink-cheeked and smiling.

"Good morning, Dory," Nixie said, unable to muster a smile for her friend.

But Dory did not seem to notice. She leaned closer to Nixie and spoke in a whisper. "They didn't get in the way."

Nixie blinked. "I'm sorry. What did you say?"

Dory grinned. "My teeth. They didn't get in the way." She giggled. "When Theo kissed me."

Nixie thought of the kiss she and Jed had shared on the darkened path, and where it had eventually led them. Had Dory felt such trembling passion when Theo embraced her? Nixie wanted to warn her friend not to open herself up to such heartache. But the advice would be useless, just as it would have been useless for anyone to have cautioned Nixie. How could anyone know the danger until they reached a point where there was no turning back?

"I'm happy for you," she said instead, patting Dory's arm as they started down the stairs. "He's a very nice man."

The dining room was full by the time the two women took their places. Nixie let out a sigh when she saw that Jed had not yet arrived. Perhaps he sought to spare her feelings by sleeping in this morning.

Or maybe he was suffering ill effects from his near-drowning in the pool. The thought sent a rush of panic through her. After breakfast, she should go and check on him. He might be lying alone in his wagon, delirious with fever, naked . . .

No, she quickly amended. She'd send Pete to see if Jed was well.

"And how are you this morning, Mrs. Merchant?" Dr. Dengler took his place at the head of the table and beamed at the woman to his left. "If I'm not mistaken, I believe you danced every dance last night."

To Nixie's astonishment, Dinah Merchant actually smiled. "I believe you might be right, Dr. Dengler," she said. She looked around the table. Overnight, she had been transformed. Her cheeks glowed pink, and she'd abandoned her mourning garb for a dress of striped lavender, which Nixie was sure belonged to Dory. She'd even loosened the knot of her hair, and combed a few curls around her face. "I'll have to say dancing is certainly beneficial to one's health," she said. "I feel wonderful this morning."

"I wonder where Mr. Hawkins is?" Nadine Dengler sat and nodded at the vacant chair across from Nixie. "Won't he be joining us for breakfast?"

"I haven't seen him since he left the dance early last night," Pete said. "Maybe he's tired and sleeping in."

"We'd better start without him, then." Mrs. Dengler bowed her head, the signal for her husband to say grace.

Nixie was spooning shirred eggs onto her plate when the door to the dining room flew open, rattling the crystals of the chandelier over the table with the breeze it stirred.

She dropped the spoon, and felt the breath leave her as she stared at the man in the doorway. Jed Hawkins stood illuminated by a beam of sunlight, his white suit gleaming, light playing off the gold streaks in his hair. His arms were full of flowers, scarlet and orange zinnias and golden poppies and pink dahlias against a fan of dark green ferns.

"Good morning," he said, bowing before them. "I apologize for my tardiness, but it took me a while to persuade Mrs. Frisco to sell these out of her yard." He approached the table and presented a small bouquet to Mrs. Dengler.

"Why thank you," she said, smiling and burying her nose in the posy.

"And these are for you." He held the rest of the flowers out to Nixie, who stared at them, dumbfounded, struggling to breathe. What did he think he was doing?

Smile never wavering, he laid the flowers alongside her plate, then came to stand behind her chair. She felt his hand come to rest on her shoulder, heavy and warm. She swallowed hard at the slight pressure of his fingers as he squeezed her tense muscles, but found herself leaning back in her chair, toward him. She no longer held her breath, but waited to see what the next act would be in this show Jed Hawkins seemed intent on performing for them.

"Dr. Dengler, I wonder if I might have a word with you?" he asked, his voice carrying across the room the way it had projected over the crowd at the fair.

Her father looked surprised. "Now?" He laid aside his fork. "Here?"

"I don't mind if the others hear," Jed said. "After all, we're all friends."

Dr. Dengler cleared his throat. "All right, then. What do you have to say?"

Nixie felt his hand tighten on her shoulder. "Dr. Dengler, Mrs. Dengler, I'd like your permission to court your daughter."

Every head in the room turned toward them. Nixie felt the color drain from her face and opened her mouth to speak, but no words came out.

Nadine Dengler let out a cry of delight and brought both hands to her chest, still clutching her napkin.

A broad grin spread across Ham Dengler's face. "I did not realize young people still observed these old courtesies. But since you asked, why by all means you may court our Nixie."

"What a romantic gesture." Nadine leaned forward and patted her daughter's hand. "Don't you think it's romantic, Nixie?"

Nixie cleared her throat. "Isn't anyone—" she began, then tried again, louder this time. "Isn't anyone going to ask me what *I* think?"

Dr. Dengler chuckled, then an awkward silence settled over the room. Jed took Nixie's hand and pulled her from the chair. "If you'll excuse us," he called over his shoulder as he led her toward the door. "I'll have a word with Nixie *alone*."

He didn't release her until the parlor door was securely closed behind them. She fled to the other side of the room, anxious to put as much distance between herself and this man as she could. "What do you think you're doing?" she asked. "Trying to embarrass me like that in front of my family and friends? How can I possibly refuse you now without looking like a fool?"

"Don't refuse." He leaned against the door, arms across his chest. "Say yes."

The casual pose emphasized his powerful shoulders and forearms, and his long, strong legs. The image flashed through her mind of his body, naked and hovering over her in his bed last night. She looked away. "You don't have to do this," she said. "It's not as if you ruined me."

"We all make mistakes, Nixie. There's nothing that says you have to spend the rest of your life paying for yours."

"My mistake was thinking that for even one night I could forget the past and live in the moment."

"I'm willing to forget the past—mine and yours. Let's start over, Nixie. Don't you think we could be friends?"

She shut her eyes, as if she might have more power to resist what she could not see. "You don't have to court me for us to be friends."

"Why wouldn't I want to court a woman who's gentle, kind, intelligent..." With each word he moved closer to her. When she opened her eyes, he was standing in front of her, barely a hand's breadth between them. "I'm thirty-one years old. Don't you think it's time I found a wife and started a family of my own?"

She opened her eyes and met his yearning gaze. Yearning for her? She closed her eyes again as she felt his arms slip around her. "No." The word was a futile protest.

"You might have my baby started in you already," he said, his breath moist against her ear. "Hawkins men are known for their potency."

Her stomach flip-flopped at the thought that she might already be pregnant.

"Maybe I should discuss this with your father some more," Jed said. He started for the door. "If I can't persuade you, maybe he can."

"No, wait!"

He turned toward her once more. "We'd be good together, Nixie. I'm not such a bad man, you'll see."

She looked at Jed—really looked at him, trying to see past his handsome face into his mind and soul. Was he a bad man or a good one? He was a show-off, able to work a crowd, whether it was a bunch of Saturday fair-goers or the group in her own dining room. On the good side, she had to admit he was kind, thoughtful even. And he was handsome, she couldn't forget that. She swallowed hard. "All right. If you're so dead set on courting me, go right ahead. But don't think anything will come of it. I know we'd never work out together, even if you can't see it."

He smiled and pulled her close, head bent as if to kiss her. She gasped. The memory of last night still burned on her skin, leaving her too vulnerable. One caress might melt away her carefully marshalled resistance.

A knock on the door stayed the threat to her defenses. "Nixie? Mr. Hawkins?" Nadine Dengler spoke through the closed door. "Won't you join us now? Breakfast is getting cold."

"We'll be right there, Mother." Without a backward glance, Nixie started toward the door. But she felt Jed's gaze burning into her all the way to the table. Settling into her chair once more, she ignored the amused looks of the others in the room and pushed the ruined breakfast around on her plate. If only she could find a way to cool her passion for Jed as thoroughly.

Caesar picked his way carefully through the blackberry patch, searching for the plumpest fruit. Who needed paradise when one had sunshine and fresh air and the company of two lovely young women to share the day with? He glanced ahead to where Nixie and her friend Dory gathered berries, long gloves and canvas aprons protecting them from the brambles. Too bad his comely companions couldn't acknowledge his presence.

All the better for his purposes, he supposed. Since Jed was being so thoroughly disagreeable about Caesar's generous offer of help, Caesar had decided to see what he could do to foster things on Nixie's end.

He slipped up behind the two women now and deposited a handful of fat berries in Nixie's pail. My, but she was a pretty one. Definitely more pleasant company than his grumpy son.

"I scarcely recognized Dinah at the breakfast table this morning," Nixie said, adding her own handful of fruit to her pail. "What in the world came over her?"

"I guess she realized the fun she'd been missing out on all this time." Dory's laugh sounded strained. "This has certainly been a summer full of odd happenings."

Nixie glanced at her friend. "What do you mean? What else odd has happened?"

Dory shrugged. "I'm sure it's nothing. Just something strange that happened after I came in from the dance last night."

Nixie straightened and brushed a thorn from her apron. "What happened?"

Another nervous laugh. "Oh, it's silly really, but ... Well, do you know if your house might be, well, haunted?"

Haunted. Caesar came close to laughing out loud himself at that one. Grinning, he moved nearer.

"Haunted?" Nixie sounded alarmed. She put a hand on her friend's arm. "Oh, Dory, if you're still worried about the séance, don't be. I told you Jed—"

"No, no, this doesn't have anything to do with the séance. I don't think."

Caesar frowned. He still couldn't believe Jed had told Nixie that he was responsible for Caesar's "manifestation" at the séance. The boy was trying to take all the fun away from his old man. Caesar could have told him Nixie would take it wrong. That was the trouble with associating with proper young ladies with high ideals. They didn't have nearly well-enough developed senses of humor.

He followed Nixie and Dory into the shade of a tall hackberry. Dory continued her story. "Last night, I'd just gotten in from the dance, and I was getting ready for bed. Not that I thought I'd get any sleep, mind you." She flashed a smile. "I was still positively giddy with happiness over the evening I'd spent with Theo. But I went ahead and washed my face and changed into my nightclothes anyway. Dinah was already in bed, snoring as usual." She covered her mouth with her hand, a guilty blush coloring her cheeks. "Oh, don't tell her I said that. She positively refuses to believe she snores, but she does. Quite loudly."

She had that right, Caesar thought. Her sister sounded like a boar hog rooting for supper!

"You're stalling," Nixie said. "Tell me what happened to upset you."

Dory plucked at her apron with one hand. "Well, I sat down at the dressing table and began to brush out my hair. I looked up in the mirror and—Oh Nixie, it sounds impossible to believe!"

"Tell me, Dory."

Dory took a deep breath, like a swimmer readying herself to plunge into icy water. "I swear I saw a man looking over my shoulder in the mirror!"

Nixie gasped. "A man?"

Dory nodded. "It startled me so badly I cried out. Dinah woke up and grumbled at me to keep quiet. I sat there for a long time, then I decided I must have been wrong, so I went to brush my hair again, and I couldn't find my brush. I looked everywhere for it, and finally had to borrow Dinah's."

"It was dark. Maybe you just didn't see it."

"That's what I thought, but then this morning, I opened the wardrobe and there was my brush—in my shoe!"

Caesar clutched his stomach, struggling to hold in his laughter. He hadn't had this much fun since he and Fats Fleshman had replaced a carnival ticket taker's hair dye with a bottle of Gentian violet. The awful woman had had to wear a wig for the next six months.

"Maybe it fell down in there," Nixie said doubtfully.

"No." Dory shook her head. "I'm positive I had it in my hand when I saw the man watching me in the mirror." She leaned toward her friend. "That wasn't the only thing odd, though."

"Tell me what else."

"When the man was watching me in the mirror, well . . ." She lowered her voice to a whisper. "I swear he winked at me!"

Nothing wrong with giving a girl a thrill, was there? Caesar grinned. This one might be homely, but he admired her spirit. There was a lot to be said for a woman with spunk. After all, looks faded, but personality didn't.

Nixie put her arm around Dory's shoulders and hugged her close. Caesar added a few more berries to Nixie's bucket, then drifted away. She had a good heart, Nixie did. Perhaps a little on the timid side, but that could be overcome with encouragement from his boy. All the more reason for Jed to pay attention to his old man. He sighed. *Young people today. You couldn't teach them anything.*

Jed didn't like having to resort to manipulation in order to win Nixie's love, but he wasn't above a few tricks if that's what it took to get her attention. So he waited until he spotted her on her front porch with her mother and father the next Sunday afternoon before he approached her with an invitation to accompany him to the ice cream parlor.

"No thank you," she said, refusing to meet his gaze.

"Oh, go with him, dear." Nadine Dengler gave her daughter a nudge in Jed's direction. "It's a lovely day for an outing."

Eyes still focused on the toes of her boots, she smoothed her skirt. "I . . . I'm not dressed for an outing."

"Nonsense. You look beautiful as always." Dr. Dengler grinned at Jed. "Doesn't she, Mr. Hawkins?"

His heart hurt for Nixie, for the way her parents tried to

push her on him, like a spavined horse to be sold at a bargain price. Any man who couldn't recognize that Nixie was beautiful without prompting didn't deserve her company. This afternoon she wore the lavender-striped gown she'd put on the day Pete broke his arm—the day Jed first realized he might be falling in love with her. "Nixie will always be beautiful to me," he said softly.

He didn't know if his words or his tone surprised her, but she jerked her head up. For a brief moment, a softness stole into her gaze, quickly replaced by a shuttered look, like a protective veil drawn around her feelings. "It's only ice cream," he continued in the same soft, coaxing tone. "What harm could there be in that?"

Without another word, she led the way off the porch. He fell into step beside her, matching his stride to hers, resisting the urge to take her hand. They walked past the Willkommen Inn and out to the road, then toward the pavilion. In spite of the summer heat, the town was alive with activity. Couples strolled along in front of the shops, the women shading themselves with brightly colored parasols. Boys in knickers and girls in skirts and bloomers played tag in a vacant lot beside the livery stable, while a group of older men engaged in a game of dominoes beneath a gnarled live oak next to the post office. A trio of matrons sat on a bench in the pavilion, drinking water dispensed from a free fountain, and talking among themselves.

Welcome Springs couldn't rightly be called a "one horse town" much longer. Once Dr. Dengler's boardinghouse opened, and publicity started spreading around the country, more and more people were bound to visit and even settle in the pretty little town. It had everything people were looking for: a healthy climate, churches and schools, pleasant scenery, adjacent farmland, good roads, and friendly people.

Jed glanced at the woman walking beside and a little ahead of him. Right now, Welcome Springs had the one thing he wanted: Nixie. "If you keep speeding up, people are going to think I'm chasing you," he said.

She stopped, so suddenly he almost collided with her.

"Are you that ashamed to be seen with me?" he asked, scarcely able to hide his bitterness.

She shook her head. "I don't want people to talk."

He looked around them. Everywhere he saw other couples, many younger than he and Nixie. A stranger might have thought the spring waters contained a secret love potion. "Why should they talk? Isn't it normal for young people to walk out together?"

"Things are different for me." Two bright spots of color blossomed on her pale cheeks.

He did take her hand, then, and patted it awkwardly. "Do you really think anybody remembers that drummer? After all, it happened a long time ago."

"You'll make them remember." She jerked her hand away. "You're so much like him."

That accusation hurt. "Am I?" he demanded, capturing her hand again.

"You're good looking like him. And you make your living on the road."

"But I would never treat you that way." He tucked her hand in the crook of his arm and led the way toward the ice cream parlor, deliberately changing the subject. "I caught Mrs. Frisco out by her fence this morning. She was pretending to prune her roses, but I noticed she was trying to hear what your father was saying to the woman in his consultation room."

"She's done that for years. Sometimes half the town will know when a woman is expecting before the mother-to-be makes it home to tell her husband."

"I crept up behind her and asked if she wanted me to go inside and ask Dr. Dengler to open the window a little wider so she could hear better."

"You didn't!" Nixie rewarded him with a smile.

"I did." He grinned and held open the door to the ice cream shop. "She called me a scoundrel and threatened to cut off my coattails with her pruning shears. To tell you the truth, I think she liked the attention."

"From you, she would!" Nixie swept past him into the shop. She glanced over her shoulder as he followed her into the cool, vanilla-scented cafe. "No wonder you sold so much tonic. You could convince a Navaho he needed snowshoes."

"Aha! Then you admit I'm good at what I do."

"I never said you weren't good at it."

"What is it then?" He followed her to the front counter.

"Do you have strawberry today, Myrtle?" Nixie asked the woman behind the counter.

"No strawberry. Got peach."

"I'll take peach, then."

"Peach for me also," Jed said. He waited until the woman brought out two dishes of gold-flecked ice cream before following Nixie to a table and pursuing the conversation. "Answer me, Nixie. Why that tone of disdain in your voice whenever you talk about what I do for a living?"

She shook her head and savored a bite of ice cream. "People like you don't have any idea what it's like to live an ordinary life, in the same place day after day, year after year, surrounded by the same people. What you see as 'entertainment' or 'telling people what they want to hear' we'd see as outright lies."

He bristled. "Are you saying I'm dishonest?"

"I'm saying knowing you'll have to stick around to suffer the consequences of your actions makes a person think twice about what they say and do."

She ate another bite of ice cream, her lips closing around the spoon as it exited her mouth. The tip of her tongue darted out to capture a wayward drop of cream and Jed's own mouth went dry.

She plunged the spoon into her dish once more and left it there. "What are you staring at?"

He shifted in his seat, trying to get comfortable. He didn't dare confess the real nature of his thoughts, at least, not here in public. Instead, he focused on ice cream. "You surprise me. Looking at you, anyone would think you were a plain-vanilla kind of girl."

The shuttered look returned, as effective as any mask. "There's lots you don't know about me."

"But so much I want to know."

He might have thought she didn't hear the words, if not for the white-knuckled way she clutched her spoon, and the fierce concentration she suddenly put into eating. "What will you do when your ingredients come in?" she asked.

Did the answer matter to her? "I'll mix up another batch of Curative."

She traced her spoon around the rim of the bowl. "Then what?"

He gave her a thoughtful look. "That depends."

She gazed up at him through the screen of her lashes, a look that might have been coquettish on someone less serious. "Depends on what?"

He bit back a smile of triumph. "On . . . a number of things."

She didn't speak again until they got ready to leave the ice cream parlor. He was content to sit in silence and watch her eat, his mind inventing half a dozen fantasies involving her luscious lips and a bowl of peach ice cream.

At last she pushed her empty dish aside. "We'd better get back," she said.

"If nothing else, I've proved you can survive an afternoon in my company with your reputation intact," he said as they stepped out into the street once more.

She crossed her arms underneath her breasts. "That doesn't mean we have any reason to spend more time together."

He moved closer, brushing against her side. "Now who's lying? Or did the other night mean nothing to you?"

"We were both upset . . . caught up in the moment . . . acting rashly."

She tried to walk away, but he caught her arm and pulled her near. "No more running, Nixie. You feel *something* for me or you never would have stayed in my wagon the other night. And I sure as hell feel something for you."

"Let me go." She struggled in his grasp.

"Not until you answer me. With the truth this time."

She grew still, and raised her eyes to meet his. "All right. Maybe I do feel a *physical* attraction for you. But I have sense enough to know two people need more than passion to keep them together."

"What makes you so sure we don't have more?"

"If you had any *idea* what's important to me, you wouldn't keep playing your sideshow tricks on my friends."

Her scorn stung him. "What are you talking about?"

"I don't know how you've done it, but you've managed to convince Dory our house is haunted."

That again! He released her and stepped back. "I already apologized for the séance. If you want, I'll tell Dory myself."

"I'm not talking about the séance. I'm talking about the other tricks you've been playing on her—hiding her things and sneaking into her bedroom. Did you think she wouldn't tell me?"

"She told you I was in her bedroom?"

"She didn't recognize you, of course, but *I* knew." She shook her head. "Tell me however much you want that it was meant in fun, but life is not all fun and games. Not to me. And because you'll never understand that, we might as well stop this . . . this whatever you want to call it between us . . . before it goes any further."

He scarcely heard her words for the anger clouding his senses. Nixie had admitted she had feelings for him, and now *this!*

"I'm sorry if I've upset you, but I felt it was best to speak the truth," she said. "Say what you will, but you can't change my mind."

He glanced at her. "I'm sorry, Nixie, perhaps we can talk more later. Right now, I need to get back to camp."

He took her arm and hurried her along the road. "Wh-what's your hurry?" she stammered.

He curled his fingers into a fist, and quickened his pace. "I have to find someone . . . and *discuss* a few things with him."

Chapter Fourteen

"Papa!" The door bounced back against the side of the wagon as Jed jerked it open and charged through. "Papa, you'd better answer me now." He knew Caesar was in the wagon. He could sense it in the unnatural silence and stillness in the air.

"I don't know that I should answer someone who doesn't even have the manners to say please." Caesar's voice floated down from the rafters.

Jed glared at the wagon's ceiling. "What kind of manners do you have, spying on Miss Evans and her sister?"

"Oh. Is that what this is about?"

Were his ears playing tricks, or did Caesar yawn? "Then you admit it! You were actually sneaking around women's bedrooms."

"I didn't realize it was their room until the younger one, Dory, spotted me."

Jed frowned. "Whose room did you think it was?"

Caesar moved closer. *"Why, Nixie's of course. I learned later that hers is down the hall."*

The blood pounded at Jed's temples. He'd always known his father considered himself the Casanova of the carnival circuit, but to think he would stoop so low as to spy on a decent young woman like Nixie . . . "What were you doing looking for Nixie's bedroom?"

"Sit down, Son, and take a few deep breaths. You look ready to pop a vessel any minute now." A bottle of Great Caesar's Celebrated Curative slid across the table. *"You'd better have a slug of this."*

Jed snatched up the bottle. "Answer me. What were you doing in any woman's bedroom?"

"Not what I'd like. Let me tell you, the accident has seriously hampered my style."

"Father!"

"I wanted to make sure she was all right. I saw her running from this wagon—running, mind you—and I could have sworn I heard her crying. Since you weren't seeing to her welfare, I thought it was the least I could do."

Guilt rushed in to crowd Jed's anger. He'd known Nixie was upset, yet he hadn't gone to comfort her. Had that been a mistake? He pulled the stopper from the bottle. "And you ended up in Dory's room instead?"

"Yes. She saw me in the mirror and—"

Jed froze, bottle halfway to his lips. "Wait a minute. I can't even see you. How could she?"

"You don't need to see me. You already know what I look like. But I thought I'd give her a little glimpse, just in the mirror."

"Did you want to frighten the poor girl out of her wits?" Jed took a long slug of Curative. It tasted good going down.

"She didn't strike me as the panicky type. Much too sensible a girl for that. She was startled, but to show there were no hard feelings, I winked at her."

Jed choked, coughing up a mouthful of tonic. "You *winked* at her?"

Caesar pounded Jed's back. *"Women always loved my wink."*

The old man was incorrigible! "Why did you hide her things?"

"Oh that. A little harmless mischief. I have to take my entertainment where I can find it, you know."

Jed sank into a chair. "Stay out of the Denglers' house. All you'll do is cause trouble." The less said on that subject, the better. He stared at the bottle in his hand. "Those ingredients should be here by now. I'd better telegram the supply company."

Caesar coughed. *"That won't be necessary."*

Jed took another swig of Curative. He felt a headache coming on. "What is going on, Papa? You *did* send in the order, didn't you?"

"It may have . . . slipped my mind. In all the excitement of being here. And my memory . . . Well, you know it's not what it once was."

Neither was anything else. Except his damned obstinant nature. Jed straightened and set the bottle aside. "I'm going to say this once, but I want you to know I mean it. Either give me the recipe for the Curative or there won't be any more Great Caesar's Medicine Show."

Caesar fell silent. Jed could hardly believe the words had come out of his mouth. He certainly hadn't planned to say them, but maybe it was for the best. He waited, every muscle tense, stomach in a knot. The sound of the Denglers' back door slamming drifted to him. He wondered if he'd just slammed a door in his own life.

Then a pen hovered from the inkwell at the desk in the corner. A piece of paper slid from a stack of old receipts, and the pen began to move. Jed watched, fascinated, as words filled up the page. He couldn't read them from here, but he recognized Caesar's flamboyant script.

The pen plunked back into the inkwell. A rush of wind across the paper, like someone blowing on it. Then it sailed across the room and into the table in front of Jed. *"There's your recipe. I hope you're happy now."*

Jed scanned the lines of script. *Five gallons fresh water. One gallon honey (clover is best). One tablespoon cinnamon oil. Three inches ginger root, pounded to release essence. Oil of cloves. Blackberry leaves.* He looked up. "These are all items I could buy at any grocer."

"All except my secret ingredient."

Jed scanned the list again, all the way to the bottom. The final words fairly leapt from the page to taunt him. *Great Caesar's secret ingredient*. He grabbed up the paper and shook it. "This doesn't mean anything without the secret."

"Which is exactly what your threats mean to me." His voice sounded smug. *"I gave you what you asked for, and all that you deserve."*

Jed sat back. He couldn't believe they were having this conversation. He and his father sounded like two ten-year olds trading taunts. Time for an adult to step in and separate them. "Fine. I can't waste any more time on this. I've got work to do." He pushed back his chair and stood.

"Then you admit I'm right." Caesar followed him to the door.

"I'll admit that you think you are. You always do." He left the wagon, shutting the door firmly behind him. Let the old man think about that for a while. For once, Jed wasn't giving him the last word.

Nixie squinted at the note in her father's cramped script. Did it say "Red Spicer—bullet in arm" or "Received—pullet on farm"?

Giving up, she laid the note aside to ask her father about later and picked up the next scrap of paper she'd gleaned from her father's bag. William trotted across the desk and tried to tug the note from her hand. "Don't eat it before I've had a chance to read it," she scolded. She coaxed the bird onto her finger and lifted him to her shoulder, out of the way.

The door to the parlor *cum* office opened, startling William. "Nanny goat! Nanny goat!" he squawked, hurtling toward the intruder.

"Be careful! Don't let him out!" she called, jumping to her feet.

Dr. Dengler slipped inside the room and rolled his eyes upward at the bird who now sat atop his hat like a fancy ornament. "You think to get past me, do you, you little fugitive?" He shooed the bird away. "And do not leave any calling cards up there, either." He smiled at Nixie. "What are you doing inside on such a lovely afternoon, young lady?"

"Trying to make sense of this paperwork." She held up the "Red Spicer" note. "About this, Papa—"

"Later, Nixie, dear." He waved the note away and hurried across the room to her. "Wait until I show you what came for us in the post today." He reached into his coat and pulled out a sheaf of letters.

Nixie fought a sinking feeling. But then, her father wouldn't be so elated over a bunch of bills, would he? "What is it?" she asked as he deposited the letters in a heap in front of her.

"They are from people wanting to reserve rooms at the Willkommen Inn."

She stared at the mail. There had to be at least a dozen letters here, postmarked from all over. Her legs wouldn't hold her up anymore. She sank into the chair. "How would all these people know about the inn?"

"I have taken advertisements in large newspapers across the state." He selected a letter from the pile and unfolded it. "See. This woman from Dallas would like to come as soon as possible."

"But . . . the inn isn't ready—"

"It will be soon. Very soon. Jed has the downstairs almost completed, and the rest will follow. I am planning a grand opening celebration in only one month."

"So soon?" The words came out a whisper. In one month, Jed would be finished with the boardinghouse. In one month, his commitment to her father would be fulfilled. He'd have no more reason to stay in Welcome Springs once his order arrived from the pharmaceutical supply house, as it surely would soon.

I could intercept the order. Or convince Papa to add to the inn . . . The thoughts barely entered her mind before she pushed them away. Why did she care if Jed was through with the inn or not? She already knew he would be leaving; the question had never been if, but when. He would return to the color and confusion of the carnival circuit, and she would spend the rest of her life here in this house, alone and pitied, like her aunt Hilda.

It wasn't fair! She gripped the edge of the desk and swallowed her rage. If she couldn't have love, couldn't she at least have *something* to look forward to, the way Jed had the medicine show and the adoration of the crowd?

"There will be much to do to prepare for the opening of the inn," her father said, sifting through the letters. "I am thinking of asking Mrs. Frisco to do the cooking. And we will need to find someone to help clean. And supplies—we will need so many things."

"Why not let me manage the Willkommen Inn?" The words burst from her, but as soon as they were out, she knew she'd said the right thing.

"Of course. Of course." Dr. Dengler nodded. "You may help all you like."

She cleared her throat and sat forward in the chair, this new exciting idea taking shape in her head. She didn't need Jed's love. She just needed something that was hers, that she could be responsible for. "I'm talking about *managing* the *business*. Taking care of the books, collecting the rent, letting the rooms to boarders."

Dr. Dengler shrugged. "I know you will be a great help to me, as you always are."

"I'm not talking about just 'helping out,' " she said. "You've said yourself over and over again what a big business the Willkommen Inn will be. Your medical practice will keep you too busy to devote your time to it. You need someone who can keep a close eye on things."

He smiled. "And we all know what a good head you have for numbers, don't we? Of course you may see to the books, just as you do for me now."

Nixie stood, trying to make herself as tall as possible, and cleared her throat. William flew to perch on her shoulder. At least *someone* around here was on her side. "I want to be paid a salary, like a real manager."

Dr. Dengler looked up at last from the stack of letters. His smile drooped into a look of sadness. "I hope you do not think I have been taking advantage of you all these years."

Ouch! She hurried to soften the blow. "Of course not, Papa. I've always enjoyed helping you with your medical practice. But I'd like to be able to earn some money of my own, so I can be independent."

He smiled fondly. "And what about a family, Nixie? Surely it will not be long before you are married and having children. You will be too busy taking care of them to manage a business."

She knew he was thinking of Jed. Ever since he had arrived here, her parents had been plotting her marriage to him. At last, a man for Nixie. Someone to take their troubled daughter off their hands. She looked down at the desktop, so that he wouldn't see the hurt in her eyes. "Don't you think it would be good for a woman to bring money of her own to a marriage?" she asked.

He relaxed and chuckled to himself. "You young people, with your modern ideas. Or are you worried I will spend so much on the inn there will not be enough left for a proper wedding?" He leaned forward and patted her hand. "You do not have to worry, Nixie girl. When the time comes, I will see to it that you are married in proper fashion."

She stared at him, dumfounded. He wasn't taking her seriously. But then, why should this surprise her so? No one ever took her seriously around here.

He glanced up from sorting the mail. "Is something wrong, child? You look a little peaked. Perhaps I should mix you a tonic."

She shook her head. "No, Papa. I'm fine. I . . . I'll just go up to my room and rest a while."

Grabbing up William's cage, she hurried out of the room and up the stairs, before he could see the tears in her eyes. He'd never begin to understand why she was crying. She wasn't sure if she completely understood herself. Merely that she was sick to death of being so ordinary, so . . . taken for granted.

She had barely closed the door to her room when a knock

startled her. Surely her father hadn't changed his mind so soon. Setting William's cage on its stand, she went to open the door.

"Oh, Nixie, please help me." Dory rushed past her into the room, the ribbons from her dress and hair ornaments fluttering behind her like pennants from a steamer. "You're the only one I can talk to!"

"What is it, Dory?" Nixie closed the door. "Why are you upset?"

Dory twisted a handkerchief in her hands. Tears streaked her carefully powdered face. "It's Dinah. Oh, I'm so worried."

Nixie had never seen Dory so agitated. She hurried to put her arm around her friend. "Come here and sit down. Tell me what's happened."

Dory allowed Nixie to lead her to the bed, where the two friends sat. "Ever since the dance, Dinah's changed." Dory blotted her eyes with the handkerchief. "She's gone all the time now, and I have no idea where. She keeps secrets from me, and she never did that before."

"Then you don't have to worry about her interfering with you and Theo." Nixie hugged her close. "That's a good thing, isn't it?"

Dory worried her lip between her teeth. "There isn't anything to interfere *with*. He and I had such a good time at the dance, but he's hardly spoken to me since." She sniffed. "I've even wondered if he isn't . . . *avoiding* me."

Nixie frowned. She would have sworn Theo Stebbins was as enamored of Dory as she was of him. But who was more ignorant than herself when it came to true love? "I'm sure Theo is just shy. He's probably working up the courage to speak to you about a . . . uh, more serious relationship."

Dory nodded. "He . . . he is shy, isn't he? And very self-conscious about his looks."

Nixie patted her shoulder. "I'm sure that's all it is. He needs a little coaxing to express his feelings."

Dory nodded, and even managed a small smile. "He certainly isn't like your Jed. Jed hasn't got a shy bone in his body—asking to court you in front of everyone at breakfast. What would he have done if you'd said no?"

He's not my *Jed*, Nixie wanted to say. But no one wanted to believe her. "I couldn't have said no without embarrassing myself in front of everyone," she said. "I'm sure he was counting on that."

"But you wouldn't have done that!" Dory looked alarmed. "Said no, I mean. Any woman would be lucky to get such a kind, handsome man for a beau. And it's easy to see he's crazy about you—and you him."

"Is it? And here I thought I was hiding my feelings well." She purposefully kept her tone light and teasing, but Dory's remark raised a new fear. Would Jed see that her feelings for him were fueled by more than passion? Would she make a fool of herself over Jed, the way she had with that salesman in her youth?

She closed her eyes against the thought. She'd have to work hard to keep from losing her heart to Jed. Otherwise, it would hurt too much when it came time for him to leave.

When Jed opened the back door of the Willkommen Inn, the smell of fresh paint assaulted his nose. Pete looked down from his perch at the top of a stepladder. "What are you doing here?" the boy asked.

"I was about to ask you the same question." He surveyed the half-painted kitchen wall.

Pete shrugged and laid his paintbrush carefully across the top of the paint can. "I figured I might as well go ahead and paint this wall. I didn't expect you to show up, seein' as how you were busy courtin' Nixie."

"I still have a boardinghouse to finish." He moved further into the room and began unbuttoning his shirt. "Besides, courting isn't a full-time job."

"It's not?" Pete scratched his nose, depositing a streak of paint on his cheek in the process. "That's good. I reckon a fellow needs time for doing fun things."

"I suppose that depends on your idea of fun."

Pete shrugged. "You know, guy stuff."

Jed picked up a brush. "Courting can be fun when done

properly." *And when the woman in question will do her part to cooperate. Unlike a certain female I could name.*

"You don't look too happy about it."

He slapped paint on the wall. "Happy? Of course I'm happy. Why wouldn't I be happy?" *Even though my father is determined to ruin everything between me and your sister, who is, by the way, one of the most contrary-minded, baffling females I have ever met.*

"I guess women must be born experts at confusing a fellow," Pete said.

Jed jerked his head up. "And what do you know about it?"

Pete shrugged and turned back to painting.

They worked in silence for a few moments. Jed concentrated on making even strokes with the paintbrush, but his mind was too full of Nixie. How could a woman be ecstatic in his arms one moment, and pushing him away the next? Did his father have anything to do with it?

"Jed, do you think you could teach me how to kiss a girl properly?"

Jed's paintbrush went sliding down the wall, landing in a wet *splat!* on the floor. He stared up at Pete. "What did you say?"

The boy flushed crimson. "I was wondering if you could tell me the right way to kiss a girl."

Jed deposited the paintbrush back in the can and sat down on the bottom step of the ladder. "I wasn't aware that there was a wrong way to go about it." He looked up at the boy above him. "Do you have a particular young lady in mind?"

Pete laid aside his brush and turned to look down on Jed. "Becky Simmons. I was thinking when I was dancing with her the other night, that maybe it wouldn't be so bad to kiss her." He swallowed hard. "Joe Sudbury says sometimes people stick their tongues in each other's mouths when they kiss."

Jed choked back laughter at the look of disgust on Pete's face. "It's not as bad as it sounds," he said. He remembered Nixie's tongue darting across his teeth, caressing his lips.

He put his hands on his knees and cleared his throat. "But that's not really how you want to start off with a girl."

"So how do you want to start off?" Pete moved down a rung on the ladder.

Jed shrugged. "Just do what feels right. Put your lips on hers."

Pete frowned. "I did that. And she slapped me. I figured I must not have been doing it right."

Jed could not hold back his laughter. He could imagine pretty Miss Becky slapping a startled Pete. "I'd say that slap is a good sign you were doing it exactly right."

Pete looked doubtful. "She didn't seem too terribly mad about it. But why would she hit me if she liked it?"

Jed shook his head. "Women can be pretty contrary creatures. They say one thing and do another. And then they expect us to figure them out. I'm not even sure they know what they want sometimes."

"Is Nixie like that?"

He nodded, recalling the whirlwind of emotions she'd put him through in the last few days. "Maybe all we need to do is slow down," he said, half to himself. He glanced back at Pete. "Take things slow and easy with Becky. Women don't like to be rushed. And I'll bet next time you kiss her, she won't slap your face."

The soundness of this advice hit home. The flamboyant, "sweep them off their feet" approach of a showman like his father worked with carnival queens, but maybe a quiet woman like Nixie required a more delicate touch.

"I guess I'll leave the rest of the painting to you." Pete climbed down the ladder and balanced his brush across the paint can. "Unless you can talk Nixie into helping you."

"What do you mean?"

Pete nodded toward the door. "She's headed this way right now." He grinned. "I'll get out of the way so you two can practice kissing. Not that I figure a fellow like you needs much practice, but my sister's always been so standoffish with men, she might need a little extra schooling." He laughed and loped out of the room, passing Nixie on her way in.

She glanced over her shoulder at Pete, then hesitated in the doorway. "I didn't know you were here." She took a step back. "I'll go and let you get on with your work."

"No, it's all right." Jed resisted the urge to reach out and take her hand. He was going to go slow this time, and wait for her. "What can I do for you?" He picked up a rag and wiped off his hands.

Nixie's gaze focused somewhere about mid-chest. "I just came in to look around." A pink blush warmed her cheeks as she turned away and fumbled in the pocket of her skirt. "I wanted to make a list of furnishings we'll need for the rooms," she said, drawing out a pad of paper and a pencil.

Jed reached for his shirt and put it on, taking his time buttoning it. Nixie was trying not to look at him, but her gaze kept flitting back in his direction. He began tucking in his shirttails.

She turned away, facing the wall. "I'm going to be managing the inn . . . for my father."

"You manage all your father's affairs, don't you? I wonder if he realizes how fortunate he is not to have to hire outside help."

"It's more practical this way, having me take care of things."

He walked up behind her, so close her skirts brushed his legs. He started to put a hand on her shoulder. But no, he would let her make the first move. Instead, he let his voice caress her the way his hands wanted to. "Practical Nixie. Don't you leave any room in your life for fun?"

She looked back at him, the full sleeves of her dress just missing his shirtfront. "What do you mean?"

"You know, fun. Magic. The unpredictable." He captured the edge of her wide collar between his thumb and forefinger. "All the lace and frills that make life exciting."

Worry lines creased her brow. "Not everyone can go through life being irresponsible."

"So you think I'm irresponsible, while you are always

practical." He chuckled. "Then I'd say together we make a pretty good team."

"This isn't a game, or a medicine show routine."

"What's important to you, Nixie? What do you take seriously?"

"This job. Now, if you'll excuse me, I have work to do."

She tried to push past him, but he blocked her escape. "What's your passion, Nixie? What do you care about more than anything?"

She looked at him as if he'd lost his mind. And perhaps he had. The questions he asked Nixie were ones he'd avoided asking himself for a long time now. She made him want to find the answers.

"I have to go," she said. "It's time for supper."

"What about the inn?" He moved with her to the door.

"I'll come back later."

She meant she'd come back alone. Without him. He sighed and followed her out of the inn and across to the house. "If you like, I'll walk a few steps behind so people won't mistakenly believe we're together," he said.

She frowned and quickened her pace. He laughed. *That's right, Nixie. I'm out of my mind. Between you and my father, I've been driven crazy.*

Nixie tried to ignore Jed as he followed her into the house and through the kitchen, but her every nerve thrummed with awareness of the man. What did he mean with his talk of magic and passion, as if life could be lived on those kind of terms?

She eased open the door into the dining room, steeling herself for the embarrassment of arriving with him on her heels. Her parents would look pleased and her brothers would giggle and tease.

But no one looked up as she moved toward her chair. In fact, most of the usual occupants of the table were missing. Only Theo Stebbins, Mr. Chapman, Pete, Lou, and Dr. Dengler sat in their usual places, glum expressions on their faces.

"Where is everyone?" Jed asked, pulling out his chair and looking around the room.

Dr. Dengler cleared his throat. "Upstairs."

"Upstairs?" Nixie asked.

Her father nodded. "The women are upstairs with Miss Evans."

"Dory!" Nixie half rose from her chair. "Is she ill?"

Her father motioned her to keep her seat. "Only upset. It is her sister who has everyone in such a state."

"I don't understand." Nixie settled into her chair and looked around the table. "What has Dinah done to upset Dory?"

"I doubt it was done intentionally," Mr. Chapman said. "It seems Mrs. Merchant has run away. With Mr. Harrison."

Chapter Fifteen

Nixie stared at Mr. Chapman. "Run away? Are you sure?"

He nodded. "Left her sister a note. Said they were going to elope."

Jed choked on the water he'd been drinking. Nixie glanced at him as his coughing fit shook the table. "Are you all right?" she asked.

He nodded, and wiped his face with his napkin. "I saw Dinah and Archie downtown when I went to see if my order of wainscotting had come in."

"You did?" She leaned toward him. "What were they doing?"

"They were over at the livery stable."

"You saw them and you didn't say anything to anyone about it?"

He shrugged. "I thought they were going to rent a buggy to take a drive in the country." He ladled peas onto his plate from the bowl in front of him. "It wasn't any of my business."

"I saw Archie this morning, packing up his camp," Theo

Stebbins volunteered. "I thought at the time he was leaving rather suddenly. Then again, he seems to have fully recovered, so I assumed he had decided to go home early."

Nixie wadded her napkin in a ball and threw it down beside her plate. "Men!" She shoved back her chair and looked around the table. Her dinner companions gaped at her, forks halfway to their mouths. "Dory is up there probably crying her eyes out over this, and if either of you had asked a few simple questions, you could have prevented it."

"Now, Nixie," Jed began. "I don't think—"

"Of course you don't." She glared at him. "Men never think about anybody but themselves. They never stop to consider other people's feelings. You go right on doing whatever pleases you, no matter that you might be breaking some poor woman's heart."

Before he could answer, she stormed out of the room. *I don't want to hear anything he has to say*, she told herself as she raced up the steps. *Let him leave and go sell his confounded Curative to every gullible soul in Texas. I'll be just fine without him.*

Nixie stopped at the top of the stairs to catch her breath, and to brush away the tears that suddenly sprang to her eyes. She was going to comfort Dory. No time now to dwell on her own problems.

She found the women in Dory's bedroom, all gathered around the figure lying prostrate on the bed. Someone had pulled the drapes, and the sound of weeping filled the gloom. "I just heard the news," Nixie said, joining the others around the bed.

"I can't believe she didn't even tell me!" Dory wailed.

"There, there, child, you mustn't take on so." Mrs. Chapman leaned over and stroked Dory's brow. "I'm sure you'll hear from your sister again soon."

They all murmured in agreement.

Dory nodded, her face contorting as she unsuccessfully fought back more tears. "She took half my clothes," she sobbed. "She said she knew I wouldn't mind. I'd understand a woman couldn't wear mourning on her honeymoon." She shut her eyes and beat her fists against the bedspread. "She took the lace mantilla I was saving to wear as my wedding veil."

Nixie's heart ached for her friend. Certainly, she knew what it felt like to be abandoned by someone you trusted. "She should have waited." Nixie took her friend's hand. "It wouldn't have hurt Dinah to wait a few weeks longer for you."

"Maybe she knew the truth. If she waited for me, she'd be waiting forever!" Her shoulders shook with sobs.

Mrs. Chapman hugged Dory to her and murmured in her ear.

"What are you talking about—waiting?" Mrs. Dengler asked Nixie. "Was Dory planning on eloping, too?"

Nixie sat on the edge of the bed and looked at Dory. Her face was puffy and reddened from crying, and her hair was half-fallen from the knot at the top of her head. "Dory, can I tell them about you and Theo?"

"There's nothing to tell." She sat up straighter and dabbed at her eyes with a sodden handkerchief. "I thought he liked me, and we've kissed a few times." She sniffed. "I thought maybe he'd even ask me to m-marry him. But I might as well be his *sister* for all the interest he's shown lately."

Nadine leaned over and patted Dory's shoulder. "Maybe Mr. Stebbins has cold feet. But what does Theo have to do with Dinah and Archie?"

"I think I know," Mrs. Chapman said. She sat on the bed across from Nixie. "Dory was hoping she'd be started on her first marriage before her sister commenced her second."

A knock on the door startled them. "Who is it?" Nadine Dengler called.

"Jed Hawkins, ma'am."

Nixie felt everyone's eyes on her as she went to open the door. "What do you want?"

Jed stiffened. "I thought you'd want to know I rode over to the post office and sent a telegram to Rock Ridge to see if anyone there could catch them."

"You did?" Nixie stared at him, a curious fluttering in her stomach. Why hadn't someone thought of this before? She held the door wide. "Come in and tell us."

He stepped into the room, hat in hand, and surveyed the mournful group around the bed. "Did you find out anything?" Mrs. Chapman asked.

He shook his head. "The buggy they rented was in the livery stable there, but they'd already gone."

"Where?" Nixie put her hand on his arm. "Hadn't anybody seen them?"

He cleared his throat. "Oh, lots of people saw them. Saw them getting on the train headed east." He nodded toward Dory. "Sorry ma'am. I wish I had better news for you."

"I appreciate your efforts, Mr. Hawkins." Dory sat up and sniffed.

He nodded again and stepped backward toward the door. "Excuse me, ladies, I'll leave you to your . . . uh, I'll leave you."

Nixie shut the door softly behind him. She felt bad now about her outburst downstairs. She owed Jed an apology. At least he had tried to help. Heavyhearted, she returned to the group around the bed. "I'm sorry, too, Dory. If Jed had found Dinah and Archie, they might have at least been persuaded to come back here and have a proper wedding."

Dory began to sob anew. "I know it's terribly selfish of me," she said. "I shouldn't begrudge my own sister's happiness. But just once I wanted her to be the bridesmaid at *my* wedding, and the guest in *my* home." She buried her head in her hands. "I don't know if I can bear to always be the plainer, older, spinster sister."

"You don't know that Theo won't still ask you to marry him," Nixie said. "This might be exactly what he needs to spur him on." She leaned closer. "What did he say when you came downstairs with Dinah's note?"

Dory shook her head. "Nothing! He didn't say anything at all—just stood there staring at me!"

"Men!" Nixie shook her head in exasperation. "You let me get alone with that Theo Stebbins and I'll tell him exactly what kind of a good-for-nothing scoundrel I think he is."

"Theo is not a scoundrel!"

Nixie blinked at her friend, who was sitting straight up in bed, glaring at her. "Just because he's too shy to say what he feels, doesn't mean he isn't as honest and good as the day is long. I mean—"

Nixie began to laugh, low giggles that tickled her throat, rising to full belly-shaking guffaws. "Oh, Dory, if you could only see yourself. Like a lioness defending her mate."

Dory blinked, then choked back a chuckle. "I suppose it does sound funny, after what I said before."

"That's part of being a woman, I suppose." Nadine Dengler leaned over and took Nixie's hand, one arm still around Dory. "You think you can't stand a man because he drives you crazy. But then again you love him, because, well . . . because he drives you crazy."

They leaned against each other, laughing, Mrs. Chapman's wheezing snicker harmonizing with Nadine's melodious chuckle. Nixie felt the sounds vibrate through her, smoothing over her worries for the future and the petty annoyances of the afternoon. She took comfort in knowing she wasn't the only one baffled by love. If women like her mother and Mrs. Chapman could hold on to that passion, in spite of its uncertainties, then maybe she'd be able to come to terms with the challenges her own heart faced.

Caesar stretched out along the porch railing, his back against the corner post, and watched Jed put the finishing touches on the sign next to the road. Jed had covered over the old faded letters with a coat of sky blue paint and now he was down on his knees wielding a smaller brush to sketch a new message in brilliant white outlined in black. *Willkommen Inn, estab. 1892*, Caesar read.

The boy always has had a flare for the artistic, he thought. Take the painting on the side of their wagon. A stroke of genius if he did say so himself. He frowned. *Had* he ever said so?

He hopped off the railing and made his way down the walk. Jed was his son. He didn't have to shower the boy with compliments for him to know his old man was proud of his talent.

Jed stepped back and studied his work. Chin in hand, Caesar did the same. Was it his imagination, or was that second *L* a little crooked? Ah—he'd fixed it now.

Yes, Jed was a fine son. If only he wasn't so incredibly stubborn. Take this latest disagreement of theirs, over the formula for the Curative. The memory filled Caesar with restlessness. He began to pace. He fully intended to divulge his secrets to the boy when the time was right, but it was too soon. He was still fine-tuning the recipe. And he wanted Jed to realize the importance of the formula.

He glanced over his shoulder to where his son knelt in the dirt before the sign. He hated to say it, but Jed, well he didn't always show the right amount of *enthusiasm* for the Curative. Caesar had tried to teach him, but—and he was sure he was imagining this—sometimes he worried the boy didn't have the heart for the medicine show business. That he'd be happier clerking behind a counter somewhere.

Preposterous! He halted behind Jed and stared down at him. Jed had Mona's dark blond hair, true enough, but even a half-blind man could see the boy was a Hawkins, through and through. He'd been weaned on Great Caesar's Celebrated Curative. The essence of it flowed through his very veins.

Hmmm. Maybe that was the problem. Caesar stroked his chin and considered this angle on the dilemma. Perhaps Jed had been away from the tonic too long. He'd forgotten the satisfaction of mixing up a batch of that glorious golden nectar, of decanting that magical formula into their signature amber bottles, of wielding the glue brush to apply their specially printed labels. Ah, the thrill was enough to put new life into any man.

Triumph surged through Caesar, the heady feeling of a problem solved. He wasn't ready yet to turn over control of the business to Jed, but to show there were no hard feelings, he'd see to it the boy got the ingredients for another batch. Smiling broadly, he went to gather the materials he needed. It wouldn't do to collect too much. Just enough for a single batch. Enough to remind Jed of the magic of his heritage.

It was almost eight by the time Jed made it back to his wagon. He'd finished the last of his work by lantern light, tacking carpeting along the stair risers until he couldn't see the tacks anymore. Stopping just inside the door, he slipped his suspenders off his shoulders and stretched. Lordy, he was tired. And he'd give half a day's pay for a hot bath to soak in.

Of course there was always the springs. He wouldn't even have to venture into the pool itself. He could sit in one of the tubs. He shook his head. He was too tired to walk that far.

He turned up the wick on the lamp on the table and lit it. He couldn't remember when he'd last worked this hard. Dr. Dengler had already sent out invitations for the grand opening on the seventh, which didn't leave Jed much time to get ready. Besides, working on the house meant he could be close to Nixie. She was bustling in and out of the place all the time now, hanging draperies and arranging furniture and stocking cabinets. She didn't say much, but he'd caught her watching him a time or two when he was busy hanging a light fixture or scraping putty off a window. Just as often, he'd found himself mesmerized by her trim figure as she bent to tuck in the linens on a bedstead or straighten a rug.

Ah, Nixie. He smiled and stripped off his shirt and undershirt. He wasn't very good at this patience business. More than once he'd been tempted to grab hold of her and kiss her senseless, until she agreed to run away with him and elope, the way Dinah Merchant had with Archie Harrison.

He washed his face and under his arms, then reached for the towel on the hook by his bed. Something lying on his pillow caught his eye. He rubbed the water from his eye and looked again. Lamplight winked off blue glass. He picked it up, the glass cool and familiar in his hand. "Great

Caesar's secret ingredient," he said. He didn't need to ask who had left this here for him.

"I discovered it quite by accident when I was looking on a shelf."

This was the first time Caesar had spoken to him in almost three days. Jed hated to admit it, but he'd missed his father's voice. "What were you looking for?" he asked.

"Why . . . a book. I was searching for a book to read."

He suppressed a smile. Caesar Hawkins never read anything longer than a broadside if he could help it. He might have "discovered" the secret ingredient today, but Jed felt sure it had been no accident. He set the bottle aside and reached into the wardrobe for a fresh shirt. "That's nice."

"What are you going to do with it?"

He studied the bottle as he buttoned the shirt. "Do? Why would I want to do anything?"

"But we're almost out of Curative! You need to make more."

"Oh, I'll get around to it one day."

An invisible hand clamped down on his arm. *"Why not now? People here in Welcome Springs might be in need of a tonic. You can never have too much on hand."*

Jed bit his cheek to keep from laughing. "I'm busy getting ready for the grand opening now."

"All the more reason to brew up a batch!" Caesar was practically roaring now. Jed only hoped those camped nearby couldn't hear. *"Folks attending the grand opening will want to try the Curative."*

He took pity on his father at last. "Then I'll have to make time to brew up a batch."

"Good." His father released him. *"You can ask Nixie to help you,"* he added.

"Nixie?" The idea of working with her on anything appealed to him, but what was Caesar up to now? "Why should I ask her?"

"It will give her a chance to see what it's all about. Help her understand why the Curative is so important."

Why is the Curative so important? The question startled Jed. He'd always taken for granted that his work—his father's work—mattered because it helped people. He'd said as much to Nixie the day he'd first come here.

But now Jed wondered: Why was the Curative important to him? "I *will* ask Nixie to help me," he said aloud. Maybe she'd be the one to show him the answer to the question he'd never before dared to ask.

"Nixie, I've been looking all over for you."

Lost in thought, Nixie hadn't noticed Jed slip into the office behind her. Now he stood so close she couldn't have moved without brushing against him. His breath stirred the loose strands of hair at her temples, setting up a corresponding flutter in her heart.

"What do you want?" She raised her head, but dared not look at him.

"What I want and what I can have may be two different things right now." He chuckled, the sound dancing down her spine.

She turned her head to study his profile, her eyes tracing the masculine curve of his nose, the strong chin, the full, gentle lips. She could recall the exact feel of those lips on her skin, she knew the way his eyes darkened with passion or glinted with laughter. She recognized the way the skin around his eyes crinkled at the corners when he was deep in thought, and how his throat relaxed when he projected his voice to carry over a vast crowd.

In a few short weeks she had memorized every physical feature, habit, and trait of this man. If only she could know his mind as well. What did he think of her, really? What would he do if he discovered the depths of her feelings for him? Would he welcome the news, or laugh at her naïveté, and flee as far from her clinging hands as possible?

"I'm hoping to persuade you to help me with something."

She made a pretense of shuffling the papers before her on the desk. "Really? I'm very busy right now."

He glanced at the open ledger and the neatly stacked pieces of paper. "I need you to help me mix up a batch of Great Caesar's Celebrated Curative."

"Surely you don't need my help." She flipped back through the ledger, pretending to search for something.

"It's much easier with two people."

A lot of things were easier, even preferable, with two people. Those were the activities she wanted to avoid. "Then get one of the boys to help you."

"No. They won't do." He walked around to the front of the desk and leaned over it, his shadow darkening the papers in front of her. "I want you."

Heat curled within her and she tried to quench the building fire with anger. She wouldn't allow him to manipulate her this way. "I don't have time for word games with you today."

He straightened, his shadow drawing back, though she could still feel his eyes on her. "Even the vilest accused is granted a trial. I'd think you'd do me the same favor."

She shoved aside her ledger book and glared up at him. "What are you talking about?"

"You once accused me of being a charlatan, someone who cheated people out of their money and sold them worthless concoctions. In fact, you said as much in this very room."

She squirmed in her chair. "I apologized."

"Yes, but you never really believed, did you? I want you to see for yourself that the Curative isn't some quack formula designed to fool people."

She hunched her shoulders. "What does it matter what I think?"

"I matters to me."

She'd expected an argument or some glib persuasion. These words, stark and rich with feeling, shook her, like a barbed dart slipping through the single flaw in her stout defenses. He leaned over and took her hand. "Come on. Let me show you."

She followed him outside and across the yard to his wagon. Though he beckoned her inside, she hesitated on the doorstep, remembering the last time she'd been here, the night of the dance, when they'd made love. If Jed remembered, he showed no sign of it. He opened the door and pulled her in after him.

The room smelled of herbs and lamp oil, and had the familiar jumble of assorted papers, leaning towers of books, wrinkled shirts, discarded boots, and rumpled bedclothes that women took to be disorder but men protested was merely comfortable.

"Let me clear off a space here." Jed raked everything off the table into his arms and deposited it in the single armchair beside the bed. The bed again. Nixie couldn't stop looking at it. Resolutely, she turned her back to the folded-down quilt and indented pillow.

Jed consulted a slip of paper and began pulling bundles of herbs from their hooks overhead and arranging them before him. "Let's see. Here's pennyroyal and camomile. Lemongrass, blackberry leaves. What else do we need? Rosemary." He pulled down another bundle. "Ginseng and ginger root."

Nixie stared at the bunches of plants. "How do you remember everything?"

"Um, that's why I write it down, of course." He consulted his recipe again, then picked up a bundle of dried plants and held it out to her. "The ginseng, for instance, lends energy. And the blackberry leaves help purify the system."

She brought the bundle of plants to her nose and sniffed. "And you think this really works?"

He frowned. "You may have kept your father's books, but you obviously weren't paying very much attention to the medical side of his practice. My father taught me that most of the medicine we have comes from plants and herbs. In the Orient, they've studied medicinal plants for years."

Properly chastised, she stepped back. "I promise to pay attention. Now tell me what else goes into the Curative."

He surveyed the bundles of plants on the table before him. "That's almost everything, except—" He reached up and plucked a blue-glass bottle from atop the wardrobe.

Nixie recognized the bottle that had brought Jed Hawkins to Welcome Springs in the first place—the bottle containing Great Caesar's secret ingredient. Had this been another of his tricks? "I thought you were out."

"I discovered this one the other day." He uncorked the bottle. "There's only enough here for one batch."

One batch and then he'd have to leave? She pushed the thought away. "What do we do?"

"First, why don't we sample a little of the last batch? That will give you an idea of what we're aiming for."

He opened another cabinet and selected an amber bottle. He unscrewed the cap and held it out to her. "Ladies first."

She took the bottle, but paused before tasting the Curative to inhale its sweet fragrance. This was the aroma that had surrounded her as they clung together in the heat of passion. As she breathed in that herbal perfume, she felt her nipples harden in response, and a corresponding tension in her loins.

"Try it and tell me what you think," Jed prompted.

She took a tentative sip. The combination of honeyed sweetness and minty herbs was a pleasing one. She looked up and found Jed watching her. "Well, what do you think?" he asked.

The boyish eagerness of his question touched her. Could it be that her opinion was really so important to him? Avoiding his eyes, she studied the colorful illustration on the front of the bottle. "Great Caesar's Celebrated Curative," she read out loud. "The all-purpose tonic. Drink daily for good health." She returned the bottle to Jed. "Maybe you ought to market this as a beverage instead of a tonic," she said. "It tastes too good to be medicine."

He glanced at the bottle in his hand. "What do you mean?"

She shrugged. "I imagine half the people who buy the Curative probably buy it because they like the taste. You'd have to charge less if you sold it as a drink instead of as a tonic, but then you could sell more to make up the difference."

He settled one hip on the edge of the table. "You mean instead of sarsaparilla or root beer, people would drink Curative?"

She nodded. "You could even sell the syrup to ice cream parlors and places like that. They could add their own water." *And then you could stay here in Welcome Springs with me,* she wanted to add.

"Hmmmm." He picked up the bottle again and frowned at it. "What would I call it? Great Caesar's Celebrated Curative sounds too medicinal."

She shrugged. "I don't know. I'm sure you could think of something." She fought to keep the excitement she felt from her voice.

He set the bottle aside and shook his head. "No. My father developed his formula to help people. I don't know if he'd approve of selling it as a drink."

What does it matter if he's dead? she wanted to say, but of course she didn't. She tried not to let her disappointment show as she turned away from him. "Are we ready to make the Curative now?"

"First, we have to crush the herbs." He opened a cabinet to his right and pulled out a marble mortar and pestle. "Here. I'll measure. You crush."

Soon the wagon was filled with the heady perfume of the mingled herbs. To Nixie, the fragrance held no reminders of the Curative itself. Instead, it conjured memories of Jed, of the scent of his skin, imbued with the very essence of his product.

"Be sure and crush them very fine. Almost to a powder." He put his arms around her and covered her hands with his own to demonstrate. "Like this." He leaned his weight into his work, and into her. She felt the muscles of his arms bunch and the planes of his stomach tense. Her own body tightened in response. He rocked forward, weilding the pestle in the mortar, taking her with him, their bodies pressed together. His breath was warm in her ear, as warm as the heat of his arousal pressed into her back.

There was nothing innocent in the posture; the very illicitness of it inflamed her already heated emotions. Didn't this prove she would never fit the virtuous mold she'd tired to force herself into?

She licked her lips, searching for some reply to turn the

course of their conversation around. But every nerve was alert to his touch, yearning for him.

She sighed as his lips grazed the back of her neck. "What . . . what do we do next?" she gasped. "To make the Curative?"

"The Curative?" He raised his head. "Oh. We boil some water."

She reached for the kettle, but he took it from her and filled it from the pail by the door. Then he set it on the gas burner. "We'll steep the herbs," he said, raking the contents of the mortar into the pot.

"What do we do after the herbs have steeped?"

"Then we'll strain it, add honey and more water, bottle it and put on the labels."

He opened the cabinet and took down a half-full jar of honey. "This might be enough." He removed the lid and stuck his finger in the sticky sweetener. "Hmmm. Good. But it's starting to sugar."

He scooped up a fingerful of the honey and offered it to her.

Her mouth watered, and she started to protest, but as soon as her lips parted, Jed slipped his finger between them. "Isn't that delicious?"

The honey was sweet and wild-tasting, with a trace of the flavor of Jed himself. Her tongue brushed across his calloused finger, dragging against the rough skin. She heard the quick expulsion of his breath, and caught the spark of desire that flashed across his eyes.

"Nixie," he breathed, and pulled her close. He grabbed her hand and dipped it in the honey jar, then transferred the fingers to his mouth.

She lost all consciousness of time and place as he suckled her fingers, all of her senses focused on the passion that jolted through her with each stroke of his tongue or movement of his velvet lips. When at last he released her, it was only to pull her closer. She tasted the honey again in his kiss. The overpowering smell of herbs filled her with each breath, until she was dizzy, blood whistling in her ears.

"The teakettle," Jed whispered. Reluctantly, he released her. "I'd better get the kettle."

She sagged against the edge of the table, gripping a chair for support. A shiver ran down her spine, as if Jed had taken all her warmth with him. *Don't leave me*, she wanted to cry out. *Not just now, but never.*

The traitorous words echoed through her head as she watched him pour the water over the crushed herbs. Even while her body still ached for him, her mind rebelled. What was it about the man that made her forget herself so completely, to abandon all pride and common sense in exchange for momentary passion? After all, Jed Hawkins had never even hinted that theirs might be a more permanent situation. Yet here she was, ready—*wanting* even—to give herself to him all over again.

She turned away, ashamed that she'd been ready to so easily surrender to her baser passions. Would she never win this battle with herself? "I have to go," she said, moving to the door.

"But we haven't finished yet."

"I have." She hurried away, walking quickly, and then running, imagining all the while that he was close on her heels. She didn't dare slow down, afraid that if Jed so much as touched her shoulder, she would melt against him, and surrender everything, like a moth dying blissfully in the bright candle flame.

Chapter Sixteen

Nixie devoted herself over the next several weeks to setting up the ledger for the Willkommen Inn, devising a registration system, and helping her father with arrangements for the grand opening at the start of the next week. The work interested and challenged her, but most importantly, it kept her from coming into too close a contact with Jed. Though these days merely looking at him across the supper table could set up a smoldering inside her. The night her mother served biscuits with honey she had to ask to be excused. She was willing to withstand only so much temptation and the sight of Jed licking honey from his fingertips would have driven a saint to want to drag him off into some dark corner where they could be alone.

Preoccupied with this thought, Nixie opened the front door one afternoon on her way out and came face to face with Theo Stebbins. "Miss Dengler! Excuse me, I had no idea you were coming out, I . . ." he stammered, his face a deeper shade of crimson than usual.

Nixie hadn't spoken to Theo since Dinah Merchant's disappearance. But she hadn't forgotten the pain he'd caused her friend. "Mr. Stebbins, what are you doing?" she demanded.

"I . . . I was looking for, that is I'd hoped to find . . . uh, have you seen Miss Evans this morning?"

Nixie debated with herself a moment before deciding it would be all right to reveal Dory's whereabouts to Theo, on the chance that he might truly care for her and just be feeling awkward about expressing himself. "I saw her headed down to the pool a little while ago. Would you like me to give her a message?"

He shook his head. "No. I thought, well, I was going to see if she'd like to go for a walk with me."

He started to turn away, but Nixie reached out and took his arm. "Perhaps you'd walk with me instead," she said. "We haven't had much of a chance to get to know each other."

His eyes widened. "Well, no, I . . . that is . . ."

She patted his arm. "Actually, I've been looking for an opportunity to talk to you. Why don't we walk toward town? I have to buy a registration book for the inn."

They walked in silence for a quarter of a mile. Nixie squinted into the bright sunlight, wishing she'd brought a parasol or at least taken the time to stop for a hat. Heat-lakes shimmered on the dusty road and grasshoppers shot out of the tall grass along the roadside at every step.

"Uh, what did you want to speak with me about?" Theo asked after a while.

She brushed a grasshopper from her skirt and glanced at Theo. He had relaxed a little, his face was not such a fiery red. "How well did you know Archie Harrison?" she asked.

He blinked. "Oh. Not well at all, really. We were camped next to each other, and we played dominoes a few times. Why?"

"I just wondered." She shook her head. "I believe Dory might be worried that he's not, well, suitable for her sister. They'd known each other such a short time and all." She glanced at him. "What if he's, well, a criminal or something?"

Theo looked alarmed. "Oh, I don't think so. He told me he owned a bakery back East, and sold the business to come west for his health. He seemed quite honest, very gentlemanly."

"Had he ever been married before?"

"I think he mentioned he was a widower."

"He struck me as a very nice man." She smiled. "Isn't it remarkable about him and Dinah running away together? But then I suppose it happens for some people that way—they know they're meant for each other right from the start." Not that *she'd* had any experience in that area.

He nodded and fell silent, as if pondering this idea. "Still," he said after a moment. "You wouldn't want to rush into something and perhaps spend your life regretting it."

Was this the problem then? Did Theo Stebbins merely have cold feet? She squeezed his arm. "I think we're much more inclined to regret the things we don't do in life," she said. "A lost opportunity is so seldom regained."

He nodded again. "I confess I've not been a man to take advantage of the opportunities that have come my way. Sometimes I've regretted that more than others."

"I wouldn't want to grow old, knowing I'd passed up a chance at love," she said. "Would you?"

She thought she heard him sigh, but when she looked his way, his face was impassive. "No, I wouldn't want that," he said softly.

They walked the rest of the way to the mercantile in silence. When they reached the entrance, Nixie removed her hand from Theo's arm. "Thank you for walking with me," she said. "If you head back to the house now, I imagine Dory will be finished with her swim by the time you get back."

Theo shook his head. "Then she'll certainly want to rest a bit before dinner." He nodded toward a trio of men gathered in the shade beside the livery stable across the street. "I see some friends over there. I think I'll join them for a game of dominoes." He touched the brim of his hat. "Good day, Miss Dengler. I enjoyed visiting with you."

Nixie put her hands on her hips and watched him cross the street to join the domino players. Hadn't the man heard a word she'd said? After all their talk about love and lost opportunities, she'd fully expected him to be in a rush to get down on his knees and propose to Dory.

"Men!" she huffed as she turned to climb the steps into the store. Why did they have such a hard time seeing what was right in front of their eyes?

Caesar had seldom seen such chaos in his life, and that was saying something, given that he'd traveled the show circuit for more than thirty years. He'd weathered a back-lot fire in Fort Worth, tornadoes tearing through the main tent up by Abilene, and flooding in the Louisiana swamps. But those natural disasters paled next to the man-made ruckus of the grand opening of the Willkommen Inn.

Around him, men worked as if possessed. The flurry of activity made him weary as he walked the grounds around the inn. Jed hammered away at a viewing stand for visiting dignitaries, men from town hauled furniture into the boardinghouse. Even that nosy neighbor, Mrs. Frisco, had been pressed into service planting flowers along the front walk. Nixie Dengler darted in and out of the house, giving orders to everyone.

"Careful with that highboy there!" she called to two men heading up the walk with a tall chest of drawers. "I don't want it scratched."

Caesar jumped out of the way, narrowly escaping being run down by Nixie as she darted after the movers. He'd be better off relaxing down by the ladies' bathhouse, but unfortunately, Nixie wasn't the only one who had work to do around here.

He turned to look at Jed, up on the speaker's platform. Just as he'd suspected. The boy was staring after Nixie, mooning after her like a stricken schoolboy.

Caesar followed his son's gaze to the young woman in question. She wasn't much better. As soon as the chest of drawers was safely through the door of the inn, she looked back over her shoulder toward Jed. When their eyes met, there was enough heat between them to boil water. But, of course, they both immediately looked away. Jed proceeded to attempt to hammer the wrong end of a nail while Nixie developed a sudden intense interest in the trim on the front door frame.

I ought to wash my hands of the both of them, Caesar thought indignantly. *I've never met two such contrary young people in all my born days.* He stalked over to the speaker's platform, where Jed was packing up his toolbox. *"Are you going to do anything about that young woman or not?"* he demanded.

Jed jerked his head up, but said nothing. Caesar glared at the boy. Maybe a good swift kick . . . "Afternoon, Travis. Reckon that'll hold 'em."

"It'll have to do." Jed's helper, whom Caesar had scarcely noticed before now, walked past them and down the steps to the ground.

As soon as Travis was out of sight, Jed spoke. "If you're talking about Nixie, there's nothing *to* do."

"Blast it! Ask the girl to marry you! Don't you know that's what she's waiting for?"

"Hah!" Jed picked up the toolbox and jumped to the ground. "We've been over this before. She can't stand me. Why make a fool of myself by proposing?"

Caesar stared after his son. Was it possible that the Great Caesar Hawkins could have raised a son who was so thick-witted? *"Then what are you going to do?"* he asked. *"Just keep mooning after her on the chance you can change her opinion of you from a safe distance?"*

Jed stiffened, and got a tight look around the eyes that Caesar didn't like to see. Trouble was coming. He knew it. "I'm not as stupid as you think, Papa. I know when to move on to greener pastures."

"Just what is that supposed to mean?"

"I've boxed up the batch of Curative we made the other day and I'm heading out right after the grand opening celebration."

The words froze Caesar in place. *"What?"* He had to race to catch up with Jed. *"You're leaving?"*

"Nixie doesn't want me here so why should I stay? You didn't mean for us to hide here forever did you?"

"I certainly hadn't intended for us to leave alone," he huffed.

"You traveled alone for thirty years and I never heard you complain."

But it wasn't the same. He had always had Mona's memory with him, and the company of many a willing female. Jed didn't have his father's appreciation of the temporary. He was a man made for commitment. Because he hadn't yet found the right person to commit to, he'd lived almost as solitary as a monk.

He watched the boy walk on alone, shoulders squared, head up, but Caesar knew the pose was a sham. Jed tried to act like a flamboyant showman, but at heart he was as practical as a bank clerk.

He turned away, scowling, and headed back toward the inn. Nixie was just as bad. She had the heart of a dance-hall diva hidden beneath that prim schoolmarm exterior. He'd recognized that the first day, when she'd sauntered across the stage and pulled her chair up next to Jed. The girl had fire in her soul but she kept trying to douse it with a dulling conventionality.

Caesar had never met two such dense young people. What was it going to take to get through to them that they belonged together? He slammed his hand into his palm and scowled. He had two more days to figure it out and by thunder he would or his name wasn't the Great Caesar Hawkins!

"I had no idea there were this many people in the whole county." Nixie looked out the front window of the Willkommen Inn, at the huge crowd gathered on the lawn.

"Isn't it exciting?" Dory leaned over her shoulder for a better view. "Like a big party."

A very big party, Nixie thought as she watched a half-dozen men climb down from a wagon and approach the boardinghouse. Her father had been beside himself for days now, overseeing the decorating of the house with bunting, and the procuring of refreshments for those who would help mark this milestone in his life.

Even the weather had cooperated, with an unseasonable spell of cool temperatures, hinting at the fall to come.

"Look," Dory said in her ear. "Is that a newspaper reporter?"

Nixie studied the balding man bent over the camera that sat on a tripod in front of the inn. As she watched, he shouted something to the crowd and her father stepped up beside the Willkommen Inn sign and struck a pose.

She searched the crowd for some sign of Jed but could not spot him in the press of people. For days she'd been torn by this unbearable desire to be near him, and yet when he was close by, she could hardly bring herself to look at him. To make matters worse, after all the effort he'd spent "courting" her, he suddenly didn't appear to want anything to do with her.

"Nixie! Nixie, are you here?" Her mother hurried into the parlor from the back. "Come along, dear. That reporter wants to take our pictures—the whole family in front of the Willkommen Inn."

Sighing, Nixie straightened and followed Dory out of the house, and into the festival atmosphere of the front yard. A German band blared polkas and schottisches over the crowd, and the sound of laughter and cheerful conversation provided a pleasing counterpoint to the music. Men, women, and children, dressed in their Sunday best, stood in groups beneath the shade of the tall hackberries and oaks. They sipped lemonade and munched on teacakes that Mrs. Frisco, in a flowered hat, handed around on trays.

A group of dignitaries in tall beaver hats and cutaway coats—including the county judge, Emil Herrmann—stood before a bunting-draped dais and posed for the photographer. Then it was Nixie and her mother's turn to stand with her father and brothers. A frozen moment, a blinding flash, and they were captured for eternity on a glass negative.

"All right, everyone. Listen up now." Her heart pounded

at the sound of Jed, calling to them from the speaker's dais. The crowd grew quiet. "I want to start by welcoming you all here today," he said in his showman's voice. "It is indeed a great day in the history of Welcome Springs."

He waited until the cheers and applause had died. Nixie glanced at her father. He was rocking back and forth on his heels with excitement, his ruddy face glowing. His smile widened when he saw her watching him. "What did I say, Nixie girl?" he said to her. "Welcome Springs will be a great resort now that we have a fine place for people to stay."

Nixie returned his smile and faced the dais once more. "In years to come, when people think of health, when people think of a place to come for rest and relaxation and the healing benefits of pure mineral water, they'll think of Welcome Springs," Jed was saying. The words flowed so effortlessly from his lips, carrying over the crowd. Whether he was touting Great Caesar's Celebrated Curative or the Willkommen Inn, Jed looked and sounded at home on a stage. "We all have one man to thank for this," he continued. "One man has seen the potential of this town from the very first. His strength of character, his persistence in holding on to his dreams, has made all of this possible. Ladies and gentlemen, I give you Dr. Hamlin Dengler."

Nixie swallowed a lump in her throat as the crowd roared their approval. Hands reached out to pat her father on the back as he made his way to the dais. Those who had laughed at him behind his back now cheered him.

Dr. Dengler moved to the center of the stage and beamed at the people gathered before him. "Welcome to Willkommen Inn," he said. "And welcome to the future of our little town. I am so happy you are all here to celebrate this day with me."

More cheers filled the air, and Dr. Dengler raised his hands to quiet the crowd. "I have many people to thank, people who helped make this day possible. But I especially owe a debt of gratitude to Mr. Jedediah Hawkins here." He put his arm around Jed's shoulders.

Nixie's heart swelled with pride as she watched Jed with

her father. Jed was wearing his white suit, his head bared. The sun shone on the gold streaks in his hair, echoing the glint in his eyes.

"This is the man we should all be thanking today," Ham said, clapping Jed on the back. "He worked hard all summer finishing the Willkommen Inn with his own two hands." He looked up at Jed and Nixie thought she saw tears glittering in her father's eyes. "But most importantly, Jed helped me to see that my dreams were not just an old man's fantasy, that they could be reality."

She could not hear Jed's reply over the roar of the crowd, and could no longer see him for the tears that blurred her own vision. To think that at one time she had accused Jed of being a bad man, a charlatan out to dupe a gullible crowd and disappear before they discovered his ruse.

Watching him now, she saw a different sort of person entirely, a good man who believed in the miracles of an herbal potion and the dreams of a small-town doctor. A man raised to know the freedom of the open road, who traveled, not because he was running away, but because it was the only life he knew.

The newspaper reporter took a photograph of her father and Jed standing together as the crowd cheered. Before the halo of the flash had faded from her eyes, Nixie's mother grabbed her and pulled her toward the refreshment table. "Help circulate these among the crowd," she said, handing Nixie a plate of teacakes.

She carried the heavy silver tray with both hands, offering the iced cakes to those she passed. She and her mother and Mrs. Frisco had worked well into the night baking the delicate pastries, icing them with buttercream and decorating each one with a nut or bit of sugared fruit. Mrs. Frisco had pronounced them the best she'd ever tasted, and their guests seemed to agree, devouring the cakes as fast as Nixie could distribute them.

She was refilling her tray when Pete and Lou descended on her, each grabbing up a handful of the fancy cakes. "Stop that!" she cried, slapping at their darting hands. "These are for our guests."

Lou grinned, his mouth rimmed with the sticky evidence of past forays to the refreshment table. "Awww, Sis, you can spare a few," Pete said with a slyer smile.

She sighed and shook her head in mock exasperation, but she couldn't help but smile in return. Pete looked very grown-up in his new long trousers, and his arm was finally free of the plaster cast.

She watched Pete as he walked away from the table, and wasn't surprised to see him approach Becky Simmons with his offering of cakes. In the space of a summer Pete had transformed from bratty brother to this handsome young man courting his first sweetheart. Everywhere she looked, change hurtled toward her like a lightning express. And Jed Hawkins might have been the engineer, driving them all into the future.

She stood on tiptoe, trying to find Jed in the crowd. She wanted to memorize the way he looked this day—like a gold-washed genie capable of granting wishes and turning dreams into reality. Except that he couldn't make Nixie's dream come true without giving up his own.

She found him at last, standing behind the boardinghouse sign with Mr. Chapman. As if feeling her eyes on him, he turned, and flashed a smile.

Embarrassed at being caught staring, she spun around, and collided with a man in a gray-striped suit. "I'm terribly sorry," she stammered, struggling to right her tray. She hastily rearranged the teacakes, which had slid to one side.

"Well, if it isn't Nixie Dengler." The man chuckled and reached out to steady her, but he kept his hand on her shoulder long after the time it would have been proper for him to pull away.

Her stomach quaked at the sound of her name spoken by a familiar voice. His hand was heavy on her shoulder and she fought the urge to cry out and back away. Slowly, she raised her eyes and looked into a face she'd prayed she'd never have to see again.

"Ah, you still recognize me." He smiled, a languid curling of his lips beneath a thick moustache. "And I'd have known your lovely shape anywhere."

She stiffened and took a step back, but he merely moved forward, as if they were partners in a dance. "Mr. Norwich," she said, her voice sounding thin, and too high-pitched. "What brings you to Welcome Springs?"

"What if I said I'd come in search of my long-lost love?" He arched one dark eyebrow in question.

She stared up at him, taking in the black hair that curled about his collar. His eyes glittered like jet stones, and his lips curved into a knowing smile beneath the luxurious moustache.

"Ah, I can see we're past that sort of pretense." Norwich nudged his shiny bowler back on his head. "Actually, I'm here at the behest of the Texas and Pacific Railroad." He nodded toward the boardinghouse. "They're thinking of building a spur through here and, since I'm familiar with the area, they sent me to check things out."

She was grateful for the tray she held, which kept him from completely closing the gap between them. She scanned the crowd, searching for help. But why should anyone rescue her? They wouldn't know the terrible secret she'd kept so long. "Then you're not still selling shoes?"

He shook his head. "No, I moved on to bigger and better things a long time ago." He gave her a look that once would have set her heart to fluttering, but now only made her feel sick. "But I've never forgotten you, Nixie dear."

"Nixie, can I help you with something?" She breathed a sigh of relief at the sound of Jed's voice, and looked up to see him standing by her side. He looked pointedly at Norwich's hand, still resting on her shoulder. "Why don't you introduce me?"

"Um, this is Alan Norwich," Nixie choked out the introduction. "Mr. Norwich, this is Mr. Jedediah Hawkins."

Norwich removed his hand from her shoulder and took a step back. He clutched the lapels of his suit coat and gave Jed a sweeping look. "Ah yes, I heard. Single-handed small-town savior to hear Ham Dengler tell it. What do you do when you're not a . . . what was it, a carpenter?"

"I sell Great Caesar's Celebrated Curative. Perhaps you've heard of it?"

Norwich laughed. "One of those patent medicine tonics, isn't it?" His eyes widened. "Hey, I *do* know it. You must be related to Caesar Hawkins."

"He was my father."

Norwich barked another laugh. "Now there's a character for you." He winked at Nixie. "Fancied himself quite the ladies' man, old Caesar did. Had a girl in every town." He glanced at Jed again. "I see you take after the old man."

The words sailed past Nixie's numbed ears. She didn't care what he said; she only wanted him to leave.

"What are you doing here, Norwich?" Jed growled the words.

Norwich struck a pose, thumbs hooking his suspenders. "I work for the Texas and Pacific Railroad. We're thinking about building a spur to Welcome Springs."

Jed nodded. "Dr. Dengler mentioned something about that." She heard the tension in his voice and looked up. He was watching Norwich the way one would watch a snake stretched across a path.

"Of course, I jumped at the chance to come back to Welcome Springs for a visit," Norwich said. His smile was just short of a leer as he looked at Nixie again. "After all, I have such *fond* memories of the times I spent here before. I've been looking forward to renewing my acquaintance with Nixie here."

Every humiliating memory of the past washed over her in waves, shaking the calm she'd fought to maintain. Five years ago, a year ago even, she would have dissolved into tears and blamed herself for the way she felt. But today rage replaced guilt, and words boiled up to fill the silence.

"How dare you!" she roared. "How dare you pretend I could ever feel anything but *disgust* for a . . . a *liar* like you." She raised the heavy silver tray and hurled it at his chest, smashing the sticky cakes into the fine fabric of his suit.

Shaking, she stepped back. A hush fell over the crowd around them and she looked up at a sea of shocked faces. Jed touched her arm and she pulled away, not wanting to see the same shock in his eyes. "Nixie—" he began.

"I'm all right," she said, clenching her hands into fists to stop their shaking. "I'm fine. I'll . . . I'll just go freshen up. If you'll excuse me."

With as much dignity as she could muster, she forced herself to walk past Jed and past the stares of her family and friends. On legs that felt like lifeless pegs, she headed for the sanctuary of her bedroom, unshed tears choking her like a hand at her throat.

Chapter Seventeen

Jed stared after Nixie. He'd never seen her so upset. Watching her from across the yard, he'd sensed that something was horribly wrong. Her face had gone all gray, and she'd drawn back her shoulders as if she were flinching. He'd practically vaulted over the crowd in his haste to reach her side.

"I'll have you know I intend to send you the bill for this suit your lunatic girlfriend just destroyed." Jed looked back and saw Alan Norwich attempting to scrub the remains of the teacakes from his coat with a handkerchief. Pink and green and white frosting smeared in streaks on the fine wool fabric. Norwich glanced up from his efforts. "I always knew there was something not quite right about that girl. Women like that are only good for one thing—"

Jed grabbed him by the collar, twisting the fabric until Norwich gasped for breath, the black moustache jerking back and forth as he worked his mouth. Jed's first instinct was to beat the man until his face was a bloody pulp. Even then, his suffering wouldn't be enough to make up for the pain he'd caused Nixie.

One look at the mixture of terror and revulsion on Nixie's face and Jed had suspected Norwich was the drummer who had seduced her years before. The first leering gaze the man had cast toward Nixie confirmed the identification. Jed had known his type before. Once they'd taken a woman to bed, they assumed they had a lifelong claim to her. The thought of this vermin so much as touching Nixie made his skin crawl.

"Oh my dear. Is something wrong?" Nadine Dengler eased her way through the curious bystanders who had gathered around them. "Why did Nixie leave?"

Jed transferred his hold on Norwich from the throat to the drummer's arm. "Nothing to worry about," he said, watching Norwich's face. "Just an accident. Nixie tripped and spilled a tray of teacakes."

Norwich opened his mouth and Jed tightened his grip. He saw the flash of pain in the other man's eyes. "Er, yes, an accident," the drummer said in a strained voice.

Mrs. Dengler studied the two men for a moment before she nodded. "Well, Jed, you seem to have things under control here," she said. "I'd better go see about Nixie."

"No. I'll go." He shoved Norwich away, then stooped and picked up the fallen tray. "You stay and take care of your guests." He handed her the heavy silver piece.

This time, he didn't hesitate to climb the stairs to Nixie's room. To hell with the kind of people who'd see evil in anything Nixie could say or do. And to hell with anyone who'd try to keep him from comforting her now.

He paused outside her bedroom and knocked. The sound of her muffled sobbing echoed loudly in the still house. The pitiful noise made his heart ache. "Nixie, let me in," he called.

When she didn't answer, he opened the door and stepped inside. She lay across the bed, sobbing into a pillow. An agitated William marched up and down her back, twittering loudly. "Hello! Nanny goat!"

Jed sat on the edge of the bed. "Nixie, it's all right." She continued to cry, her tears soaking the pillows. Pain knotted in his chest as he watched her. If everything were truly "all right" then she wouldn't be weeping, would she?

"Come here." He reached out to gather her into his arms.

She rolled out of reach, curling herself into a ball with her back to him. William fluttered to the headboard, and glared at him. *Now what did I do?* Jed wanted to cry out in frustration.

He shook his head and tentatively placed one hand on Nixie's back. When she didn't pull away from his touch, he began smoothing his hand up and down in a soothing gesture. He traced the intricate bones of her spine with his palm, and felt her skin warm beneath his touch. If only he could reach her heart so easily.

"That was him, wasn't it?" he asked after a moment. "Norwich was the drummer you told me about—the one who seduced you when you were younger."

She nodded into the pillow. "When I saw him, it was as if I was nineteen all over again," she said, her voice breaking. "Hearing him tell me he was going away, listening to him say those awful things about me—"

He stilled his hand and leaned down until his mouth was next to her ear. "Listen to me. It doesn't matter now. It was a long time ago."

"It hurts like it was just yesterday," she sobbed. "How could I ever have been so stupid!"

"You weren't stupid. You were young and naive. There's a difference."

"I thought he *loved* me. I didn't know anything about love."

And what do you know about love now? he wanted to ask. *Have you learned anything from me?*

Do you love me, Nixie? He longed to whisper those words in her ear. But fear held his tongue. What if her answer was no?

He resumed rubbing her back. "Do you want me to run him out of town? Or maybe I should beat him within an inch of his life. Would that help you feel better?"

She rolled over to look up at him, and he managed a smile. "Shall I make him walk the plank, or should we coat him in tar and feathers and ride him out of town on a rail?"

She struggled to a sitting position, wiping her tears with the hem of the blanket. William fluttered to her shoulder and made soft cooing noises against her cheek. "No. Don't do anything. Don't attract any more attention to him than I already have. What if he said something more about me—about us?"

"Then he'll live to regret it," he said, menace in his voice.

"We should ignore him." She shook her head. "He won't stay long, I'm sure." She moved over to cradle her head against his chest. "But thank you for offering," she whispered.

He kissed the top of her head, sending William fluttering to the headboard once more. Easing his arms around her, he fought the urge to crush her to him. He wanted to banish every memory she had of Alan Norwich and replace them with a desire for him that would equal his love for her.

Brushing his lips against her damp cheeks, he tasted salt, and the chalk and perfume of her face powder. She sighed, her breath hot against his throat, warming him throughout. He clasped her head and tilted it back, until she was looking up at him. Her eyes still glittered with tears, but he recognized the spark of passion within the green-gold depths. Her pupils widened, and her lips parted, moist and inviting as the velvet petals of a flower to a bee.

He dipped his head and kissed her, plundering the recesses of her mouth with his tongue. He sought to brand her with his lips, to possess her as his and his alone.

There was only now, only Nixie, and the fierce longing to join together so that time and distance and everyday cares could never break them apart.

Nixie ended the kiss, though she continued to cling to him. Jed smoothed his hand down her side and thought of her bedroom door behind him. Did he dare get up and lock it?

"What did Alan mean, when he said you took after your father?"

The question jarred him, like a heckler intruding on his spiel. He pulled away enough to look down on Nixie's upturned face. He knew good and well what Norwich meant, that he was every bit the Casanova his father had been, but it wasn't true. "I suppose he meant I look like my father," he said slowly. He tried to make his voice more convincing. "Or maybe he meant I was like him on the stage. I learned everything I know about selling from him. People say he was the best and I'm following in his footsteps."

"Oh." She looked troubled. "I think you'd better go now." She pushed him away. "Before someone comes and finds us together like this."

So much for locking the door. He thought of arguing with her, but she was right. It wouldn't do either of them any good to take this any further. Especially since he was leaving.

The thought squeezed his heart like a giant hand. "Is there anything I can get you?" He stood and backed toward the door, unable to take his eyes from her.

She shook her head. "No. I'll just lie down a while. Alone."

He thought of all the nights he'd be lying alone from now on. *Nixie, stop me!* he wanted to cry out. *Don't let me go and leave us both miserable.* But, of course, she wouldn't stop him. She preferred misery to him.

He jerked open the door and marched down the hall with as much dignity as he could muster. He looked every bit the master of the situation, but inside he felt about three inches tall.

Nixie awoke the next morning with the stuffy-headed feeling of one who has cried too much, and then slept too long. She sat up in bed, clutching a pillow to her chest, and tried to come fully awake. William sang a cheerful melody.

She wished she felt half as cheerful. But the return of Alan Norwich cast a black pall over the day. His presence reminded her over and over again of how foolish she'd been to mistake lust for love, and casual endearments for eternal promises.

She threw back the covers and climbed out of bed. Maybe Alan would take care of his business in Welcome Springs quickly and move on. He was a painful reminder not only of the past, but of her bleak future.

Things might have been so different, she told herself as she took a clean pair of stockings from the drawer and sat on the edge of the bed to smooth them on. For a moment yesterday, when Jed had first raced to her rescue, and again when he'd come up to her room to comfort her, she'd dared to hope things might work out differently between them. But then he'd reminded her he belonged on the road, following in his father's footsteps. Leaving her behind.

Jed and Alan had more in common than she liked to admit. They were both handsome, flamboyant showmen, with a taste for travel and adventure. And both Alan and Jed had spent their lives avoiding commitment.

"A girl in every town." Her voice broke as she said the words. Alan had said Jed took after his father, who was a "ladies' man." Jed might think she was too innocent to know *that* was what Alan meant, and that *she* was the "girl" in Welcome Springs—for Alan, for Jed, for any smooth-talking man who might come along.

She stood and jerked a brush through her hair, then hastily pinned it up. "Well, Mr. Jed Hawkins and Mr. Alan Norwich have another think coming if they believe I'm going to fall for their lines again. I'm older now, and I'm definitely wiser."

Late for breakfast, she raced down the stairs and through the kitchen, almost colliding with Jed in the hall outside the dining room.

"Ah, you're up." He smiled at her, a breathtakingly handsome smile that made her weak in the knees despite her resolve to remain unaffected. "Ready for a big day?"

It took her a moment to realize what he was talking about. "The boarders. Of course, they're moving in today." She nodded. "What with everything else, I'd almost forgotten."

He put his hands on her shoulders and looked at her, eyes full of concern. "You're not still upset about Norwich?"

"Of course not." She raised her chin and assumed a disinterested expression. She didn't want to discuss Alan with Jed, or with anyone else. "He'll be leaving soon anyway."

"The sooner the better, as far as I'm concerned."

They entered the dining room just as everyone else was taking their seats. Nixie settled into the chair Jed held for her, then looked down the table to smile at Dory. What she saw made her gasp.

In Dinah Merchant's former place, at Dr. Dengler's left, sat Alan Norwich, dark hair shining with pomade, handlebar moustache waxed and curled. "Good morning, Nixie," he said. "You're looking lovely as ever this morning."

She looked away, unable to speak. It was bad enough, knowing Alan was in town again. She'd never expected to have to eat at the same table with him.

"Wasn't the party yesterday wonderful?" Dory exclaimed as soon as Dr. Dengler had ended the blessing.

"It looked as if half the county turned out to celebrate the opening of your new boardinghouse." Alan helped himself to a link of fried sausage. "Or maybe they just came to see all the pretty women you've surrounded yourself with."

To Nixie's dismay, he looked across the table at Dory and winked. The young woman blushed and fluttered her eyelashes. Nixie suddenly felt sick to her stomach. *No, Dory don't!* she wanted to shout.

"The Willkommen Inn is already an outstanding success," Dr. Dengler said. "All the rooms are rented and we're getting requests for more."

"Elspeth and I have decided to take up residence there ourselves," said Mr. Chapman. He smiled at his wife. "After all this time, the town feels like home to us."

"I'm thinking about laying out more campsites between the house and the inn," Dr. Dengler said. "If things work out, we plan to enlarge the bathhouses come spring." He attacked his sausage and eggs with a knife and fork. "Our little town is growing."

"That it is." Alan took a sip of coffee and looked around the table. "I have some wonderful memories of my visits here. It's good to be back."

"Were you with the railroad when you visited here before?" Mr. Chapman asked.

Alan shook his head. "No. I was a shoe salesman then. Floreham's Finest Shoes. I was with them for five years, then my uncle told me about this opportunity with the railroad. It seemed like the perfect job for a young man with no family, who likes to travel."

"How long has it been since you were through here last?" Dr. Dengler asked. "Five years?"

"Almost six." He scooped up a forkful of grits. "Hard to believe that much time has gone by, isn't it?"

"Well, I hope it won't be another six years before we see you again." Dr. Dengler laughed. "Why, at one time, I almost thought you'd end up one of the family. You were sweet on our Nixie, if I do recall."

Nixie choked on a mouthful of biscuit. Everyone turned to stare and she wished the floor would open up and swallow her.

Alan smiled, showing a mouth full of sharp white teeth. "Yes, I was quite fond of Nixie," he said. "I've thought of her often over the years, wondering if I made the right decision when I didn't come back, at least to visit."

"I'd say you made the right decision," Jed grumbled under his breath and scowled down the table at Alan.

"I must say, there doesn't appear to be any shortage of attractive young women in Welcome Springs." He smiled at Dory once more. "Perhaps there's something in the water. What do you think, Miss Evans?"

"Oh, I'm sure I wouldn't know, Mr. Norwich," Dory said.

Theo Stebbins cleared his throat and shifted in his seat. Nixie glanced at him and saw that his face was the red of a harsh sunburn, though his knuckles where he gripped his fork were a bloodless white. His eyes were fixed on Dory as she giggled and blushed at Alan Norwich's outrageous flirtations. But he said nothing.

Nixie laid aside her fork. Suddenly everything on her plate tasted bitter. She couldn't believe Dory was falling for Alan's phony charm. She was old enough to know better, yet she was simpering at him like a girl.

Like the girl I once was, Nixie thought.

She glanced across the table at Jed. His eyes practically snapped with sparks as he glowered at Alan. Nixie wouldn't have been surprised if the tablecloth had suddenly burst into flames from the heat of that glare.

But Alan seemed oblivious to either Nixie or Jed or Theo's discomfort. No one else noticed, either, since they were all looking at Alan, hanging on his every word.

"My superiors are very interested in the possibility of running a spur line through Welcome Springs," he said, polishing off a plateful of eggs and sausage and grits as he talked. "One of the officials got a hold of your flyer advertising the town. I think they have visions of bringing carloads of bathers here to take the waters."

"I have no doubt they would have plenty of business," Dr. Dengler said. "Why, hydrotherapy is the most modern method of treatment for a host of ailments, and I have chemical analysis to show the benefits of Welcome Springs water. And of course I, as a medical doctor, personally oversee the course of treatment of every person who comes here for purposes of improving their health."

"And don't forget the vacationers," Mr. Chapman added. "This is the perfect climate for year-round entertainment for the entire family."

"And we've had a number of inquiries from wealthier individuals from the northern states interested in spending the winter here," Dr. Dengler said.

Nixie began to feel dizzy from directing her attention back and forth between her father and Mr. Chapman and Alan. With every breath, their vision for Welcome Springs enlarged. She had not even had time to grow accustomed to the idea of the boardinghouse being open, and already they were talking of train cars full of tourists and streets full of rich Yankees. Fulfilling one dream apparently wasn't enough for her father. He'd already moved on to bigger fantasies.

Didn't he realize how dangerous such dreams were? What if people didn't flock to the town the way he envisioned? What if water therapy fell out of fashion? What if the railroad decided not to build the spur line?

She glanced at Alan. He sat listening to his host, a self-satisfied smile on his face. Her skin crawled to think that this man might have her family's future in his hands. With a few unfavorable words to his superiors at the railroad, he could dash her father's hopes.

Just as he had destroyed her own happy dreams those long years ago. She turned her eyes to Jed once more. When Alan had left, she'd thought she'd never marry. Who would want a woman who had given herself so freely to a man who was, after all, practically a stranger?

But mistakes in the past didn't seem to matter to Jed. He was a man who looked to the future. To the next town, the next show, the next sale.

Take me with you, she had the sudden urge to plead. *I don't want to be here to weather these changes alone. I just want to be with you.*

She looked away, a feeling of heaviness descending on her as if someone had handed her a lead weight. She couldn't go where she wasn't wanted. A wife, and possibly children, would be an anchor for a man who was used to traveling light. Better to stay with the home and family she knew. Whatever the future held for her and Welcome Springs, she'd have to struggle through and find her proper place in it. Just as Jed had to find his place, even if it was in a wagon rolling from town to town.

Caesar scowled at the newcomer in their midst, this interloper, this usurper, this Alan Norwich! Oh, he'd seen slick tricksters like him before, sly con men who exercised an oily-edged charm to gather a crowd around them. They cheated people out of their money, their property, their dignity—or all three—and slipped away under cover of darkness like the slimy snakes they were.

Caesar rubbed his hands together, his palms itching to grab Norwich up by the collar and pitch him into the nearest mud puddle. Preferably one pigs had been rolling in. He'd wipe that smirk off the odious man's face!

His scowl deepened as Norwich called to someone on the path up ahead. Caesar looked and saw Miss Evans greet the shyster with a beautiful smile. So ruining one woman wasn't enough for him, was it? Caesar groaned aloud. *"You wait until I find you alone, mister,"* he mumbled.

A door slammed and Caesar turned to see Jed striding across the yard toward the Willkommen Inn. *"Wait up there, Son,"* he called, hurrying after him. *"I want to talk to you about this Norwich fellow."*

"I don't have anything good to say about that weasel," Jed growled.

"My sentiments exactly. What I want to know is what are we going to do about it?"

Jed stopped in his tracks and glanced around the empty yard before addressing his father under his breath. "We aren't going to do anything."

"You don't mean you're going to let him carry on like this, upsetting dear sweet Nixie and who knows who else? Surely you don't want a man like that to get away without being punished."

"What I want is for you to stay out of this. You've gotten me in enough trouble already."

Caesar flinched at the harsh tone of his son's voice. *"What do you mean, I've gotten you into trouble?"* he asked. *"I've done nothing but try to help you since we came to Welcome Springs."*

Jed moved on toward the boardinghouse. "Did you hear what Norwich said to me when we met yesterday afternoon? When Nixie was standing right there?"

Caesar shook his head, then, remembering Jed couldn't see him, added, *"No. What did he say?"*

"He asked me if I was related to the Great Caesar Hawkins."

"Well of course he did. You should take that as a compliment, my boy. I—"

"He said you had quite a reputation as a ladies' man. That you had a girl in every town. And that I obviously took after you." Jed's voice crackled with anger. "He leered at Nixie like she was just another notch on my belt. As if because I was *your* son, I couldn't possibly have real feelings for her."

Jed's face was white with rage. Caesar shrank back. He'd never seen the boy like this before. As if . . . as if he *hated* his father. *"Now I'm sure Nixie is much too sensible a girl to believe such unfounded accusations. Perhaps if I spoke to her—"*

"You stay away from her!" Jed jabbed a finger in the air, about where Caesar's chest would have been, had he been standing in front of the boy, which he was not.

"I only thought—"

"Don't think! Don't *do* anything! Just go away and leave me alone!"

Caesar decided he'd come back later. When Jed could talk more reasonably. Though judging by his current state, that might be quite some time. Next month perhaps.

Caesar straightened and headed across the yard, toward where he'd last seen Alan Norwich and Dory Evans. He intended to make life very difficult for that two-legged python for the remainder of his stay in Welcome Springs.

It was the least he could do for Nixie. And for Jed, who still needed his father, whether he liked to admit it or not.

Chapter Eighteen

Jed paced the length of the Willkommen Inn's front porch. Exactly twenty-three and one-half paces. He knew because this was the third time he'd counted them off this afternoon.

"Jed, what are you doing?" Nixie paused in the open front door and looked out at him.

He stopped at the end of the porch and made a precise turn. "Nothing," he said. "Absolutely nothing." That, of course, was the problem.

"Well, goodness, you spent all morning taking down the speaker's dais and cleaning up the yard. Why don't you sit down and rest?"

He shook his head. "I'm not tired."

She shifted the thick ledger she was carrying onto her other arm. "Why don't you chop some firewood?"

"There must be two cords back there already."

"Maybe my father needs your help with something."

"He's visiting a patient."

Two men approached, carrying a large trunk between them. Nixie stepped aside to allow them to enter the house.

"I don't know what to tell you, then. I've got to get back to helping our boarders settle in. But please, stop pacing. You'll scare people off."

She moved back out of sight once more. He leaned against a porch post and looked out over the yard. It was as neat and orderly as he could make it. After months of work, the boardinghouse was complete, down to the last nail and hinge.

For the first time in memory, he had absolutely nothing he had to be doing at this moment. No show to prepare for, no spiel to perfect, no town to reach by sundown. The idleness was as uncomfortable as shoes that were three sizes too big.

After a few weeks in one place he was usually itching to get back on the road, to find what adventure lay over the next hill. But lately whenever he walked by the parked wagon, it was as if a cloud passed in front of the sun. The prospect of setting out alone held no attraction for him. After years of not knowing what it meant to have a home, he had finally found a place that fit the definition, and he was now compelled to leave it.

In any case, he wouldn't think of leaving until Alan Norwich was safely out of town.

The thought of the man made him curl his fingers into fists. He'd like nothing better than to wipe the leer off that scoundrel's face. It had been all Jed could do this morning at breakfast not to lunge over the table at the man when he'd started grinning at Nixie.

He shoved himself away from the post and ambled down the steps and into the yard. What he needed was something to take his mind off Norwich and Nixie and his approaching departure from Welcome Springs.

The front door of the Denglers' house opened and he spotted Theo Stebbins coming out. "Theo!" he called, hurrying toward him.

Theo looked up. "Oh, Jed. How are you?"

Jed mounted the steps to the Denglers' front porch. "Are you busy right now?" he asked.

Theo shook his head. "I was looking for Dory. Have you seen her?"

Jed shook his head. "Maybe she's swimming. Or she might have gone into town, shopping."

He nodded, his expression even more dejected. Jed clapped him on the shoulder. "What say we get up a game of Moon?"

"All right. Who will we get for a third?"

Jed looked around the yard, but there was no one else about. A movement on the far side of the campground attracted his attention. His eyes narrowed. "What about Norwich?" he asked, nodding toward the man who had stepped out from behind a buggy.

Theo scowled. "I don't much care for the man."

"Neither do I," Jed said. "But if we engage him in a game we can find out what he's up to—how long he intends to stay in town and all that."

Theo pondered this a moment, then nodded. "All right. I suppose forewarned is forearmed."

Norwich was polishing the harness on his buggy, buffing the metal buckles, then studying his own reflection in the mirrored surface. "Sorry, I can't play now," he said when Jed extended the invitation to join them in the domino game. "I'm getting ready for an assignation with a delectable female."

"Who?" Jed asked, wary.

Norwich grinned. "Why, Miss Evans, of course. You saw how she went for me at breakfast this morning, didn't you?"

"Dory!" Theo looked as if he were choking on the word, his face a vivid crimson.

Norwich nodded and fingered the end of his moustache. "Sort of a horse face I admit, but her figure's ripe enough, and I hear she's got loads of money." He leered. "I can always close my eyes when I'm making love to her."

"How dare you insult Dory that way! Why you—"

Jed grabbed Theo around the waist to keep him from launching himself at Norwich. The drummer took a step back and pulled a whip from its socket by the buggy's front seat. "Lay one hand on me, Stebbins, and you'll regret it."

"You'd better apologize for your remarks about Miss Evans or I'll see that *you're* the one with regrets," Jed said.

"And stay away from Dory!" Theo demanded, still straining against Jed's hold.

Norwich studied them both, seeming to weigh the cold anger in Jed's eyes and the barely controlled fury of Theo Stebbins. After a moment, he shrugged. "I'm sorry if I said anything offensive in regards to Miss Evans. As for whether or not I continue to see her, she's a grown woman, free to see whomever she pleases. Now if you'll excuse me, I have work to do."

Theo sagged against Jed's arm. Jed gave Norwich one last hard look, then turned away. "Let's get out of here," he said. He led the way around the back of the Dengler home, down the steps that led to the root cellar beneath the kitchen.

"Where are we going?" Theo asked as Jed swung open the heavy wooden doors leading into the cellar.

"I know where the good doctor keeps his beer." He climbed down into the cellar and grabbed two glasses from a shelf against the back wall. Crossing to a keg in the corner, he filled both glasses to the brim, then led the way out to a bench that encircled a thick-limbed oak.

He handed Theo one of the glasses, then took a long sip of the frothy dark brew. "Ahhhh. That's more like it," he said, resting his head against the tree trunk.

Theo sipped from his own glass. Both men were silent for a long while. Jed listened to the sounds of activity inside the Dengler kitchen: the muffled ring of pots and pans and the low murmur of women's voices. Further in the distance, children shouted and splashed in one of the springs. Sunlight filtered through the canopy of leaves overhead, dappling the bench and making him lazy with its heat.

"I guess I ought to thank you for saving me from making a fool of myself," Theo said, pulling Jed from a half-doze.

"What?" He took another sip of beer. "How is that?"

"I'm not much of a fighter. Norwich probably would

have killed me." He sighed. "I can't blame Dory for choosing a good-looking fellow like him."

Jed glanced at his friend. Theo was slumped against the tree trunk, his chin resting on his chest, staring into his half-empty glass of beer. "That's it?" he asked. "You're going to let her go that easily?"

Theo turned his head to look at Jed. "What else am I supposed to do?"

Jed looked away. "I guess you're right. After all, it's not as if there was anything serious between the two of you. You're probably better off without her."

"I love her."

Jed took another drink of beer.

"I love her," Theo repeated.

"And you told her that and she's still choosing Norwich over you?" Jed shook his head. "Women."

Theo slumped even lower. "I never told her." He took a long drink. "Why would she want me? I'm just a poor schoolteacher. I'm not handsome or witty or—"

"I suppose she told you that—about her wanting a man with money and looks and wit. Women usually take pains to point those things out to a man early in the relationship."

"She never said anything like that."

"She didn't strike me as the type who would." He set his empty glass on the bench beside him. "But I wouldn't be surprised if she weren't feeling pretty desperate now, what with her sister having run away and left her all alone. She might even decide to do the same and elope with Alan Norwich."

"She wouldn't!" Theo sat bolt upright.

"Women aren't exactly predictable. Or hadn't you noticed that?"

"I've got to find her." He drained his glass and jumped up from the bench. "I've got to talk to her."

Jed watched him hurry around the side of the house, but made no effort to rise and follow. A numbing lethargy had replaced his earlier agitation. Warm sun and beer and the labors of the morning left him in need of a nap. So he stretched out on the bench and shoved his hat down over his eyes and slept.

"Alan Norwich, I want a word with you!"

Caesar was pleased to see Norwich make a mess of knotting his tie and have to start all over when Caesar's "stage voice" boomed down from the ceiling of his room in the Willkommen Inn. "Who's there?" Norwich demanded, looking around the empty room.

"No friend of yours. I'm here to order you to leave this town at once."

"No one orders me around." His gaze continued to dart around the room. "Especially someone who's not man enough to come out and face me."

The nerve of the man! *"I'm more of a man than you are!"* Caesar huffed. He drifted down from the ceiling to stand behind Norwich. *"Don't think I don't know your type—preying on innocent young women. You ought to be run out of town on a rail. I ought to do it myself."*

"You and what army?" Norwich's expression relaxed. "Is that you, Hawkins?" He craned his neck to look behind the wardrobe. "What is it, some kind of trick built into the rooms, like those speaking tubes in fancy hotels?"

"If you are referring to Jedediah Hawkins, I am not him. And this is no trick. I'm right behind you."

Norwich turned, slowly, as if he could care less what anyone said or thought. "Then why can't I see you?"

Caesar wished he could wipe that smug expression off the scoundrel's face. *"I suffer from the effects of a rather unfortunate accident. But I am as capable as ever of teaching you manners."*

Norwich barked a laugh. "This act's so funny you ought to take it on the road." He turned back to the mirror and began adjusting his tie once more. "I haven't got time to discuss this with you now. I've got an important rendezvous with a certain rich miss."

Caesar ground his teeth together. Of all the impertinent— *"You'll have to change your plans."* He opened the wardrobe and swept all the conniver's clothes from the rod.

They landed in a heap on the bed, a fine linen shirt on top slithering to the floor. Caesar stepped on it, grinding it into the carpet.

But Norwich didn't seem to notice the shirt. He stared at the suits on the bed, face slack. Then his mouth shaped into a scowl. "You'd better watch it, Hawkins." He picked up an armful of suits and returned them to the wardrobe, pausing for a moment to examine the rod. "What did you do—fix this up with some kind of spring?" He nodded. "I know about you carnival types."

Being run out of town was too good for the man. He ought to be horsewhipped! Caesar flung open the wardrobe again, almost wrenching the doors from their hinges, and hurled the suits to the floor.

Norwich flinched, but continued to smooth his hair with a comb. "I'll deal with you later. I don't have time for your fun and games now. And don't think you can outsmart me. I know every trick in the book."

Norwich never even looked back when he left the room. Caesar was tempted to pitch the clothing out the window after him, but what good would it do? Norwich obviously had visions of Dory's money buying him all the clothes he'd ever need. Some might say the man was fearless; Caesar preferred to think him too big a fool to be afraid.

He sank down onto the bed. Was he reduced to this, then? Dismissed as a mechanical trick, useless to everyone, including his own son?

He straightened. *"I am the Great Caesar Hawkins."* But the words had a hollow ring to them. What good was greatness if he lost everything else that mattered? An unaccustomed pain clutched at his chest, and a black cloud hovered over his spirits that even Great Caesar's Celebrated Curative could not dispel.

"I'm sorry to bother you, but I remembered that you had some ribbon that would make the perfect trim for this hat." Dory stood in the hallway outside Nixie's room, a straw bonnet and a bunch of silk flowers in her hands. "I know you're terribly busy with your work at the inn, but I'll only keep you a minute."

"Nonsense. I'm ready for a break." Nixie took her friend's hand and pulled her inside. "I was about to go down to the kitchen and fix a cup of tea. Do you want to join me?"

"No, I can't stay long. I'm in a rush to get this hat fixed before supper."

"Oh? Why is that?" Nixie pulled open the top drawer of her dressing table and rummaged among the handkerchiefs and hat pins and fans for the length of ribbon.

Dory sat on the end of the bed. "I'm meeting someone after supper." She paused, then added. "A man."

Nixie watched her friend in the mirror. Dory's eyes were bright with excitement, and she clasped her hands together like a young girl trying to hold on to a secret she couldn't wait to reveal. "Who?" Nixie asked, turning around.

"Alan Norwich." Dory grinned. "Can you believe someone as handsome as him asked me to go out with him?"

Nixie's knees no longer had the strength to hold her. She sank down on the stool in front of the dressing table. "Where are you going?" she asked weakly.

Dory shrugged. "Out for a drive. But I want to look my best." She held out her hand for the ribbon.

Nixie refused to relinquish the strip of satin. "Dory, no! Not Alan Norwich. You mustn't go out with him."

Dory's smile faded. "Why not? He's a perfectly nice man."

"Oh, but he isn't," Nixie blurted. She shook her head. "He really isn't a nice man."

"How can you say that?" Dory frowned. "Or is it because he used to be sweet on you? I never thought you'd be the type to be jealous of an old beau."

"It's not that." Nixie twisted the bit of ribbon in her hands. What would persuade Dory to abandon the idea of going out alone with Alan? "You don't know Alan like I do," she said. *He seduced me and made me believe he would marry me and then said awful things and abandoned me,* she thought. But the shameful words stuck in her throat.

Dory looked away. "He's handsome and he's charming. Why shouldn't I enjoy an evening in a handsome, charming man's company if I want to? Or is that something only pretty, young women get to do?"

Nixie flinched at the hurt tone of Dory's words. She tried a different tack. "What about Theo?"

Dory sniffed. "What about him? He obviously doesn't care two cents for me or he would have said so by now. He was just using me. Well, a woman can play that game as well as a man."

She let her hands lie still in her lap. "What are you saying?"

"I'm saying I can enjoy myself with a man without expecting anything in return. Why not? Men do it with women all the time."

She gasped. "Dory, you don't know what you're saying."

Dory stood and looked down on Nixie, her face a mask of unhappiness. "What do you know about it?" she asked, her voice trembling. "You're so pretty and you have a wonderful family and a handsome man who's obviously crazy about you. You don't know what it's like to look into the future and see nothing but loneliness. Why shouldn't I take my chance for a little happiness when I can find it?" She turned away. "Just leave me alone. I don't need your advice or your stupid ribbon."

She rushed out the door. "Dory, don't leave," Nixie called, going after her.

But Dory fled the room, her feet pounding along the hall and down the stairs. Nixie sank onto the bed, sick to her stomach. *I should have told her what happened to me,* she thought. *Why didn't I speak up when I had the chance?*

She lay back on the pillow and closed her eyes. Jed was the only one who knew the truth about her relationship with Alan Norwich. She'd had no trouble confiding in him. But now, when it mattered most, stubborn pride sealed her lips.

She opened her eyes and stared at the cluttered dressing table. The desperate look on her friend's face was burned into her mind. *Maybe it's not too late*, she thought. *Maybe I can still do something to save Dory from making the same mistake I once made. And this time, I won't hold back from saying what needs to be said.*

Jed lit the gas burner and dumped a tin of stew into a pot. The gray mess didn't exactly make his mouth water. Sighing, he poked at a supposed potato with his fork. Guess this was his penalty for sleeping through the supper bell at the Denglers. Either Dr. Dengler's beer was stronger than he'd supposed, or he'd been working harder than he thought.

A pounding on the door shook the whole wagon. He hurried to answer it and found Nixie on the steps, agitation pinching her face. "What is it?" he asked, immediately alarmed.

"Jed, you've got to help me." She stepped inside without waiting for his invitation.

"What is it? What's wrong?" He smoothed his hands along her arms, puzzled. The fact that she didn't draw away from him spoke of the depth of her distress.

"It's Dory. She's going out driving with Alan Norwich this evening. We have to stop her."

He dropped his hands. "Last I checked, Dory was a grown woman. It's not our place to interfere in her life."

"But she doesn't know what Alan is up to. I do." She turned away, wringing her hands. "Dory thinks this is an innocent little buggy ride. I know better."

She began to pace the length of the small room. "I talked to her this afternoon. She's still upset about Dinah running away, and she's all but given up on Theo ever declaring himself." She stopped and looked at Jed, her eyes filled with pain. "She feels like there's nothing to look forward to but loneliness for the rest of her life. A woman who feels that way will take chances—chances that won't lead to anything but hurt with a man like Alan."

She spoke about Dory, but Jed knew the words came straight from Nixie's heart, like arrows sent out to strike him where it hurt the most. He could see plain enough that

Nixie would never forgive herself if she didn't help her friend. And if he didn't help her . . . Well, he wouldn't be very good company for himself for the next few months or years.

"What do you want me to do?" he asked.

"Let's get your horses and follow them. If nothing happens between them, then fine. But if Alan tries to pressure Dory into anything she might later regret, we can interrupt."

"Don't you think that will look suspicious?" he asked. "Norwich and Dory will both be angry if they think we followed them."

"We can say we were out for a ride."

"At night?"

"We're supposed to be courting. We can say we thought a moonlit ride would be romantic."

He raised one eyebrow. "Don't you think your parents would object?"

"Why should they? They never objected to my going out with Alan."

If they had, they wouldn't be in this mess now. But that was another story. "Can you ride?"

"Some. And Mr. Carruthers at the livery stable will lend us a sidesaddle."

Jed shook his head. "What if I say the idea's crazy and we should stay home and mind our own business?"

She raised her chin and fixed him with a solemn look. "Then I'll go by myself."

She meant it, too. She'd ride off like the devil after Norwich without a thought for herself. Jed loved her even more that moment than he had before. "All right. I'll go with you. Change clothes and I'll meet you back here in fifteen minutes."

Half an hour later, Jed followed Nixie as she led the way around the side of the livery stable. She had traded the white dress for a brown riding skirt and jacket and covered her hair with a tartan scarf. Though she'd drawn back when confronted with one of the big grays he used to pull his wagon, she'd refused his offer to take her back home. "I can do this," she said, as she stepped onto the mounting block and swung up into the sidesaddle.

"How do you know they'll even come this way?" he asked, as she looked down the road leading back toward the boardinghouse.

"They will."

She had hardly finished speaking when they heard the distant rumble of buggy wheels and a horse's hooves. And then a vehicle appeared on the horizon. "That's them," Nixie said.

"How do you know?"

"I can see Dory's hat, and I recognize the dress."

Indeed a woman's white dress glowed against the dark upholstery of the open-fronted buggy. As the vehicle drew nearer, Jed could make out Dory's face, and Alan Norwich's moustache.

He and Nixie drew back into the shadows beside the livery stable as the buggy passed. "Now what?" Jed asked. "How are we going to keep up with them without being seen?"

"Follow me." She nudged her horse forward, and turned in the opposite direction the buggy had traveled.

"What are you doing?" he asked as they swung onto a riding path leading into the hills. "We'll lose them."

"I know where they're going."

"How—" Jed bit off the words as realization settled over him like a dash of ice water. Nixie was taking him to the place where she and Alan had gone to . . .

He swallowed and gripped the reins until his knuckles whitened. The thought of Norwich and Nixie . . . of his hands on her satin skin . . . of his mouth . . . Anger clawed at Jed, choking off breath and clouding his vision. He cursed the day Alan Norwich had ever heard of Welcome Springs. The sooner the man was run out of town, the better.

He spurred his horse to catch up with Nixie. If only he could chase the memories from her head as easily as he could banish the man.

• • •

GREAT CAESAR'S GHOST

Nixie clung to the saddle horn, concentrating on staying on the horse as it climbed the rocky path over the hill. The moon bathed the landscape in silver, making the streaks of quartz running through the rocks sparkle like diamonds. Tall plumes of bear grass rustled in the night breeze, which carried the faint perfume of blooming sage.

Any other night, Nixie would have found the scene enchanting. But tonight, her stomach was in knots, her heart pounded with fear. She was nineteen all over again, riding in Alan Norwich's buggy for the first time. She had been more excited than afraid then, feeling reckless and daring to be sneaking out of the house without her parents' knowledge—alone with a handsome, charming man.

Even when Alan had put his hands where he shouldn't, and begun to unfasten her clothes, she had told herself it was what she wanted. She wanted to know what went on between a man and woman. Even so, in the back of her mind, she had known what was happening to her was not quite right. It was not what love ought to be like.

Alan had been a skillful enough lover. He had made sure she experienced as much physical pleasure as he could give her, though later he'd condemned her for daring to express her pleasure. For years, she'd blamed herself for failing to supply the mysterious missing ingredient to that first lovemaking.

She'd been shocked to discover how different things were with Jed. His tenderness and passion had touched her somewhere deep within, so that when they came together, it was more than a physical joining, but more like the union of two spirits.

With Alan, it had been as if she'd just been wading at the edge of a pool, enjoying the coolness of the water and thinking that was all there was to it. With Jed, she had dived to the depths, surrounding herself with the silken water and coming to know its magical ability to sooth her soul.

The horses began to ascend the hill and Nixie saw the grove of trees that was their destination. Slowing her horse, she signaled Jed to ride up beside her. "There's a clearing in the center of those trees," she said. "We'll hide on the edge of it and watch from there."

Jed swung down off his horse, then helped Nixie dismount and led the way down the path to the edge of the trees. They tied the horses, then started into the grove.

The thick growth of oak and cedar shut out almost all the moonlight, and they had to feel their way through the trees. Without a word, Jed took her hand and led the way. She was thankful for his firm handclasp, lending strength to shore up her shaky courage.

"We can watch from here," he said, halting as the undergrowth gave way to the leaf-carpeted clearing.

She leaned against the sloping trunk of an oak, and stared into the clearing. Nothing about it looked familiar, but then she'd hardly been concentrating on the scenery back then.

Jed brought his hand up to caress her shoulder and she fought the urge to lean back against him. It would be so easy to surrender everything to him. But then, giving in to those feelings had gotten her in this mess in the first place.

"I think they're coming now," he whispered.

The buggy rolled slowly into the clearing, leather creaking and traces jingling. Nixie held her breath as Dory half-turned in her seat to look around. "It's beautiful," Dory said, her voice carrying clearly in the still air. "Like a secret room in the woods."

"Romantic, isn't it?" Alan said. "The perfect place for two people to get to know each other better."

Nixie flinched at the sound of the familiar words. Jed squeezed her shoulder.

Alan did the same with Dory, who gave a cry of surprise as he lowered his head and kissed her.

Nixie stiffened, but Jed held her back. "He hasn't done anything yet," he whispered, his mouth very close to her ear. "Dory looks as if she might like it."

Indeed, Dory had put her hands on Alan's shoulders but was not pushing him away. He raised his head and Nixie heard his low chuckle. "That's a nice start isn't it?" he said. He brought his hand up to caress her cheek. "Has anyone told you what absolutely gorgeous eyes you have?"

GREAT CAESAR'S GHOST

Nixie could not make out Dory's comment, but Alan replied by pulling her close once more. This time his kiss was less gentle, more forceful. Dory squirmed in his arms, pushing him away.

"Oh come now." Alan laughed. "Don't be shy. You know you want it." He pulled her toward him once more.

Nixie struggled also, to free herself from Jed's grip. "He's hurting her!" she cried.

But before Nixie could act, a great crashing in the bushes across from them drew their attention. Alan and Dory froze as a man on horseback bolted from the screen of trees and narrowly missed colliding with the buggy.

Chapter Nineteen

Theo!" Dory gasped as Mr. Stebbins fought to control his excited mount. She drew further away from Alan. "What are you doing here?"

Theo succeeded in calming his horse, then reached into his coat and withdrew a pistol. "Get out of that buggy, Norwich, and leave Miss Evans alone."

"Theo, put that gun away." Jed stepped out of the clearing, Nixie following on his heels.

Dory stood and looked at the new arrivals. "This seems to be a popular gathering place," she said drily. She turned to Theo once more. "What do you think you're doing?"

Theo straightened and took a firmer grip on the gun. "I won't see you hurt by the likes of him," he said. "You're too much of a lady for a . . . a scoundrel like him."

Dory raised her chin and glared at him. "What difference does it make to you what happens to me?"

"I . . . I care for you a great deal," he said.

She put her hands on her hips. "You have a strange way of showing it."

Alan reached up and put his hand on her arm. "Dory, perhaps we should be leaving," he said.

She frowned at him and shook off his hand. "Not yet. Theo and I have things we need to discuss."

Theo lowered the gun to his side and glanced around, as if aware for the first time that Jed and Nixie had joined them. He cleared his throat. "Perhaps we should continue this conversation another time—" he began.

"No. We can discuss it now. I'm tired of waiting. I've waited twenty-seven years to meet the right man for me. I've waited weeks and weeks for you to make up your mind. I'm not waiting any longer."

For once, Theo's face lost its characteristic flush. "What are you saying?"

She took a deep breath. "I'm saying if you want to marry me, Theo Stebbins, then you'd better say so now. Or tomorrow I'm packing my bags and buying a ticket away from here." She sniffed and raised her hand to dash away a tear. "You'll never see me again."

Theo swallowed hard and looked around the clearing. "I didn't think," he began. "That is—"

Jed walked up and slapped him on the leg. "The man is supposed to do the proposing, so get on with it."

He nodded and offered the gun to Jed, who took it. Then Theo swung down off his horse and walked up to the buggy. Dory sat and he took her hand. "Miss Evans, will you marry me?" he asked, his voice loud and clear, ringing through the clearing.

"Yes!" She shouted her answer and enveloped him in a hug.

Nixie cheered and threw her arms around Jed. Alan Norwich scowled and looked away.

Holding Nixie's hand, Jed walked over to Norwich and glared up at him. "I'd say your business in Welcome Springs is about finished, wouldn't you?" he said.

Norwich looked at Nixie, who forced herself to meet his gaze. Standing here, with Jed's hand firmly clasping hers, she found her old lover no longer had the power to wound her with a disdainful stare or snide remark. "Good-bye, Alan," she said.

He touched a finger to his hat brim and nodded, then turned and gathered up the buggy reins. Theo helped Dory out of the buggy, and the two couples stood together, watching as Alan Norwich drove away.

"Congratulations!" Nixie cried, embracing Dory.

Jed pumped Theo's hand. "Yes, congratulations. I know you two will be very happy together."

Theo grinned and nodded. "Well, I guess I'd better take Dory home now." Theo swung up behind the saddle of his horse and Jed made a step with his hands and helped Dory into the saddle. The couple set off on the path for town.

When Theo and Dory were out of sight, Nixie turned to walk back through the trees to their horses. Jed wanted to stop her, to pull her into his arms and tell her she was beautiful. He wanted to kiss her. But he was afraid those things would echo Norwich's insincerities too much. So he kept silent and waited for her to speak.

She didn't say a word until they arrived back at his wagon and she was untying the scarf from her head. "When will you be leaving us?" she asked.

When. Not "Will you?" but "When will you?" The words fell on his ears like brickbats. He stared at her numbly. "Do you want me to go?"

She turned so that he couldn't see her face in the shadows. "I don't see how I have anything to do with it."

You have everything to do with it. But the words clung to his tongue like felt.

She stepped back and looked up at the wagon. Moonlight splashed across her face, washing it porcelain white, silvering her hair. "Great Caesar's Medicine Show," she read. "Great Caesar Hawkins, proprietor." Her gaze darted to him. "You ought to get that sign changed. Since it's your show now. You don't want to go misleading your public." She stepped back into the shadows. "I'd better be going now."

He stood there, struck dumb and immobile, as she turned and headed up the path toward the house. He was about to turn and go inside when she called to him. He looked up and saw her waiting at the first curve in the path. "Thanks for helping me tonight," she said. "I know you didn't have to but . . . I was glad to have you there."

Then she was gone, slipping into the shadows, only her softly fading footsteps reminding him she was more than a figment of his fevered imagination.

Inside the wagon, he hunted for the bottle of brandy, stumbling over the crates of Curative as he searched. The bottles chimed together in discordant notes. He stared down at them, remembering the first day he'd met Nixie, and the way she'd looked, holding up the bottle on his stage, taunting him with it.

"It's my show now," he whispered, echoing her words to him. Seizing a bottle of Curative, he stared at the ornate lettering. He'd learned to read by picking out the words on this label. Before he was tall enough to see over the table he'd helped his father wash old bottles and paste on labels. While other children memorized nursery rhymes and Bible verses, Jed had labored to learn his part in Caesar's varying medicine shows. He'd preached the benefits of Great Caesar's Celebrated Curative from New Orleans to Ozona, until he could recite his spiel in his sleep. He'd devoted his whole life to the contents of this little bottle and for what?

The truth shook him like a revelation. Replacing the bottle in its slot, he hoisted the crate to one shoulder and carried it out of the wagon and down the path to the springs. He didn't dare wait a moment longer.

Caesar was awakened by the sound of splashing water and the conviction that something was terribly wrong. Foreboding drove him, heart pounding, to the wagon to look for Jed, but the brightly painted vehicle sat empty. He hovered just inside and again heard the sound that had awakened him. Definite splashing, like water being poured out of a bottle. Water or . . .

Caesar flew toward the sound, away from the campground down the path to the springs, to the light of a single lantern set on the rocks beside the lower pool. Even from a distance, he recognized Jed standing there, arm outstretched, emptying bottle after bottle of Great Caesar's Celebrated Curative into the water.

"What are you doing?" Caesar rushed toward his son, hands outstretched as if to catch the precious tonic in his fingers. *"Why are you wasting the Curative? Is there something wrong with the batch?"*

Jed looked up. The lantern light cast harsh shadows over his face, deepening the lines around his mouth, hollowing his eyes, and lending a grimness to his expression that surely Caesar only imagined. "There's nothing wrong with it. Except that this is your dream, not mine."

Caesar gaped at him. *"Everything I've done. All my work. My whole life means nothing to you?"* His voice rang with anguish. The Curative splashed across his palms, cool and slightly sticky. The perfume of it hung in the mist around them.

"It's your work." Jed set an empty bottle aside, picked up another and uncorked it. "It was a great work. But I have to find my own great work now."

"I gave you my work to carry on."

Jed shook his head. "I'm sorry, Papa." His voice grew softer. "It . . . it wasn't enough."

Caesar sank onto a nearby rock, too weak to stand. He watched as Jed emptied bottle after bottle of Curative into the water. He'd only wanted the best for the boy—his whole life he had worked to make Great Caesar's Medicine Show truly great so that he could pass on something his son would be proud of. He'd tried to give Jed his passion for selling the Curative, instead of letting him go to find his own passion.

He closed his eyes and brought his fingers to his nose, inhaling deeply the scent that was like his own life's blood draining from those bottles. He was losing the Curative, but worse, he was losing Jed. How would he ever get him back?

Nixie slept fitfully, disturbed by dreams of Jed. He'd looked so bereft when she'd left him last night. Twice she'd started to go back to him, but stopped herself in time. What good would it do to make a fool of herself with him again? Better to let him go without making a fuss.

She rose and went through the motions of getting dressed. "Hello! I love you," William chirruped when she uncovered his cage.

I love you. Three simple words. But not so simple in their meaning, or their importance. Since their first night together, Jed had never uttered them again.

And why should he? she thought, staring at her face in the mirror. Dark shadows rimmed her eyes and lines of tension creased her forehead. What kind of a wife would a small-town spinster like Nixie Dengler be for a showman like Jedediah Hawkins?

She went down to breakfast, but the empty chair across from her seemed to mock her. She tried hard to smile and join in congratulating Dory and Theo, but she was grateful when the meal was over.

After breakfast, Dory waylaid her outside the dining room, and wrapped her in a perfumed hug. "I'm so happy this morning, I could burst," she announced.

Nixie wondered if she could somehow borrow some of that happiness for herself. "Come into the front parlor and tell me about your plans," she said, leading the way to the little room.

"Theo is looking into a teaching position here in Welcome Springs," Dory said as she settled beside Nixie on the horsehair sofa. "Won't it be wonderful if we can stay here? We've set the wedding date for two weeks from today. That's enough time for Theo's parents to travel here. Oh, Nixie, I can hardly wait."

"I'm very happy for you," Nixie said sincerely. She shook her head. "When I think of you going off with Alan Norwich—"

"I was only hoping to make Theo jealous." Dory grinned. "And it worked. He teases me about proposing to him, but I had to do *something*. Theo's so shy, if I hadn't come out and said something, I might still be waiting on him. Instead, I'm planning a wedding." She sighed contentedly. "I guess sometimes a woman has to come right out and ask for what she wants."

"Hmmmm." *And what if the woman isn't sure what's best for her?* Nixie wondered.

"Come on, I want you to help me pick out some things for the wedding," Dory took her hand. "I've got so much to do."

Thinking the distraction might lift her spirits, Nixie spent the morning with Dory, combing the shops in town for material and trim for a wedding gown. They consulted with Mrs. Frisco about what flowers she thought would be available, and asked Mr. Hodgkins to stock up on confectioner's sugar so there'd be plenty for the wedding cake.

By the time they returned to the house, they'd missed lunch. Dory went in search of Theo, to show him her purchases. Nixie laid down and took a nap. She woke feeling worse than ever and only picked at her supper. The chair across from her was empty once more and the general uneasiness she'd been feeling all day edged toward panic. She couldn't recall Jed ever before missing all his meals with the Denglers. After all, a man had to eat.

After supper, she decided to go for a swim. A dip in the springs would be the best thing to soothe her frayed nerves and on the way she could walk by Jed's wagon.

Just to make sure he was all right.

She had absolutely no intention of stopping.

She thought at first her eyes were playing tricks on her as she approached the campground. But as she hurried closer, she saw that the space where Jed's wagon had sat all summer was empty. The cold fire ring and a rectangle of dead grass were the only evidence of its time there.

Heart in her throat, she stared down at the shallow indentations where the wagon wheels had once rested. Surely Jed had not left already? How could he leave them without saying good-bye? Tears stung her eyes, but she blinked them back. She wouldn't give way here in the open. She wouldn't let everyone see that she'd foolishly given her heart to a man who had no use for her. Better to let her tears mingle with the waters of the springs, which had eased so many sorrows over the years.

The sun had already set, and the air had the sting of fall in it. Though the water of the springs remained the same temperature no matter the time of day or season of the year, most people stayed away from the water during the evening hours. In the cool darkness the public pools became her private refuge.

So she was surprised to see an old man shuffling toward her on the path. She didn't recognize the hunched figure, but perhaps he was newly arrived in town, come to visit the healing waters. He certainly looked in need of medicine. He was paler than any man she'd ever seen, and he looked exhausted. "Sir, are you all right?" she asked as they met on the path.

He looked up at her and smiled. A smile that sent a shock of recognition through her. As if she'd seen it somewhere before . . .

"Ah child. Going for a swim, are you?" He nodded at the towel draped over her arm. *"All alone?"*

The words sounded so forlorn. *Alone. All alone.* "I like to swim in the evenings when it's quiet," she said.

He nodded. *"I thought you were looking for someone. A young man perhaps?"*

"What made you think that?"

"Oh, every pretty young woman should have a young man. Especially one as pretty and sweet as you." He leaned toward her, eyes searching her face. *"Tell me child, are you in love?"*

Was she? Her heart pounded in answer. What a strange question.

He didn't wait for an answer. *"I've been in love,"* he said. *"The real thing. It was a long time ago, but I still remember. We were married, but she died young and left me with a son to raise."* His gaze, which had drifted away as he spoke, focused on her again. *"You haven't answered me yet—are you in love?"*

She looked away. What harm would it do to tell this old

grandfather the truth? "I think I am—but I've made a terrible mistake."

"A mistake? What kind of mistake?"

"I . . . I didn't speak up and tell my love, and now it's too late." The truth of her words settled like rocks in her stomach. How many times had others advised her to speak her mind, and yet she'd held back, until there was no time left to say what she needed to say—that she loved Jed, and wanted to be with him.

"Nonsense. It's never too late."

"It is for me. He's gone." Her voice choked on the last words. She swallowed hard, afraid of embarrassing herself completely by bursting into tears.

"Gone?" The old man frowned.

"His . . . his wagon is gone. He must have left earlier today." She shook her head. "It doesn't matter. I'm not the right person for someone like him."

He took a step toward her. *"But you're perfect!"*

She supposed he was only being sweet, though he sounded so sure. "No. He needs someone—more exciting and flamboyant. Someone who could be famous."

"You could be famous." He nodded, seeming so definite.

"I thought so once but . . ." She looked down at the towel folded across her arm. "I just want to be me. Not a dutiful daughter or a proper young lady, but me. Nixie."

He looked thoughtful. *"I suppose that's the best any of us can do. Be ourselves."* He rubbed his grizzled chin. *"Excuse me, dear. I have to go now. I'd better hurry. I have to catch someone before it's too late."*

He hurried past her. She looked back over her shoulder after him. "What a strange old man," she thought. He'd seemed so . . . familiar somehow. She shook herself and went on down the path toward the pool.

Jed pocketed the money from the sale of the wagon and the horses and turned toward the new mare he'd just purchased. He'd bought some camping gear from Mr. Hodgkins and would put together more of what he needed later.

"So it's true then. You are leaving."

He turned and saw his father standing by the stable door. Really *saw* him, for the first time in a long time. Great Caesar looked much the same, though a little paler. Older perhaps. Not as . . . Great. The thought touched him, that a man he'd always thought of as invincible might have a few weak spots. "Hello, Papa."

"I stopped by to say good-bye."

Caesar smiled at him. Jed couldn't help but return the look. He hadn't realized how much he'd longed to see his father's smile again. "Aren't you coming with me?"

"No. I have someplace else I ought to be. Someplace I'm long overdue for, really. But first, I have to give you this." He held out a scroll, tied with a bit of blue ribbon.

"What is it?" Jed asked as he took the paper.

"It's the formula for Great Caesar's Celebrated Curative."

What was the old man up to this time? Wary, Jed unrolled the scroll and read words that were familiar to him from before, except for one change at the end. He looked up at his father. "Passionflower?"

Caesar nodded. *"The secret ingredient."*

And as common as thorns. Why, Mrs. Frisco had them growing up one side of her house. "Why didn't you tell me before?"

Caesar looked at the ground. If an old man could be said to hang his head like a boy, then that's what he did. *"Because I'm a very foolish old man."*

Jed rolled up the scroll. He didn't have it in him to be angry anymore. Not over this. "How come I can see you now?" he asked.

Caesar shrugged. *"Maybe because you need to see me."* He straightened and looked him in the eye, with that clear blue gaze Jed had both dreaded and craved as a child. Dreaded because it meant he was about to be on the receiving end of one of his father's many lectures. Craved because for that time at least, he would have his hero's undivided attention. *"There's one other thing,"* Caesar said. *"I know you don't want to hear it, but I have to say it. I want you to listen."*

Jed stuck the scroll inside his coat. "I'm listening."

"Don't pass up a chance for happiness with Nixie." He reached out and clasped Jed on the shoulder. *"She's at the springs now. Go to her."* He cocked his head, a faint smile on his lips. *"I have to go now. Good-bye son. I . . . Well, you know I always loved you. Always will."* He began to fade, until he was no more than a silvery shimmer in the air. *"Yes Mona, I'm coming dear."*

And then he was gone. Jed knew he'd never see him again. He was on his own now. Alone. He thought of what his father had said—about Nixie and about mistakes. He'd never be the showman his father was, or the smooth charmer, or even the skilled herbalist with a knack for concocting tonics and remedies. But he could say he had his father's will and the drive to go after his dreams. Maybe Nixie was part of that dream.

He knew one thing. He couldn't leave without finding out for sure.

A single lantern cast a circle of light into the water, dancing and shimmering with the pulsing current of the springs. Jed moved toward the light, the crunch of gravel beneath his feet echoing in the still, humid air. His heart pounded in rhythm with his steps as he set his lantern next to the other and stepped back to wait.

At first he didn't see Nixie. Then she moved out of the darkness, swimming toward him. She cut through the water with silent, sure strokes. When she reached the shallows, she stood, water streaming from her unbound hair, flowing over the curves of her body like a loving caress.

He held his breath, paralyzed by love and desire and awe. Was this really Nixie, or some goddess from the deep, come to possess him, body and soul?

"I thought you'd left," she said.

"I had to come back."

She pushed damp hair back from her face and studied him, indecision in her eyes. "Why?"

Don't be afraid he wanted to tell her. *I've got enough fear inside me for both of us.* But he didn't say anything.

He sat down on the damp stone edging the pool and began to untie the laces of his boots.

She stared at him. "What are you doing?"

"I want you to teach me to swim."

He waited for her to say something, anything to bolster his fading courage, to let him know he was right to take this risk.

Instead, she climbed up out the water and knelt beside him, pushing his clumsy hands away. She removed his shoes, and his socks, then stood and took his hand and led him toward the water.

At the first sensation of wetness against his toes, he hesitated, fear colder than the water paralyzing him. But her warm grasp pushed back the fear. She tugged at his hand and he moved forward until he was almost up to his knees in the pool. She stopped and looked back at him. "Are you nervous?"

The water was soaking his pants, weighing him down. The constant current nudged him, lapping at the back of his legs. He could imagine himself falling, pulled under by the weight of his wet clothing and the force of the current, sinking beneath the dark water. He swallowed and nodded. "Yes."

She turned and put her hands on his shoulders and looked up at him. "I'm afraid sometimes, too. Of different things." She smoothed her hands down his arms, and laced her fingers with his. "Maybe together we don't have to be afraid anymore."

She moved closer, until their bodies touched, her thighs against his thighs, the tips of her breasts brushing his chest. He could see himself reflected in the dark pools of her eyes. "Trust me," she whispered. "I want to trust you."

She stepped back, pulling him with her, until the water lapped about his waist. "Lie back in my arms," she commanded.

He did as she asked. Cold fear stole his breath as he felt the water wet his back. But Nixie's hands and arms were warm, supporting him and guiding him. "Now lift your legs," she said. "The water and I will hold you up."

He couldn't move, paralyzed by old memories and dread. He closed his eyes, thinking to gather his courage by shutting off his senses. But Nixie leaned close and whispered in his ear. "Jed, look at me. Trust me."

He opened his eyes and she fixed him with a look so full of love and tenderness it left no room for fear or doubt. He relaxed in her arms and stretched out his legs, floating in the water.

He stiffened when she began to move out into the pool, but she calmed him with a smile of encouragement and a gentle squeeze of her hands at his back and thighs.

She carried him to the middle of the pool, where the water was deep and he knew if he stood he would no longer be able to find footing. Water soaked his hair and clothes, warm against his skin. As the warmth seeped into him, he was aware of his fear retreating. The tightness in his chest eased, and his breathing returned to normal.

Nixie guided them back to shallower water and released him to stand beside her. "How was that?" she asked.

He looked down at the water around his waist. "I haven't stood in water this deep in years." He pulled her close. "Other people offered to teach me to swim, but I was too proud to let them know I was afraid. And too independent to want anyone to think I needed help."

She smiled, eyes sparkling with unshed tears. "We are two of a kind, aren't we? And I thought we were too different to ever be happy together."

He cradled her head on his shoulder, tenderness tightening his voice and making it difficult to draw deep breath. With Nixie, he could dare to do anything. Be anything. Even himself. "All I know is, I'm never going to be happy apart from you. I love you, Nixie."

"Oh, Jed, I love you. I promise I'll never again wait to say it." She stood on tiptoe to kiss him, her arms around his neck, drawing him to her. Her mouth was softest velvet beneath his own, warm and pliant and tasting as sweet as honey. He would never get enough of the taste of her, of the feel of her. The inside of her mouth was like satin against the sweep of his tongue, her teeth slick glass. Aching to feel her closer, he gathered her up into his arms, still keeping his lips on hers.

Now he could feel the soft curve of her bottom against his arm, and the pebbled tip of one breast against his chest. He left the pleasure of her mouth for even greater pleasures elsewhere, trailing his lips along the curve of her jaw, resting them for a moment against the strong steady pulse at her throat.

He dipped his head further, down the long line of her neck, across the curve of her bosom, to one beckoning peak. Closing his mouth around the damp serge, he moved the rough fabric against the sensitive nipple until she writhed in his arms and let out a moan of passion that sent a thrill through him.

She brought a hand up to stifle the sound, but he raised his head and looked at her, into eyes dark with passion and longing. "You don't have to be quiet for me," he said. "I want to hear how much you love me. And how much you love the things I make you feel."

Tears pooled in her eyes and she shook her head. "I can't," she whispered.

"Why not?"

"It isn't . . . Only prostitutes make noises like that."

His heart contracted, compassion and anger doing battle in his chest. "Did Norwich tell you these lies?"

She didn't answer, but he saw the answer in her eyes. "It's not true!" he said, with unaccustomed fierceness. He hugged her closer. "You can say anything you want, Nixie. Feel anything you want. There's nothing wrong or ugly about any of it, anymore than laughing or singing or crying out for joy would be wrong."

She was silent for a long while, her face pressed against his chest. He wondered if she was crying, but when she raised her head at last, he saw no tears. "Make love to me here," she whispered.

He cocked his head toward her. "I'm sorry, I can't hear you."

A shy smile curved her lips. "Make love to me now," she said with more confidence. "Here." She began undoing the buttons of his shirt. "As naked as the day God made you."

He started to move out of the water, but she did not even allow him that. She finished the buttons on his shirt, then started in on the fastenings of her bathing dress, peeling back the wet serge to reveal skin like captured moonlight. Droplets of water slid down the curve of her breast and beaded the tips, until he bent and captured the moisture in his mouth, and felt the shudder of her breath in his ear and the shiver of her soft flesh in his hand.

She squirmed away from him, out of his arms liked a mermaid ready to flee. But she only parted long enough to strip the rest of the way out of her clothes, and to help him out of his. Then they stood naked before one another, in water up to their knees, mist swirling around them.

Words escaped Jed as he stared at her. No artist could do her justice, no fantasy could be as complete. After a moment he noticed the gooseflesh pebbling her arms, and felt a chill breeze across his own shoulders. "You're cold," he said, taking her hand and leading her into deeper water. The fear he'd known earlier had vanished, driven away by his love for Nixie.

The water flowed like silk around them, warming, caressing, coaxing them to new heights of arousal. When he held out his arms, she moved into his embrace as naturally as a dancer matches the steps of a longtime partner.

They kissed long and hard, kisses stoking the fire within them. Nixie tilted her head back and lost herself in the pleasure of those kisses. When at last his mouth left hers, she opened her eyes and stared up at the shadowed canopy of trees and the swirling mist—a world as topsy-turvy and fantastic as the riot of feeling within her. Jed loved her. He loved her and wanted to stay with her. Forever.

He lavished attention on her breasts now, his mouth hot against her night-cooled skin. Pleasure jolted through her as he licked and suckled. A half-wild moan echoed in her ears, and she realized with embarrassment the moan came from deep within her. She tried to hold back the sound, stiffening her body against it.

Jed grew still. He raised his head to look at her. Mist beaded his lashes and shone in his hair like glitter, like some supernatural being. But the voice that spoke to her was a man's, low and commanding, sending tremors through her at its very sound. "I want to hear you when I love you," he said. "Don't hold back." He slid his hand under the water, along the curve of her hip, then across her thigh. "Don't hold back ever again."

She gasped as he slid his finger inside her, and she could not have held back the sharp cry that followed as he began to move, in and out, his thumb delving in her wet curls and finding the point where she was most sensitive. "That's it," he whispered as her head fell back against his arm once more. "Don't hide how I make you feel. You don't have to hide your feelings with me."

His words faded against the roaring in her ears, and the indescribable sensations that rioted through her. The warm water flowed around her while Jed's arm supported her and his hand . . . his hand! Her heart did a wild dance in her chest, in time with the chorus of animal cries that came from her throat unbidden. Faster and higher the sounds rose, with the throbbing tension within her. How much more could she stand. But please don't stop!

"Oh God, Jed!" she screamed, and fell back in his arms, surrendering to him and to the springs and to the pleasure that had replaced the blood in her veins.

But she had little time to rest. Guiding her hands to his shoulders, he grasped her hips and gently lifted her in the water, until she was straddling him, his arousal hot and silken against her thigh. "Guide me in," he whispered.

She clasped him with one hand, smiling at the grunt of pleasure he made at her touch. He hesitated and she thought he meant to enter her slowly, carefully. But she was past being careful now. She moved forward, and impaled herself on him, crying out in pleasure as he filled her completely.

They came together in a frenzy of passion and need, churning the waters with the fury of their lovemaking. Nixie wrapped her legs around his waist and shuddered as her climax took her once more. Then Jed shouted out her name as he found his own release.

Afterward, they lay side by side on the bank, naked, legs and arms entwined. He rested his cheek against the tangled softness of her hair and let out a sigh from deep inside himself. Here was where he belonged. No town, no people, no building would ever give him what Nixie had. In her, he had found his home, a sanctuary he would never leave.

Epilogue

GILLESPIE COUNTY, TEXAS, MAY 1895

Nixie made her way through the crowd on the midway, praying she wouldn't be late for the show. A second soda, and her rather advanced pregnancy, had necessitated a trip to the latrines. Now she was worried she wouldn't make it back to the stage in time to hear Jed speak.

"Come on, Zeke, we don't want to miss Daddy's show." She turned to the little boy holding her hand and smiled. The toddler grinned back at her, chocolate-brown eyes shining from beneath a shock of almost white hair.

They arrived at the foot of the stage just as Dory stepped out from behind the curtain. Nixie waved to her friend. Dory looked smart in her new orange and white walking suit. One would never suspect she'd given birth to her second daughter only two months before.

Then the curtain moved again and Jed walked to the center of the stage. Nixie's heart leapt at the sight of him. He wore his new white suit with the broad shoulders and narrow lapels. Sunlight glinted off his gold-streaked hair and shone on the pristine fabric, so that he appeared to be standing in a halo of light.

An angel, or the devil himself, she thought, remembering her first sight of her husband years ago. She smiled. Maybe Jed was a little of both. But all man. And all hers. Just the thought warmed her to her toes.

"Papa! Papa!" Little Zeke jumped up and down and waved at his father. Nixie picked him up and cuddled him against her hip so he could have a better view of what was happening on the stage.

"Ladies and gentlemen," Jed began, his voice carrying over the crowd. "I'm here today to talk to you about one of the most refreshing wonders of nature." He took the bottle Dory handed him and held it up. Sunlight sparkled on the amber glass. "What I have here is a new beverage. Not a seltzer, not sarsaparilla or root beer or lemonade. But a uniquely tasting, refreshing, and yes, *healthy* beverage for all ages."

He turned the bottle so that the label showed. The colorful logo featured a smiling blond with a bouquet of herbs and flowers. "*Nixie.* A deliciously different refreshment," Jed announced. "Only a nickel a bottle, my friends. Available ice cold at all the beverage stands at this fair. And when you get back home, don't forget to ask your favorite druggist or ice cream vendor if they carry this new and unique drink."

Dory reappeared at Jed's side, carrying a tray of the amber bottles. "And for today only, free samples, to acquaint you with this new taste," Jed said. "Step right up, folks. One to a customer, please."

Nixie moved to the side as the crowd surged forward. Jed and Dory distributed bottles to a sea of outstretched hands. "Don't worry, there's plenty for everyone," Jed assured. He paused at the end of the stage in front of Nixie and winked. She grinned and returned the gesture.

Jed straightened and spoke to the departing crowd. The

GREAT CAESAR'S GHOST

familiar words never failed to thrill her, and Zeke clapped his hands and giggled with delight.

"Remember the name, folks," Jed called. "No matter where you go or what you do, there's only one *Nixie*."

Presenting all-new romances—featuring ghostly heroes and heroines and the passions they inspire.

❤ Haunting Hearts ❤

- ***A SPIRITED SEDUCTION***
  by Casey Claybourne — 0-515-12066-9/$5.99

- ***STARDUST OF YESTERDAY***
  by Lynn Kurland — 0-515-11839-7/$6.50

- ***A GHOST OF A CHANCE***
  by Casey Claybourne — 0-515-11857-5/$5.99

- ***ETERNAL VOWS***
  by Alice Alfonsi — 0-515-12002-2/$5.99

- ***ETERNAL LOVE***
  by Alice Alfonsi — 0-515-12207-6/$5.99

- ***ARRANGED IN HEAVEN***
  by Sara Jarrod — 0-515-12275-0/$5.99

Prices slightly higher in Canada

Payable in U.S. funds only. No cash/COD accepted. Postage & handling: U.S./CAN. $2.75 for one book, $1.00 for each additional, not to exceed $6.75; Int'l $5.00 for one book, $1.00 each additional. We accept Visa, Amex, MC ($10.00 min.), checks ($15.00 fee for returned checks) and money orders. Call 800-788-6262 or 201-933-9292, fax 201-896-8569; refer to ad # 636 (10/99)

Penguin Putnam Inc.
P.O. Box 12289, Dept. B
Newark, NJ 07101-5289
Please allow 4-6 weeks for delivery.
Foreign and Canadian delivery 6-8 weeks.

Bill my: ☐ Visa ☐ MasterCard ☐ Amex _____ (expires)
Card# _____
Signature _____

Bill to:
Name _____
Address _____ City _____
State/ZIP _____ Daytime Phone # _____

Ship to:
Name _____ Book Total $ _____
Address _____ Applicable Sales Tax $ _____
City _____ Postage & Handling $ _____
State/ZIP _____ Total Amount Due $ _____

This offer subject to change without notice.

DO YOU BELIEVE IN MAGIC?

MAGICAL LOVE

The enchanting new series from Jove will make you a believer!

With a sprinkling of faerie dust and the wave of a wand, magical things can happen—but nothing is more magical than the power of love.

❏ *SEA SPELL* by Tess Farraday   0-515-12289-0/$5.99

A mysterious man from the sea haunts a woman's dreams—and desires...

❏ *ONCE UPON A KISS* by Claire Cross

0-515-12300-5/$5.99

A businessman learns there's only one way to awaken a slumbering beauty...

❏ *A FAERIE TALE* by Ginny Reyes   0-515-12338-2/$5.99

A faerie and a leprechaun play matchmaker—to a mismatched pair of mortals...

❏ *ONE WISH* by C.J. Card   0-515-12354-4/$5.99

For years a beautiful bottle lay concealed in a forgotten trunk—holding a powerful spirit, waiting for someone to come along and make one wish...

VISIT PENGUIN PUTNAM ONLINE ON THE INTERNET:
http://www.penguinputnam.com

Prices slightly higher in Canada

Payable in U.S. funds only. No cash/COD accepted. Postage & handling: U.S./CAN. $2.75 for one book, $1.00 for each additional, not to exceed $6.75; Int'l $5.00 for one book, $1.00 each additional. We accept Visa, Amex, MC ($10.00 min.), checks ($15.00 fee for returned checks) and money orders. Call 800-788-6262 or 201-933-9292, fax 201-896-8569; refer to ad # 789 (10/99)

Penguin Putnam Inc.
P.O. Box 12289, Dept. B
Newark, NJ 07101-5289
Please allow 4-6 weeks for delivery.
Foreign and Canadian delivery 6-8 weeks.

Bill my: ❏ Visa ❏ MasterCard ❏ Amex _____ (expires)
Card# _____
Signature _____

Bill to:
Name _____
Address _____ City _____
State/ZIP _____ Daytime Phone # _____

Ship to:
Name _____ Book Total $ _____
Address _____ Applicable Sales Tax $ _____
City _____ Postage & Handling $ _____
State/ZIP _____ Total Amount Due $ _____

This offer subject to change without notice.

TIME PASSAGES

- ❏ CRYSTAL MEMORIES   *Ginny Aiken*   0-515-12159-2
- ❏ ECHOES OF TOMORROW   *Jenny Lykins*   0-515-12079-0
- ❏ LOST YESTERDAY   *Jenny Lykins*   0-515-12013-8
- ❏ MY LADY IN TIME   *Angie Ray*   0-515-12227-0
- ❏ NICK OF TIME   *Casey Claybourne*   0-515-12189-4
- ❏ REMEMBER LOVE   *Susan Plunkett*   0-515-11980-6
- ❏ SILVER TOMORROWS   *Susan Plunkett*   0-515-12047-2
- ❏ THIS TIME TOGETHER   *Susan Leslie Liepitz*
  0-515-11981-4
- ❏ WAITING FOR YESTERDAY   *Jenny Lykins*
  0-515-12129-0
- ❏ HEAVEN'S TIME   *Susan Plunkett*   0-515-12287-4
- ❏ THE LAST HIGHLANDER   *Claire Cross*   0-515-12337-4
- ❏ A TIME FOR US   *Christine Holden*   0-515-12375-7

All books $5.99

Prices slightly higher in Canada

Payable in U.S. funds only. No cash/COD accepted. Postage & handling: U.S./CAN. $2.75 for one book, $1.00 for each additional, not to exceed $6.75; Int'l $5.00 for one book, $1.00 each additional. We accept Visa, Amex, MC ($10.00 min.), checks ($15.00 fee for returned checks) and money orders. Call 800-788-6262 or 201-933-9292, fax 201-896-8569; refer to ad # 680 (10/99)

Penguin Putnam Inc.	Bill my: ❏ Visa ❏ MasterCard ❏ Amex _____ (expires)
P.O. Box 12289, Dept. B	Card# _____
Newark, NJ 07101-5289	Signature _____
Please allow 4-6 weeks for delivery.	
Foreign and Canadian delivery 6-8 weeks.	

Bill to:
Name _____
Address _____ City _____
State/ZIP _____ Daytime Phone # _____

Ship to:
Name _____ Book Total $ _____
Address _____ Applicable Sales Tax $ _____
City _____ Postage & Handling $ _____
State/ZIP _____ Total Amount Due $ _____

This offer subject to change without notice.

FRIENDS ROMANCE

Can a man come between friends?

❑ **A TASTE OF HONEY**

by DeWanna Pace   0-515-12387-0

❑ **WHERE THE HEART IS**

by Sheridon Smythe   0-515-12412-5

❑ **LONG WAY HOME**

by Wendy Corsi Staub   0-515-12440-0

All books $5.99

Prices slightly higher in Canada

Payable in U.S. funds only. No cash/COD accepted. Postage & handling: U.S./CAN. $2.75 for one book, $1.00 for each additional, not to exceed $6.75; Int'l $5.00 for one book, $1.00 each additional. We accept Visa, Amex, MC ($10.00 min.), checks ($15.00 fee for returned checks) and money orders. Call 800-788-6262 or 201-933-9292, fax 201-896-8569; refer to ad # 815 (10/99)

Penguin Putnam Inc.	Bill my: ❑ Visa ❑ MasterCard ❑ Amex _____ (expires)
P.O. Box 12289, Dept. B	Card# _____
Newark, NJ 07101-5289	Signature _____
Please allow 4-6 weeks for delivery.	
Foreign and Canadian delivery 6-8 weeks.	

Bill to:

Name _____

Address _____ City _____

State/ZIP _____ Daytime Phone # _____

Ship to:

Name _____	Book Total	$ _____
Address _____	Applicable Sales Tax	$ _____
City _____	Postage & Handling	$ _____
State/ZIP _____	Total Amount Due	$ _____

This offer subject to change without notice.